THE SECRET LIFE OF
LADY LUCINDA

THE SECRET LIFE
OF LADY LUCINDA

A Summersby Tale

SOPHIE BARNES

AVONIMPULSE
An Imprint of HarperCollinsPublishers

Excerpt from *Lady Alexandra's Excellent Adventure* copyright © 2012 by Sophie Barnes.

Excerpt from *Three Schemes and a Scandal* copyright © 2012 by Maya Rodale.

Excerpt from *Skies of Steel* copyright © 2012 by Zoë Archer.

Excerpt from *Further Confessions of a Slightly Neurotic Hitwoman* copyright © 2012 by JB Lynn.

Excerpt from *The Second Seduction of a Lady* copyright © 2012 by Miranda Neville.

Excerpt from *To Hell and Back* copyright © 2012 by Juliana Stone.

Excerpt from *Midnight in Your Arms* copyright © 2012 by McKinley Hellenes.

Excerpt from *Seduced by a Pirate* copyright © 2012 by Eloisa James.

EPub Edition DECEMBER 2012 ISBN: 9780062225399

Print Edition ISBN: 9780062225405

10 9 8 7 6 5

For Helene, because I know you'll squeal when you see this!

Constantinople, 1811

"Run, Lucy, run—as fast as you can!"

Rounding a corner, Lucy looked back over her shoulder to see the absolute terror in her mother's eyes. Footsteps were coming fast behind them. Surely there wasn't enough time.

"Through here." Eugenia grabbed her daughter's wrist and gave it a hard tug, pulling Lucy backward and through an archway. They stopped in the open space beyond to listen, their chests rising and falling rapidly as they fought to catch their breaths.

"Mama?" Lucy was shaking with fear. She'd been fast asleep in bed when she'd suddenly found herself startled awake by her mother urgently shaking her. When she'd told Lucy to hurry up and come with her, her voice had been filled with unmistakable panic.

"Hush," her mother now cautioned in a soft whisper as she pressed her hand firmly over Lucy's mouth.

A door swung open further down the hallway, revealing muffled voices—Turkish, as far as Lucy could tell. She stiffened, her heart pounding in her ears as she clutched her mother's hand. A moment's silence followed, and then . . . the steady click of deliberate footsteps coming closer and closer.

"Come," Eugenia whispered, ushering Lucy forward toward an open doorway. "Just a little bit further and we'll be safe."

The strain in her mother's voice did little to reassure her. Why was this happening? Lucy had no time to ponder before her mother ushered her inside a room that had always been reserved for informal visits. She watched as her mother closed the door softly behind them and locked it firmly in place. "We don't have a moment to lose."

"But what about Papa?"

She saw the answer in her mother's eyes but failed to believe it. "Those men . . ." Lucy's voice quivered and broke before she could get the rest of the words out. A tremor swept along her spine and her eyes pricked with the onset of tears as her mother swiftly shook her head.

"Your papa will not be joining us, my love," Eugenia said, her face filled with despair as she answered Lucy's unspoken question. "Now come along." Hurrying across the mosaic-tiled floor, Eugenia quickly reached the window. She swung open the delicately carved shutters and glanced out over the rooftops before lowering her gaze to the alley below. "You will have to jump. Do you think you can manage it?"

Lucy peered out over the ledge of the window. They were only one floor above the street, yet such a leap seemed practically impossible. She shuddered at the thought of it, just as a loud bang sounded against the door to the chamber. The next thing she felt was her mother's arms about her in a tight embrace, her lips grazing her cheek in a succession of quick kisses.

"Take this," Eugenia said, shoving a small leather pouch into the palm of Lucy's hand. She then lifted her startled daughter up onto the windowsill. "It isn't much, but it will help you return to England. Run as fast as you can, and whatever you do, do not look back."

"But where will I . . ." Everything was happening so fast. With her feet dangling over the edge, Lucy half turned in the opening. "Mama, what about you? I won't leave you!" Life without her parents was unthinkable—she couldn't do it.

"You must, my love. If we both go, they will catch us and all will be lost. I will try to delay them as long as I can." Eugenia's voice was calm, in stark contradiction to her tear-drenched cheeks. "Stay away from the family. If you go to them, they will find you."

"Who will, Mama?"

Another bang resonated through the air to the sound of angry voices.

"There is no more time. Find my friend Constance. You remember? She will take good care of you. Just promise me that my sacrifice will not be for nothing."

"I . . . Mama . . . I . . ."

"Promise me," Eugenia insisted, her fingers clutched tightly around her daughter's shoulders. All Lucy could do was stare back at her in confusion. She didn't understand what was happening, much less why. "Promise me!"

The seconds seemed to stretch into minutes until Lucy eventually nodded. "I promise, Mama."

Relief flooded Eugenia's face. She hugged her daughter against her once more, as if the memory of it would have to last her a lifetime. "Remember that I love you." It was the last thing she said before pushing her unsuspecting, twelve-year-old daughter out of the window to face her fate alone. A moment later the door sprang open, giving way to five armed men, each wielding a yatagan as they moved forward to face her. A tall figure garbed in a crisp black suit, his white cravat tied to perfection and a beaver hat placed neatly upon his head, followed in their wake. Upon his face, he wore a mask that concealed his every feature—a shiny black thing, the sight of which made Eugenia shudder. He cast a careful glance about the room before asking the only question that seemed to concern him, "Where is she?"

"I cannot possibly imagine to whom you might be referring," Eugenia said as she bravely straightened her spine and silently prayed that her daughter would be saved from the fate she herself was about to suffer.

CHAPTER ONE

London, 1817

William Summersby stared into the darkness that surrounded the terrace of Trenton House. He'd stepped outside with his father in order to escape the squeeze inside the ballroom. Taking a sip from the glass of Champagne in his hand, he shot a quick glance in his father's direction. "I've made up my mind, Papa."

Bryce said nothing in response to this, but merely waited for his son to continue, the cigar he held in his hand seemingly forgotten for the moment.

"I've decided to marry."

"Oh?" His father's surprise was clear. "I suppose you must have some candidates in mind then?"

William turned away from the darkness to face his father, knowing that what he was about to say would probably be met with disapproval. "I have done far better than that, Papa. In fact, I have already proposed." He paused for a moment, allowing his father to digest this surprising piece of news. "It may please you to know that the lady in question has accepted, and that we hope to marry before the year is out."

"I . . . er . . . I see," his father muttered in a half-choked tone that did little to conceal how astonished he was. "I always imagined that you would consult me first when it came to choosing a bride. However, you're grown, undoubtedly capable of making such a decision on your own. What, if I may ask, is the name of the lady who has so suddenly captured your heart, William?"

"Lady Annabelle—Lord and Lady Forthright's daughter, if you recall."

An immediate frown appeared on his father's forehead. "Yes, I know her well enough, though it did not occur to me that you were so well acquainted with her."

William merely shrugged. "I'm hardly getting any younger, you know. It's bad enough that both of my siblings are now married. I'm your heir, and, as such, I have a certain responsibility."

His father's frown deepened. "You aren't even thirty years of age."

"Perhaps not, but I've attended enough social gatherings by now to have met all the eligible young ladies, and I am forced to admit that not one has made my heart beat faster. Thus, my decision has been based on logic. Lady Annabelle will make a most agreeable wife. She is from a very respectable family. She has a level head on her shoulders, and I dare say that her looks suggest that our children shall not be lacking in physical attributes."

Bryce stared back at his son with sad eyes. "I always hoped that you would marry for love, William. I was fortunate enough to do so, and it is quite clear that Alexandra and Ryan were as well."

"We can't all be that lucky, Papa. First comes duty, however unfortunate that may be. But I will not run from it. I've tried long and hard to make a match that would put Romeo and Juliet's love to shame but with no success. I see no point in wasting any more time. Lady Annabelle will suffice. She's quite pleasant, really."

"Well, if your mind is made up, then the least I can hope for is that you might, in time, find more appropriate words with which to describe your bride. 'Most agreeable' and 'quite pleasant' are rather lacking, if you ask me. And don't forget that if you both live long and healthy lives, you will be stuck with each other. Do you really wish to spend the remainder of your days with a woman who merely *suffices?*"

William let out a lengthy sigh. He'd always longed for the sort of happiness his father and mother had shared, but as time passed he'd gradually been forced to acknowledge that he would be denied that sort of marriage. The woman he longed for didn't exist. "There's no one else. Besides, I've already proposed, and she has accepted. It would be badly done if I were to go back on my word now."

"Perhaps." His father patted him roughly on his shoulder. "But whatever you do, you have my full support. I hope you know that."

Lucy Blackwell's gaze swept across the ballroom like a hawk seeking out its prey. She'd barely made it through the door before finding herself assaulted by a hoard of young gentlemen, all wishing to know her name and why they'd never seen or heard of her before. She'd favored each of them with a faint smile but had otherwise done little to enlighten them. She wasn't there to elaborate on her pedigree in the hopes that one of those young gentlemen might find her eligible enough to merit a courtship. No, she'd done her research as meticulously as any detective, and, consequently, she already knew whom she planned to marry. All she had to do now was make his acquaintance.

Moving forward, she slowly made her way around the periphery of the room until she found her path blocked by a small gathering of women who appeared to be quite caught up in whatever subject it was that they were discussing. Lucy was just about to squeeze past them when one of these ladies—a lovely blonde with bright blue eyes, stopped her. "Please excuse my ignorance," the woman said, "but I don't believe that you and I have been formally introduced."

Lucy stared back at her, making an admirable attempt to hide her annoyance. How many people would delay her this evening?

"I am the Countess of Trenton, and these ladies who are presently in my company are the Marchioness of Steepleton and my sister-in-law, Lady Cassandra."

"It is a pleasure to make your acquaintances," Lucy told them, managing an even broader smile at the realization that the woman before her was not only her hostess but also Lord Summersby's sister. "My name is Lucy Blackwell. I am Lady Ridgewood's ward."

"I had no idea that she had a ward," Lady Trenton said, looking to her companions as if to see if either of them had ever heard of such a thing. Both ladies shook their heads.

"As you may know, Lady Ridgewood favors the country,"

Lucy told them by way of explanation. "And since I have only recently turned eighteen, there hasn't been much reason for us to come to London until now. But her ladyship has most graciously agreed to grant me a season, so here I am."

"And not a moment too soon," Lady Cassandra blurted out. "One can never start scouring the masses quickly enough. Finding a good match can often take more than one season." She followed her statement with a nervous giggle, which led Lucy to believe that Lady Cassandra had probably been on the marriage mart for some time.

Lucy responded with an awkward smile. "I dare say that I hope it won't take more than this one."

"Have you perhaps set your sights on someone already?" the marchioness asked with a great deal of curiosity as she moved a little closer.

"I was practically stampeded on my way in here," Lucy remarked, unwilling to divulge any important details to these women for fear that they might sabotage her plan. "Surely there must be a potential husband among them."

All three women nodded in agreement.

"But for now, I am actually searching for a certain Lord Summersby, for he and I are meant to dance the next set together, and with the crowd being as dense as it is, I'm finding it rather difficult to seek him out."

Lady Trenton served her a bright smile. "I would be delighted to be of service. Are you not aware that he is my brother?"

"Forgive me, my lady, but I really had no idea." It was a small lie perhaps but one that Lucy deemed necessary.

"Well, he most certainly is. And if I am not entirely mistaken, I saw him not too long ago on the terrace with our father. Come; I will take you to him directly."

"That is most kind of you, my lady, but really quite unnecessary. I should hate to impose."

"First of all," Lady Trenton began, linking her arm with Lucy's, "you shall call me Alexandra from now on, for I am quite certain that the two of us shall be wonderful friends. Second of all, it is no imposition at all."

Lucy could think of nothing more to say. She was quite certain that she and Alexandra would be far from friends once she put her plan into motion, but she couldn't help but admit that she did need her, if for no other reason than to lead her to the right man.

"Shame on you, William," Alexandra teased moments later as she stepped out onto the terrace with Lucy in tow. "It seems that you've quite forgotten your dance partner— a bit out of character for you and rather ungentlemanly, I might add."

If Alexandra continued speaking, Lucy found it impossible to focus on what it was she was saying, for the man who presently turned toward her, the very one she planned to ensnare, would undoubtedly be capable of taking her breath away ten times over. In short, he was the most perfect, the most handsome, the most memorable of any man she'd ever set eyes upon. That Mother Nature had taken it upon herself to create such a fine specimen must surely be a crime against all the other poor creatures who'd have to walk in his shadow. She drew a sharp breath.

"Lucy?" a distant voice from a far-off place seemed to ask.

Lucy's first instinct was to ignore it, but then she felt Alexandra's hand tugging gently on her arm, hurtling her with startling force right back to reality. "Hm?" She couldn't for the life of her imagine what she might be expected to say, much less overlook the puzzled expression on Lord Summersby's face.

"I don't believe we've ever met, Miss Blackwell."

Panic swept over her from head to toe until she realized that the words had been spoken not by Lord Summersby but by an older gentleman who stood to his right. He wasn't quite as tall as Lord Summersby, but he still had an imposing figure, and Lucy considered how terrifying he must be when he was angry. Thankfully, he looked rather cheerful at present. His eyes were a tone lighter than Lord Summersby's, his chin a little rounder around the edges, and his nose slightly bigger.

"Please allow me to introduce myself. I am the Earl of Moorland. It seems I must apologize for detaining my son from his prior engagement."

There was a flicker of something in the old man's eyes that was by no means lost on Lucy. Mischief perhaps? *How odd.*

Lord Summersby, on the other hand, had taken on a rather stiff stance, his gray-blue eyes regarding Lucy with a mild degree of interest.

"It is a pleasure, my lord," Lucy responded, offering the earl a graceful curtsy.

"William, you've not said a single word to Miss Blackwell as of yet." Lord Moorland's voice was stern—the mark of a man who was used to being in command. "I dare say you'd do rather well to make your own apology. A lesser woman would already have had a fit of the vapors in response to your lack of attention."

There was a momentary pause. Lucy held her breath, wondering if Lord Summersby would act as a gentleman or declare her a liar before all. Her heart hammered and her palms grew sweaty, but then, like her very own knight in shining armor, he gave a curt nod and took a step toward her, not only saving her from utter humiliation but unwittingly helping her realize the next part of her plan.

"Forgive me, Miss Blackwell." His eyes bore into hers, holding her captive as he spoke. "It seems that I was so engrossed in the conversation I was having that I must have had a complete lapse in memory. Indeed, it is so severe that I might just as well not recall having asked you at all. I do apologize with the sincerest hope that you will still allow me to make good on my promise."

Lucy almost lost her nerve. Not in a million years would she have imagined that any man would make her feel so small and wretched. His tone had not been mocking, but his meaning had been clear. He thought her a charlatan, and why wouldn't he? After all, they'd only just met, and she'd hardly done anything to make him think highly of her. Quite the opposite. She groaned inwardly, knowing that what she planned to suggest would sound ludicrous to him. She hoped he'd accept without a fuss however, for if he didn't, he'd likely hold a harlot in higher regard than he would her once the night was over.

Pushing all sympathy from her mind, she squared her shoulders and strengthened her resolve. "Nothing would please me more, my lord," she replied, allowing him to take her by the arm and lead her back inside the ballroom.

Taking up their respective positions for the start of the quadrille, Lucy shot a quick glance at Lord Summersby who was standing right beside her. "Thank you," she whispered as the music started and two other couples began their turn about the dance floor.

"I cannot say that you are welcome," he muttered in response, "for I despise deception."

"I'm sorry, my lord, but I saw no other way in which to make your acquaintance."

"Really?" Though his face remained fixed upon the other awaiting couple across from them, his irritation was quite apparent. "I'm not sure what game you're playing, Miss Blackwell, but I can assure you that I am far from amused."

Before Lucy could manage a response, he'd taken her by the arm and led her forward, turning her about before leading her in a wide circle while the other couples looked on. As soon as they were back in their places, Lucy pulled together every ounce of courage she possessed. This was the reason she'd come, and she would have only one chance at getting it right. "I have a proposal," she whispered. "Indeed, I am in need of your service."

For a moment, she wasn't entirely sure if he'd heard her. Her heart hammering in her chest, her legs growing weak with expectation, she feared she might suddenly collapse from sheer nerves.

"And what service might that be?" he finally asked, leading her forward once again.

"I've done my research, my lord, and am quite familiar with your career. In fact, you are regarded as the best foreign agent that England has to offer, and, as it happens, I am in need of precisely such a man. I will pay you handsomely enough, of that I promise you." She wondered if there would be enough money in the world to pay him for participating in her mad endeavor.

Lord Summersby shot her a sideways glance. "As *tempting* as your offer may be, I fear you must take your business elsewhere. You see, Miss Blackwell, I am soon to be married and have every intention of settling down to a peaceful family life in the country, away from all the excitement that the Foreign Office has to offer."

Lucy blanched.

Marry?

Apparently she had far less time to set her plan in motion than she had hoped for. If Lord Summersby married someone else, then . . . She had intended to let him in on her scheme, but if he'd already proposed to another woman, then she might have to resort to more desperate measures.

Her mind reeled as he steered her smoothly back toward their places. The music faded, and all the couples bowed and curtsied—all but Lucy. She was far too busy making a hasty change of plans.

"I take it that your so-called *research* didn't mention that I am betrothed?" He was leading her back toward the periphery of the ballroom.

"It did not."

"Well, it has been a rather hasty decision, I suppose."

Lucy stopped walking, forcing Lord Summersby to a halt as well. Staring up at him, she searched his eyes for the answer to a question that she dared not ask.

Until that very moment, William had paid very little attention to the physical attributes of the woman with whom he'd been dancing. Not only had the lighting been quite poor outside on the terrace, but he'd also been so angry that she'd had the audacity to slither her way into his life through lies and deceit that her looks had been the last thing on his mind.

Since then, he'd barely glanced in her direction, but now that he was given no choice but to take a good look at her, he couldn't help but feel his heart take an extra beat—a rather disconcerting feeling indeed, given the fact that he intensely disliked her. However, as well as that might be, he could not dismiss her exceptional beauty. Her hair was fiery red, her eyes intensely green, and her bone structure so fine and delicate that she could have worn a sack and still looked elegant. But the gown that Miss Blackwell was wearing was by no means any sack. Instead, it showed off a figure that boasted of soft curves in all the right places.

Clenching his jaw, William swallowed hard and forced himself to ignore the temptation. He would marry Annabelle, and that would be that.

"Do you love her?" Miss Blackwell suddenly asked, her head tilted upward at a slight angle.

By deuce, even her voice was delightful to listen to. And those imploring eyes of hers . . . No, he'd be damned if he'd allow her to ensnare him with her womanly charms. She'd practically made a fool of both his sister and his father; she'd get no sympathy from him. Not now, not ever. "You and I are hardly well enough acquainted with each other for you to take such liberties in your questions, Miss Blackwell. My relationship to Lady Annabelle is of a personal nature and certainly not one that I am about to discuss with you."

Miss Blackwell blinked. "Then you do not love her," she said simply.

Good grief, but the woman was insufferable. Had he at any point in time told her that he was not in love with his fiancée? Why the devil would she draw such a conclusion? It was maddening and quite beyond him to understand the workings of her mind. "I hold her in the highest regard," he said.

Miss Blackwell stared back at him with an increased measure of doubt in her eyes. "More reason for me to believe that you do not love her."

"Miss Blackwell, if I did not know any better, I should say that you are either mad or deaf—perhaps even both. At no point have I told you that I do not love her, yet you are quite insistent upon the matter."

"That is because, my lord, it is in everything you are saying and everything that you are not. If you truly love her, you would not have spent a moment's hesitation in professing it. It is therefore my belief that you do not love her but that you are marrying her simply out of obligation."

Why the blazes he was having this harebrained conversation with a woman he'd only just met, much less liked, was beyond him. But the beginnings of a smile that now played upon her lips did nothing short of make him catch his breath. With a sigh of resignation, he slowly nodded his head. "Well done, Miss Blackwell. You have indeed found me out."

Her smile broadened. "Then it really doesn't matter whom you marry, as long as you marry. Is that not so?"

He frowned, immediately on guard at her sudden enthusiasm. "Not exactly, no. The woman I marry must be one of breeding, of a gentle nature and graceful bearing. Lady Annabelle fits all of those criteria rather nicely, and with time, I am more than confident that we shall become quite fond of each other."

The impossible woman had the audacity to roll her eyes. "All I really wanted to know was whether or not anyone's heart might be jeopardized if you were persuaded to marry somebody else. That is all."

"Miss Blackwell, I can assure you that I have no intention of marrying anyone other than Lady Annabelle. She and I have a mutual agreement. We are both honorable people. Neither one of us would ever consider going back on our word."

"I didn't think as much," she mused, and before William had any time to consider what she might be about to do, she'd thrown her arms about his neck, pulled him toward her, and placed her lips against his.

CHAPTER TWO

It was by no means a kiss of legend, though it did have the desired effect that Lucy was hoping for. As she pulled away from him, Lord Summersby's eyes were not the only ones filled with shock. Indeed, the entire ballroom had fallen into a hushed silence, interrupted only by the low whispers that were making their way from person to person.

Straightening her spine, Lucy turned to face their assessing gazes. "Ladies and gentlemen," she began, "as surprising as this may be in the light of the fact that most of you have yet to make my acquaintance, Lord Summersby has just now asked me to be his wife, and I have accepted."

The clapping was a bit slow and hesitant at first but eventually took on a louder tone until the whole ballroom was resonating with applause.

"A word, if I may?" Lord Summersby's tone was curt in Lucy's ear. For a moment there, she'd almost forgotten his presence, though it was difficult to do so now that he was dragging her away toward the terrace, his grip so tight that she was quite certain she'd bruise from it.

"What the hell was that?" he fumed as soon as they were outside, away from the curious gazes of the *ton*.

"I told you that I was in need of your service, and—"

"Good God, woman. Are you insane? You couldn't have what you wanted so you decided to trap me into marrying you? Have you any idea of the kind of scandal you've brought upon my family? Lord and Lady Forthright will be furious, and rightly so. Lady Annabelle will be furious. Everyone will think me a complete cad, though the fault lies not with me but entirely with you."

"I am sorry, my lord, I did not—"

"Sorry? The devil you're sorry, though I shall make bloody certain that you are indeed quite sorry by the time I'm through. I will not marry you."

"Indeed you will, my boy," Lord Moorland stated as he walked up to them with Alexandra and another gentleman at his side. "I don't believe you've met my other son, Ryan."

"Mr. Summersby," the younger man corrected as he stared Lucy up and down. He was the tallest of Lord Moorland's three children, and while he was certainly as handsome as his brother, he almost looked angrier, if such a thing was possible. Lucy shuddered, knowing that she'd crossed a family that was not to be trifled with.

"Papa, you cannot possibly be serious. We can still find a means by which to call this disaster off."

"And how exactly do you plan to do that without making things worse? As it is, Lady Annabelle will no longer have you, of that you can be quite certain."

Lord Summersby raked his fingers furiously through his hair. "There has to be a way."

"None that I can see," his father told him. "And since that is the case, we have come here to congratulate you instead."

Lord Summersby groaned. Lucy, who stood beside him, was doing her best to avoid eye contact with any of them. She knew she'd done an abominable thing, but marrying Lord Summersby was necessary. She couldn't very well travel to Constantinople on her own, much less with a man she wasn't related to, without bringing scandal upon Lady Ridgewood. Besides, he needed a wife. He'd said so himself, and since he didn't much care for Lady Annabelle anyway, then what harm was there in him marrying someone else? Her, to be precise.

"I must say that you surprised us all," Alexandra stated.

Looking up, Lucy noted the hard glare in her eyes, accusing her with the swift precision of an executioner's sword. Mr. Summersby's expression had not grown any less severe.

"Well then," Lord Moorland said. "Why don't you join us for tea tomorrow afternoon, Miss Blackwell. I am quite sure that we would all like to become better acquainted with you. As for the wedding arrangements—I'm certain that my sister will be more than happy to oblige."

With a quick succession of bows and curtsies, the Summersbys took their leave of Lucy, leaving her alone on the terrace, a little closer to her goal, but perhaps more miserable than she'd been in a very long time.

CHAPTER THREE

Having strategically placed himself by the window, William stared out of it in a deliberate attempt to feign disinterest in the woman seated on the sofa next to his sister. He knew he was being extraordinarily rude, but he couldn't seem to help himself. The lovely redhead had just deprived him of his freedom, and part of him wanted to lash out at her for the audacity.

"I understand from my daughter that this is your first season in London?" he heard his father say from the other side of the room.

"Yes, my lord," Miss Blackwell responded, her voice a little shaky. "When I turned eighteen, Lady Ridgewood thought it time for me to venture out into society."

Only eighteen and yet so conniving? William thought as he groaned.

"William," his father said in a tone suggestive of his growing impatience with him, "won't you join us?"

Knowing better than to argue, William turned his head and, seeing the dark glare in his father's eyes, decided it might be best to comply. Still, he saw no reason to pretend that he was pleased about doing so. With a shrug of his shoulders, he walked across to the nearest armchair, sat down, and crossed his arms and legs. "If I must." He made a point of staring directly at Miss Blackwell as he said this, hoping she would catch the double entendre. With her teacup rattling against its saucer, she hastily looked away. *Good*. Let her suffer a little discomfort for her arrogance.

His sister, brother, and father all stared back at him with open mouths, apparently stunned by his lack of manners. Did they really expect him to be pleasant, given the situation at hand? He could understand his father, for he certainly seemed to have fallen under Miss Blackwell's spell, but considering that Alex and Ryan had happily criticized Miss Blackwell the night before, he would have thought they'd be more understanding. Undoubtedly their father's words of warning prior to Miss Blackwell's arrival had affected them more than they had him.

"Lady Ridgewood, you say?" Bryce had turned his attention back to Miss Blackwell. "It's been years since I've had the pleasure of her company."

"Her ladyship hasn't ventured out much since the death of her late husband," Miss Blackwell told him in a quiet voice as she returned her teacup to the table and folded her hands in her lap.

"Quite right," Bryce muttered. Then, in a brighter tone, "Well, I do hope we'll have the pleasure of her company for the wedding. As far as I recall, she's a lovely lady."

Miss Blackwell responded with a weak smile and a slight nod. "Yes. In fact, she did regret that she was unable to join me here today, but unfortunately she was otherwise engaged. My apologies, my lord—I realize that under the circumstances and as my guardian she should have been here."

Bryce smiled. "Well, considering how quickly things have progressed, I completely understand if she was unable to alter her plans."

"And yet, I was able to alter mine," William muttered. He knew he was being childish, and as much as he disliked himself for it, he disliked Miss Blackwell more for bringing out the worst in him. This was not the sort of man he believed himself to be. He prided himself on being a gentleman in every aspect of his life, and yet the current situation was proving a difficult test of his courteous and honorable attributes.

What he didn't expect was for Miss Blackwell to raise her chin a notch and turn her attention on him. "My lord, I realize how displeasing this situation must be for you. I apologize for ruining your plans in regards to marrying Lady Annabelle, but I needed your help and saw no other way . . . Had you married her, you—"

"I what?" William asked as he leaned forward in his seat, his eyes focused intensely on Miss Blackwell's face.

"You would have retired to the country. You said so yourself."

"And?"

He saw her hesitate—watched as her eyes shifted about before focusing on a spot on the table. "You would not have been in a position to help me."

Her voice was so low he barely heard her. Whatever it was she wished for him to do, it must be important to her. But the way in which her eyes had darted around the room before she'd answered him suggested that it was a matter she wished to keep private. He doubted she'd say more with the rest of his family present, so he decided to let the matter rest for the moment. They would have plenty of time to discuss it later. Instead, he determined to show her that he would not be her lapdog. "Very well. The wedding shall take place next Saturday by special license. You will arrive at St. George's at precisely ten o'clock, or the deal is off and you may consider yourself free to find another unsuspecting fool who'll marry you."

"Did you just call yourself a fool, William?" Alexandra asked.

"Do not test me, Alex, or you may find yourself joining Miss Blackwell on my current list of unfavorable people."

Biting down on her lip, Alexandra wisely chose to keep quiet this time.

"Once the ceremony is over, we shall reconvene here for a small reception and wedding breakfast, and when I say small, I mean it. We will be no more than twenty people at most."

Miss Blackwell blinked. "I had hoped we might marry at the Grosvenor Chapel."

There was no reason for William to deny her such a wish, provided that the Grosvenor Chapel was available at such short notice. But, seizing the opportunity to give her a taste of her own medicine, he found himself saying, "Considering that you've had a say in everything else so far, I do believe I'll be the one deciding this."

Miss Blackwell drew a breath as if to add something but apparently decided against it, for she quickly closed her mouth again and merely nodded. "As you wish, my lord."

Were her eyes glistening? Damn it all, but he felt awful.

He was trying to formulate an apology of sorts when the door to the parlor opened and his aunt marched in. "I hope you haven't begun planning the wedding without me," she said, sounding far too chipper for William's liking.

"What a pleasant surprise," William said as he rose to greet her, though his eyes remained fixed on his father. This was undoubtedly his doing.

His father smiled. "You did say that she would be able to help with the preparations."

"Did I? As far as I recall, that was your idea."

His father seemed to consider this for a moment, eventually shrugged, and said, "Ah yes, now that you mention it, I do believe you're right."

"Oh my," Aunt V exclaimed, "is this your betrothed?"

William gave himself a mental kick. Once again he'd managed to forget about protocol, and while he might get by without it in his father's company, his aunt was another matter entirely. Stepping forward, he held his hand out toward Miss Blackwell, who mercifully took it, allowing him the gentlemanly gesture of helping her rise. "Aunt V, it is my pleasure to present to you Miss Blackwell. Miss Blackwell, this is my aunt, Virginia Camden, the Viscountess of Lindhurst."

"It is an honor to make your acquaintance, my lady," Miss Blackwell said as she performed a perfectly executed curtsy.

The corner of Aunt V's mouth drew upward to form a crooked smile while her eyes swept over Miss Blackwell's entire form. By the time she was through, William felt confident that his aunt might have unnerved his betrothed more than he had done, for she looked far more concerned about her fate now than she had ever looked before—whatever confidence she'd had seemed to have vanished entirely under his aunt's scrutiny.

But then Aunt V's smile broadened, and her eyes took on that gleam that meant she was getting excited about something. "I have just the gown in mind for you, my dear, and with that hair and those eyes . . . William, you've no cause for concern as far as your children go—with a mother this stunning, they'll be very precious indeed!"

"I . . . er . . ." was all William managed to get out before his aunt cut him off.

"Bryce, you must be so pleased, so very pleased indeed."

"Oh, I can assure you I am," Bryce said, beckoning for his sister to claim the remaining seat on the sofa. When they were once again comfortably seated and Aunt V had been offered a cup of tea, he said, "Virginia, I do believe you arrived at exactly the right moment. William was just telling us about his plans for the wedding."

He wanted to strangle his father. This was clearly an ambush. His father must have known that he would try to make a stand against Miss Blackwell and had apparently decided to champion her cause against him—why, he could not imagine. And he'd certainly picked the right person for the battle, for when his aunt raised her eyebrows and said, "Pfft! Weddings are not for men to plan," he knew he'd lost his footing.

Aunt V barely drew a breath before rattling off a list of things that would have to be attended to in preparation for the big day. Alexandra's jaw dropped when she was issued orders to visit the florist, while Ryan began to squirm in his seat when he was told to accompany William to the jeweler's. Apparently Miss Blackwell was deserving of a lovely new set of earrings for her big day.

Bloody hell!

And through it all, his father just sat there with that annoyingly smug expression upon his face, right until Aunt V, bless her heart, decided that he should be the one to hire the musicians. Served him right.

But as the minutes ticked by, William began to feel an urgent need to assert himself before the situation got completely out of hand. "Aunt V, we are not planning a big event, just a small function with the closest family."

His aunt tilted her head a little and frowned. "You are the heir to an earldom, William. Surely you must realize that there are notable members of the *ton* who must be invited for the sake of propriety."

William groaned.

"Now then," Aunt V continued, "where were we? Ah, yes . . . the menu . . ."

His aunt had just begun suggesting some sort of seafood roulade when Miss Blackwell unexpectedly said, "I do apologize, Lady Lindhurst, but I think I may be in need of some fresh air. Would you mind terribly if I stepped outside to the garden for a moment?" Even more unexpectedly, William found her turning to look directly at him. "Perhaps you would care to escort me, Lord Summersby?"

Would he ever? Trying not to look too happy about the promise of escape, he made a stoic effort not to smile as he offered Miss Blackwell his arm. "Certainly."

Lucy drew a sigh of relief the minute they stepped out onto the terrace. She'd accepted an invitation to tea only to find herself swept away in a dizzying array of wedding preparations. Noticing that Lord Summersby had looked quite put out by his aunt's sudden interference, she'd waited as long as she'd thought necessary before excusing herself. Not that a stroll in the garden with a fiancé who held a grudge against her was much better. Hazarding a glance in his direction, she realized that he was looking at her a bit oddly. "What is it?" she asked, fearing that a piece of her attire might be out of place.

He frowned. "I was under the impression that you were unwell, and yet you look surprisingly healthy now."

Oh . . . that.

"May I be honest with you?"

"Now would be as good a time as any," he said, his eyes narrowing.

"Right." Good Lord, he was making her nervous. "Well, it did seem a bit overwhelming in there and I . . ." He raised an eyebrow, and she felt the words cram together in her throat. He seemed far more imposing today than he had last night at the ball. She took a deep breath. "Well, the thought of fresh air did seem awfully tempting, and since you looked like you wouldn't mind rescuing, I thought I'd ask you to join me."

He stared at her for a moment. "Miss Blackwell, I have no idea what to make of you. Your actions last night were extremely selfish, you lie as if it is second nature to you, and you seem quite without regret about either. But still, there's something . . . desperate about you. I have a feeling this doesn't come as easily as you might want it to seem. What is it that you wish for me to do?"

Lucy wished she'd kept her mouth shut. She feared for

her life and would now have to worry that the little she'd said in his family's presence might place her in even greater danger. This was a family of spies; it was second nature for them to question everything, and she'd just offered them all a puzzle. If word got out that she was still alive . . . No, she couldn't risk saying more until she was certain that they were in private and that he could be trusted. Turning back toward the house, she said, "My lord, I do believe it's time for us to venture back inside. I've no desire for your aunt to think that I deliberately tried to avoid her company."

He caught her by the arm. "Avoiding the truth will not endear you to me," he told her firmly.

She looked down at where his hand touched her, hating the way her heart was responding. Forcing a serious expression, she looked up and met his gaze. "Sometimes, there is no choice."

He let her go, but as she started making her way back inside, she heard him mutter, "On the contrary, Miss Blackwell, there is *always* a choice."

CHAPTER FOUR

"This is not what your parents would have wanted for you, Lucy." Constance's eyes were filled with concern as she watched the young woman who'd been in her care for the past six years. "You've made a tremendous sacrifice, and on top of that you've forced an unsuspecting man into marrying you. What were you thinking?"

"You know the answer to that," Lucy said. As soon as the cake had been cut, she and Constance, the Countess of Ridgewood, had retreated to the parlor of Summersby House for a quiet chat while the rest of the guests continued to enjoy the celebration in the ballroom. "For six years I've been planning my revenge, and I swear to you, I *will* have it, no matter the consequences."

"Even if it means destroying the lives of others? What has Lord Summersby done to deserve a lot such as this?"

Pacing the room, Lucy ignored the question, offering only a reproachful glare in response. "He's rated the best agent within the Foreign Office. If anyone can find the man I seek, then it surely must be him."

"But to go as far as marriage?" Constance couldn't hide her shock. She recalled how sweet and quiet Lucy had been as a child. The tragedy surrounding her parents' deaths had made a detrimental impact on her. It was understandable of course, but she still worried that the path that Lucy now felt compelled to follow would only lead to more pain and suffering.

"You and I both know that it would be highly unseemly for a young, unmarried woman to travel alone with a single man whom she's not related to and has only just met. My reputation would be ruined, but, most importantly, so would yours."

Constance knew that she was right of course, but that was hardly enough to make the situation any better. It certainly didn't excuse what Lucy had done, though she was finding it difficult to make her see that. "I worry for you, my dear," she said softly. "All of these years, your heart has been so full of anger . . . I shudder to think of what you will do once you find the man you seek—if indeed you find him. More importantly, I fear for your safety. For whatever reason, he killed your parents and probably would have done the same to you if your mother hadn't helped you flee."

"I am reminded of Mama's sacrifice every day." Her voice was hard and unwavering as she turned her gaze on Constance, but as she briefly closed her eyes, Constance couldn't help but notice the tears that were pooling beneath her lashes. "Sooner or later, I *will* find him, of that you may be quite certain."

Constance sighed. She knew there was little point in trying to dissuade her; the whole affair had become a fixation. "What makes you think that Lord Summersby will even be willing to help you? The man will not be likely to grant you any favors in the near future after what you did to him."

"I've still to find a solution to that problem," Lucy agreed.

"I know that I am not in a position to change your mind, but please promise me that you will be careful. If anything were to happen to you . . ." Tears began to prick at Constance's eyes as she thought of Eugenia. It was still difficult for her to believe that she was dead. "I would never forgive myself." Lucy was the closest thing she'd ever had to a child. She was thirty-six years old. Her husband had died eight years previously, leaving her a widow—the two had never managed to conceive. Caring for Lucy had given her life purpose; she loved the girl with all her heart and considered her task a huge responsibility.

From her place by the window, Lucy offered Constance a sad little smile. Walking across to the sofa on which she sat, she took a seat beside her and pulled her into a warm embrace. "I promise," she whispered.

"Will you tell Lord Summersby who you really are?" Constance then asked, easing away a little so she could meet Lucy's eyes.

There was a pause, as if Lucy was weighing the pros and cons of doing just that. "I doubt it would be wise," she finally said. "I've no way of knowing how well I can trust him. The entire *ton* thinks me dead, and if word gets out that I am still alive . . . Well, I should hate for the news to reach Constantinople before I do."

A soft knock at the door sounded.

"Enter," Constance called out.

The door opened to Alexandra who, on the occasion of her brother's big day, had bought a lovely new gown—a lilac creation that suited her blue eyes and blonde hair rather well. "My apologies for interrupting," she said, her tone too clipped to be deemed polite. She'd clearly not forgiven Lucy for whisking her brother so hastily off to the altar. "William wishes to know if you are ready to depart for Moorland Manor."

Lord Moorland had gifted the great estate to William upon his marriage to Lucy, insisting that Summersby House in London would offer more than enough space for himself while Moorland Manor would be put to far better use by the young couple. He'd made it abundantly clear that he hoped for the place to teem with a multitude of grandchildren, thereby adding to Lucy's guilt since the matter of producing babies was presently the furthest from her mind.

Lucy nodded somewhat numbly. She'd no desire to spend the next three hours confined to a carriage with a man who clearly despised her. What choice did she have though? She'd made her bed, and now she must lie in it—however flea infested that proverbial bed might be. "Yes, I shall be right there," she replied, straightening her spine and squaring her shoulders. No time for regrets now.

The first hour of their journey was spent in complete silence. As much as Lucy kept trying to come up with something to say to her husband, she could think of nothing that did not sound pitiful or stupid. Eventually it was William who spoke. "Did you enjoy the ceremony?" he asked. He'd been looking out of the window but had now turned to face her, his eyes lacking any emotion whatsoever.

Lucy nodded. "Yes, thank you, my lord."

"Do not thank me, for I had nothing to do with it. It was entirely my aunt's doing."

As calm as his voice sounded, there was a level of annoyance to it that made Lucy cringe. "Yes, I know . . . I mean . . ." She shifted nervously in her seat. When she'd first met him, she'd barely been able to keep her mouth shut, yet now it was practically impossible for her to speak to him at all without her tongue tying itself into knots. "I merely meant to show my appreciation."

"You may do so tonight, my dear—in the bedroom." He gave her a meaningful smirk.

Lucy gasped. "Have you no sense of decency, my lord?"

"When it comes to my wife? None." He leaned slightly toward her, his arms crossed, with his elbows resting on his knees. "May I remind you that I did not enter into this marriage willingly? However, since I do find myself in the undesirable predicament of having you as my wife, and since I really have no means of escape, I will at least take whatever pleasures I may get out of it, no matter how loathsome that may be for you. Do I make myself clear?"

Lucy could barely breathe. Her immediate instinct was to punch the insufferable man for saying such outrageous things to her, but it was his right—he was her husband. An unusual feeling assailed her, as if she was falling from a very high place and with no one to catch her. She tried to compose herself. "As I mentioned before, my lord, all that I request from you is a little assistance. As far as this . . . undesirable union goes, I would not have forced it upon you without being able to offer you some means of escape."

Raising an eyebrow, William leaned back in his seat and fixed his gaze upon hers. "Go on."

"If you help me, then I shall grant you an annulment. You will be free to marry another lady of your choosing, and considering how eligible you are, I dare say you won't have much trouble with that, scandal or not."

A smile of amusement spread its way across William's lips. "And pray tell, how will you manage that?"

"If we do not consummate the marriage, then . . ."

William grinned in open amusement. "Is that your great plan?" Lucy stared back at him with a large degree of uncertainty. The sarcasm that dripped from his words made her edgy. "You stupid woman—lack of consummation is hardly grounds for an annulment. Where the devil did you get such a harebrained notion?"

"But I thought . . ."

"There are only three possible grounds: fraud, incompetence, and impotence. Let's examine each of these, shall we? I trust that Lucy Blackwell is your actual name?"

Lucy nodded, for she could not under any circumstances give him her real name; he'd know who she was immediately.

"Now, I know that Lady Ridgewood gave her consent to our union, for I spoke to her myself, so no grounds there I'm afraid. As to whether or not you are of sound mind . . . If you ask me, then you are undeniably as mad as a March hare, though I doubt any judge or jury will agree. As for impotence, I assure you, that I would rather hang myself before declaring anything of the sort, especially since such a claim would be matrimonial suicide. So there you have it—it seems that you and I are very much stuck with each other."

Lucy gaped at him. His expression was one of arrogant condescension. It was unfathomable. She'd been so sure of herself, so quick to act with the assumption that it could all be reversed. He'd assist her, she'd compensate him for the trouble she'd caused, and they would part ways. What a bloody little fool she'd been—too rash and blinded by her own purpose. The result: she'd trapped herself as much as she'd trapped him, as it turned out. Ironically, the last thing she wanted was a husband. She'd forced the marriage out of necessity alone, but once she found her parents' killer and exacted her revenge, she'd hardly be able to return to a quiet family life at her husband's side. Besides, what did she and her husband even know about one other? Nothing, absolutely nothing. It was galling.

"Feeling faint, my dear?" William's tone was mocking, and Lucy couldn't help but spot a look of pleasure in his gray-blue eyes. She couldn't blame him—not after what she'd done. They were now in the same boat, however heartbreaking that might be.

A blend of panic and fear swept through her. Not only would they be stuck with each other for life, but he'd already alluded to his marital rights. After everything that had happened thus far, she doubted that he would be gentle with her and nothing terrified her more. "If that is indeed the case, then I am doubly sorry for my actions. I will do my best to make you both happy and proud, of that you may be quite certain, my lord." She paused, carefully considering how best to phrase her next sentence. She needed to pacify him because if they could become friends somehow, then he might be more willing to allow her requests. "Perhaps it would be wise of us to become better acquainted with each other."

He regarded her thoughtfully before saying, "Yes, I think that would be a splendid idea. I'm very curious to discover if you have any singular trait that I might find agreeable."

She let the jibe slide, confident that he would respond better to a gentle wife than an argumentative one. "Promise me that you will stay with me a while at Moorland and that you will not hasten back to London at the first opportunity." What she wasn't ready to tell him was that she feared being alone—her days plagued by memories and her nights by terrible dreams.

Suspicion flickered across his face, eyes narrowing as he pinned her with his gaze. "For a moment there you almost had me fooled, yet I believe your real intent is to have me do your bidding. That's why you wish to keep me by your side, and you're hoping to do so under the pretext of desiring to better our acquaintance. You are sly in your attempts at manipulation, but you forget who you're dealing with."

Of course he was right, but Lucy knew better than to admit as much. Her only hope right now was that of retreat. "Let's forget about my reasons for wanting to marry you for now. It's nothing that cannot wait a while longer. Considering that we are bound to each other for life, whether it be for better or for worse, I think it prudent for both of us to try and make this marriage work—don't you?"

William pondered that for a moment. In truth, he longed for nothing more than to dump the wretched woman at Moorland and then head back to London in the hopes of forgetting all about her. However, he couldn't deny that the duration of his marriage might be made a little more bearable if he and his wife were given the opportunity to make amends and move past this bumpy beginning of theirs. "What do you have in mind?" he asked.

"I thought perhaps a wedding trip might be a good start—an escape from all of this and a chance for us to spend some time together."

William stared at her in horror. A wedding trip? Who the devil had ever conceived of such a ghastly thing? "You do realize that I'm a man and not a girl in a frilly dress?"

His wife's cheeks colored instantly. "Yes," she muttered with a hint of awkward embarrassment. "It would indeed be difficult for me not to notice as much, my lord."

Something about the way in which she said that pleased him immensely. "Ah, a compliment at last." His smile, as brief as it was, was at least genuine. His curiosity peeked, he narrowed his eyes on her. "If I were to agree to such a thing, might I ask where you'd like to go?"

Lucy's eyes met his in a deadpan stare as her lips curved into a charming smile that instantly made him feel as if his heart had just been dislodged from his chest. "Constantinople," she told him sweetly.

"Constantinople?" Well, the woman was certainly full of surprises. "A tad bit further than I'd imagined. Why the devil would you want to go there?"

"It has long since been a dream of mine," Lucy told him, her eyes straying to the window of the carriage. She was quiet for a moment, her thoughts clearly elsewhere until her gaze returned to him, and she said, "I've read a great deal about the people there, the culture, and the history. It intrigues me."

William was stumped. Perhaps there was more depth to her than he'd imagined. Indeed, he doubted that Lady Annabelle would have cared to venture across the Channel at all, much less as far as the Ottoman Empire. His own adventurous spirit relished the notion, though he wasn't about to let his wife know it just yet; she still deserved to languish a little. "Hm . . . I will think on it, my dear, and give you my answer in the morning." The carriage rolled to a sudden halt, rocking it abruptly from side to side. "In the meantime, it does appear as though we have arrived at our destination."

Lucy looked startled, as if she'd been so caught up in their conversation that she'd lost track of both time and place. She picked up her reticule, which had been lying on the seat next to her. "Thank you," she said just as William was readying himself to alight, "for considering my request. It's most gracious of you."

He couldn't help but feel as if he was missing something, and it filled him with uneasiness. "Make no mistake—as tempting as a trip to Constantinople in your company might be, I do not make a habit of handing out free favors. You will repay me for this, and you will begin to do so by committing to your wifely duties."

Lucy opened her mouth to speak, but William stopped her. "One word of protest and Constantinople will remain but a dream. My motive for marrying was to produce an heir. I would have been perfectly content to let Lady Annabelle see to that task, but you were determined to interfere.

"There is a lesson to be learned from all of this, and I suggest you learn it well: actions have consequences." His bearing was stiff as he stepped down onto the graveled driveway and turned to offer her his hand. She took it without hesitation or complaint, her chin tilted dignifiedly as she smiled down at him. But her eyes glistened with the sadness of a woman who'd resigned herself to her fate, and he realized that her bravado was not directed at him but at the servants who'd been assembled to greet their mistress.

William had never felt like more of a cad. He'd been harsh with her, threatened her even when she was barely more than a child, yet it was she who'd risen above the disastrous situation, saving them both from losing face. Damn it all to hell—she'd lured him into the parson's mousetrap against his will, he reminded himself as she settled her hand upon his arm. Nobody in his right mind would be able to blame him for his conduct toward her. If anything, he'd been more civil than most men in his situation would have been, and yet he could not shake the guilt that now gnawed at his conscience.

CHAPTER FIVE

There was no denying it. Lucy was terrified.

Upon their arrival, William had quickly retreated to his study under the pretext of having to see to some ledgers, not to mention the correspondences that must have accumulated and about a dozen other things that required his immediate attention. Lucy rather thought he'd been seeking an excuse to escape from her for an indefinite amount of time. Sadly, she hadn't minded in the least; in fact, she'd been rather relieved to take a break from his constant condemnation. Instead, she'd allowed the housekeeper to show her upstairs, marveling at the grandeur of the house as she went.

Dinner had been a lonely affair with no sign of William, and while she'd enjoyed her afternoon spent in solitude, she had hoped that he would make an appearance in the dining room, if for no other reason than to make her feel less absurd about being the only person seated at a table long enough to fit twenty. The sound of her cutlery clanking against her plate had resonated through the room so that by the time she was done eating, she found herself immensely relieved at the prospect of escaping back upstairs to her room.

But then her maid had come to attend her, selecting a nightgown that, to be frank, was really too flimsy and transparent for Lucy not to blush at the mere thought of donning such a garment. It had been selected by William's aunt, Lady Lindhurst, as part of Lucy's trousseau. The second her maid had finished combing out her hair and departed, Lucy had jumped up and grabbed her dressing gown—she wasn't about to let William find her lounging on the bed as if she actually looked forward to what was about to transpire between them.

Instead, she now stared at the heavy oak door with as much foreboding as a prisoner awaiting the executioner. Her knowledge pertaining to the more intimate aspects of married life was limited—not because Constance hadn't made an attempt to enlighten her, but because Lucy had been too embarrassed to listen. She now wished that she'd paid more attention, for her mind imagined an experience wrought with pain and suffering, not too dissimilar to what she expected childbirth to be like, albeit in a reversed sort of way. In fact, she was convinced that the whole affair might even be quite harmful, especially to someone like her with no experience. She instinctively crossed her legs and clamped her buttocks tightly together.

William had told her that he expected her to perform her wifely duties without complaint, but would he force her? Would it even be fair of her to put him in a position where he might consider doing so? She shuddered. No, she'd treated him badly enough already. The least she could do would be to keep her end of the bargain and submit to his baser instincts.

Perhaps if she managed to play the part of an agreeable wife, then he might grant her wish and tell her that they'd soon be off to Constantinople. Besides, she'd been through far worse, she told herself, and yet she still clutched her robe against her chest with trembling hands. She really wasn't as courageous as she'd hoped.

A soft rap at the door sounded. Lucy flinched but quickly recovered. "Come in." Her words sounded calmer to her ears than she'd expected.

The door eased open, and William entered, dressed in a deep blue velvet robe. Pausing for a moment, his eyes sought Lucy's, and as they did, a crooked smile forced the corners of his mouth upward. Whatever apprehension she felt about what was to happen, she couldn't help but suck in a breath. Her husband was truly a feast for the eyes with his dusty blonde hair, gray-blue eyes, and well-defined jawline. "You look lovely," he told her as he nudged the door closed behind him.

"Thank you, my lord." Her words were softly spoken.

William cursed beneath his breath. A better man would have thought of a far more appropriate word than *lovely*. To be fair, the woman who sat before him in her white dressing gown, her head held high while her fiery red hair cascaded over her shoulders, deserved better than that. In truth, she was completely and utterly mesmerizing—indeed, it was enough to make a wave of heat wash over him.

William's body tensed. This was ridiculous. He'd been with countless women before. Why then did he suddenly feel as nervous as a young lad about to have his first encounter with a female? Lucy was his wife after all, and he was merely following procedure—doing his duty so to speak. They both were. He drew a tight breath and made his way toward her. "I trust the room is to your liking?"

Looking flustered, if not a bit shy, Lucy dropped her gaze to the floor. "My lord, I couldn't have asked for better accommodations. Thank you."

William steeled himself for a moment, reminded that however calculating Lucy had been, she was still an innocent. She was on unfamiliar ground, about to embark on a life-altering experience with a man she barely knew. It couldn't be easy for her. Not to mention that he'd practically run off like a coward the minute they'd arrived, avoiding her completely until this moment. Truth was, it had all been so overwhelming—the rushed wedding; a manipulative wife who, in spite of his better judgment, still made his blood pump faster through his veins; the fact that, regardless of his best efforts, he'd had no say in anything for the past week, save for his own attire. And with both his aunt and father on her side, he'd also found himself saying his vows at the Grosvenor Chapel rather than at St. George's. He felt as if she'd laid siege to his life, and all he could do was stand by and watch it crumble around him. Still, he ought to have given her a tour of her new home rather than leave her to herself for hours on end. She was after all in an unfamiliar place, surrounded by unfamiliar people, and with a newly acquired husband who, from her point of view at least, wished to have very little to do with her outside of the bedroom.

With this in mind, he approached her with greater caution, and as he reached her side, he held out his hand, allowing his fingers to glide across her cheek, fascinated by the softness of her skin. Gently lifting her chin to force her gaze upward, the quivering lips and tear-filled eyes that greeted him were like a blow to his stomach. What on earth did she imagine he might do to her?

Without a word, he sank down next to her on the bed and put his arm around her, pulling her gently against him until her head came to rest upon his shoulder. "What are you so afraid of?" he whispered, brushing his fingers gently through her hair the way his mother had done when he was a small boy and needed soothing. A loud sob was all he heard in response to his question. "We got off to a terrible start, you and I, but we are married now, Lucy, and what we are about to share is only natural. I won't lie to you—there is bound to be a little pain involved, but it will be brief, and after that . . ." Dear Lord, she was actually trembling with fright. Swallowing hard, he forced himself to continue. "After that, Lucy, I promise you that you will enjoy it. At least I shall do whatever I can to make it so."

Raising her head, her eyes locked onto his, and William instantly caught his breath. Even his heart was beating a little faster than usual. He closed his eyes for a second. It was absurd. This woman had treated him most unfairly. She'd been entirely selfish, taking away his freedom without a single thought for his wishes. And yet . . . and yet somehow, she was having a far greater effect on him than any other woman he'd ever known. Did he resent her? Of course—it was difficult not to in light of everything that had happened. But what was done was done. The best they could do now would be to make the most of it, like she'd suggested earlier in the carriage, and try to move past it. After all, the rest of their lives would depend on it. That wasn't to say that he was about to forgive and forget from one moment to the next. She would still have to prove herself to him, and, unfortunately for her, doing so would be much more difficult now that he knew what she was capable of.

"I . . ." Lucy began, but her voice faltered. She paused, then took a deep, quivering breath. "All of this . . . I have no idea what to do, what to expect, or what *you* might expect of me. What if I disappoint you? And the mere thought of . . . of getting undressed in front of you when I've never even kissed anyone before kissing you at Trenton House that night . . ." Her words trailed off while her cheeks flamed with visible embarrassment.

William felt his heart tighten. The last thing he wanted was for her to feel uncomfortable. However, they were husband and wife now, and this was their wedding night. Part of him feared that if they couldn't get this part of their marriage right, then they'd stand no chance at all with the rest of it. Hoping to reassure her, he said, "I think you'll find that your mind has turned this into a far greater ordeal than it is likely to be for either one of us." He shifted a little in order to face her. "And, if I may make a suggestion, a kiss does seem like a lovely way to begin." Lucy's eyes roamed over his face. It was almost as if she was searching for something. He couldn't tell if she found what she was looking for, but to his relief, she eventually nodded her agreement. "I'll let you set the pace," he then said, forcing a calm and soothing tone that he hoped might put her at better ease. "I've no intention of rushing you into anything that you're not ready for, especially not when this is your first time."

She blinked as if she could scarcely believe that he was being so kind. Good God, he'd made her think him the very devil the way he'd chastised and mocked her in the carriage. It had been unavoidable though, for he'd been furiously angry with her—had wanted to hurt her somehow—and since he wasn't one to beat a woman, he'd chosen to do it with words.

He watched her now as she took courage and leaned toward him, her lips pursing as they met with his for the briefest of kisses—the most chaste he'd experienced in years. A rich scent of roses wrapped itself around him as she lingered, and there was something about the intimacy of the moment that sent his heart racing in his chest while a rich, velvety heat surged to his groin. Lord help him, he hadn't even seen her naked yet.

As she leaned back and met his gaze, he took her hand in his and gently squeezed it. "That was . . . a good beginning, though perhaps a bit timid." He noticed the look of despair in her eyes and quickly continued. "I believe I may have a little more experience in this department. Would you mind terribly if I gave you a small demonstration?"

With a shake of her head, she gave her approval, upon which he wasted not a second more. Drawing her against him, he lowered his mouth over hers and held her firmly in place, the silk of her robe rippling beneath his fingers.

This second kiss was as soft and gentle as her attempt at first, but then he drew her bottom lip between his own, teasing it apart from the upper. It took but a moment for her lips to part of their own accord, and once they did, his tongue was swift to slip between them.

He felt her tense beneath his hold and immediately

stopped before allowing himself to get carried away. He wanted her, though he doubted she'd noticed the proof of his growing desire. He'd assured her that he wouldn't rush her into something that she wasn't ready for, and he intended to keep his word. Besides, he wasn't the sort of man to take a woman against her will—not even his own wife.

Pulling away, he searched her eyes for the smallest hint that she wasn't doing this for his sake alone but that she wanted him as desperately as he now wanted her.

Disappointment gushed into his stomach at what he saw. He found no sign of hunger in her eyes, but something far worse. She looked determined, like a good little girl intent on doing her chores for fear of being punished. Was that really what he'd turned this into—a burden to be overcome? Releasing her completely, he increased the distance between them. "There's no need for us to be hasty." His voice sounded foreign to his own ears. "Let's take some time to adjust—get to know each other a bit better like you suggested. We have the rest of our lives ahead of us for this."

"But, my lord . . ."

"Don't worry. You've shown yourself to be a most obedient wife." He failed to mask the bitterness in his voice as he got up and walked to the door, his hand reaching for the handle. With his mind made up, he could barely get away from her fast enough. "Perhaps this trip to Constantinople will be just the thing to help our marriage onto the right track, but in return I want you to make me a promise."

"Anything at all, my lord."

"Don't ever deceive me again, or I swear to you that I shall make your life miserable." His tone was harsher than he'd intended, but it couldn't be helped. His unrequited desire had made him angry again, and besides, he couldn't abide lies, especially not when they came from his own wife. He wanted a partner, someone he'd be able to trust with his life if it ever came to that. Perhaps it was his experience as an agent that made this so vital for him. He knew the risk that came with trust; he'd learned that in Paris upon discovering a trusted colleague had deceived both him and England two years earlier. No, when it came to his wife, he needed to know that she would not betray him. Anything else would be intolerable. "Be loyal and honest, and the two of us might be able to get along."

Lucy watched him go while a cold shiver raced down her spine. William had shown her nothing but kindness and understanding in return for her dishonesty. He was a good man, she realized, but if she lied to him again, she'd feel his wrath—of that she had no doubt. But how could she be honest? He'd never allow her to go through with her plan if he knew what it entailed. And what if he found out who she really was? She didn't know him well enough to trust him not to tell anyone, and she knew, beyond any shadow of a doubt, that if word got out that she was still alive, not only would her life be in immediate danger, but she'd also be running the risk of failure.

She rose from the bed and walked across to the window, pulled back the curtain, and peered out at the starry sky. Small pools of water began to gather in her eyes. She'd hoped to remain indifferent and cold toward William, but the kindness he'd shown her was making her feel like the worst sort of ogre imaginable. If only they'd met under different circumstances—if they had, she knew that he was precisely the sort of man that she might consider falling for.

Turning her back on the darkness outside, she removed her dressing gown and climbed into bed. Unfortunately, with her plans just beginning to move into action, falling in love with her husband would be just about the worst idea in the world. The last thing she needed right now was to become some doe-eyed female who couldn't think straight because her heart was too busy going pitter patter. On a deep sigh of agitation she tried to push the image of William from her mind, but however much she wished it otherwise, she couldn't deny that her stomach had fluttered when he'd kissed her.

CHAPTER SIX

"I understand you'll be off soon?" Andrew Hutchins, otherwise known as the Earl of Fairfield, asked as he took a sip of Champagne.

William nodded in response to his friend's question. "It seems as if her ladyship has a desire to visit Turkey, though I can't for the life of me understand why."

"Consider yourself lucky, William. There are far worse places to travel to. When my brother Rupert got married for instance, his wife insisted that they spend a whole month at some distant relative's estate in Tuscany. I suppose it may have had its charm and all that, but if the countryside was what she wished for, then I don't see why they couldn't just as well have remained at home and saved the money." He leaned closer to William's ear. "Don't you dare tell them I said that."

William chuckled. "I wouldn't dream of it, old chap."

"So when are you leaving anyway?"

"Two weeks from today, though I have the distinct feeling that her ladyship would have liked to be on her way already. Personally, I can't see the urgency—must be one of those female notions I'll never comprehend. In any event, I told her that it might be wise of us not to hurry off before we'd had a dinner in her honor—get her better acquainted with my family and friends and so on. After all, things have been rather rushed around here lately. I see no harm in allowing our lives to settle a bit first."

."I rather imagine that you are trying to put your foot down. You can't do it soon enough, you know, or she'll be running you ragged. After all, I very much doubt that a house full of guests is what you really desire, thus confirming my suspicions, though I dare say you may have traded one evil for another."

William frowned. Perhaps Andrew was right. Perhaps he *had* used the idea of a house party as an excuse to show Lucy that, although he would grant her the trip to Constantinople, they'd leave when he was ready to do so and not a moment sooner. But there was a little more to it than that. He was the master of Moorland Manor now—a place that had once been alive with music and laughter. All of that had died with his mother, and it was something that he greatly missed. Now that he was married, he'd decided that it might be time to breathe some life back into the old estate.

He'd invited his family and his good friends Lord Fairfield and Lord Reinhardt. Following a run-in with Lord Galensbury at White's, Lord Fairfield had conversationally mentioned his invitation to Moorland, upon which Galensbury had immediately written to William, politely asking if he might join. Well, why not?

Another letter had soon followed, wherein Galensbury mentioned that he'd had a run in with Lord Stanton, and would William mind terribly if he came as well? Of course not—the more the merrier, William had decided.

Mary and Alexandra had in turn invited a couple of young ladies each in order to even the numbers between the gentlemen and the ladies—not that he much cared for a bunch of young hens parading about in the hopes of impressing one of his friends, but his aunt had insisted. In any event, it did appear as though everyone was having a jolly good time, though they were still two men short, Lord Galensbury and Lord Stanton having yet to arrive.

"I dare say you've made quite a catch with this one," Lord Reinhardt said as he strolled over to where William and Andrew were standing. "I just spent a good fifteen minutes in conversation with her ladyship, and I have to say, her knowledge regarding the political state of Europe is quite commendable. There's a lot more substance to her than to any of the young debutantes, that's for sure." He nodded discreetly toward Lady Amanda, Miss Scott, Lady Hyacinth, and Miss Cleaver, all of whom must have taken his momentary attention as a sign of interest, for they all turned into a bunch of snickering imbeciles a second later.

William ignored them and darted a look across the room to where his wife was seated, animatedly discussing something or other with his aunt and Lady Ridgewood. "Surely you must be joking, Charles." His gaze returned to Reinhardt.

If Charles was put out by his friend's lack of confidence in his judgment, he failed to show it. "Be that as it may," he said, "she knew all about Tsar Alexander's orders to have the Jesuits removed from Russia as well as the formation of the senate in Finland. In fact, she was quite opinionated about both matters."

William could say nothing to that. Lucy was clearly full of surprises, and this, he decided, was a rather pleasant one. He didn't mind having a wife whose head wasn't merely filled with what he considered to be fluff. On the contrary, he felt relieved to know that he might be able to have a meaningful conversation with her, though it did irritate him a little that Charles had been the one to discover this instead of him. Then again, he and Lucy had barely spoken more than two words to each other since their rendezvous in her bedroom, despite their agreement to improve upon their acquaintance.

That was five days ago now—the longest five days of William's life, especially since he couldn't seem to get the feeling of her body pressed against his out of his mind. It drove him half mad whenever he saw her. The desire to fling himself on top of her and ravage her was growing stronger with each day that passed. Yet he couldn't very well do so without terrifying her. Thankfully, there was a cold lake on the property for him to jump into; indeed, he'd never taken so many swims in all his life.

"What the devil's keeping Stanton and Galensbury?" he suddenly asked, for lack of anything better to say, if not to take his mind off the fact that his own stupid sense of chivalry was now keeping him from the marriage bed. "They should have been here an hour ago."

"Well I hope that they arrive soon and remove some of the attention from the rest of us," Charles said, just as Miss Scott raised her hand and waved at him teasingly. He responded with a scowl that immediately resulted in another burst of laughter from the young women.

"Do try to enjoy yourself, Charles," William said, though he couldn't help but sympathize. He knew all too well what it felt like to be hunted; he'd endured it himself for the last few seasons and had consequently grown attuned to which women posed a threat to him, avoiding each of them in the same way he might avoid an enemy in the field. He'd made his plans, certain that he would never be trapped.

Well, so much for that. In the space of half an hour, perhaps even less, Lucy had swooped into his life and claimed him as her own. She might as well have bound and gagged him, for there had been just as little chance of escape. His eyes flittered past Charles again to where she was sitting—laughing now at something his aunt had said. He had an urge to march over there, pick her up, and give her a good shake for all the nuisance she'd brought to his doorstep.

"Easy for you to say, old chap," Andrew remarked, forcing William's attention away from Lucy. "You're already off the market—no need for you to fear the toll of the church bell anymore."

William grimaced. "They don't look all that bad . . . the blonde one for instance, Lady Amanda I believe, she's very pretty. Perhaps . . ."

"Not in this lifetime," Charles ground out. "Those ladies are nothing but trouble—apples from the forbidden tree, so to speak. Extremely tempting, I grant you that, but take one bite and you'll find your arms cast into irons, your legs shackled, and your back whipped for the remainder of your days. No thank you, I say. I'll stick to my little opera singer if you don't mind."

"I'll drink to that," Andrew said, raising his glass and clinking it against Charles's.

William glowered.

"You on the other hand needn't worry," Andrew told him hastily. "Lucy's a winner, just as Charles says. I'm sure you'll be very happy together."

William wasn't so sure about that, though the discussion had renewed his interest in learning more about the woman who'd so quickly altered the path of both their lives. Still, she had yet to tell him why she'd sought him out in the first place. She wanted something from him, and the more time that passed without her telling him what that something was, the more worried he became.

As much as she tried to feign interest, Lucy was becoming increasingly tired of listening to William's aunt recount the latest fashion trends. Thankfully, Constance was there to add to the conversation so that all Lucy was required to do was nod her head on occasion and laugh at the appropriate moments. She had no desire to entertain all of these people for the next week, the mere thought of which only added to her impatience to be gone from England altogether. But William had insisted, and having no desire to raise his alarm by being too pushy, she'd managed a smile and agreed.

Since her arrival at Moorland, she'd spent most of her time in the housekeeper's company. Mrs. Barnes seemed like a good-natured woman and had eagerly helped her become acquainted with the many responsibilities that would now become Lucy's. Together, they had decided on the menu for the house party, and when Lucy had suggested buying only two cases of Champagne, Mrs. Barnes had diplomatically suggested a much larger quantity, saying, "Better to have too much than too little—especially if you still intend to host that ball you mentioned."

Hosting a ball for all the neighboring estates had been William's idea, but now that Lucy had begun planning for it, she had also started to look forward to it with great enthusiasm. Moorland Manor was the sort of home that begged to be filled by a crowd of people, all dressed in their finest evening attire while music sifted through the air. And since this would be her first event as Lady Summersby, she intended to make it a smashing affair.

"Aunt V, Lady Ridgewood." Lucy's thoughts faded as she looked up in response to her sister-in-law's voice. "Would you mind terribly if I stole Lucy away from you for a while?"

The second Lucy's eyes met Alexandra's, she knew that she wasn't just doing her a favor out of the goodness of her heart. She breathed a heavy sigh, hoping that there might be some escape from her sister-in-law, but when Lady Lindhurst replied, she knew she'd been a fool to think herself so lucky.

"Not at all, my dear," Lady Lindhurst cooed and then looked at Lucy. "We'll continue our discussion later."

Lucy could barely manage a *yes* or *thank you* before Alexandra had pulled her through an archway to a vacant spot by the window, their position partially concealed by a tall pillar. "I think it's time you dropped the act," Alexandra whispered, the smile on her lips a stark contrast to her tone.

"I beg your pardon?" Lucy tried to pull away, but Alexandra's fingers held her arm tightly in place.

"Look, it's inconceivable that you married my brother because you love him. None of us had even heard as much as the whisper of your name before you showed up at my house. I dare say that you pulled the wool over all of our eyes that evening when you told us William had invited you to dance. My poor brother was too much of a gentleman to call your bluff, and though I've questioned him about it since, he still insists that I'm mistaken in my assumption that the two of you had never laid eyes upon each other before then. I'm not a fool, Lucy—I know you intentionally trapped him, though I cannot begin to understand what your motive might have been for doing so."

Turning her gaze away from Alexandra's, Lucy stared out at the torch-lit driveway, the many flames casting an orange haze upon the ground. "I need his help," she muttered. At least that much was true.

"So you took it upon yourself to condemn him to an unhappy marriage?"

At that, Lucy reeled on her. The woman was out of line and far too blunt for Lucy's liking. "I didn't plan for it to be permanent, you know. Indeed, I intended to have the whole thing annulled on the basis of . . ." She shook her head, abandoning all hope of a decent explanation, for there was none—none that she was prepared to give anyway. "There's no telling that we won't be happy together. Besides, he won't be any less happy with me than he would have been with Lady Annabelle."

"You don't know that," Alexandra hissed. "Lady Annabelle was his choice—a choice you deemed yourself superior to. You had no right!"

As much as she wished it, Lucy could do nothing but agree that she did not. It only compounded her misery.

"I've given the matter a lot of thought," Alexandra continued, "and have managed to reach only one conclusion. Whatever your reasons, it does appear as though you have an alarmingly devious agenda."

A cold shiver ran down Lucy's spine, her eyes still fixed on the driveway. She dared not look at Alexandra, dared not so much as utter a single word in response for fear of giving herself away.

"I intend to make it my mission, Lucy, to find out precisely what that agenda entails."

"Please don't," Lucy whispered, but her words were lost to the sound of neighing horses as a carriage pulled up to the front steps. She watched as two masculine figures climbed out, their greatcoats twirling about their legs. A few moments later, the door to the parlor opened and two striking young men appeared, each handsomely dressed in black evening attire.

"I do apologize, Summersby," one of them was now saying as he happily accepted a glass of Champagne from one of the footmen, "but we were forced to stop in Craften when one of the horses lost its shoe—so sorry."

"An unforeseeable delay that couldn't be helped," William responded as he shook the hand of the other gentleman. He then looked around until his gaze met with Lucy's. "This way if you please."

With her jaw still tightly clenched from her altercation with Alexandra, Lucy knew that her smile must have seemed forced as she came forward to greet her newly arrived guests.

"I'd like you to meet Lord Galensbury and Lord Stanton," William said as he came to stand beside her. His demeanor led her to believe that they were not as close friends of his as Lords Fairfield and Reinhardt but merely acquaintances.

"It is a pleasure to meet you," she said, to which they each offered her a broad smile.

"The pleasure is entirely ours, I assure you," Lord Galensbury remarked as he reached for her gloved hand and raised it to his lips. He was the sort of man whom Lucy presumed many women would find attractive, for his face seemed perfect in every way—pretty almost. Lucy had to admit, however, she had a much stronger preference for a man with more rugged features, like her husband.

Straightening, Galensbury met William's gaze. "I see now why you married her as quickly as you did, you scoundrel. The minute you saw her you must have realized that she'd be available for only a matter of days before some other fellow made her his wife. However, I can't say I'm overly pleased by how swiftly you snagged her for yourself. From what I hear, nobody but you even managed to so much as dance with her."

Lucy instantly felt her cheeks grow hot from embarrassment. She'd never enjoyed being the center of attention and liked it even less now in the company of strangers, but when she raised her gaze to gauge William's reaction she couldn't help but notice that he was looking at her with something akin to appreciation. Feeling a surge of warmth in her belly, she returned her attention to Lord Galensbury. "You are entirely too kind, my lord," she replied.

"Oh do tell us that we'll have the opportunity to dance with you now, Lady Summersby," Lord Stanton said with a gleam of anticipation in his eyes. He was a little taller than Galensbury, though neither man was quite as tall as William. He suddenly smiled, and it was a smile so pleasant and kind that Lucy couldn't help but imagine that he must have tempted dozens of women with it. "We'll be terribly disappointed otherwise."

"I do believe that there are four other ladies present who'd be more than eager for your attention," William stated jovially yet with a note of possessiveness—something that surprised Lucy, considering how little she'd seen of him since her arrival. She hadn't thought that he cared for her at all. He lowered his voice before adding, "In fact, I am of the opinion that your arrival will be considered most welcome by Andrew and Charles. They both fear the toll of that infernal church bell."

"You make it sound like a funeral," Lucy said, her tiny moment of pleasure at feeling wanted by her husband ripped away. When he made no attempt to rectify his statement but merely stood there staring at her in bewilderment, she forced a smile to the best of her abilities, directing it at Galensbury and Stanton. "It was lovely to meet you both, and I do look forward to getting to know you better during the course of the next few days. Perhaps we shall have that dance after all. Actually, I do believe a waltz would be just the thing. If you'll please excuse me." And just like that she walked away, confident that she'd left her husband to seethe a little. Served him right.

Chapter Seven

Seated at the head of the long dining room table, William regarded his wife who was sitting at the opposite end. She looked so tiny with all of that space between them, her laughter ringing through the air in response to something his father had said.

He was still annoyed with her for walking off the way she had, offering to waltz with both Stanton and Galensbury if given the chance to do so. She'd intentionally tried to irritate him, though he still wasn't entirely sure what her motivation had been. After all, he'd practically declared her off limits to other men; she should be flattered. And yet, her eyes had been filled with sadness and her voice with pain as she'd taken her leave. He didn't understand it, but it had touched a place somewhere deep inside of him all the same—a place he hadn't even known existed, and that worried him. He couldn't afford feeling pity toward her, much less anything that bordered on a more emotional response.

Still, he'd been trying to give their marriage a genuine try—had, in light of what the consequence would be, determined to make a real attempt at building a life together, with the hope that they might one day develop an affection for each other. An affection—ha! What a ridiculous aspiration when the woman he'd married was clearly not to be trusted. Only an idiot would give her a second chance.

A future image of himself back in London, cavorting in the arms of a mistress while his wife kept house in the country, shot through his mind. An estranged marriage—hardly what he'd imagined or hoped for himself, not when his own parents had loved each other so dearly. A bitter taste filled his mouth, and he quickly took a sip of his red wine to rid himself of it.

Taking a bite of his food, he eyed his sister, sitting to his left, as he remembered something. "Lucy looked rather upset after talking to you. What did you say to her?"

Alexandra shrugged as she raised her gaze to meet his. "Not much."

"Not much?" He served her a frown that had oftentimes been used to intimidate the fiercest of men, yet it seemed to have little effect on his troublesome sister.

"I mean, I did badger her a bit I suppose. In fact, I told her that I know she married you with an ulterior motive in mind and that I plan to do what I can to discover what it is."

William stared back at her with incredulity. What was it with women? He swore he'd never understand a single one of them. "Alex, when will you learn to keep your nose out of other people's business?" His voice was tight, but there was still a hint of brotherly affection to it. He loved his sister dearly after all, in spite of her eccentricities.

"I'm sorry. I know I probably overstepped my bounds, but I was just trying to look out for you, William."

He shot her a smile of reproach, but secretly, he couldn't help but appreciate how much she cared. "I'll let you know if I need looking out for. Until then, I do hope you'll remember that I'm a grown man. I can take care of myself, so please don't say or do anything else in regards to Lucy unless you've spoken to me first." He waited for his sister to acknowledge his order, which she eventually did, albeit a little begrudgingly, then found himself asking, "You don't like her much, do you?"

Alexandra shot a glance in Lucy's direction and then shook her head. "No," she said simply. "Her dishonesty cancels out any positive attributes that she might have."

William considered this but found that he didn't entirely agree with his sister's sharp judgment. Alexandra was loyal to the bone, however. It was in her nature to protect the people she loved with fierce determination and had proved as much when she'd ridden to France two years earlier on a harebrained mission to clear his name of treason.

But, she did have a point. Lucy had made it clear she had an ulterior motive for marrying him, and he was now forced to consider if it was a powerful enough reason to merit her dishonorable actions. He found the spy in him rising to the challenge and wondered if he might be able to unravel the mystery behind his own wife. Why was it so important to her that they get married? His marriage had suddenly become the kind of intriguing puzzle he'd built his career on, and, for the life of him, he couldn't help but smile.

"One might have said the same of me." It was his sister-in-law, Mary, who was seated on his right, who suddenly spoke and brought him stumbling out of his daydream.

"I beg your pardon?" he asked as he raised his glass in response to a toast made by Andrew from further down the table.

"Forgive me," Mary said, giving him an odd little smile. "But I couldn't help but overhear Alexandra's comment in regards to your wife. If you'll both recall, I kept a great deal hidden from Ryan as well when we first met, yet you both seemed rather keen about the two of us getting married."

"But your secret was something to be admired," Alexandra stated. She lowered her voice to a whisper. "For heaven's sake, Mary, you were riding to the rescue of ladies in distress, performing operations with the competence of an excellent surgeon. Your actions are quite heroic!"

William noticed the flush that rose to Mary's cheeks as she said, "You think so only because you were aware of my actions, but suppose you hadn't been. Wouldn't you have worried that your brother was getting involved with a dishonest woman—one who appeared to be leading two separate lives?"

Choosing to ignore the question, Alexandra said, "Let's not forget that you probably wouldn't be married if it weren't for me—honestly, the amount of times I had to champion your cause with Ryan . . . countless!" Reaching for a grape, Alexandra pointedly popped it in her mouth while William did his best to hide his grin. This little repartee was becoming more amusing by the second.

"Granted," Mary agreed. "But that is beside the point, and before you say otherwise, Alexandra, for I can see that you are quite eager to do so, I merely think it prudent to suggest that you ought to give Lucy the benefit of the doubt. It is true that what she did was wrong, but I still believe that it would be wise to refrain from calling the kettle black."

William choked back a laugh while Alexandra simply gaped at her sister-in-law, apparently unable to comprehend her candor. "Excuse me?"

"All I am saying," Mary continued blithely, "is that from what I've been told, you weren't exactly forthright yourself when you first met your husband. Indeed, if anyone here is a master of deception, then it surely must be you."

Alexandra responded with a pout. "I didn't trap him against his will."

"You did other things that we'd best not discuss at present," William muttered. "May I remind you of a certain duel?"

"That was . . ." His sister wisely clamped her mouth shut in order to avoid saying anything else. And while they didn't discuss Lucy or his marriage any further during the course of their meal, William had to admit that both women had given him something to consider.

Retiring to the parlor with the ladies while the gentlemen enjoyed their after-dinner drinks in the library, Lucy decided that dinner had gone quite well. Everyone seemed to have had a pleasant enough time, and considering how hungry they'd all been thanks to Stanton and Galensbury's delayed arrival, Cook's bountiful feast had been met with unsurpassed greed.

She herself had had a lovely conversation with Lord Moorland about agriculture—not that she knew a great deal about it for that matter, but her Uncle George, who'd managed her parents' estate before their departure from England, had spoken to her at great length about various varieties of corn, when to harvest, and how to determine what to plant for the following year's crop. She couldn't have been more than seven or eight years old at the time, but she still had fond memories of riding out into the fields with him.

From what Lord Moorland had told her, Moorland Manor dealt mainly with wheat, while her uncle had shown a clear preference for barley. Her father hadn't seemed to care one way or the other. He'd been much too busy advancing his political career from what she recalled. She closed her eyes momentarily as the memory of both him and her mother came rushing back to her. It hardly seemed as if the time that had passed since that terrible night had healed the wound that ran so deep inside her chest.

Sucking in a breath of air, she opened her eyes once more only to find Constance staring back at her with concern. "Are you all right?" she asked with the beginnings of a frown.

Lucy nodded as she took her by the arm and steered her toward a couple of chairs that seemed forgotten in a corner. "Yes, thank you—just one of my flashes."

"I worry about you, Lucy. It doesn't appear as though the . . . incident . . . is getting any easier for you to deal with." Taking her seat, she patted the one next to her and watched while Lucy sat. "Keeping all this anguish and hatred inside you cannot be good for you. Perhaps if you were to confide in your husband . . ."

Lucy expelled a deep breath. Things were rocky enough between the two of them without her giving cause to further arguments. "I know that I will have to do so eventually if I am to ask for his help, but I find that it's a difficult issue to approach at the moment—especially with the state of our relationship in mind."

"And what exactly is the state of your relationship, if you don't mind my asking?"

Lucy breathed a heavy sigh. Looking around, she noted that all of her guests were otherwise occupied with one another and were therefore unlikely to pay the least bit of attention to the fact that she and Constance had secluded themselves. A maid stood by the doorway, and Lucy quickly waved her over, asking her to bring a hot cup of tea for each of them, which she swiftly did with great efficiency. Once this had been accomplished, she returned her attention to Constance. "He resents me."

"That is hardly surprising." The words were gently spoken, and yet they still stung.

"I realize that, though I hadn't expected to feel quite so miserable about it."

Picking up her cup of tea and taking a slow sip, Constance sought out Lucy's gaze. "I gather you like him then, perhaps more than you'd expected?"

"I don't know." It was the truth really. Since they'd met, her relationship with William had been a frantic rise and fall of emotions. At times he seemed cold and distant toward her, perhaps even angry and irritated by her, while at others he appeared quite caring and considerate. On top of this, there was the fact that he somehow seemed capable of weakening her knees with a mere smile or quickening her heartbeat with no more than a touch—not that he did so that often, yet it was making her feel not only uncomfortable but incredibly uncertain of herself as well.

Constance studied her for a moment. "He's quite handsome, you know."

A helpless laugh escaped Lucy's lips, as if she hadn't noticed.

"Have you . . . ?"

Lucy looked at her friend in confusion. "Have I what?"

"You know . . ."

Lucy gasped when she realized her friend's implication. "Heavens, Constance!" She noticed that Lady Hyacinth had turned her head to stare at her in surprise, so she immediately lowered her voice and leaned closer to Constance. "I cannot believe that you would address such a thing over a cup of tea and with guests present no less. It's highly improper!"

Constance shrugged her shoulders. "Perhaps." She paused for a moment before saying, "Well?"

With a sigh of defeat, Lucy shook her head. "Not yet."

"Well, then I do believe it's high time you give it your best try. A lot of marital conflicts can be resolved between the sheets, you know—or at the very least be momentarily forgotten."

Although Lucy thought she might soon die of embarrassment if they didn't change the subject of their conversation, she also knew that Constance had a point. She'd been married to William for a full week now, and he hadn't once tried to approach her since their failed liaison that first night together. It was disastrous. The worst part was that she'd no idea how to broach the subject with him. In fact, she completely lacked the nerve to do so, especially when they'd barely spoken to each other since. If only *he* would approach *her*, because if they continued to carry on in this manner, like two complete strangers who wished to have nothing to do with each other, their future together did look rather bleak to say the least.

CHAPTER EIGHT

Settling back against his favorite chair in the library, William raised his glass of brandy toward his father and uncle, standing by the fireplace enjoying their cigars. They immediately responded to his toast by raising their own glasses in return.

"I'm so glad you invited us," Andrew said, walking over and plopping down on another chair. "It was a splendid idea of yours, this house party."

"Yes, I must say that I'm rather happy to be here myself," Galensbury added as he joined them. "Any excuse to escape the season is most welcome, if you know what I mean."

"I couldn't agree more," Andrew said, tossing back the remainder of his drink and reaching for the bottle that was standing on the side table next to his chair. "And your wife is lovely, William, absolutely lovely. Honestly, I couldn't be happier for you."

William groaned. Apparently everyone thought her the most wonderful creature in all of Christendom. If only they'd stop singing her praises so repeatedly—it was not only tiresome to listen to but served to make him that much more aware of the fact that she wasn't who she appeared to be. "Thank you, both. I'm pleased to know that you're enjoying yourselves." What else was he to say? He certainly wasn't about to tell them that Lucy wasn't nearly as lovely as they thought her to be. Whatever issues the two of them were having, they were a private matter—not something that he was prepared to discuss with anyone other than his closest family.

"So tell us, William," Stanton said as he and Charles claimed the last remaining seats across from William, each with his own drink in hand, "how's married life suiting you?"

"You've definitely won the grand prize as far as her ladyship is concerned," Charles added, "beauty and brains all tied up in a neat little package."

"I couldn't agree more," Andrew said as he raised his glass. "It really does seem as though we must toast your good fortune, William." And raising their glasses, his friends proceeded to do just that.

William smiled to show his appreciation but said nothing.

"It was rather hasty, come to think of it," Andrew suddenly blurted out. "Are we to assume that there's a little Summersby on the way?"

"Good God, Andrew," Charles exclaimed. "Do you always have to say the first thing that pops into your head?"

Andrew shrugged. "We're all friends here, and besides, I'd rather be firm and direct and leave the wishy-washiness to the ladies." He then arched a brow and turned to William, one big question mark adorning his handsome face. "Well?"

William couldn't help but smile. As peculiar as he was,

he loved Andrew and his boyish ways. "As far as I am aware, that is not the case. It certainly wasn't the reason for my hasty decision to marry. No, I merely decided that my time was up and . . . having come across her ladyship at a private function, decided that she would do very nicely as my wife."

Andrew nodded understandingly as he sank back against his seat. "Well, congratulations then. I'm sure you'll be very happy together."

"Here, here," the rest of the group added, all raising their glasses for yet another toast.

"So, Charles tells us that you're off on your wedding trip soon," Galensbury remarked. "Mentioned you'd be heading to Constantinople?"

William nodded, noting with some curiosity the spark of interest that flared in his friend's eyes. "You were there yourself some years back, were you not?"

Galensbury nodded, a pleasant smile drawn across his lips while his eyes took on a distant gaze. "I found the Turks to be a very loveable people—wonderful cuisine and a culture unlike any you've ever seen north of the Alps. It's a long journey to be sure, but in my opinion very much worth it. And, if this was her ladyship's idea, then you really are a fortunate man. Most women would choose to go to Paris and shop for the latest fashion," he said as he shuddered.

"My words exactly," Andrew added.

The door opened and Ryan entered, followed by Alexandra's husband Michael, the Earl of Trenton.

"Where the devil have you two been?" William asked as he stared at both men.

"Michael was telling me about his newly acquired mare

during dinner. It was quite obvious that he was eager to show her off, so I suggested we take a walk over to the stables. I have to say that it was well worth it. She's a stunning creature, William. You really must see her."

"I shall look forward to it, though I do believe it will have to wait until tomorrow if that's all right with you. In the meantime, why don't you come and join us?"

"We were just discussing William's rapid rise from veritable bachelorhood to responsible patriarch, though I'm sure the two of you must have a great deal more to say on the matter, seeing that you're practically a pair of veterans in that department yourselves. After all, you've been married for what . . . one and two years, respectively? Surely your experience must be vast or, at the very least, vaster than ours," Andrew remarked.

Ryan grinned as he walked toward the assembled group. "You're always ready with a quick remark, aren't you Fairfield?"

"And yet he does make a valid point," Galensbury said, to which Stanton nodded. "Surely you must have some advice to offer."

Taking a seat while Trenton headed for the sideboard, Ryan glanced across at William, hesitating only for a second before saying, "It is my belief that all marriages require a great deal of effort from both parties. It is vital to be honest, to listen to each other, and to respect each other's opinions."

William watched as Trenton handed Ryan a glass of claret.

Andrew stared back at him. "That's it?" he asked with open disbelief. "That's all there is to it?"

Trenton slumped into the last remaining armchair. "Did you think perhaps that there might have been a magic formula?"

"No, but perhaps something that required a bit more . . . shall we say craftiness?"

"I don't believe there's a married man who'd dare attempt such a thing," Trenton said. William couldn't help but notice the sparkle of mischief in his eyes. "Not unless he desires to find his home transformed into an open battlefield—and don't be fooled by the inferior size of your opponent, for women are built that way primarily to deceive us. Mark my words, gentlemen: cross any woman and you'll find yourself opposing a formidable adversary. But be honest with her, listen to her, and respect her opinion on matters of importance, and she will be far more likely to listen to reason and to follow your sound judgment."

"Ah, so we *are* talking about being crafty then," Andrew said with an air of marked relief present in his tone.

"I . . ." Trenton began. He must have realized that there was little point in discussing the matter any further, for rather than continue he simply shook his head and took a sip of his drink.

"It seems the trick is simple enough," Stanton ventured after a momentary pause. "Be honest with her ladyship, William. Treat her as an equal, and I dare say you'll be thoroughly rewarded. Is that the gist of it?"

"It is, " Trenton said.

"Then I shall endeavor to do the opposite," Charles remarked, raising his glass in salute. "For I dare say the very last thing I desire is for any woman to conceive of the ill-begotten notion that she can get along with me. I'm having a deuced hard time fending them off as it is!"

William couldn't help but notice that both Ryan and his father were rolling their eyes. He stifled a grin.

"Anyone up for a game of cards?" It was Charles who'd spoken, no doubt tired of the topic of conversation.

"Sounds like an excellent idea to me," Stanton remarked. "Perhaps the ladies would like to join us. What say you, Summersby?"

Turning his head, William regarded the man sitting next to him. Like Galensbury, he didn't know him very well. They didn't share the same kind of history that had always strengthened his friendship with Andrew and Charles, and then of course there was the age difference. It wasn't much, but it had been enough to ensure that they had moved in different circles and missed each other entirely during their studies at Eton. "I'm sure they would be delighted," he said, knowing that his sister in particular would be more than happy to participate. He couldn't help but wonder if the same would be true of his wife.

As it turned out, Lucy wasn't the best Bridge player in the world, though she certainly seemed to enjoy the game regardless of whether she won, and William had to concede that this spoke well of her character.

Naturally, Ryan and Trenton had won hands down, much to the annoyance of Alexandra who'd clearly been hoping to best them both—a feat made so much more unlikely by the fact that she'd been partnered with Aunt V, whose interest in card play seemed somewhat lacking. She had continuously interrupted the bidding with all kinds of remarks, most of them pertaining to fashion.

Still, it had resulted in a most entertaining evening, but the hour had grown late, and with most of his guests now in the process of turning themselves in, William walked across to his father who was still discussing some issue or other with his Uncle Henry. None of the ladies remained, not even Lucy who had stayed behind a bit longer than the rest, for when he'd suggested that she go to bed too, the look of exhaustion upon her face had turned to one of relief, and she had quickly said her goodnights.

"Forgive me for interrupting," he now said, addressing both gentlemen, "but there is a matter of some importance that I would like to discuss with you, Papa. I do apologize, Uncle. I hope you don't mind."

"Not at all," Henry replied. "I'm feeling rather tired myself. It's been a long day."

"Why don't you go ahead, William? Prepare a couple of drinks for us, and I'll be along in a few minutes." The stern look in Bryce's eyes told William that no matter the subject he wished to discuss, it would be quite rude of them both to depart so hastily when Bryce and Henry had been right in the middle of a conversation. William knew that his father was right, of course, so nodding his head in agreement, he slipped quietly out of the door, determined to find his favorite bottle of cognac.

It was a good ten minutes before the door to William's study finally opened and Bryce entered, his broad frame blocking out the hallway that lay beyond. Acknowledging his son's presence, he stepped inside the sanctuary and closed the door smoothly behind him. He stood there for a moment as if pondering something then made his way toward one of the deep leather armchairs, took a seat across from William, and drew one of his favorite cigars from his jacket pocket. "It's been a while since we've sat like this."

Leaning back in his own seat, the leather squeaking, William raised his glass to his father before taking a sip. "It truly has," he replied a moment later then paused as if contemplating what to say next. "I'm having a difficult time determining whether my marriage is destined to be a disaster."

Bryce, his large frame leaning toward the candle on the table in order to light his cigar, stilled momentarily at his son's declaration. Returning to his task until it was completed, he then leaned back, settled himself comfortably in the armchair, and took a deep puff. "Why do you say that?"

William practically had to fight not to roll his eyes in response to such a question. "Why indeed? Because she seems to be completely wrong for me."

"Oh? And you've decided that after a mere week, have you? A bit soon, don't you think?"

"No, I don't think it's at all too soon. I know the sort of woman I would have been happy with. Lady Annabelle was that sort of woman. Lucy . . ." William raked his hands through his hair in open frustration.

"You may think that you made a mistake by marrying her, William, but the truth of the matter is that you didn't have a choice—not after such a public display of affection."

"Something I should have prevented! I never should have allowed her to take such liberties."

"Perhaps not," Bryce agreed. "Still, I think you're being dishonest with yourself in one regard."

William hurled a dangerous scowl in his father's direction.

"I think Lady Annabelle would have bored you to tears. She's too sedate, too proper, too ordinary, the exact sort of woman you've always claimed you wished to avoid. You need a bit more of a challenge and adventure, William—someone to match you as an equal. And I dare say that your wife shows great promise as far as that is concerned."

William stared at his father in disbelief. "She's a charlatan, Papa. When she speaks, I have no idea if the words leaving those pretty lips of hers are a lie. A marriage ought to be based on trust, respect, and loyalty, yet I cannot trust her or respect her, for she's given me no cause to do so, and as far as loyalty goes . . . she may be loyal, but if so, then her loyalty doesn't lie with me. If you ask my opinion, the woman is up to no good."

Bryce didn't bother to stop himself from grinning. He raised his glass to his lips and took a sip before saying, "The Summersby women generally are, you know. Consider your sister and your sister-in-law, Mary—strong women, both of them, but I dare say they gave their husbands a hard time on their way to the happily ever after that they now share. If I were you, I wouldn't give up on Lucy too quickly. She may surprise you."

"Ha! You are certainly correct in that regard. Indeed, it does appear as though she's full of surprises, doesn't it?" The bitterness in William's voice was almost palpable. "That aside, I'm more concerned with who she might turn out to be. Not only did Lucy make it clear she had a reason for trapping me into this marriage, but she herself actually hoped to eventually escape. When I told her that lack of consummation was most assuredly not grounds for an annulment, she actually seemed quite desperate, however offensive that might have been to me." Bryce raised a mocking eyebrow, which William chose to ignore. "However, that is the reason why I've asked you here. I need to know whom it is that I'm married to and if she poses a potential threat to our family. What do we really know about her?"

Bryce frowned. "Not a great deal, I suppose. After all, she's been secluded in the country for all of these years."

"And you don't think that's strange?"

Bryce shrugged. "Consider your sister. Few had ever set eyes on her before she showed up in London a couple of years ago to claim the most eligible bachelor on the market. I'm sure a lot of young ladies must have frowned at that." He got up and walked across to the sideboard. "Another glass of cognac?"

William nodded, rose, and strode across to his father, offering him his empty glass for a refill. "Mary made a similar point, and in light of the fact that Lucy and I are married . . . forever . . . I do feel as if I ought to give her the chance to prove herself. In fact, it was Lucy's suggestion that we ought to try and start over—get to know each other a bit better and so on."

Bryce nodded as he proceeded to fill their glasses. "I think that's an excellent idea, William." He handed William his glass. "Did you consider asking Lucy directly about her motivation for seeking you out? It could save you a lot of time and trouble, you know."

"Of course I have, Papa, but she and I have scarcely spoken since our wedding night." He saw the look of surprise on his father's face and, having no desire to offer any further explanation, hurried on with, "Whenever we happen upon each other, it always seems awkward and tense. Eventually one of us makes an excuse to hurry off and hide. It's really quite awful."

"I see," Bryce muttered, returning to his armchair. "I can't say I'm not surprised by this new revelation, for I rather thought that whatever attraction you might have for each other would help resolve your differences. You are attracted to her, are you not?"

William groaned. He'd tried as best he could to avoid the subject, but his father was clearly determined to address the issue. "It would be odd if I weren't. One cannot deny her beauty, but, before you say anything else on the matter, you and I both know that beauty means nothing if the woman reveals herself to be a snake. I merely wish to determine whether or not she is."

Bryce nodded. "Quite right. I'll send a letter to Percy first thing in the morning—see if we can't set your mind at ease."

Including the first secretary of the Foreign Office in their investigation did seem like a good idea. "Thank you," William said as he leaned forward in his seat, his elbows resting on his knees. "I especially want to know of her heritage. Who were her parents? Do you know?"

"I've no idea," Bryce admitted.

"For all we may discover, she's merely a servant's by-blow, hoping to live out the remainder of her days in a lap of luxury."

"You're speaking out of anger now, William. You know as

well as I that a woman like Lady Ridgewood would never have sanctioned the marriage if her ward were of inferior birth. What you've just suggested is an insult to both ladies."

"Forgive me," William said as he frowned. He hesitated a moment before saying, "I don't suppose you'd want to have a little chat with Lady Ridgewood . . . see if you can unearth anything?"

Bryce automatically arched an eyebrow. He might be old, but he wasn't too old to recognize a beautiful woman when he saw one, even if she was past her prime. And though the memory of Penelope still made his heart ache, he'd also begun to acknowledge that he wasn't quite dead yet. It had been twelve years, and now that all of his children had flown from the nest, he had to admit that he wouldn't mind a bit of companionship from time to time. "I'd be happy to, though I doubt she'll say anything to implicate her charge."

"Probably not," William agreed, "but it's still worth a try."

Bryce snuffed the remainder of his cigar in a nearby ashtray. "In the meantime, I do recommend that you give Lucy a chance. She's a pleasant enough girl, William, and intelligent to boot. You could certainly do a hell of a lot worse."

Reassuring words indeed.

CHAPTER NINE

Having said goodnight to his father, William made his way upstairs to bed, taking the steps two at a time as he went. He needed the reprieve that sleep offered, an escape from the troubling thoughts that were presently cramming his brain to such a degree that he felt a sharp headache coming on.

Reaching the top of the landing, his eyes immediately found Lucy's door, only to discover that there was a soft, flickering glow visible beneath it. He cursed under his breath. She must have fallen asleep with the light still burning. *Foolish woman.*

Tipping the door handle, he quietly eased the door open and peered inside, his eyes settling on the massive, four-poster bed that Lucy occupied. He could barely make out her figure in the dim lighting, though a sharp movement beneath the covers made him pause. "Lucy?" Another sharp movement responded, coupled with a soft groan.

Realizing that she must be asleep and probably in the middle of a dream, William closed the door carefully behind him and stepped forward, his path a straight line leading toward the oil lamp that stood on Lucy's nightstand. But the closer he came to her bed, the more agitated she became. He could see her head now, occasionally tossing from side to side as she mumbled a succession of incoherent words. She slowly quieted, and William continued on his way, moving gradually closer, his feet padding softly against the plush carpet. He'd almost reached her bedside when she suddenly muttered a loud, "No!" Her agitation swiftly increased. "No, Mama . . . no!"

"Lucy?" William voiced her name again in the hopes of urging her back to a more blissful slumber.

She didn't respond but cried out instead, "Mama!"

This was not the reason he'd come—to soothe away the nightmares of his wife. Their relationship was far too strained for such a task. But as he looked at her now, his face set in a mask of stone, he unwillingly felt his heart stir at the sight of the troubled look upon her face.

Expelling a low sigh of surrender that was tinged by aggravation, he did what came naturally. He slumped down on the edge of the bed, the mattress dipping a little under his weight, and gently brushed his fingers over the crown of her head. "Lucy," he whispered. "Lucy, wake up. You're having a bad dream."

She shrugged her shoulder and shook her head as if to rid herself of his touch, but he persisted until all of a sudden her hand whipped toward him from seemingly out of nowhere. She must have sought to push him away, but he caught her just in time. "No," she said, her voice more forceful than before. "I won't let you!"

Hardening his own tone in the hopes of breaching the

wall that separated her from reality, he told her sternly to wake up as he gave her shoulders a hard shake.

Lucy was no longer twelve years old. She was a grown woman standing in a dark alleyway, her feet bare upon the hard, gravelly dirt and her knee aching from the fall. Looking up, she saw her mother—her profile perfectly framed by the arched window. And then her back was suddenly toward her, and a man was there, a man so elegantly poised and all dressed in black, his face covered by an ugly, black mask. And then there was blood . . . lots and lots of thick, dark blood. It was flowing out of the window and down the wall toward her. "Mama?" she called out again, but all she heard in response was laughter, hideous and mocking laughter. Her mother was no longer there, but *he* was. He was looking down at her, and she realized that he'd taken off his mask. It made no difference though, for he had no face, this man who'd so often turned her dreams into nightmares. There was just a blank head.

She wouldn't run this time, she told herself—would not allow him to chase her away. This was her chance, her moment. She could hear him calling to her. "Lucy . . . Lucy . . ." Turning toward the sound, she spotted him. He was alone now and in the alley coming toward her, still holding the blade that he'd used on her mother, except *she* somehow had that blade now, and . . . oh, she could see his whole body grow tense as she served him a menacing smile. He'd already taken everything she cherished and loved away from her. She had nothing to lose, and so help her, if this was the last thing she ever did, she *would* put an end to this vile abomination of a man.

Running toward him, with her arm raised and eyes squeezed shut, she lunged at his neck, the blade sinking deep. Her eyes sprang open, and he was somehow there, unscathed, and shaking her, his hands tight about her arms as he spoke her name.

She immediately screamed and began to struggle, the bed sheets twining their way about her legs in a jumbled mess, but her attempts at escape made him grip her only harder than before. "Shh . . . shh . . . it's all right, Lucy. It was just a dream, that's all. You're safe now."

William?

Opening her eyes, she found herself staring back at her husband's handsome face. Her breathing was still ragged, her heart still pounding against her chest as he lifted her enough to hold her against him, and as he did so she lowered her head against his shoulder, reveling in the firmness of his embrace. With slow, even strokes he ran his hand over her hair, and she couldn't help but think that she had truly done him a disservice by forcing him to marry her. He was far too good a person to be burdened by her problems.

It felt good though, this moment between them. There was a tenderness about it that made her wish things could be different between them, and she suddenly realized that she was crying—whether from the shock of her nightmare or from knowing that she longed for something that would in all likelihood never be hers, she wasn't sure. All she knew was that she didn't want it to end. She wanted to stay this close to him forever, and she wondered what it might take for her to right the wrong she'd made.

Complete honesty.

He must have sensed that she'd somewhat recovered from her moment of fear, for he eased away a little and reached for the glass of water sitting on a tray beside her bed. Picking it up, he held it to her lips and helped her drink. "Are you all right?" he then asked, concern marking his eyes.

She nodded her head. "Yes. Thank you, I . . . I sometimes suffer from bad dreams."

"Would you like to share this particular one with me?"

She considered it but eventually decided against it. Their marriage would require work before she dared to share such personal details about herself with him. In fact, the thought of sharing what she'd gone through with anyone at all—of reliving each and every detail of that fateful night with a vividness that would surely be unavoidable—terrified her. As it was, the only person she'd ever spoken to about it was Constance. And even though she'd avoided going into too much detail then, it was not an experience she wished to endure again anytime soon, least of all with a husband who held her in low regard. So, rather than say anything, she slowly shook her head, averted her eyes, and fixed them upon her hands. "It was nothing really, just . . ." She shook her head again, drawing a deep breath. "Nothing."

She sensed him stiffen next to her and reluctantly looked back up at him, noting that he had eased back a little, and she quickly attempted a smile. "I'm sorry, I just . . ."

"Not to worry," he told her gently as he gave her hand a little squeeze. "Would you like me to stay for a while? Until you fall asleep again?"

She stared at him in wonder and said, "Why are you being

so nice to me?" She couldn't comprehend it. She'd acted terribly toward him, and yet he was being so wonderful in return. It only served to magnify her guilt.

"I'm not entirely sure," he muttered. His smile was warm and kind—no, sympathetic would best describe it—and the way his eyes suddenly sparkled with wonder and curiosity . . . Lucy felt her heart trip. It was as if the whole world had stopped around them. All she could see was William, a man so beautiful of both body and soul that regardless of what she'd put him through, he'd still be there, ready to stand by her side. It was a ridiculous moment—in truth, the most absurd she'd ever encountered—and yet her heart opened against her will and allowed him in just enough to claim a tiny corner of it.

Closing her eyes, she forced herself to ignore the giddy feeling that washed over her. She had to stop this ridiculous effect he was starting to have on her. What good would it do either one of them?

She paused with indecision. She did want him to stay, but she didn't want to give him the wrong impression either. Constance had advised her to get on with the matter of consummating their marriage, and while Lucy did desire to do so, she still felt as if there was a gaping canyon between herself and William. Over the next few days, she would try to make more of an effort to develop a friendship between them, and once that happened, then . . . She felt her cheeks begin to blush at the prospect of what they might then share. In the meantime, however, she simply shook her head. "Thank you, but I'll be fine," she said. "After all, it was just a dream. It was kind of you to come and see to me though."

"Well then," he said, his voice completely even and devoid of all emotion, "I wish you a good night." He rose, turned to go, and then paused. Looking back over his shoulder he added, "Should you need anything, you know where to find me."

Lucy nodded her appreciation and then watched him go, his broad frame disappearing out of sight as he closed the connecting door between their bedrooms behind him.

Pausing for a moment outside her door, William expelled a breath that he hadn't even realized he'd been holding. He'd hoped his outward display of sympathy and consideration would have chipped away at her barriers enough to grant him the opportunity to win a little more of her confidence—a confidence that had become essential to discovering her true motive for marrying him. But the determination to keep whatever secrets she had bottled up inside of her was all too apparent.

Time, he reasoned, coupled with patience and persistence would serve him far better than any display of the anger he felt coursing through his veins. It took every ounce of his will-power to stop his jaw from clenching and to stop the harsh words sitting on the tip of his tongue from spilling forth. And she made it no easier for him as she gazed back at him with a pair of big round eyes that effectively concealed her true, meddlesome nature.

As she'd sat there in bed, her slim figure propped slightly up against her pillow and her red hair fanned out behind her, she'd looked as innocent as a newborn babe. When it came to the art of deception, William knew that he had met his match, yet it made him only more determined to discover the truth about her.

Crossing the floor with heavy steps, he shrugged out of his jacket, undid his cravat, and began rolling up his shirt sleeves. He needed a drink to calm his mood. Truth was, he'd never been more confused in all his life. Considering how much he liked having a situation under his command, he hated feeling as though he'd lost all control of his own life. He thought of Lucy. Nobody had ever confounded him more, and while he wanted to give her the benefit of the doubt, he also felt it prudent to tread with caution. He wasn't about to risk having his heart broken. He scoffed at the notion, no chance of that happening as long as he didn't love her. And the way things were between them right now, it seemed unlikely that he ever would.

Forcing himself to ignore the ache in his chest, he went to the tray that always sat upon his dresser and reached for the crystal carafe that beckoned. He'd just curled his fingers around the neck of it when a loud clatter reached his ears—it had come from Lucy's room.

Without pause, he ran across to the door and yanked it open, his eyes roaming the darkness that greeted him. "Lucy?"

"I'm quite all right," she replied. She sounded moderately embarrassed if he wasn't mistaken. "Sort of, at least."

Sort of?

Returning to his own room momentarily, he grabbed an oil lamp and marched back into Lucy's room, instantly catching his breath. "What on earth happened?" he asked, making a stoic attempt at keeping his voice level. It was damn near impossible though when his wife was standing there before him in nothing but her nightgown—her very translucent nightgown. He swallowed hard and tried to focus, but the more he did, the more aware he became of the slow heat that slid over him before settling in his groin, stirring him more vigorously than ever before.

Her body was that of a goddess—slim hips below a curvy waistline and above that . . . his mouth grew dry and he swallowed again. Heaven help him if those weren't the sort of breasts that every man fantasized about—plump and perky as they strutted against the flimsy fabric in a seemingly eager attempt to escape. Well, there was a part of him that was growing more and more eager for escape by the second. He hoped she wouldn't notice.

"I was trying to go back to sleep but felt restless, so I thought I'd go for a midnight stroll in the garden, but when I tried to find my dressing gown and shawl, I stubbed my toe against the table over there, knocking over the vase."

"You were planning to go for a walk in the garden, dressed in nothing but your dressing gown? Did it occur to you that any number of our guests could have happened upon you? It would have been highly inappropriate to say the least."

"Everyone's fast asleep, William . . ."

"We're not." If he didn't want her to as much as waltz with one of his friends, did she really imagine that he might be all right with one of them seeing her in a state of deshabille?

"It's what I've done in the past whenever I can't sleep."

"Even in winter?" He couldn't imagine that she was that irresponsible, but he had to ask all the same.

"Of course not." She seemed annoyed by the question. "When it was too cold to go outside, I'd merely roam the house."

"Ah." He studied her for a moment, and felt another wave

of heat crash over him. "You're not going anywhere dressed like that, not even if you're covered up by your dressing gown. If you'd like something to calm your nerves and lull you to sleep, however, I will be happy to offer you a glass of excellent brandy as well as my charmingly good company." He saw that her lips had begun to twitch in response to what he'd said. A moment later, she actually laughed, and when she did, it was as if her whole face lit up. William felt his heart swell with inexplicable pleasure.

"Very well then," she acquiesced, "but if you don't live up to your claim, I shall be thoroughly displeased."

William found himself smiling as he waved her through to his bedroom. He'd always hoped for a wife with a sense of humor and couldn't help but wonder what other charming attributes Lucy might possess. She'd apparently forgotten all about her dressing gown now that she wouldn't be venturing outside, and as hard as he tried to refrain from ogling her, he simply couldn't keep his eyes from taking the occasional peak at her breasts. It clearly hadn't occurred to her that her nightgown might be rather see-through, for if it had he very much doubted that she'd be acting quite so casually. "Have a seat," he offered as he headed over to his dresser and filled an extra glass with brandy. He took a deep breath and then forced the air back out again before turning back to face her, closing the distance between them with a few swift steps.

Once seated comfortably, his legs firmly crossed in the hopes of concealing any further attraction he might feel for her, he raised his glass to hers. "To new beginnings," he said as their two glasses clinked together.

She smiled in response—a genuine smile, meant only for

him, and it filled his heart with hope. "To new beginnings." She hesitated a moment after taking a sip, then said, "I'm sorry about earlier, William. I hope I didn't embarrass you too much in front of your friends, but when you insinuated that marriage was such a terrible thing to subject oneself to . . . I have to admit that it hurt."

He stared at her in befuddlement. He'd thought she would ignore the issue entirely and pretend it never happened; he certainly hadn't expected an explanation or an apology, and while he hadn't understood her actions at the time, he felt like a complete cad now that he did. "I should be the one apologizing, Lucy. I only meant that Andrew and Charles are hoping to maintain their state of bachelorhood. It wasn't a jibe directed at you."

"I know that now." She let out a bit of a shaky sigh and offered him a shy smile. "You know, I actually think you're a rather wonderful man, when you're not so busy hating me— quite dashing too."

William grinned. Oh she did, did she? "You're not so bad yourself, as far as accidental brides go." She immediately smiled. "And I don't hate you, Lucy. I just don't like having important decisions in my life, like marriage for instance, decided by someone else. But everyone seems quite determined to sing your praises, so I dare say I've become a bit eager myself to discover what you're really like." And with a little more effort at gallantry on his part, he hoped she might soon grant him the opportunity to sample what she was presently keeping on such prominent display.

CHAPTER TEN

When Lucy awoke the following morning, she took more care than usual in getting dressed. Her amicable conversation with William the night before had given her a sense of comfortable companionship, renewing her hope that he might still warm to her—especially if she allowed herself to open up a little. With this in mind, she had confided in him her reason for insisting they marry at Grosvenor Chapel. Her parents had married there, and with both of them gone from her life, she'd hoped to bring them a little bit closer in spirit. William had held silent as she'd spoken, his eyes growing soft with sympathy. He hadn't said much in response—just a simple, "I'm sorry."

Donning a pale green muslin gown, Lucy asked her maid to fetch her cream-colored shawl, for although it promised to be a warm day, she didn't want to catch a chill if she happened to find herself in the shade.

Regarding her appearance with a critical eye, she wondered if William might find her appealing. Her stomach fluttered at the thought of it, and she secretly hoped that he would. It had never before occurred to her to try to win a man's affection, and she'd certainly never considered that she'd have to make a deliberate effort to do so with her own husband. He had every reason to be annoyed with her, yet last night it was almost as if he'd enjoyed her company.

Consequently, she'd spent a great deal of time later on in her bed, before falling asleep, considering how to tell William about her past. She wanted to trust him, but she also knew that men often felt they knew best when it came to matters of danger and gravity. If he knew what her real motivation was for wanting to go to Constantinople, she feared he'd insist that she remain at home where she'd be safe and try to put the entire matter behind her. Or, even worse, word would get out that the Earl of Hampstead's daughter had resurfaced, and the man who'd killed her parents would seek her out and kill her too.

She felt her hands begin to shake at the thought of it. No, she couldn't continue to live in such fear, forever looking over her shoulder. Besides, she needed the closure that the death of the assassin would offer. She only hoped that William wouldn't be too furious once he discovered that she'd chosen to deceive him even further. Of course, there was still the possibility that he'd have their marriage annulled when he learned the truth, for as he'd said, fraud would make for a valid reason, and she *had* lied about her family name. It wasn't Blackwell but rather Etheredge.

With a heavy sigh, she took one last glance at her own reflection to ascertain that she looked her best and then grabbed her straw bonnet and headed for the door.

"Would you care for a cup of tea?" Lady Lindhurst asked

as Lucy took her seat at the table in the dining room. Only the women remained, the men having apparently finished their meal already and departed for the stables.

"Yes, thank you," Lucy replied, raising her cup and allowing William's aunt to pour.

"I must say that you do look particularly lovely today."

The comment came from Alexandra and held no sense of mockery or sarcasm to it as Lucy might have expected a compliment from her to do. Instead, it seemed as if she'd given her honest opinion, which led Lucy to believe that William must have had a word with her. It unnerved her that Alexandra had so bluntly addressed the issue of her marriage to William the previous evening, but if she wished to make an attempt at amends, then it would be rather badly done on Lucy's part to ignore the olive branch she'd just been handed, so she hastily shot her sister-in-law a smile. "As do you. I especially love that shade of blue on you. It goes so well with your complexion and really brings out the color of your eyes."

"And I do so adore the color of your hair," Mary added from the other end of the table, where she'd been advising Lady Amanda and Lady Hyacinth about the uses of a variety of different herbs. "It's absolutely stunning! Has it always been so vibrant?"

"I believe so," Lucy murmured as she felt the heat rise to her cheeks. She appreciated how kind they were being, but all of the attention was making her feel more than a little bit uncomfortable. Needing to occupy herself with something so she didn't feel too much like an artifact on display, she took a sip of her tea.

"And, may I add," Lady Lindhurst remarked as she nudged

the bread basket, cheese, and jam in Lucy's direction, "few men are able to resist a striking redhead, you know."

"Aunt V, I hardly think . . ." Alexandra protested, clearly attempting to prevent her aunt from making any inappropriate comments.

"Oh for heaven's sake," Lady Lindhurst exclaimed, to which the younger women at the table stilled so as to give the countess their complete and undivided attention, expectantly hanging on her every word, "anyone with a pair of eyes in their head can see how tightly wound Lucy is, not to mention how terse William has become. I dare say that their marriage is already under a tremendous amount of strain, so it really wouldn't hurt for Lucy here to try and charm the breeches off her husband."

Miss Scott instantly burst out laughing but quickly stifled it by slapping a hand over her mouth. Everyone else looked marginally appalled, except for Lucy who felt as though she must have paled to such a degree that she feared she might fade away altogether.

"What?" Lady Lindhurst asked unblinkingly.

"Please excuse her bluntness, Lucy," Alexandra said. "She does mean well, but as you can see, she's still a little rough around the edges. Indeed, it can be quite a challenge to bring her out into polite society."

Lucy gaped. She simply couldn't believe that Alexandra had just said such a thing about a peeress, regardless of their blood ties, and in her presence no less. She knew by now that her sister-in-law was a bit . . . *different* from other young ladies, but really this was incomprehensible. She rather expected Lady Lindhurst to rise from the table and walk away in disgust, but instead she just snorted and said, "You're one to talk."

Alexandra merely cast a disapproving glance toward her aunt, as if hoping to stop any further comment from leaving the older woman's lips. She then returned her attention to Lucy. "Truth be told, we've all been hard on you for the manner in which your marriage to William came about, but in all fairness, this is between you and him. Still, I do believe that it will be much easier on both of you if you make an effort to get along."

Lucy stared back at her. Was she seriously receiving marital advice from the same woman who'd threatened to uncover her devious agenda the last time they'd spoken? She wondered how long it might take for her to grow accustomed to the many eccentricities that the Summersbys had to offer. The women, in particular, were an unusual breed.

That aside, she had to agree with Alexandra's suggestion, for she'd come to the same conclusion herself and had to admit that it did hold a great deal of appeal. A soft shiver tickled her spine. She was attracted to William. It would be pointless denying it, and since they *were* married . . . If his aunt had noted that their relationship seemed strained, then Lord only knew what the servants might be discussing below stairs. As much as it frightened her, she knew she'd have to make an effort to get them back on a smoother path, if for no other reason than to remove all speculation. For, she concluded, as long as she and William appeared to be happy together, the less likely it would be for others to question her motives for marrying him. Of course, there was much more to it than that—her growing appreciation of the man for one thing.

"Thank you," she told Alexandra. "I do believe that's very sound advice. I shall do my best to make him happy."

"Do that, and I may not have to challenge you to a duel after all," Alexandra remarked. Her eyes were deadly serious.

Lucy all but choked on the piece of bread she'd just bitten into. "A duel?"

Mary and Lady Lindhurst both rolled their eyes. "Must you always resort to violence?" the viscountess asked as she turned to Lucy. "She's famous for throwing down the gauntlet at the slightest provocation."

Alexandra started laughing. "I was joking, Aunt V. Must you always take me so seriously?" She turned her eyes on Lucy. "Treat him well, and you and I might one day be friends, but remember, Lucy, I protect those I love."

So do I.

The words, however, never left Lucy's lips. Instead, she merely nodded, understanding that if Alexandra had been in her shoes, she would probably have acted in much the same way.

After breakfast the ladies decided to take a stroll in the gardens. Walking alongside Alexandra, Mary, and Lady Lindhurst while the unattached ladies trailed behind them (undoubtedly discussing the bachelors present, if their occasional snickers were any indication), Lucy allowed her guard to slip enough to let her true personality shine. She'd never really had any friends. Truth was, in Constantinople she'd lived a secluded existence under her parents' protection, and after returning to England, her life at Ridgewood Estate had been equally devoid of companionship, albeit for an entirely different reason. Now, listening to the amicable verbal exchange of these women who were so familiar with one another, she felt a sense of longing pulling at her soul. This was what she wanted—friends, family, and love. She smiled as Mary listened to parenting advice from Alexandra.

"How old is Vanessa now?" she asked the minute a pause arose in the conversation.

"She'll be three months in a couple of weeks," Mary said, smiling the satisfied smile of a woman who'd brought a child into the world. "It's incredible how easily someone so small can command an entire household. You should have seen my husband when he held her for the very first time. Although he'll deny it, he was really quite emotional."

"So was Michael when both Richard and Claire were born," Alexandra said. "These men . . . they erect walls of steel around their hearts and put on a grave mask to conceal what they're truly thinking, yet a small, dimply chuckle from their babes will disarm them immediately. And if their child happens to fall ill or some other threat presents itself? Lord help me but not even the chains of Prometheus would be able to keep them at bay."

Lucy was stunned. They all seemed so tough and unapproachable, these men. In truth, Lord Summersby and his brother both made her feel uneasy with their serious expressions and scowls. Was William perhaps the same, she wondered—hard on the outside with an underlying thread of sensitivity? He'd already showed himself to be concerned and considerate toward her, but she now wondered if there wasn't a softer spot somewhere deep down inside of him, a place he kept protected. The thought of uncovering it made her own heart beat a little faster.

"In answer to the question you're not asking," Alexandra continued, sending Lucy a lopsided smirk, "my brother's no different, though developing closeness might be difficult in light of everything that you've done. Your actions don't exactly inspire trust, you know. However, I dare say it's not impossible for the two of you to recover from this. Just be honest with him."

Lady Lindhurst snorted and all eyes turned to her. Eyeing each of them for a moment, she finally relented. "You shouldn't be so quick to judge." Her remark was directed at Alexandra. "It's not as if you were the pinnacle of honesty when you met Lord Trenton."

"I—"

Alexandra's aunt wouldn't allow her to continue however. "He thought you were a *man* for heaven's sake. Not only that but you allowed him to continue believing so for several days. And after that . . . well, suffice it to say that you're hardly in a position to criticize anyone, much less Lucy."

"William's life was in danger at the time," Alexandra protested. "The scenario was completely different."

Lady Lindhurst waved her hand as if this last bit of information was completely inconsequential. "And you, Mary." Mary halted as if prepared to take the blow that her friend's aunt seemed ready to deal her. Lucy felt as though she ought to somehow intervene but wasn't sure of how to go about it. "We all know what you used to get up to in the middle of the night, and I know for a fact that Ryan wasn't aware of it."

Lucy's mouth dropped open as she stared at the marchioness, unable to imagine what Lady Lindhurst might be talking about. Apparently Mary felt the need to explain, for she quickly said, "She's referring to my medical practice. I'm a surgeon, you see, something which my husband had a rather difficult time digesting. It's become far more acceptable now that he and I have started work on building our own hospital, but, be that as it may, her ladyship is correct. I did keep my identity as a surgeon purposefully hidden from Ryan in the beginning, though I'd like to point out that unlike Lucy here, he and I weren't married.

"That said, I, like you, Lady Lindhurst, believe that Lucy may have an honorable reason for what she's done, and if that's the case, then she probably has cause to keep it hidden, though I really would advise you to tell William about it, Lucy, however troubling it may be."

"It's settled then," Lady Lindhurst remarked. "We shall judge Lucy based on her character and forget about the rest of it, unless she gives us a valid reason to question her conduct. If she and William are meant to be, they will surely find a way to muddle through this together. In the meantime, I for one intend to believe that she had a damn good reason for picking him instead of someone else. Let's leave it at that for now, shall we?" And while Alexandra and Mary looked on in amazement, no doubt stunned by Lady Lindhurst's use of profanity, the viscountess took Lucy by the arm and steered her away along a path that led directly toward the stables.

They arrived just as the men were returning from their morning ride, the horses panting heavily from the cross-country gallop that they'd just been subjected to. Spotting the women, William turned his mount toward them, tugged on his reins, and dismounted. "I would have thought that you might have preferred the rose garden to the smell of muck," he said, his eyes drifting past each of the women until they came to rest upon Lucy. His eyes widened. "May I say that you look exceedingly lovely today, my dear."

Her cheeks burned with self-consciousness as she grasped for an appropriate response. She knew that a mere *thank you* would suffice, but the words seemed to jam together in her throat all at once. Whatever was the matter with her? She suspected it might have a lot to do with William's appearance.

His jacket was gone, and so was his cravat. The top buttons of his shirt had been opened, the sleeves rolled up past his elbows and, wet from sweat no doubt, it clung to his back and his chest, alluding to a masculine figure that had instantly made her mouth go dry. And his hair . . . the ride had whipped away all its neatness, ruffling it into something wild and unruly. He looked more rugged than usual, and heaven help her for thinking it—utterly wicked. The debutantes must have made a similar observation, for they were all huddled together and giggling like the green girls that they were.

"She does, doesn't she," Lady Lindhurst said, coming to her rescue and filling the silence.

Lowering his voice, he added, "However, next time you choose to visit the stables, I would recommend something less . . . overt." His gaze dropped to her bosom. She'd deliberately selected her dress because of its particularly low décolletage, which she had hoped he would find alluring but apparently did not, given his sudden frown.

A rush of heat prickled her skin, in response not only to his comment but also to his closeness. It was enough to make her lose her wits entirely. Closing her eyes against his undeniable masculinity, she tugged at her shawl in an attempt to cover herself, her eyes seeking anything that wasn't her husband. Her throat had begun to tighten and her vision to blur. She'd been so looking forward to seeing him again today but now wished that she had remained in bed instead.

"William Summersby! That is no way to talk to a lady. Can't you see that you've upset her. She's practically in tears," his aunt scolded.

All Lucy wanted to do was turn and run from the ghastly situation. She'd become the center of attention now—and not in a positive way at all. She'd no desire for any of the people present to watch her crumble, least of all William. Why was he being so mean? Last night they'd laughed together over a glass of brandy, and now her heart felt as if it might crack. Somehow, she had to rise above it though. She was Lady Summersby now, and a hostess to all of these ladies. It really wouldn't do for her to fall to pieces in front of them. So, swallowing hard, she straightened her spine, pulled her shoulders back, and lifted her chin. "My sincerest apologies, my lord," she told William. "I shall endeavor to wear a more matronly gown in the future. After all, I seek to please only *you*."

There was a bite to her tone that clearly caught him off guard, for he took a retreating step backward and stared at her in surprise. Before she had the chance to examine the situation any further, the sound of male voices carried on the breeze. She turned her head, shading her eyes against the sun with the palm of her hand to find Lords Fairfield, Reinhardt, Galensbury, and Stanton approaching. Ignoring William entirely, with the intention of making a point, she left the safety of her group and stepped lightly toward her other guests. And then, attempting a smile more genuine than that of a child's on Christmas morning, she drew their attention. "It appears as though you have had quite an exerting ride!"

"We certainly did, my lady," Reinhardt replied, his step quickening as if he hoped to reach her faster. She sent her husband a meaningful look; he could learn a thing or two about gallantry from this friend of his. Her attention was swiftly returned to Reinhardt however, for he was now before her, taking her hand in his and bowing over it as he pressed a kiss against her knuckles. He straightened and offered her a charming smile. "William lent me one of his geldings—a fine specimen to be sure."

Fairfield drew up next, with both Galensbury and Stanton in his wake. "Do you ride?" he asked with genuine curiosity as soon as he'd made his address, going so far as to offer her a dandelion that he must have picked on his walk back from the stables. The cheeky expression in his eyes told Lucy that he'd done so with the express attempt at outdoing Reinhardt. Unable to help herself from warming to his mischief, she gave him a thankful smile, accepted the dandelion, and placed it behind her ear.

"Perhaps tomorrow, if my husband will be kind enough to wait for me . . ." She threw a scowl in William's direction. "You'll have the opportunity to judge for yourself."

"Nothing would give us greater pleasure," Stanton told her with a broad smile. "We're all quite keen on getting to know you a bit better."

"The thing is," Galensbury added, "that none of us ever expected Summersby to get hitched so quickly. You must be a very special woman to have managed such an extraordinary feat."

"Shall we return to the house, my lady?" Fairfield asked as he offered her his arm. "I dare say I could use a glass of lemonade."

"Me too," Reinhardt said, offering his arm as well so that she found herself pinned between the two attentive gentlemen.

Starting on their way, with Galensbury and Stanton following behind, they passed William and the ladies. Again, the debutantes erupted in a fit of annoying giggles. Lucy, however, responded to William's glare with the sweetest, most innocent smile she could manage. If he had no desire to shower her with attention, then she would simply have to seek the company of his friends until, she hoped, he'd become sufficiently jealous.

CHAPTER ELEVEN

William was in a foul mood as they walked back toward the house, mostly due to his own stupidity, he was forced to acknowledge with an even greater sense of annoyance. Why had he been so brusque with Lucy? He'd been hoping to improve upon their relationship, to make an attempt at developing true friendship, yet with one critical remark he'd as good as put himself back a thousand paces. He'd seen it in her face, seen the pain and the anger that had flickered in her eyes. For a moment he'd expected her to burst into tears and run off, but by some miracle that he couldn't possibly begin to comprehend, she'd drawn from some inner strength he hadn't even known she possessed. It had been astonishing to watch.

And then, with his friends she'd been the perfect hostess, all grace and smiles, though he imagined she'd done so while battling the urge to pummel him. He'd seen her scowl.

He knew he'd overreacted, but after seeing her last night in her nightgown, an overwhelming sense of possessiveness had come over him. He didn't want any other man to admire the creamy white skin of her bosom or to as much as consider what her bosom might look like without the restraint of her gown. He knew how it looked, and he wanted it, and her, for himself.

Watching her now as she walked ahead of him, his friends clearly hanging on her every word, he felt his stomach tighten. He couldn't ignore the feeling that crashed over him with overwhelming force, for it was as real as the ground he was walking upon: envy. William steeled himself, shook his head, and frowned. How could he possibly be jealous of the smile she was presently favoring Charles with? He watched through stormy eyes as she turned her head in Galensbury's direction and laughed in response to something he'd said. The knot in his stomach tightened as, with a heavy blow, he realized that he'd give anything if she would only laugh or smile like that with him. Last night it had happened, but then he'd gone and ruined it like the idiot he was.

"You can still win her, you know."

Startled, William's head snapped around to find his aunt keeping pace with him. She gave him a smug little smile and nodded toward Lucy. "You're married to her, William. Would it be so terrible if you tried to romance her a little? If I were you, I'd snatch her away from your rakish friends before one of them beats you to it. From what I understand, they're quite the womanizers—Fairfield included."

With concern whipping through him, William gave her a curt nod. "Duly noted. Thank you." Then, picking up his pace, he hurried forward until he was directly behind Lucy. He caught her by the elbow, effectively yanking her to a halt. "If you don't mind, there's a pressing matter that I wish to discuss with my wife," he said, ignoring Lucy's startled and very annoyed expression as he addressed his friends. "We'll meet you back at the house in roughly half an hour. Andrew, would you please see to it that tea is served on the terrace? Or lemonade for those who require something more refreshing?"

"Yes, of course," Andrew replied, seemingly a bit taken aback by William's sudden haste.

Lucy, on the other hand, wasn't afforded the opportunity to utter a single word of protest before William practically made her fly across the neatly trimmed lawn, hauling her along at a pace that many might have considered quite dangerous. He didn't care; all he knew was that he had to put a solid end to the rift between them. Somehow, they had to make it work or they would both face the very real possibility of a miserable marriage.

Not until they had passed out of sight of the others and were safely hidden away by the hedges that separated the lawn from the rose garden did William slow his pace. Looking sideways he saw that Lucy's breath was coming hard while a frosty glare had become visible in her bright green eyes. He hazarded a smile, but rather than return it as he had hoped, her frown merely deepened. "What on earth is wrong with you?" she fumed.

His own expression sobered in response to her harsh tone. "Like I said, there's a pressing matter that I wish to discuss with you."

She stopped and turned to face him, her hands on her hips and her chin jutting out in anger. "What?" Her tone was terse. "What could possibly be so important that you felt the need to humiliate me twice in the course of one morning?"

For a long moment, William just stood there, staring

down at her. She was right to be angry with him for so publicly humiliating her. He now feared that she might not welcome his advances.

Focusing on the larger picture, he forced his misgivings aside and closed the distance between them with a single step, his gray-blue eyes locking onto hers. "Merely this," he muttered, so low that it was but a rough whisper in the air. And then he claimed her, his hands reaching around her waist, locking her in a tight embrace and pulling her close as his mouth bore down upon hers. She didn't attempt to escape— didn't even flinch. Her only response was a gasp the moment he lowered his head and she realized his intent.

And then his lips were upon hers. She was just as soft as he remembered, but more accepting and, if possible, more willing. A thrill of excitement seeped through him, quickening his heartbeat. He wanted to be gentle with her—allow her the chance to adjust to the unexpectedness of the kiss— but heaven help him, he wanted her, and being denied the pleasures she offered had begun to drive him mad with desire.

Still, he wanted her to come to him of her own free will and not by force. Slowly and methodically he hoped to awaken her inner passion, offering her only the occasional taste of what he would give her, until she'd find herself consumed by lust. It was a task he'd never faced before. The women he'd known had always been more than eager to share his bed, but then again, they'd all had ample experience. Lucy was different in that regard—thankfully so, he decided—and as a result, she would require a far lengthier attempt at seduction on his part.

He ran his tongue along her lower lip, hot and beseeching. Her lips gradually parted of their own accord, allowing him entrance. With the skill of a man who'd kissed countless women before, his tongue swept over Lucy's, coaxing her into a sensual dance that meant to mimic his own wicked desires. Oh, the things he longed to do to her—his imagination knew no bounds as far as his carnal urges were concerned.

His mind was swiftly returned to the present when he felt her hands splayed widely across his back, exploring his contours with nimble fingers, fingers that he could quite easily imagine doing other far more sinful things. Heaven help him if he wasn't aroused to the point of unbearable pain, and he briefly wondered if she might have guessed what the hardness was that strained against her. She couldn't possibly know, innocent that she was. But the soft murmurs of pleasure escaping her lips as he pressed soft kisses along the length of her neck were a sure indication that he was succeeding in his task, a task to uncover the wanton that he very much suspected to be residing beneath her otherwise ladylike façade.

Warm and inviting beneath his touch, his fingers felt the silky softness of her hair, the quickening of her heart beneath her breasts. Her breasts . . . God how he longed to bare them, to strip away the fabric of her gown and sear them with kisses. His groin tightened at the thought, and he found himself wondering if he would be able to stick to his plan and not merely toss her to the ground at the first available opportunity, like right now, for instance.

With more willpower than he'd ever imagined he possessed, he forced himself to take control of his own needs. His plan made sense, but in order for it to work, he would have to stop himself before he ripped her bodice down the middle and devoured her in broad daylight. The last thing she needed was for him to cause another embarrassing moment.

Disengaging himself and pushing her gently away, he eased back a little, enough to take a good look at her face. Her cheeks were flushed, her lips swollen, and her eyelids heavy over eyes that gazed back at him with longing. In short, she looked like a starved woman who'd just happened upon a bountiful feast. Her breathing was heavy with greed.

There was no doubt in William's mind. His wife desired him, and if she said otherwise he would know that she was lying. This sort of blatant need—the sort that seeped from every pore—could not be conjured as a form of pretense, least of all by a virgin.

Satisfied and pleased beyond compare, he dipped his head to kiss the rise of her breasts, felt her breath catch and her body tremble. "What fools we've been," he murmured, nudging the top of her sleeve a little to free her shoulder. He kissed her again. "We've wasted a whole week with our stubbornness."

A sigh of pleasure was the only response she made. Blood roared through his veins. Once again he felt the overwhelming need to have her now, this very instant. Glancing sideways, he spotted one of the many benches adorning the garden, considered it momentarily, and finally dismissed the idea, marveling at his restraint as, for the hundredth time in the span of five minutes, he pulled on the reins and forced his baser instincts under control.

Stepping back, he saw the stunned look of confusion in her eyes and immediately took her hand in his, lifting it to his lips and kissing it. "Forgive me. It was not my intention to get so carried away." Nudging her sleeve back to its proper position, he offered her his arm. "Would you please walk with me for a while?"

A dreamy look of detachment settled like a veil upon her face. She nodded slowly, clearly dazed and astounded by what had just happened between them, perhaps even (he hoped) a little disappointed and frustrated by how abruptly it had all ended. With measured steps, they made their way along a path that, skirting the perimeter of the property, would eventually lead them back to the house.

"Was it a mistake?" she suddenly asked so softly that he barely heard her.

"What?"

She paused for a moment as if trying to find the right words. "What we just . . . I mean . . ." She looked embarrassed—could not quite seem to get the necessary words out.

William instantly understood. "No." He drew her closer. "You mustn't think that. Never think that. Damn it, Lucy, couldn't you tell that I was enjoying it? Rest assured that I did, very much."

She gave him a hesitant smile. "Why are you being so nice?"

"Nice? I don't believe that's how I'd define the comment I made to you earlier. It was most unkind, and I'm sorry if I hurt you in any way as a result."

She glanced in his direction before returning her attention to some far-off point in the distance. "Thank you," she said. "It was rather unexpected considering what a wonderful time we shared last night."

"I just didn't want any of my friends to look at you the way

I knew they would when they saw you in that gown. You look lovely in it," he hastily added. "But it's also rather revealing, and, well, to be perfectly honest, I would prefer that if you decide to wear it again in the future you do so for my benefit alone."

She drew a deep breath. "It was entirely with you in mind that I put it on," she admitted. "I was hoping that you might approve."

What the devil? Was she trying to seduce him then? It certainly sounded as if she'd just declared herself ready to entertain his desires. He couldn't help but smile at the notion. Perhaps they'd sojourn in bed more quickly than he'd anticipated. "I can't deny that I do. For in truth, you look ravishing," he told her. He was anxious now to make her understand his reasoning. "What worries me is that when your neckline becomes so dangerously low other men have no choice but to let their minds wander. Do you understand?"

She nodded faintly beside him. "I'm terribly sorry, William. I hadn't considered it. You must think me quite gauche."

"Not at all, my dear. In fact, I think you're the loveliest woman I've ever seen."

She responded with a warm smile, the sort he'd been longing for, and he felt his heart swell. But then she frowned and asked, "Why is it that you don't despise me, William? Most men in your situation would, and yet here you are not only complimenting me but also being so undeniably kind."

He knew she had a point. He knew that most men of his acquaintance would very likely have put her six feet under by now. However, he'd always considered himself to be far more reasonable and level headed than most, and, considering that he'd meant to marry somebody anyway and hadn't been in love with Lady Annabelle, it no longer made much difference to him who his wife was as long as she was pleasant, intelligent, and appealing enough to attract his attention.

Lucy certainly seemed to fit all of those qualifications rather nicely, more nicely than Lady Annabelle ever would have done, because as it happened, Lady Annabelle was precisely the sort of typical socialite he'd given a wide berth for so long. She'd merely been a little less vexing on the ears than the rest.

Lucy, on the other hand . . . the edge of his mouth slipped upward into a helpless smile. She was far from ordinary. "Upon reflection, I've decided that you might not be so bad after all. You didn't steal me away from a woman I was in love with. In fact, if I recall, you made a point of ensuring that you wouldn't be doing so. No hearts were broken as a consequence of your actions and, in truth, you're beginning to grow on me a little."

A pained expression flickered behind her eyes. "And yet you know it's not that simple, William. You know that for me marrying you had a purpose." She took a deep breath and then expelled it. "You're honorable to a fault, and I . . . to be perfectly honest, I don't believe that I deserve you."

He was quiet for a moment. Then, halting, he turned to look her straight in the eye. "I don't suppose that you'd be willing to share your reasoning with me? As it is, I suspect that it must concern a matter of great importance. You told me that you needed my help, but how am I to help you if you won't trust me? You're my wife, Lucy, and come what may, I'll stand by your side—of that you have my word, as a gentleman."

In spite of her qualms, Lucy had, after much reflection, decided that it would probably be best to tell him everything—to let him in and share her troubled past with him, no matter how difficult it would be for her to do so.

Her husband had made it clear to her that he valued the truth. What better way for her to make a real attempt at narrowing the distance between them than to be completely honest? She steeled herself for a moment. He had told her that he would stand by her, but he had done so blindly, and while she did not doubt that he would keep his word, there was still a very real possibility that he would not only be furious with her but that he might also demand an annulment on the basis of fraud once the truth was out. It was a chance she would have to take. "Very well," she conceded, "but you must promise not to tell another soul."

He placed his hand over his heart. "You have my word on it."

"Swear it," she insisted, "as a gentleman."

"I swear to you on my honor, Lucy, that whatever you are about to tell me shall follow me to the grave."

She nodded, satisfied with the knowledge that he would keep silent, and recommenced walking while he followed, keeping pace. "Lady Ridgewood has been my guardian for the past six years. I came to her rather unexpectedly after my parents . . ." She drew a deep breath as the memories were once again released from where she usually kept them hidden in the deepest recesses of her mind. "I'm not who you think I am, William. My real name isn't Lucy Blackwell. It's Lucy Etheredge." Turning her head to look at him, she noticed the look of surprise on his face. It was swiftly followed by one of puzzlement.

"Why does that name sound so familiar?"

"My father was the Earl of Hampstead, British ambassador to the Ottoman Empire. He was a good man, William, and my mother . . . you would have loved her, I'm sure. She . . ." Words failed her. She choked back a sob.

"What happened, Lucy?" William looked ashen, as if he didn't really desire an answer to the question he'd just posed.

She wiped at her eyes with the back of her hand. "I'll never forget the fear in Mama's eyes the last time I saw her. I didn't understand it to begin with. I was so confused. Before I knew what was going on, we were running through our house in a desperate attempt to escape the men chasing us." She took a deep breath to force away the painful tightening of her throat. "I was the only one who got away. My parents were both killed—my mother stabbed in the chest before my very eyes."

William halted in his tracks, and she turned to face him. His eyes were stricken, mirroring the pain that she felt once more as it clutched at her insides. "You . . ." Speech seemed to fail him, and he closed his eyes against the awfulness of what she'd just told him before making another attempt. "You witnessed your mother's murder?"

She couldn't look at him without falling to pieces before his eyes, so she merely nodded in response. A heartbeat later, she felt his hand close around hers, felt herself being pulled back against him, his strong arms encircling her and cocooning her in his warmth. "I'm so very sorry," he whispered.

His kindness sank below her skin where it touched her soul and squeezed her heart. A moment later the dam broke. She could do nothing to still her quaking shoulders or the cries of despair that were only slightly muffled against her husband's chest. He drew her closer, kissed the top of her head, but said nothing more. He just held her until the tears had passed. How she'd been so fortunate to marry a man as kind as he was beyond her.

On a shaky sigh, she pulled away and looked up at him through red-rimmed eyes. "I'm sorry to have involved you in all of this, to have burdened you with this pain that I carry." She took a quivering breath. "I'm sorry I lied."

He stared at her for a long moment. "You silly woman," he eventually said, drawing her against him once more and hugging her fiercely. "I'm honored to have won your trust. I only wish that you would have told me sooner. As for your true identity . . ." Lucy anxiously bit her bottom lip. "I must admit I'm happy to hear that you come from a good family, as sorry as I am for your loss. But just as I have promised to guard your secrets, you must swear to me that you will never deceive me again. Is that clear?"

Easing away from him a little, Lucy met his gaze. "On my mother's soul." She hesitated a moment before asking, "You do realize what this means, don't you?"

He didn't pretend not to, for he quickly nodded his response.

Unable to discern his thoughts, she quietly asked, "Do you wish for an annulment?"

He paused, as if considering all that she had told him, then tilted his head a little and smiled. "And ruin the chance for a perfect marriage?"

Lucy could scarcely believe her ears. "Perfect?"

His smile broadened. "Why yes. The way I see it, I am married to the most beautiful woman I've ever seen, a woman whose company I'm beginning to grow quite fond of, and on top of that, I've also been offered a rather grand adventure."

"I..."

"Isn't that the real reason for your keen interest in visiting Constantinople? To find the men who did this?"

She drew back a little in order to meet his eyes, a little stunned by his astuteness and somewhat chagrined that she hadn't expected him to discern as much. After all, it was his skill at deduction that had led her to him in the first place. "Yes," she told him firmly, "I mean to see justice served."

William knew better than to argue. Any attempt he might make to stop her would only produce a greater rift between them, or, worse, she might do something stupid like run off, thinking herself capable of settling the matter alone. He couldn't allow that happen. "Then let me help you as you intended for me to do." After all, Trenton and Ryan had eventually supported their wives in their endeavors, as unconventional as they had been, and everything had worked out well for them.

A grateful smile of relief warmed her features. "Thank you, my lord, I..."

"Please don't call me that again." His tone was quite serious. "I hope that we're familiar enough with each other now for you to call me William."

Her smile widened. "William."

The name rolled off her tongue with such tenderness that he practically felt his heart melt. Perhaps his father had been right after all. Lucy was precisely the right woman to grab his interest—and keep it. She was stronger than he'd thought, having kept her anger and pain tucked away for so long. And as it turned out she had her reasons for trapping him, reasons that were not only honorable but also commendable. It must have taken tremendous courage for her to do what she'd done. He couldn't fault her for it—not any longer, not after everything she'd just told him.

Casting a wary eye in her direction, he recalled the kiss they'd shared a short while earlier. An annulment indeed! Even now that such a thing was possible, he'd fight it with every fiber of his being. He wanted her physically, but he also felt an overwhelming need to protect her for the rest of his life. The revelation shook him to his core. He could scarcely believe it himself, but there it was: he wanted his wife, body and soul, and could only dare hope that once all of this was behind them she might want him in the same way.

CHAPTER TWELVE

"Oh do come and join us," Miss Scott insisted as she patted the seat next to her. The four debutantes were sitting on the terrace enjoying what appeared to be a large jug of elderberry juice—a good thing, Lucy decided, since she really wasn't all that fond of lemonade.

"Where are the others?" William asked as he looked about.

"Well," Lady Hyacinth said, swatting away a determined fly. "Your sister suggested a shooting match, to which Lady Steepleton, Lord Trenton, and your brother all agreed, while Lord Stanton challenged Lord Fairfield to a game of chess, but I've no idea about the whereabouts of Lord Galensbury or Lord Reinhardt."

"I see," William muttered somewhat tersely.

Lucy hid a smile. Well, he *had* asked. "What about Lady Ridgewood, Lord Moorland, and the Lindhursts?"

"From what I understand," Miss Scott remarked, "the Lindhursts decided to explore the library, while Lady Ridgewood and Lord Moorland . . . Well, I don't suppose anyone's seen either of them since breakfast. Not to worry though, I'm sure that wherever they are, they'll be back in time for luncheon."

Lucy managed a polite smile. She was happy to discover that her friend was enjoying Lord Moorland's company, but she also worried that Constance might let something slip—a small detail that could lead to further deduction. Although William now knew the truth, she had no desire for anyone else to discover it just yet. Of course she trusted Constance implicitly, but all the same, Lucy would feel more comfortable if Constance didn't spend quite so much time with her father-in-law.

"I think I'll see how Stanton and Fairfield are getting on with their game," William said. Turning to Lucy, he offered a heartfelt smile. "If you don't mind, that is."

Lucy would have been happy to join him. Following their walk together, she felt that they'd finally started getting onto the right track, and she longed to continue with their conversation, which, she hoped, signaled the beginning of a true friendship. However, it was also her duty as hostess to entertain her guests, and, truth be told, she really hadn't spoken more than a few words with any of the young debutantes since their arrival. "Not at all," she said, returning William's smile. "I'll see you again soon."

Bowing, William lifted Lucy's hand to his lips and placed a lingering kiss upon her knuckles. Her heart instantly skipped a beat, while each of the young ladies sighed and tilted their heads as if with longing. "If only I could form an attachment to a gentleman as handsome as Lord Summersby," Lady Amanda mused as soon as William was out of earshot. "You truly are very lucky."

"Yes, I do believe I am." It was impossible for Lucy to contain her smile. She hastily went on to add, "You must agree though that both Lord Fairfield and Lord Stanton are rather striking."

"Oh, they most assuredly are," Miss Cleaver hastily agreed as she nodded her head. "And one mustn't forget Lord Reinhardt. In fact . . ." She lowered her voice to a low whisper. "When I spoke to him yesterday, I was very much under the impression that, had we not been in the company of others, he might have attempted to kiss me—on the cheek of course."

"Noooo . . ." Lady Hyacinth said, sounding quite astonished. "Really?"

"Oh, indeed," Miss Cleaver assured her in a most serious tone. "Unfortunately, I haven't been afforded the opportunity to explore the situation any further, though I do hope that one will present itself soon."

"I'm sure that it will," Lucy agreed, though she very much doubted that Miss Cleaver was correct in her assessment of the situation. As far as she knew, Reinhardt had very little intention of getting himself attached to anyone, so she couldn't help but wonder if he might be seeking a dalliance and decided to say, "I do feel that I must caution you, however, for there are gentlemen who have a more rakish personality than most. I'm not saying that this is the case with Lord Reinhardt of course, for I hardly know the man, but I do think that it would be wise of you all to avoid being alone with any singular gentleman at any given time. One never can tell what might happen." Heavens, she sounded like an old matron giving advice, when in fact she was no older than them. It really was quite absurd.

"That's very sound advice," Miss Scott said, reaching for a plate of cookies and offering it to Lady Amanda who in turn passed it on to Lucy. "Naturally, it would never occur to any of us to deliberately seek the private company of a bachelor. It would simply scream ruination. However, one does hear of such things happening, so, by all means, we shall take your advice to heart, Lady Summersby. Shan't we ladies?"

"Oh, we shall," Lady Hyacinth exclaimed. "Though I must admit that I personally wouldn't mind a walk in the garden with Lord Fairfield. There's a boyish charm to him that I find very enticing."

"He's not serious enough for me," Miss Cleaver remarked. "I'd much rather set my cap for someone like Galensbury or Stanton. Both are exceedingly handsome and with that touch of enigma about them that makes you wonder whether they're actually listening to what you're saying or wondering what it might be like to kiss you."

"Heavens," uttered Lady Hyacinth. The other ladies gasped a mere second before they all erupted into a fit of giggles.

Lucy, of course, maintained her composure, wondering if she'd ever been as silly as these four women. She didn't think so, but then again, she'd never put herself on display in the hopes of capturing a gentleman's attention. Life had been too hard on her for that.

She had to wait another fifteen to twenty minutes or so before an appropriate gap in the conversation allowed her to take her leave. Luncheon was no more than half an hour away, and she'd decided that she wanted to change into another

gown first—one that she hoped William would have no cause
to take issue with.

Entering her bedroom, she immediately removed her
shawl, laying it carefully on the bed before ringing for her
maid. Walking across to her full-length mirror, she then regarded her own reflection, turning this way and that, until
she'd decided that while her bosom did seem to swell against
her bodice, William really had overreacted; it wasn't nearly
as low cut as some of the gowns she'd seen other ladies wear.
However, she did want to please him, and if covering herself
up a bit was what it would take, then so be it.

She was just about to cross to her wardrobe when something caught her attention; a small, purple box with a gold
ribbon wrapped around it was sitting on her vanity table. She
stared at it for a moment, then approached, a smile beginning
to tug at her lips while her stomach tightened with anticipation. William must have brought the gift for her while she'd
been sitting outside. A wave of warmth rushed through her.
Surely this was a sign that their time together in the garden
had meant as much to him as it had to her.

Picking up the box, she ran her fingers over the smooth
surface, her heart quickening its pace as she wondered what
it might contain. Her curiosity eventually got the best of her,
and she quickly tugged on the ribbon and eased the lid open
to gaze inside, only to stiffen, her breath caught in her throat.
A cold shiver ran down her spine as she staggered across to
the nearest chair and sank down onto it. Burning tears were
already pressing against her eyes, and when she tried to calm
herself with a deep breath, a shaky sob escaped her lips instead. With trembling fingers, she reached inside the box and

gently removed the small, gold, heart pendant that had been her mother's. It was impossible. It couldn't be here, for it was the very same one that she'd worn the day she'd died.

Lucy wanted to scream and toss the box across the floor, but it wouldn't do to draw that kind of attention, not until she figured out what was going on. Instead, she drew a ragged breath and wiped away the tears that threatened to overflow at any moment.

She was just about to set the box aside when she noticed that it wasn't completely empty. There was something else inside—a piece of neatly folded paper with her name on it. Lucy froze. For a long moment, she simply sat and stared at it, wondering what it might say and too afraid to find out. But, she also knew that she'd have to read it eventually. There was only one person she could think of who could have sent this to her, and if this letter would bring her closer to discovering his identity, she really had no choice but to take courage.

Picking it up, her hands shook as she unfolded the paper, and as she read, it became impossible for her to hold back the tears any longer.

Dear Lady Summersby,

Please accept this small gift as a token of my admiration. You have managed to elude me for much longer than I ever would have imagined possible. However, as you well know, all things must come to an end, even this little chase of ours, as enjoyable as it has been. Naturally, it goes without saying that you must mention no word of this to anyone, for if you do your darling husband shall quickly suffer the same fate as your dear Mama and Papa. To make my point clear, I suggest you consider this before acting rashly: I know you care for him, or you wouldn't have told him about your past. Oh, I suppose you thought yourself alone when you were dallying in the garden?

Think twice before you try to outwit me, my lady. It would be a foolish endeavor on your part, especially since it has come to my attention that Lady Ridgewood secretly enjoys a glass of brandy in her bedroom before retiring. How unfortunate it would be if one of these days her nightcap fails to agree with her.

Wear this pendant as a sign of your cooperation, and I promise that no harm shall come to either of these people.

With fond memories,
Your masked friend

He'd found her then. But how? Lucy didn't need to spare much thought on that. Her marriage to William had been discussed at great length among the gentry, from what Constance had told her. Like all society weddings, it had also been announced in the papers, and while she might have changed her family name, she'd not only kept her Christian one but also knew that her appearance—her hair and her eyes—was unusual enough to stand out. All the assassin would have had to do was find an opportunity in which to see her with his own eyes.

A knock on the door sounded, and Lucy practically leapt out of her seat she was so startled. "Come in," she said, taking a step backward and reaching for a pair of scissors that lay upon her vanity table. She'd last used them for cutting a ribbon that she'd felt was too long but now grabbed the tool in the hope that it might serve as a weapon in case she needed it.

"My lady, I . . ." Lucy breathed a sigh of relief. It was only her maid Marjory whom she'd called upon to help her change. "Dear me," Marjory exclaimed, closing the door and hurrying across to her mistress. "You look a fright. What on earth happened?"

"No . . . nothing," Lucy stammered, her voice still shaky from the sudden shock of discovering that the man she'd spent six years hoping to find so she could exact her revenge had not only found her instead but was presently residing in her own home. She felt ill at the mere thought of it. "I was just reminiscing about my parents. I lost them both when I was quite young, you see."

Marjory gave Lucy a sympathetic smile. "I'm very sorry to hear it, my lady. The loss of a parent can be very difficult to bear. Perhaps you ought to feign a headache for the remainder of the day. I can bring you a tray of food if you like."

"No," Lucy told her, sniffing a little as she dabbed at her eyes. "There's no need for that, though I appreciate your concern. I am the hostess after all, so I should attend to my guests unless I'm really unable to do so. Feigning a headache would be not only cowardly but also dishonest."

"Well, then we really should wash your face with some cold water. It will help reduce the redness around your eyes."

With a nod of approval, Lucy allowed Marjory to take command of the situation, while her own thoughts returned to the letter that she still held clutched in her hand. Four names crowded her mind: Fairfield, Stanton, Galensbury, and Reinhardt . . . perhaps Trenton and Mr. Summersby too, if she dared to consider the worst possible outcome. Frowning at the thought of it, she quickly dismissed them again. Neither seemed capable, but then again, none of the gentlemen did. And yet she knew, beyond any shadow of a doubt, that one of them was a cold-blooded killer.

William was standing in the parlor talking to Ryan when Lucy made her entrance. After leaving her side about an hour earlier, he'd watched Stanton beat Andrew in a very intriguing game of chess. Still, he'd found himself missing the easy companionship he'd begun to develop with his wife, and, looking to pick up where they'd left off, had arrived in the parlor early, hoping to find her there. Instead, he'd found his brother in the process of reading a medical book that his wife, Mary, had apparently recommended.

"I must admit that as captivating as this is, I'd much rather immerse myself in a novel by Defoe or Fielding," Ryan had said as he closed the book and put it aside in favor of the conversation William offered. Alexandra and Trenton had joined them soon after, followed by the rest of the guests—all except the one woman whom he now found himself eagerly awaiting.

He forced himself not to stare at the doorway, reminding himself that he wasn't a green lad in short pants. There was no reason for this ridiculous longing that he now felt in her absence. For heaven's sake, he was a secret agent for the Foreign Office, a man who'd faced countless enemies, gotten himself out of numerous near-death situations, not to mention bedded more women than he cared to remember. Surely he ought to feel a bit more together where his own wife was concerned, and yet he found his eyes straying to the door once more, except this time she was there.

An unwilling sigh of relief escaped him, and he quickly eyed Ryan, wondering if he might have noticed. Sure enough, the scamp was openly grinning at him. He served him a frown in return. "If you'll please excuse me. I do believe that I ought to escort my wife to the table."

Leaving his brother behind, he made his way over to Lucy, noting how pretty she looked in her lovely white gown. She'd apparently taken his earlier words of the day to heart, for beneath her neckline she wore a fichu, a piece of delicate white lace that framed a golden heart pendant suspended at the base of her neck.

Considering himself an imbecile for denying himself a view of her creamy white skin, he also felt his heart leap at the thought that she'd tried to please him. He could only hope that it wouldn't be too long before he caught a glimpse of her delicious breasts again. Reaching her side, he offered his arm. "You look beautiful," he told her with a smile.

"Thank you," she muttered as she returned it, and yet he couldn't help but notice that her eyes no longer held a sparkle to them. It was almost as if the light behind them had faded, giving way to a dull sense of lifelessness.

"Are you all right?" he whispered, after lowering his lips to her ear. "You seem tense or perhaps preoccupied with something."

"Yes," she said, nodding her head as her eyes surveyed the room. "Yes, I'm perfectly well, thank you. I'm just hungry, that is all."

But William knew she'd just dismissed him with a lie. It was clear upon her face and in the sound of her voice. Something had obviously distressed her since they'd last spoken.

He wanted to press the matter further but knew better than to have such a private conversation in public, so instead he announced that the food was ready and led his guests through to the dining room with Lucy on his arm.

It was the longest meal that Lucy had ever had to endure. Seated at one end of the table, she couldn't help but notice that William was watching her from the other. Somehow, she'd have to hone her acting skills if she was to keep him safe from harm. The thought of him being killed because of her was enough to send chills down her spine. She had to protect him at all cost; the alternative was simply unthinkable.

Feigning interest in what Lord Moorland was saying, she studied each of the young gentlemen in turn. All were immersed in conversation—all except Reinhardt, who met her assessing gaze. A moment later, his serious demeanor softened into a smile. "That's a very pretty pendant you're wearing, my lady," he said as he took a sip of his wine. "A family heirloom perhaps?"

Lucy felt her nerves grow taut. Was he the one then? Or had he merely tried to be polite? "It . . . it was my mother's," she replied, studying his features for any sign that he might be the man who'd tormented her for so long. When she didn't find what she sought, she allowed her gaze to flitter to the other men, but none appeared to have taken the slightest interest in her exchange with Reinhardt.

"If I recall, my mother has a similar one," Reinhardt was now saying. "Her initials are engraved upon the back of it. Is that also the case with yours?"

"I . . . er . . . yes, as a matter of fact it is." She noticed that William was staring at her again with marked intensity. She really had to get a grip of herself if she was to avoid his asking questions later. With a polite smile in Reinhardt's direction, she returned her attention to Ryan and Lord Moorland who'd begun discussing what Lucy could only deem to be Ryan's and Mary's plans for the hospital they'd soon be opening. Again, she smiled politely and nodded her head, but if either gentleman would have asked her a question, she would have been completely stumped, for she could think of nothing but how to try to beat the assassin at his own twisted game.

CHAPTER THIRTEEN

The following afternoon, while the other young ladies went to town with Lady Lindhurst, Lucy decided to go for a walk in the gardens. After another troubled night plagued by bad dreams, she knew she needed some time alone in which to think, and since the men had decided to postpone their ride until later in favor of walking out into the fields and admiring the crop, she saw this as the perfect opportunity to do so.

Passing the rose garden, she followed the path leading down toward the lake. There was a spot there beneath a willow tree that she'd frequented in the days following her wedding, when she'd worried about what the future might hold. Reaching it now, she spread a blanket on the ground and then seated herself upon it, delighting in the rays of sunshine that flittered through between the branches and the ducks that quacked merrily on the water.

With a heavy sigh, she thought of everything that had happened—of everything she'd been through so far in order to survive. It hadn't been easy, but none of it was as difficult as the challenge she was now faced with. She didn't even know the killer's intent. If he wanted her dead, she'd surely be so already—unless of course he merely found some sort of pleasure in toying with her first. Or perhaps he was just waiting for the right opportunity, a moment when she'd find herself secluded and alone.

Glancing about, she cursed her own stupidity. There was safety in numbers. How could she possibly have thought that it might be a good idea to venture so far away from the house on her own? As it was, the vegetation around parts of the lake made the spot quite secluded. If someone were to . . . The rustling of leaves in the undergrowth made her gasp. A moment later, a squirrel appeared, pausing momentarily to look around before darting up a tree. Lucy breathed a sigh of relief, shook her head, and chastised herself for being so jittery. Her imagination was clearly getting the better of her.

"Mind if I join you?"

Had it been possible for her to jump out of her skin, Lucy would have done so, she was so alarmed by the sudden sound of a male voice coming from directly behind her. Her heart knocked against her chest as she slowly turned her head to find Lord Fairfield staring down at her. "I thought you would have joined the others," she said, unable to think of anything else just then.

He tilted his head, studying her for a moment as if contemplating something, and then smiled that crooked signature smile of his. "Yes, I suppose you might have," he said, "but then again, I've always enjoyed surprising people—keeps them on their toes."

Lucy could say nothing in response to that. Indeed, it was all she could do to refrain from fainting right there on the spot from sheer terror. His words, coupled with the fact that he'd deliberately sought her out in private, had riled every instinct that told her to leap to her feet and run as fast as she could. Yet the only thing she could run toward was the cold water of the lake, for Fairfield himself was blocking the route back to the house.

Panic began to set in, but the letter she'd received gave her pause. What if Fairfield wasn't the one? She couldn't risk revealing anything in case word about her impending nervous breakdown spread. So, she clutched her hands tightly in her lap and nodded to the space beside her, forcing herself to say, "By all means, my lord, do have a seat."

"As it happens, I've no desire to venture out into all that corn—too many dratted insects, you see," he explained as soon as he was on the ground beside her. "Are you cold, Lady Summersby? You're visibly shaking. It really wouldn't do for you to catch a chill. William would have my head. Here, please take my jacket."

What on earth was she to think? Was the seemingly kind and jovial Fairfield the very same man who'd so callously murdered her parents? The more she considered it, the more Lucy found that she was having a very difficult time equating the two. And yet, she reminded herself that she must remain cautious. Similarly, it really wouldn't do to offend an innocent man, so she thanked him for his offer, accepted his jacket, and then asked in the most nonchalant tone of voice that she could manage, "Did you happen upon me by chance, Lord Fairfield, or was there something particular that you wished to discuss with me?"

"I see you've found me out, Lady Summersby," he said

with a chuckle. He must have seen her startled expression, for he immediately began to elaborate. "You see, I like to give my gentlemen friends the impression that I've no interest in marriage—the desire to maintain my image and all that." With a sigh of relief at discovering that Fairfield wasn't about to stab her or perhaps drag her into the lake and attempt to drown her, Lucy relaxed a little and tried to give him her full attention. "However, I can't say that I would oppose were I to find the right woman."

"I see. And you wished to bring me into your confidence because . . . ?"

"Well, I thought you might perhaps be able to recommend one of the young ladies. It is possible that I might enjoy their company if I give them half a chance, but I've no desire to waste my time either."

Lucy stared at him in surprise. "You don't mince words, do you?"

He grinned as he leaned back on his elbows and stretched his long legs out in front of him. "I realize I come across as a bit of a prankster at times, but rest assured, there is a more serious side to me."

"Really?"

"Well, it would have been difficult for me to keep my estate running otherwise. I doubled my income last year."

Lucy was shocked. She hadn't taken Fairfield to have any real business sense.

"My only weakness is gambling. I always get too excited and bet too high. Consequently, I generally lose, but then again, it's a small indulgence and one that I can afford." He fell silent for a moment before continuing. "What I need now,

Lady Summersby, is a wife, so if you think that any of these young ladies might suit, I'd be most obliged to hear your opinion on the matter."

Lucy considered the proposition for a moment and then decided that it was best to be honest. "The fact of the matter is that I don't really know any of them well enough to form an opinion upon which to recommend any one of them in so serious a matter. However, I am able to tell you that Lady Hyacinth did suggest that she would very much enjoy a stroll about the garden with you."

Fairfield's eyes came instantly alive with interest. "She's very pretty, but what about her character? Did she leave you with a good impression?"

Lucy had to admit she liked the fact that he was trying to assess all of Lady Hyacinth's attributes rather than focusing on her looks alone. Truth be told, she really was the loveliest of all the debutantes. Lucy nodded. "She seems both kind and gentle but with just the right touch of forwardness to make her interesting. It's quite possible that the two of you might suit, but you really must judge for yourself."

"Oh, I shall look forward to it, and I shall begin tonight at the ball. What a splendid idea that was on your part."

"Ah, there you are," another voice cut in, interrupting them. Lucy turned her head, knowing full well that the man who'd just spoken was none other than her husband. "I've been looking all over for you. Trying to charm my wife, Andrew?" He spoke lightheartedly, and yet Lucy couldn't help but hear the underlying threat. Something about it made her skin tingle.

"A little perhaps, though the truth of the matter is that I was actually seeking her advice."

"Oh?" William asked, snatching up a twig and tossing it in the water. He looked down at Fairfield. "On what, if I may ask?"

With a quick shake of her head and a rather pointed expression that was meant to suggest that she'd tell him all about it later, Lucy hoped to stop her husband from badgering his friend. Apparently it worked, for William simply smiled, waved his hand, and said, "No matter. I only came to see if you would still like to join us on our ride, Lucy. You said yesterday that—"

"Yes, yes of course!" She quickly jumped to her feet, excited not only to spend more time with William but also to show him that this was something she excelled at. "I'll just run up and get changed."

"Very good," he said, his mouth widening into a broad smile. "I'll wait for you on the terrace. Come along, Andrew, it's time to see what her ladyship is made of."

It took Lucy a little longer than she'd expected to change into her riding habit, but when all was said and done, she had to admit that she did look the part of a very fashionable peeress. She refused to wear the ridiculous hat that Marjory was trying to hand her, however, claiming that the feathers had gotten in her eyes once before and had almost caused her to lose her balance. By the time she made it downstairs, she found William waiting for her as promised, along with Fairfield, Galensbury, Stanton, and Reinhardt, all of whom looked quite dashing in their crisp, white shirts, spotless breeches, and newly buffed Hessians.

Stepping forward, William offered Lucy his arm and began leading her along the path that led toward the stables. She'd allowed herself to forget about his friends during the short time in which she'd readied herself and hadn't really considered that they'd be joining them on the ride until now. For some absurd reason, she'd envisioned only herself and William racing along side by side, but of course the other gentlemen would be there too. After all, it was technically them who'd invited her for the ride in the first place.

Clenching her jaw, she forced herself to stay calm. William would be there with her, so she wouldn't be in any real danger for now—not as long as she remained by his side.

"Nervous?"

Pushing back her thoughts of despair, she tilted her head to look up into William's stormy blue eyes. "Not at all," she replied, forcing a smile, but the frown that appeared upon his forehead told her that he wasn't going to be so easily brushed aside. He knew she was being dishonest, so she hastily added, "It's merely a slight headache. I've been suffering from it since I woke up this morning. Hopefully the fresh air that the ride has to offer will make me feel better."

"I hope it does," he replied with a great deal of sympathy. But then he dipped his head, bringing it a little closer to hers, and the tone of his voice grew husky. "For I'm rather looking forward to waltzing with you this evening."

Heat swept through her body at the sound of his words, so tenderly spoken but with an underlying promise of something far more wicked and dangerous. The effect it had upon her was immediate; her skin began to prickle, her stomach fluttered, and her legs turned to jelly. "Thank you" was all she could think to say, feeling not only addlepated but quite self-conscious as well. "I'm looking forward to it too." She didn't have to look at him to know that he was grinning.

"Why, Lady Summersby," he continued in more of a whisper, "I do believe that you are blushing."

Annoying man!

"It does appear as though I find myself quite flummoxed whenever you are near, my lord," she quickly responded. "Indeed, it's very likely that you may pose a serious hazard to my health."

"I doubt that's possible," he murmured, dropping his tone another notch. "On the contrary, I'm confident that you have just the right amount of stamina to match me in practically anything—and I do mean *anything*, Lucy."

Thankfully, they'd arrived at the stables now, with the rest of the party drawing up beside them, or Lucy might have either withered away from embarrassment or burst into flames as a result of her husband's innuendo; she wasn't sure which.

A moment later, all thoughts of her exchange with William were swiftly forgotten as she spotted Alexandra coming out of the stables to greet them, dressed like a man in a shirt and breeches. She was accompanied by Ryan who seemed completely at ease with his sister's odd choice of clothes—shockingly so, in fact.

Eyeing William, she noticed that he didn't seem to find it unusual either. She was beginning to think that she was the only one who'd even noticed that her ladyship wasn't properly attired, until she saw that the rest of the gentlemen were staring at her in open fascination. Alexandra apparently didn't care. "I asked the groom to saddle Primrose for you," she told Lucy. "She's a good horse—not as boisterous as some of the others. And since I wasn't certain of your prowess, I thought it best to play it safe. I hope you don't mind."

"Not at all," Lucy told her, grateful that her sister-in-law had shown her such consideration. And when she saw Primrose a short while later, she knew that Alexandra had chosen well, for the legs were long and the body lean. She might be gentle and obedient, but she was certainly made to run.

They started off at a trot, following the dirt road that skirted the edge of the fields and led toward the heather-covered hills in the distance. The sun was high in the sky by now, forcing Lucy to wonder if she'd made a mistake by leaving behind her hat, but as a gentle breeze tickled her skin, she knew she'd made the right decision. Elegantly perched upon her horse, she rode up next to Alexandra who'd foregone the sidesaddle in favor of riding astride. "Do you find it more comfortable, riding like that?" she asked.

"Oh, absolutely," Alexandra replied, her eyes twinkling with a spot of mischief. "Of course I use a sidesaddle when I go for rides in Hyde Park, but when I'm away from town and surrounded by friends, this is my preference. It's also much easier to maintain one's balance during a race or when leaping over a hedgerow."

Lucy supposed she might have a point, though she'd never had any trouble staying in the saddle herself. However, there was that element of doing something improper about it that somehow intrigued her, though she doubted she'd ever have the courage to attempt such a thing with other people around to witness it.

"Tell me, Lady Summersby," Stanton remarked as he came up beside them, sending an immediate shiver down Lucy's spine, "does the promise of a waltz still stand?"

For a moment, Lucy felt confused but then recalled the deliberate jibe she'd made at William when she'd first been introduced to Stanton and Galensbury a couple of days earlier. Knowing that William had no desire to see her dance in such close proximity to another gentleman and having no wish to be held in the arms of a potential killer, she frantically wracked her brain for an appropriate excuse. "I must confess that I have just agreed to dance the waltz with my husband, my lord, and since there is to be only one waltz, in deference to the débutantes who have yet to be granted permission to dance it, I fear I must decline. However, I would be happy to oblige you in a reel or a quadrille if you like."

"A pity," Stanton lamented, though his tone held a sense of humor to it. "I shall simply have to sit it out then, but while I do so I shall look forward to our reel, for a reel it shall be then, with great anticipation."

"Or, you could simply offer to dance the waltz with Lady Ridgewood. I'm sure she'd be delighted," Alexandra remarked.

"I do believe that she'll be hoping to entertain Lord Moorland's company rather than mine," Stanton said.

Lucy bristled. She still hadn't had the opportunity to speak with her friend, for whenever she went in search of her, she was nowhere to be found, apparently because she was ensconced somewhere with William's father. The thought made her very ill at ease. After all, it was more important than ever now that she avoided drawing attention.

Alexandra shrugged. "Then perhaps a lady from one of the other nearby estates. From what I understand, Lucy and William have invited everyone from near and far to attend—anyone within reasonable distance that is."

"That does sound rather promising," Stanton admitted.

"What does?" It was Ryan who'd asked the question.

"Lord Stanton here desires to waltz this evening," his sister explained, "but since all the ladies appear to be either taken or unable to oblige him, I merely suggested that he wait and see who else shows up. Lord Hackston has what . . . five daughters, all of marriageable age. I'm sure they'll be more than eager to take a spin upon the dance floor with our handsome Lord Stanton."

Ryan groaned, leading Lucy to suspect that the Hackston women had remained unmarried for a reason. He swiftly confirmed it by saying, "I advise you to steer clear of that lot, Stanton. Their mama is the sort of desperate woman who will risk anything in order to see her daughters wed."

"Duly noted, Summersby," Stanton said with a chuckle. "Indeed, it does appear as if I shall either have to choose my partner wisely or simply forego altogether."

"Ready for a bit more speed?" William shouted, his horse already quickening its step in agitation.

"Most assuredly," Alexandra responded with an edge of eagerness. "Same route as usual?"

William strained against his horse's reins to keep the beast from bolting. He nodded his head. "We'll ride out to that old cottage—you can just about spot it on the horizon—turn around, and head on back. Anyone not up to it?" His eyes caught Lucy's, and she knew that his question was directed at her. How gallant of him not to have singled her out directly. But she knew that she was up to the challenge, so she quickly offered him a nod of confirmation. "Very well then— may the best man, or woman, win!" Giving the reins some slack, he allowed his mount to take off across the moor.

The rest of the horses, clustered together as they were, whinnied and neighed, their hooves frantically shuffling about as they got ready to take up the chase. Pulling sharply on the reins, Lucy eventually managed to break free with Primrose's long legs leaping forward and picking up speed as she raced after Alexandra and Stanton. She knew that the rest of the group was now coming fast behind her, for she could hear the heavy beat of thunder drumming the ground. A moment later, Ryan drew up beside her, casting a lopsided grin in her direction as he leaned forward against his horse's neck, and passed her.

Frustrated, Lucy flicked her whip against Primrose's rump and held on tight as the mare quickened her pace, catching up to Ryan again in a few easy steps. "You'll never beat them," he yelled across at her as he nodded his head toward William and Alexandra. The pair already appeared to have made it to the cottage. "I've been trying for years!" And with a cheeky grin, he veered off to the side, disappearing out of sight.

Turning her head, Lucy saw that he'd turned about and had begun heading in the opposite direction; apparently he'd given up. But she also saw that Galensbury, Fairfield, and Reinhardt were coming up behind her fast and quickly returned her attention to the race. She might not be able to beat William and Alexandra, but she could still come in third and ahead of the other men. Tapping her whip against Primrose once more, she leaned forward, bracing herself against the agile creature while the wind whipped across her face and tugged at her hair.

Fairfield and Galensbury were the next to come up beside her, their jackets billowing out behind them. Tossing a quick glance at each of them, Lucy leaned as far forward as she dared and yelled for Primrose to pick up her pace. The loyal mare immediately complied, but the awkward position that the sidesaddle offered Lucy, prevented her from reaching the optimal speed, and a few seconds later, she was forced to concede defeat as Fairfield and Galensbury both overtook her.

Looking up, she saw William and Alexandra heading toward her on their way back to the finish line, followed closely by Stanton. Winning would now be impossible, of that there was no doubt. But she wasn't one to give up either. She would finish this race, even if she came in last. Looking back, she saw that she was still a few yards ahead of Reinhardt, and she turned her attention back to the ground that lay stretched out before her, covered by a purple blanket of heather. Another hundred paces, she reckoned, and she would reach the cottage. Fairfield and Galensbury were already turning about, both sporting smiles of boyish glee as they started their homeward run.

But as they passed her, concern began to descend upon her, wrapping itself across her shoulders and clinging to her with insistent determination. She was alone now, with Reinhardt on her heels . . . Reinhardt . . . the only person who'd remarked on her mother's pendant the night before. Was it a coincidence or something more? She dared not think of it, but she knew that he must be able to pass her just like the rest had done, if that was what he wished to do, and yet he remained behind her.

If he wanted her dead, the race would offer him the perfect opportunity. All he had to do was ensure that she fell from the saddle . . . perhaps once they reached the cottage, for as they turned about, they would be hidden from view momentarily. A cold chill dug its way beneath her skin, and she drew a sharp breath as panic swept over her. He could break her neck as soon as she was down, and nobody would be the wiser. Nobody would suspect a thing.

With fear curling itself around her, she glanced back one more time and then whacked her whip against Primrose as she tugged the reins to the left, forcing them in a wide circle that would take her back to the safety that the rest of the party offered.

"Stop!" she heard Reinhardt yell. Like the devil she would. Her heart was now beating so fast she felt it might burst through her chest. She could hear the beat of his horse's hooves coming closer, and unable to stop herself, she looked back again, only to find that he was now right on her tail.

"Get away from me," she cried as she desperately thrashed at Primrose with her whip. If she could make it only another five minutes . . . But then she sensed Reinhardt draw up beside her, and her better judgment failed her. With a sharp pull on the reins she attempted to cut him off, but she miscalculated the distance required and found herself pushed up against him instead.

Before she could think of what to do, his arm was about her waist and he had grabbed hold of her reins, pulling both animals to an immediate stop.

"What the devil's wrong with you?" he fumed, grabbing her by the arm and pulling her around to face him.

Lucy slapped Primrose's rump, forcing the obedient horse forward once more. With a hard yank, she then freed herself from Reinhardt's grasp, only to find herself pulled back once more—this time by her gown—and it dawned on her that Reinhardt must have reached down and grasped the fabric, knowing that it would either bring her to a standstill or send her tumbling from the saddle. With a sense of impending doom bearing down on her, she tried to kick him away.

"For the love of all that is holy, would you please sit still?"

Turning her head to face him, intent on offering the scoundrel a string of oaths, she instantly stilled at the sight of the blade that now flashed in his hand. In that moment, it was almost as if her heart had stopped beating. She couldn't breathe, couldn't move, couldn't scream. All she could do was sit there and stare as he leaned toward her, his forehead creased in a frown of serious determination. She was going to die, and she very much doubted that there was much she'd be able to do to stop it, but she was damn well going to give him one hell of a struggle.

Balling her right hand into a tight fist, she leaned back and away from him before sending the upper half of her body forward, adding force behind the punch that she delivered a second later to his left cheek. He instantly dropped the knife, his eyes wide with shock as he stared back at her in wonder. But then his eyes grew dark, and she saw his jaw clench in anger.

Unwilling to give up just yet, she dealt him another blow, but he moved aside too quickly, and it landed against his shoulder instead. Hoping to give it another try, she readied herself, but he anticipated her this time and caught her tightly by the wrist. "What on earth has gotten into you, Lady Summersby?" he asked between bursts of air. "You rode like a madwoman, beating your poor horse until her hide was practically raw. I tried to stop you, but you refused to listen. Why?"

"You know well enough, Lord Reinhardt," she replied, her eyes flickering momentarily to Primrose's backside, only to see that it was indeed marked with angry red lines. Her throat tightened at the sight of it. How could she have been so cruel?

"No, I don't, but what I do know is that you very nearly caused what could have been a fatal accident, trying to intercept me the way you did. You got the skirts of your gown caught in my stirrup in the process—a terrible mess if you'll only care to take a look yourself. But when I tried to cut you lose, you decked me like no other woman I've ever seen. In all honesty, I'm inclined to think you're completely mad!"

"Is everything all right?" With a small gasp of surprise, Lucy turned to find William trotting up behind her. "Bloody hell, Charles, you look like you've just been in a tavern brawl! What the devil happened?"

"A slight misunderstanding, I believe," Reinhardt offered in response to his friend's question, though he served Lucy a chastising gaze as he did so.

"Lucy?" William then asked. His tone was soft but stern.

"I . . ." Her mind boggled. She'd been so certain that he was after her that she'd acted completely out of character. She'd been spurred on by fear. Of course it was still possible that he was the assassin and that he was merely toying with her the way a cat might play with a mouse before gobbling it up. Truth was, she no longer knew what to think, but what she did know was that this did not look good, and it most certainly was not in accordance with the assassin's request to avoid drawing attention. Actually, she'd just caused quite a scene, and she wasn't at all certain about how to explain it to William.

"Lord Reinhardt was only trying to assist, but when he drew his dagger, I'm afraid I had a moment of panic . . . ever since the incident that I mentioned to you yesterday, William, knives and the like have a tendency to terrify me. I hope you'll forgive me." She turned to Reinhardt who was staring at her with great intensity. "You too, my lord—my actions were terribly inappropriate. I'm really sorry. If we hurry back to the house, we should be able to put a piece of meat on your bruise so you won't look too terrible tonight at the ball."

Reinhardt blinked, as if he couldn't quite comprehend that she would even be thinking of the upcoming ball at a time like this. He opened his mouth to speak, but William cut him off, saying, "I was surprised to see you fall behind, Charles. Is everything all right?"

Reinhardt held silent for a moment, his mouth set in a tight line while his eyes shifted first to Lucy and then to William. "I dislocated my shoulder in a boxing match last week. It's still a bit sore—forces me to take things slow."

William drew a deep breath and let it out again in a loud gush of air. "Come along then, you two. The sooner we tend to that bruise of yours, Charles, the less likely you'll be to frighten away the ladies." Turning Primrose about, Lucy felt like the stupidest simpleton ever to have walked the earth. Reinhardt had kept pace with her because he'd been in pain, yet in addition to a recently dislocated shoulder, he now sported a black eye as well, thanks to her. She groaned inwardly as she plodded back toward Moorland Manor. This was the second time in the course of one day that she'd allowed her imagination to get the better of her. Whatever it was the assassin had in mind, if he hoped to rattle her, then he was doing a very fine job indeed.

CHAPTER FOURTEEN

Stepping into his study, William was not in the least bit surprised to find Alexandra, Ryan, and his father waiting for him. After all, he'd been quite clear when he'd told them that there was a matter he wished to discuss. Closing the door firmly behind him, he walked across to the side table and, noting that everyone else had already been served a drink, proceeded to pour himself a brandy.

Upon returning from his ride, he'd escorted Lucy up to her room and requested that a hot bath be drawn for her. He'd then told Marjory to ensure that Lucy got some rest as soon as she'd eaten the sandwiches that he'd ordered one of the footmen to send upstairs to her. It was his hope that all of this would help soothe her nerves, for in spite of the explanation she'd given him, there was no dismissing the fact that she'd suffered a panic attack, and he very much suspected that there might be more to it than what she'd told him.

With all eyes upon him, he walked across to one of the leather armchairs and took a seat. "I'm concerned about Lucy," he then said, taking a slow sip of his drink as he regarded the only people that he dared trust with such a delicate matter. "She seems . . . skittish and easily frightened. I was wondering if any of you might have noticed the same thing."

"She looked distraught when she returned from her ride," Alexandra offered. "I can't imagine what might have gotten into her, but I dare say that Reinhardt wasn't the only one to suffer at her hands. It will take poor Primrose several days to fully recover from such a lashing."

"I know," William muttered with a sigh. "I hope you're not too angry. Whatever the reason for her behavior, I do believe that Lucy must have thought herself to be in real danger. From what she told me, the sight of Reinhardt's knife threw her into a fit of hysterics."

"I suppose that might make sense, but only if she was already too alarmed to listen to reason," Ryan pointed out. "After all, she'd already been riding Primrose hard for some time before then, as if she was already convinced that Reinhardt was chasing after her with ill intent."

William shook his head, unable to comprehend any of it. "Charles is suffering severe discomfort due to an injury he received last week. Lucy had no reason to be frightened of him—none that I can find, at any rate."

"You know," Alexandra muttered with a frown as she leaned forward in her seat, "now that I think of it, she also seemed a little tense and uneasy before the race, when we were talking to Stanton and he offered to waltz with her."

William took another sip of his drink as he considered this. "Her response was probably dictated by the fact that I'd suggested she should dance the waltz only with me."

"Oh dear," Bryce chuckled, "getting a bit possessive, are

we? There's no need for that, William. The girl's completely mad for you, you know. You'll only push her away if you start acting the part of the jealous husband."

"I don't believe that William needs to act, Papa. He's made it quite apparent that Lucy belongs to him and to no other—not that there was ever any doubt, although one might say that you're the one who belongs to her."

Alexandra snorted a little in her attempt to bite back a laugh, while William merely glowered. His wife had trapped him; that was true. But he wasn't about to allow anyone to make a mockery of his marriage, especially not when things appeared to be looking up. "One can only commend her for realizing so quickly that the two of us would make a perfect match, and rather than allow me to suffer an endless bout of courting—or worse, marrying the wrong woman— she swiftly took matters into her own hands. Quite farsighted of her really, if you think of it."

But rather than nod their heads in agreement, Ryan and Alexandra both looked ready to erupt into a fit of laughter. William just rolled his eyes and decided to give up; whatever he might say from this point on, it would only compound the fact that he was rapidly turning into a lovesick puppy.

"And here I was, thinking that you might be filled with regret over the loss of Lady Annabelle," Bryce mused. "I'm so happy to see that you've changed your mind."

William groaned. "That's neither here nor there, and it definitely doesn't help resolve the issue at hand."

"No, I don't suppose it does." He frowned. "I did send that letter to Percy by the way. I suspect he's probably put an agent on the case already, but it will likely take another couple of days before we hear anything back from him."

William cursed himself for forgetting about that letter. Lucy had made him promise not to share what she'd told him with anyone, but having asked Percy to investigate her past, it might be difficult to keep it a secret. While William didn't doubt the Foreign Office's discretion, he and Lucy would no longer be the only ones privy to her true identity, and it was too late to call off the investigation now. Still, he decided that it would be best to keep quiet on the matter. If his father was to discover anything, he would do so from Percy and not from him. No, William would keep his word to Lucy though he did make a mental note to tell her that her secret might not be safe for much longer.

"She acted a bit odd at dinner last night as well, don't you think?" Ryan suddenly remarked.

William nodded as he recalled the drawn look upon her face and her strained smile. She'd seemed worried about something. "You were sitting directly beside her. Did she happen to say anything out of the ordinary or respond to something somebody else might have said in an unusual fashion?"

Ryan frowned. "Not exactly, but . . ."

"When Reinhardt addressed her, complimenting her on the pendant she was wearing, she seemed to lose her composure a little," Bryce said, cutting straight to the chase.

Charles again . . .

William had of course noticed the gold heart pendant that Lucy had worn but hadn't commented on it. She'd worn it again today, he realized, and he suddenly wondered why he'd never noticed it before. She must have worn it for the first time yesterday, but why would discussing it with anyone make her ill at ease? It didn't seem to make any sense.

"What about, Lady Ridgewood, Papa? Has she said anything that might give us a better understanding of Lucy's peculiar behavior?"

Alexandra gaped at William. "You've asked Papa to entertain Lady Ridgewood with the purpose of garnering information?"

"And you've agreed?" Ryan asked, sounding equally appalled.

"As it is," Bryce said, "I happen to respect the woman a great deal, and I also enjoy her company."

"You're using her with the express hope that she will betray her charge!" Alexandra shot out of her chair and began to pace, anger flashing in her eyes. "She's a lovely woman, Papa. She does not deserve this, and neither does Lucy."

"Two days ago you didn't even like Lucy," William said, offering her a hopeful smile that was not returned. "I'm happy to see that you've changed your mind."

Alexandra served him a scowl and then turned on her father. "Don't do this," she said, "for if you keep it up and Lady Ridgewood discovers your true intent, I dare say she won't like you as much as you like her. In fact, she'll probably never speak to you again."

Bryce frowned, picked up his glass, and took a long gulp. "Giving your old papa advice on how to treat the ladies?"

Rolling her eyes in frustration, Alexandra flopped back down onto her chair and expelled a deep breath. "No, just trying to keep *you* out of trouble for a change."

Bryce chuckled. "I appreciate that, my dear, but there are

times when we must put other people's best interests before our own, and in this case, it is my belief that finding out what we can about Lucy may be the best way for us to protect her against whatever it is that she's so terrified of. And I am willing to sacrifice Lady Ridgewood's good graces for such a cause."

William steeled himself. He already knew what it was that frightened her—the masked assassin that she hoped to find with his help in Constantinople, the very same man who haunted her dreams at night.

Wrapped in her cream-colored, silk dressing gown, Lucy stared out of her bedroom window at the garden below, berating herself for allowing fear to take control. Somebody was likely to get hurt as a consequence. She closed her eyes against the bright and colorful scenery outside, knowing that she'd never forgive herself if that were to happen. Whatever it was the assassin had in mind, she hoped he'd act soon and cease this game of his.

A knock sounded at the door, startling Lucy out of her bleak reverie. Heaven help her, she'd never been this jumpy before in her life. "Who is it?" she called out, making a firm attempt at keeping her voice level.

"It's me, Constance," her friend's voice replied.

With a sigh of relief, Lucy crossed the floor, unlocked her bedroom door, and pulled it open, allowing Constance to enter. "I can't tell you how happy I am to see you right now."

"Yes, it does seem as though we have a great deal to discuss," Constance said as she gave her a warm smile. "I brought these for you, and I've asked your maid to bring up some tea."

"Thank you." Realizing how hungry she actually was, Lucy gratefully accepted the plate of cucumber sandwiches that was being offered to her. She then gestured toward one of the armchairs in the corner. "Come, let's sit."

"So, I understand that there was a bit of an incident during your ride earlier," Constance remarked as soon as they were both comfortably seated. "Would you like to tell me what happened?"

Of course she did, but she couldn't; the risk was too great. So instead, she settled for the same tale that she'd spun for William's benefit. "You know that I don't react well to knives, Constance, and while I realize now that Lord Reinhardt was no threat to me, the sight of him drawing that blade sent me into a panic. I was alone with him after all, and it terrified me." She shook her head in a self-deprecating manner. "William must think I'm such a fool. I acted like a complete madwoman, going so far as to hit Lord Reinhardt for heaven's sake. It's deplorable!"

Reaching for Lucy's hand, Constance gave it a tight squeeze. "Nobody thinks ill of you, Lucy—not as far as I can tell. But, we are worried. This isn't normal behavior." She stared long and hard at her before asking, "Is there something that you're not telling me?"

Swallowing hard, Lucy shook her head definitively. "No."

Constance did not look convinced. "What about your nightmares? Are you still suffering from them?"

"Yes," Lucy managed to say, adding a weak nod. "Yes, they still plague me most nights."

"Oh, Dearheart," Constance murmured, "nobody should have to suffer like this. There's so much pain and anguish in your eyes, Lucy. It breaks my heart to see you like this."

"I just hope that it will all be over soon," Lucy muttered, her voice tripping a little.

"You still intend to find this man, don't you?"

"More than ever." She turned to Constance with renewed determination. "Don't you see? I'll never have a moment of peace until he's brought to justice."

There was a knock at the door and Marjory entered, carrying a tray with a pot of tea and two cups. She set it down between the two ladies, bobbed a curtsy, and then excused herself.

"And what about William?" Constance asked as she reached for the teapot and began to pour for each of them.

"I spoke to him yesterday as you suggested."

Constance stilled for a moment while her eyes widened. "Really? What did he say?"

"That he will help me as best he can." She met Constance's gaze. "I told him everything."

"He's a good man, Lucy. I believe you are right to trust him with this. You'll see. It will bring the two of you closer." She smiled as she reached for Lucy's hand, giving it a gentle squeeze.

Lucy took a sip of her tea. How much everything had changed since yesterday afternoon. The concern she'd had about sharing her past with William, with the potential problem of the news spreading, seemed silly compared with the threat she now faced. She couldn't help but wish she'd told him sooner, for she'd apparently lied to him for no reason.

The assassin had found her anyway and was using the very same method of attack that she herself had hoped to apply. Nothing could possibly be more ironic. She grimaced at the thought of it. Her greatest concern right now was that of protecting those nearest and dearest to her. Without thinking, she allowed her hand to drift to the gold heart pendant about her neck.

"That was your mother's, wasn't it?" Constance quietly asked.

Lucy blinked. Of course Constance would recognize it. This was not something that she could so easily dismiss. "Yes," she replied, picking up a sandwich and taking a bite. She needed to keep her hands occupied, or they'd be twisting at the fabric of her dress.

Constance frowned. "I didn't realize that you had it. In fact, come to think of it, I do believe that this is the first time that I've ever seen you wear it."

"I know, but when I opened my jewelry box yesterday and saw it lying there, it seemed appropriate somehow. I'm not sure that I can really explain it." It hurt that she couldn't be honest, but what else could she possibly have said?

Constance's expression brightened. "Perhaps it's a sign that you're beginning to put this whole matter behind you and heal. Your wound is deep, but it does appear as though there's still a chance for recovery."

If only it was that simple.

"Maybe," Lucy agreed, adding a smile for good measure, "but enough about my troubles—let's talk about you and Lord Moorland instead."

"Heavens, Lucy! That is not the sort of thing a woman

my age discusses." There was no mistaking the bright pink hue that had settled upon Constance's cheeks. "We're merely acquaintances; that is all."

"Really?" The skepticism behind Lucy's voice was quite palpable, but, then again, she'd deliberately exaggerated the intonation of her question. "Because for two people who are nothing more than mere acquaintances, you certainly do seem to be disappearing out of sight together quite often."

"We simply enjoy each other's company," Constance said, looking away. "Besides, he's still not over the loss of his late wife, and, more to the point, I doubt he ever will be enough to consider courting a middle-aged woman like myself."

"Middle aged? Are you really that old?"

Constance rolled her eyes, upon which they both erupted with laughter. "I was your mother's best friend after all. We did grow up together, so you surely must have realized by now that I'm a little closer to forty than I care to admit."

"Well, you don't look it," Lucy told her, and it was the truth. As far as she could tell, Constance didn't look more than thirty at most, and there was no doubt that she must have been the belle of the ball in her day. As it was, she'd captured the heart of the Earl of Ridgewood, a man she claimed to have been the handsomest bachelor in all of England.

Lucy knew that their love for each other had been very real, but unfortunately their marriage had been barren, and then one day the earl had gotten sick. Constance had buried him a year later and never remarried.

"You know," Lucy cautiously continued after a moment's silence, "he'll never get over her, Constance, just like you won't ever get over your husband. But that's not to say that he wants to go on with the rest of his life alone. You'll never be able to take her place, but that doesn't mean that there isn't space in his heart for you as well. His children are grown now. Your charge has married and gone off to live a new life. I don't think anyone would protest if you both chose to move on with your own lives and find happiness with each other, if that's what you wish to do."

There were tears in Constance's eyes when Lucy was finished talking. "When did you become so old and wise?" she asked with a chuckle.

Lucy shrugged. "It's just an observation, that's all."

Constance drew a heavy breath. "Well, in this case, I do believe that you are spot on." Brushing away the tears with the back of her hand, she favored Lucy with a bright smile. "Now, how about if we decide on what to wear for the ball this evening?"

Lucy nodded, warming to the idea, for not only would it serve to distract her from the troubles she faced, but it would also grant her the opportunity she so often craved these days: to impress her husband. For no matter what happened, she knew that his regard for her was of the utmost importance, and if she looked deep enough inside herself, she'd find that it was because he'd captured a larger part of her heart than she'd ever planned to share.

Chapter Fifteen

Music rose and fell through the air, blending with the chatter of a hundred people. Having spent well over an hour greeting his guests with Lucy, William had removed himself to the periphery of the ballroom and was now enjoying a glass of Champagne with Andrew, Ryan, and Trenton. "Your wives look splendid this evening," he said, nodding in Mary and Alexandra's direction. Both women were having a very animated conversation with his aunt, though he dared not imagine what they might be discussing.

"As does yours," Trenton replied.

Turning his head, William immediately spotted Lucy and found himself breathless by her beauty for the second time that evening, the first time being when she'd appeared in the parlor a couple of hours earlier as he'd waited to escort her into the ballroom where they'd taken their places by the door in anticipation of their guests.

She was turned slightly away from him now, listening to something that Lady Ridgewood was saying and affording him a moment in which to admire her without detection. Her gown was of the softest green silk, so slippery in appearance that he couldn't help but envision it falling off her shoulders and pooling on the floor. He drew a tight breath in response to the sudden, unbidden heat that whipped through him.

Instinct told him to march on over there and carry her off right away before anyone else happened to visualize a similar occurrence, for although they were married in name, he had yet to claim her in the most important way of all. Tonight, he decided, he'd make a true attempt at it.

His heart quickened in response to the idea, while his skin began to prickle with sudden anticipation. What if she didn't want him? Heaven help him, but he'd never felt more inexperienced or awkward before in his life. The task at hand was not one that was new to him, and yet the thought of potential failure gave him pause and filled him with growing concern.

As far as he could tell, they shared a mutual attraction for each other, judging from the way she blushed and smiled whenever he was near. And the kiss . . . well, there could be no denying the impassioned heat of *that* moment, and still . . . the failure of that first night together had made him hesitate more than once.

He watched now as she turned her head toward him. Their eyes met across the distance, and she offered him that stunning smile of hers that he'd come to crave. A moment later, her smile fell away, and he saw that Stanton had approached her. He had no idea what they might be saying to each other, but, whatever it was, he sensed Lucy's tension as if it were his own. She suddenly nodded, and with a few words directed at Lady Ridgewood, took the arm that Stanton offered her.

William automatically started forward, only to feel a staying hand upon his arm.

"You cannot keep her from dancing with anyone else, you know." The voice was his brother's. "Especially not when she's the hostess."

"Besides," Andrew added, "I don't believe she'll look too kindly on being coddled."

William hesitated a moment but eventually chose to remain where he was. They were right of course. He couldn't charge in and declare his wife off limits to anyone seeking a dance partner—not without causing a scene. "I'm still worried about her," he offered by way of explanation.

"She does look a lot better than she did earlier in the day, you know. Actually, I dare say she's made a full recovery from her . . . ahem . . . episode," Trenton said with a bit of a frown.

William had to agree, for Lucy was smiling and chatting as if the incident had never occurred at all, and yet there was something in her eyes that warned him against blindly believing what he saw. He'd worked for the Foreign Office long enough now to recognize an act, although this was definitely one of the best he'd ever seen.

"Oh look," Andrew remarked, pointing toward the dancers. "It does appear as though Galensbury's taken pity on Miss Cleaver. I hadn't thought that she would enjoy dancing at all. She comes across as much too serious."

"And yet, she certainly seems to have come out of her shell for that reel. Even Galensbury looks as if he's having a splendid time," Ryan commented.

"Perhaps we should do our duty then and make a deliberate attempt to entertain the young ladies. After all, William, we do want everyone to have an enjoyable evening, if not for our own sakes then at least for Lucy's," Andrew said as he strained his neck and looked around. "Oh look, there's Lady Hyacinth. I dare say I'll ask her to join me for the next set."

William watched his friend disappear into the crowd, feeling more confused than ever. Andrew never danced with anyone, not even his own sisters. What the devil had gotten into everyone today?

"Fairfield's right, you know," Trenton said. "It really is quite badly done of us to stand about here in the corner when I'm sure that there are plenty of young ladies who would love to dance. And, if I may add, now that we're married, we really have nothing to fear from any of them. In fact, it will very likely place us in our wives' good graces if we shower a desperate wallflower or two with some attention."

William knew that he was right of course, and yet there was only one lady whom he had any desire to dance with at all, but she was presently turning about the dance floor with Lord Stanton.

Making an effort to mask his annoyance, he followed Ryan and Trenton, all the while hoping that the waltz he planned to dance with Lucy would not be too far away.

In spite of the smile that she wore upon her face, Lucy was *not* enjoying her reel with Lord Stanton. Far from it. In fact, now that she was out in public once more, she found herself assessing everyone, as she wondered if they might pose a potential threat. She hadn't spoken to Reinhardt since their altercation during the ride, but his eyes had briefly met hers, upon which he'd quickly looked away as if hoping to avoid having anything further to do with her.

And then there was Galensbury, whom she'd caught staring at her on several occasions; Stanton, who, in spite of his gallantry and charm, seemed to lack some inner warmth; and finally Fairfield, whose otherwise jovial demeanor was apparently a façade, concealing a man more serious and sharp than she'd expected. It was all quite unsettling really, not to mention terribly confusing.

The dance drew to an end, and she watched Stanton bow while she curtsied. "Thank you for doing me the honor," he said as he took her by the arm and led her away from the dance floor. "If you don't mind, I think I'll retire to the card table for a bit and try my luck there."

"In that case, I certainly do hope that you win."

"Lady Summersby," he said, releasing her arm and raising her gloved hand to his lips. He looked up at her and offered her another smile before straightening. "I *always* win."

"Well," she said, not knowing exactly what to say to that, "thank you for the dance."

He bowed again before heading toward the library, now a gaming room for the duration of the evening, while she in turn began her search for William. She'd seen him looking at her earlier from across the room, but then Stanton had come along and claimed her for the reel that she'd promised to dance with him. Scouring the ballroom now, she saw no sign of her husband. Perhaps he'd gone off to play cards as well?

She was just about to turn away and have a look in the library when someone caught her by the arm. It was Alexandra, who appeared to be in the best of moods. "Have you seen?" she asked with much excitement in her voice while her eyes shimmered with merriment.

"Seen what?" Lucy asked, noticing that the crowd around the dance floor was now much denser than before.

"Come and take a look for yourself." And with no other word of warning, Alexandra whisked Lucy off toward the growing wall of spectators. Skirting the masses, they managed to find a spot where they could squeeze through, and once they'd done so, Alexandra leaned close to Lucy's ear and whispered, "They may appear tough, but each of them is a gentleman through and through—even Lord Fairfield as it turns out."

Lucy caught her breath, for there before her was not only William but Lord Trenton, Mr. Summersby, Lord Galensbury, and, indeed, Lord Fairfield too, each paired with a lady that most men would probably have ignored. But Lucy knew that by simply dancing with these women, her husband and his friends had afforded them the opportunity they needed to get noticed and, she hoped, make a good match. She couldn't have admired them more, for she was well aware that as far as these gentlemen were concerned, dancing was on the very bottom of the list when it came to favored pastime activities.

Except for Lord Fairfield, of course—he e was also the only one whom she knew to have real motivation. It certainly seemed as if he planned to take her advice where Lady Hyacinth was concerned. Turning about as he switched partners, he looked across at her and winked. It was impossible not to be taken in by it all, especially now when the crowd had begun clapping and cheering.

Lucy felt her smile widen into a grin, but it was the smoldering look in William's eyes as he turned his head to catch her stare that took her breath away. And as the dance ended and the crowd began to disperse, it was his slow, deliberate approach that sent sparks of heat skittering across her skin. She knew in that moment that she loved him, more desperately than she ever would have imagined possible, and the realization of it terrified her half to death.

"I believe this next one is ours," he said as he stood before her, his gray-blue eyes locked with hers in a silent plea.

Swallowing hard, she reminded herself that it really wouldn't do at all if her legs turned to jelly now when the waltz was about to commence. Nodding, she accepted the arm he offered her and drew a deep breath with the hope that it might somehow calm her racing heart. "Indeed, it is," she then said, putting all the love she felt for him behind the smile she gave. He remained quite still for a moment, as if in a daze, but then the spell was broken, and he shook his head, placed his hand upon her waist, and readied himself for the first step.

"You dance beautifully," he told her after a few easy turns about the dance floor. His lips were close to her ear.

Goosebumps spread their way along her arms and down her back, and Lucy feared that if she didn't concentrate on her steps, she might very well stumble over her own feet—or even worse, over *his*. "Thank you. So do you." Was she really such a dolt that she could think of nothing better to say? She had to pull herself together somehow. "To be honest, I've been looking forward to dancing with you all day."

He tightened his hold on her as he led her in a wide circle. "As have I. Of that, I can assure you."

Lucy felt her stomach tighten in response to his words,

for there was something in the way he'd spoken them that made her think he was talking about something else entirely. Was he flirting with her or perhaps trying to seduce her? The thought sent fresh waves of heat racing through her, but it also intrigued her, and she found herself rising to the challenge. "Do you know, I do believe that I would enjoy doing it again later."

If she wasn't entirely mistaken, William actually misstepped, but if he did, he quickly recovered, so it was difficult to tell. Again, he tightened his hold on her. Heavens, if they moved any closer they'd practically be one and the same person. "Later?" his voice was low and gravelly as he spoke.

"Hm, yes . . . I thought we might enjoy another moment together in your room . . . like last time." William looked perplexed, and it was almost impossible for her not to laugh— almost, but not quite. "Except this time we'll dance of course."

He cleared his throat, sounding somewhat agitated. "Dance . . . I suppose we might, though there really isn't much space for a waltz in either of our bedrooms."

"No, I don't suppose there is," she said, pretending to contemplate the dilemma as he swept her past Ryan who was dancing with his wife Mary. Looking up at William, she gave him her most innocent stare. "My gown *is* quite voluminous . . . perhaps if I were to take it off? I could perhaps dance in my chemise."

"Lucy . . ." His voice was hoarse as he clasped her against him. "What exactly are you suggesting?"

She knew that the time for playing games was over, so she took all the courage she possessed and put it all into the next few words, saying, "Merely that whatever it is you desire to do for the remainder of the night, I shall be more than happy to comply."

A moment later, she couldn't help but fear that she might have taken her coquettish behavior a step too far, for her husband's breath was now coming in rapid bursts while his eyes had narrowed into something of a predatory stare. As the music slowed and they glided to a stop, he held on to her with possessive firmness, forcing her to realize that there was only one thing on his mind right now and that he was busily trying to figure out how to best go about whisking her off and having his way with her. Leaning toward him, she thought it prudent to say, "All eyes are upon us, William. We cannot remain in such an intimate embrace now that the dance is over. We must move to the side."

He blinked, nodded, and stepped away from her a little before offering his arm. "Would it be terribly rude if we were to make our excuses and retire for the evening?" he asked as he led her toward the refreshment table.

"We are the host and hostess, William, so I do believe our guests would find it rather odd, if not quite poor behavior on our part, if we were to abandon them so soon."

He frowned as he picked up a glass of punch and offered it to her, the wheels in his head spinning with obvious rapidity. "My sister can take over—or my father perhaps."

"Not unless there's a valid excuse. Besides, I don't quite understand your sudden rush to escape. I for one am having a splendid time."

She was only teasing him of course, but the look of annoyance that he gave her warned her that he was not in the mood to be trifled with. "Am I mistaken, Lucy, or did you not just suggest that we . . ." He drew her back a little for the sake of privacy. When he spoke again, his voice was a low whisper. "That we stop ignoring the way in which we respond to each other, and . . . and . . ."

"Shh . . . don't say another word," she said, doing her best to reassure him with a smile. "Not here. As it happens, I do feel a headache coming on. Perhaps you'd be kind enough to escort me upstairs to my room?"

He let out a deep and shaky breath. "I would be happy to," he told her with a nod, his expression still a bit tight around the edges. It dawned on her that he might not be as confident as he generally let on.

Was it possible that he feared her rejection? The possibility filled her with incredulity, not to mention a strong sense of guilt for toying with his emotions. Setting down her half-empty glass on the table, she placed her hand upon his arm, squeezing it a little as she met his gaze. "Let's find your sister and make our excuses."

CHAPTER SIXTEEN

In his excitement to get on with the matter at hand, William gave the bedroom door a hard shove, closing it behind them with a loud bang that drew a gasp from Lucy. Taking a moment to gather his wits, he quietly watched as she moved further into the room, the slippery green silk of her gown sliding across her backside as she walked. A mischievous smile spread its way along his lips, and he moved toward her with measured steps, unable to stop himself from saying, "I had no idea that a woman as innocent as you would be able to engage in the sort of exchange we shared downstairs. I must admit that it caught me completely off guard."

She eyed him for a second and then looked away, cheeks flaming, and he suddenly had the distinct impression that she wished to flee. He shouldn't let her of course, but her visible mortification forced him to remember that she wasn't nearly as brave or as worldly as she was attempting to let on. She was most likely more confused and embarrassed by all of this than she'd ever been by anything else in her life, and yet she'd encouraged him—of that there could be no doubt. If only they could find a way to return to that easy flirtation they'd shared.

Swallowing hard, William took a tentative step toward her. "Tell me, Lucy . . ." he said as he reached out and ran the pad of his thumb along her jawline, pleased when her breath shuddered in response. "Tell me what you're thinking."

"I couldn't possibly," she muttered on a breath of air that drifted toward him and sank beneath his skin.

Cupping her cheek, he gently caressed her, allowing her to relax against his touch. "Please, Lucy, I need to know that I'm not the only one consumed by this desperate desire that I feel for you. Tell me that you feel it too."

She responded with the slightest of nods. "I do," she whispered, and he felt his heart soar with elation. "My heart pounds in my chest whenever you are near, and whenever I think of you I . . ."

His stomach tightened and his skin prickled as he contemplated her next words, but they trailed off into silence, and she looked suddenly quite embarrassed. Pulling against him, she made an attempt at escape, but he held on fast, tightening his grip instead. "What were you about to say?"

"Nothing." Her eyes darted sideways, and he knew that it wasn't *nothing* at all.

"Have your thoughts of me been . . . improper in any way?" Dear God, he hoped so.

Her eyes closed against his words. "How can you ask me such a thing? It's not appropriate."

He grinned at that, loving her innocence. "I beg to differ, my dear, for you see, I am your husband, and I simply wish to know what excites you, and given the situation that we are in, it is really *very* appropriate." He paused as he toyed with a lock of her fiery red hair. "Do you understand?"

It took a while before she nodded, the simple movement sending sparks of pleasure across his skin. "I fear you might think me wanton."

He leaned closer, so as to whisper in her ear. "I'll tell you a secret, Lucy. You may be as wanton as you wish when it's just the two of us." He leaned back to meet her eyes, which were now as large as saucers, but there was something else in them too—hunger, he reckoned. "In fact, I would encourage it."

Pulling her toward him, he settled his hands about her waist, saw the expectant look upon her face, and leaned forward, gently kissing her upon her lips. There was no hesitation on her part. On the contrary, she practically flung her arms about his neck, tugging him closer as she drew his lower lip between her own, startling him to no end with her brashness. Apparently he'd not only found himself a very astute pupil but also a delightfully passionate woman.

Taking advantage of the opening her move offered, he slipped his tongue between her lips, coaxing hers until she followed suit. Liquid heat pulsed through his veins, built by the fire she so eagerly offered. He lowered his hand to the firmness of her bottom and pushed her hard against his growing arousal, extracting a gasp from somewhere deep inside her.

Her hold on him tightened and William felt her squirm ever so slightly as she adjusted her position against him, allowing him the access he craved. It was almost too much for him to bear. He wanted more, needed more, and knew without a shadow of a doubt that so did she, and yet he forced himself to remember that he must be careful with her.

Running his fingers along the length of her spine, his fingers toyed with the small, silk-covered buttons of her gown, pushing them through their buttonholes one by one until he felt the fabric fall away from her back.

With a deep kiss, he ran his hands back up her sides. They hesitated against the curve of her breasts, and again he felt her move restlessly against him. Intent on denying both of them a moment longer, his hands continued on their upward path. Disengaging himself from her, he then stepped back a little and, with his gaze holding hers, slipped the small capped sleeves off her shoulders and down her arms until her gown lay pooled at her feet. "Turn around," he muttered, and she did as he asked without question or the slightest bit of hesitation.

For a moment, his eyes simply ran over her, feasting on her every curve. He reached out his hand and allowed it to slide across the plump swell of her bottom, but when he gently gave her a squeeze and she arched her back in response, he had to fight to maintain his composure. He would have her soon enough—but not in a rushed and insensitive way. No, Lucy deserved better than that. So he drew a tight breath instead and went to work on her corset, pulling on the ties until it, too, fell away from her.

Stepping back a little so as to better peruse her, it was impossible for him to hold back the heavy breath that unwillingly escaped his lips, for her chemise, much like the nightgown she'd worn the other evening, left nothing to the imagination. Indeed, she might just as well have had nothing on, and he almost staggered at the incredulity of it—and of her. Circling around in order to face her, he made no attempt to hide his admiration. Her breasts were larger and fuller than he recalled—or perhaps they simply appeared so due to the much tighter chemise.

Her nipples, however, were hard like pebbles, beckoning for his touch, while her waist was slim and her hips well rounded, with an alluring patch of red between them. She was perfect in every sense of the word—absolutely perfect.

Watching her face, the desire in it, he reached for the hem of her one remaining garment, found it, and proceeded to pull it up, so slowly and deliberately that he was certain that her expression turned to one of pure torture. A satisfied smirk lifted the corners of his mouth as the flimsy fabric came up to bunch around her waist, his fingers sliding over her soft and enticing curves. Lifting her right leg, he settled it upon a small bench that stood by the foot of the bed. Her eyes widened in response, and his smiled broadened into a roguish grin. "How do you feel?" he asked in a gruff tone as he ran his fingers along her extended thigh in small circular motions that left gooseflesh in their wake.

She sighed in response, her back instinctively arching once more, forcing her breasts against the taut fabric that was still covering her upper half. "Sinful beyond compare," she muttered.

A deep throaty chuckle escaped him. "This is only the beginning, my love." He lowered his lips against her neck to plant a row of kisses there. "By the time I'm through with you, you'll feel just about ready to burst into flames." His teasing fingers skirted along the place where he knew she desired him the most. She groaned, tried to move herself toward him, but his fingers moved on up and over her hip, crawling beneath her chemise and over her naval. With determined fingers, he grasped the delicate fabric that still encased her, and then with a quick upward sweep, he pulled it away from her body and tossed it on the floor.

Lucy immediately sucked in a breath, and he felt her shiver. Reaching up, his hand found her breast. He squeezed her nipple, gently at first, and then more insistently as she arched her back further, her eyes glazing over. By God he could kick himself for wasting this much time on what led to their marriage. This . . . what she had to offer was exquisite pleasure beyond belief. She was innocent, yes, but the way she responded . . . he'd never find another woman more erotic than her. The effect she had on him . . . Lord help him. If he didn't remove his breeches soon he felt certain that the buttons would begin to fly right off.

Lucy was in heaven. There could be absolutely no other explanation, she reasoned. The way he touched her . . . the feelings and sensations those nimble fingers of his evoked was completely maddening.

The juncture between her thighs had long since grown hot with need—the ache there almost impossible for her to bear a moment longer without losing her mind. What sort of woman would think such deplorable things? Good heavens, she actually wanted him to touch her there, in her most private of places. Indeed, she was quite prepared to beg for him to do so. It was appallingly inappropriate to say the least!

But of course the blasted man seemed quite indifferent to her need. In fact, his fingers had danced right past her most urgent desire and . . . She let out a small gasp as he pinched her nipple. Apparently the pleasure that waited between her thighs would have to delay a while longer, for she felt her whole body tremble as he touched her and . . . Dear merciful God, his tongue . . . that devilish tongue of his was licking at her breasts, sending bursts of scorching heat along her flesh. Lucy whimpered; it was unavoidable. And then she felt his whole mouth descend upon her, suckling with ferocious need as his hand swept down along her midsection. Down, down, down, until . . .

Lucy practically buckled, the sensations were so over-whelming, but he held her firmly in place, cradling her against him with his left arm while his right hand stroked the soft folds of her womanhood.

"Bloody hell, Lucy," he murmured against her ear, "you're so incredibly wet . . ."

She wanted to ask him what he meant, but the words wouldn't come. She was beyond speaking, beyond chastising herself for this utterly divine and alarmingly uncivilized behavior. All she could do was enjoy it. So she did—every second of it.

Pressing against his hand, she reveled in the odd yet delightful feel of the caress that his fingers offered as they feathered inside her, stroking her toward a place of wondrous glory.

Tugging on her nipple with his teeth while his fingers continued to work their magic, she suddenly felt herself burst like fireworks erupting in the night sky, and for a moment there was no doubt in her mind that she would crumble from the force of the waves that shook her. But William held her firmly in place, allowing her to lull in his embrace. "Good gracious," she muttered, her breath still coming in heavy pants.

She felt him nuzzle her neck. "There's so much more," he murmured.

Her eyes grew wide with wonder. How much more could there possibly be? She felt dizzy just contemplating it but was afforded little time to consider the matter any further before finding herself lifted off the ground. A moment later, William settled her down on the bed, straightened himself, and then looked at her in much the same way that a hungry lion might view a gazelle. He was all but salivating. His eyes were hooded, his breath coming fast as he ripped his shirt from his shoulders and flung it across the room. Next, he started popping open the buttons of his breeches, one by one.

Lucy stared, mesmerized and incredibly curious. The bulge at his crotch appeared to have grown in size, if such a thing was even possible. Perhaps her eyes deceived her?

Bending at the waist, William drew both his breeches and his unmentionables down over his long, lean legs, and Lucy's mouth grew instantly dry at the sight of the flexing muscles he revealed. Pulling the garments over his bare feet and kicking them away, he then righted himself and turned to face Lucy. She couldn't help but gasp at the sight that presently greeted her. William merely grinned, eyes sparkling like those of a young boy about to do a world of mischief.

Never in her life had she seen or imagined something like this. It was huge—much larger than his fingers had been. And yet as horrified as she was at the prospect of him coming one step closer with that . . . *thing* jutting toward her, she was also somewhat intrigued. Feeling the need to say something—anything at all—she suddenly asked, "Is that . . . normal?"

Looking up, she saw that his lips had begun to twitch ever so slightly and knew that he was trying to stop from erupting into a fit of laughter. Well what was she expected to think? She frowned and crossed her arms, feeling a bit put out, not to mention rather embarrassed that she'd asked what apparently appeared to have been a rather silly question.

"Yes," he told her gently as he came toward her. The signs of humor that had played upon his face a moment earlier had now been replaced by something more serious. "This is the evidence of the desire that I feel for you, Lucy."

Her eyes returned to the swollen flesh, only to discover that her concerns had now been replaced by wonder and awe. Leaning forward, she tried to take a closer look while William in turn remained perfectly still, apparently not caring in the least that his wife was giving him a thorough inspection. Wondering what it might feel like, Lucy eyed her husband warily as she edged a little closer to where he stood. "Would you mind terribly if I"—she paused as she considered how best to ask but then gave up on all hope for propriety and decided on complete candor instead—"touch it?"

An odd expression settled upon William's face, and Lucy immediately regretted how brazen she'd just been. In truth, she was quite appalled by herself. But when she opened her mouth to apologize, William quickly cut her off, saying, "Lucy, if you're so brave on our first intimate encounter, then I dare say that our future together looks most promising." With his eyes locked on hers, he reached for her hand and placed it upon him.

He was softer than she'd expected, and for a moment she simply ran her fingers gently across him, but when she heard him draw a ragged breath and looked up to find that his eyes were squeezed shut—a look of intense pleasure upon his face—she took courage and closed her fingers around him.

William's eyes flew open, and she thought for a moment that she might have hurt him somehow, but rather than turn away from her, he placed his own hand over hers, guiding it back and forth until she became accustomed to the motion.

"Enough," he suddenly muttered as he pulled away from her. He must have seen the startled expression in her eyes, for he followed his brusque remark with a warm smile. "If you keep touching me like that, I'll only spend myself in your hand, Lucy, and I've no intention of letting that happen." And then he surprised her by pushing her backward against the mattress, and crawling up between her legs while he kissed his way along her inner thighs.

Lucy held her breath for what seemed like an eternity. Of all the sinful things they'd done so far, this was by far the most illicit. Reaching down, she tried to block access with her hand. William paused, raised his head, and stared up at her, arching an eyebrow in question.

"You . . . you . . ." she stammered, "you can't do that. It's completely inappropriate behavior, perhaps even illegal come to think of it."

He offered her a cheeky grin. "If it is, then I am about to commit a felony." And then he simply lifted her hand ever so gently, bowed his head, and licked her—one long heavenly lick that sent shivers scurrying across her skin as liquid heat pooled between her thighs. It felt divine, and, though it was probably beyond aberrant, Lucy was powerless to stop it. All she could do was stretch back and enjoy it.

He licked her again, and her hips rose to meet him. She felt that same aching need begin to build and knew that she was once again restless for more. If this would send her plummeting straight to the pits of hell, then so be it. She was damned if she cared.

Lifting his head, William moved his body forward until he was resting directly above her. His breath was heavy, the muscles in his arms straining as he held himself suspended. "This is bound to hurt a little," he murmured, "but it will be over quickly. I promise." Settling himself between her legs, he then eased forward slowly.

Lucy felt herself tense but caught his gaze, and as she held it, began to relax, for he was telling her not with words but with his eyes that this would work—that it would be all right. As if to reassure her even further, he gave her all the time that she needed in order to adjust to the new sensation. And then he kissed her, plundering her mouth as he drove her to the brink of madness—to a place where she forgot what he'd just told her, to a place where all thoughts of pain vanished and only bliss existed. She flinched momentarily as he buried himself deep inside her, a sharp pain tearing itself through her until she feared she might be ripped apart. But then it passed, and whatever sounds of protest that she might have made were swallowed by their kiss.

He moved out a little, and she instinctively gripped his shoulders in an attempt to bring him back against her. Without hesitation, he obliged her, kissing her a moment longer. Then, raising himself above her once more, he looked her straight in the eye and said, "Move with me, Lucy." And she did. Wrapping her legs around him, she followed his lead until she found herself moving in perfect time to his rhythm.

Heavenly—absolutely heavenly.

"God, you're beautiful," William muttered before lowering his head against her breast to flick his tongue against her nipple.

Feeling the same tingling heat from earlier begin to build once more, Lucy clung to him more tightly than before. "William . . ." His name was faint upon her breath, and yet he seemed to know precisely how to respond. Picking up pace, he plunged harder and deeper until she felt the first ripple of pleasure tickling her insides. Another followed swiftly after, and then she shattered as she cried out his name.

With one last forceful push, William let out a guttural groan before dropping his head against her chest. He remained quite still for a while after—his breath hot against her skin—before turning his head to place a reverent kiss upon each breast.

"That was . . . far beyond any of my wildest expectations," she whispered a short while later when they both lay wrapped in each other's arms.

"Mine too," he told her, adding a tender kiss to the top of her head.

"Perhaps we can do this more often?"

William offered her a mischievous smile. "We can do it as often as you like, love—preferably several times a day."

"Heavens!"

"Indeed." He turned on his side and began trailing his fingers over her hip. "But right now, there's a ballroom full of guests downstairs, and since you've claimed a headache, I believe it falls on my shoulders to return to them as host."

"Dear me, I'd completely forgotten."

"But perhaps later . . . after they've all gone?" He leaned forward and gently kissed her.

"If I'm asleep," she said, already eager for him to return so he could ravish her once more, "wake me."

"I promise," he said as he chuckled, climbed from the bed, and began to retrieve his clothes. "But until then, I suggest that you try and rest, for it promises to be a very long night indeed." And then he sent her a wink that she feared would likely melt her heart, but as he left her with the promise that he would soon return, her soul felt heavy with the burden of the secret she was now forced to keep from him. The man who'd killed her parents was not only a guest in her own home but had deliberately sought her out, threatening the people she cared about most.

Settling back against her pillow, she drew the covers up to her chin and stared back at the darkness surrounding the bed. Whatever the assassin's plan might be, she had to try and fight him if she hoped to remain at William's side. Forcing back the fear and allowing her six-year-long hatred for the man to settle in its place, she made her decision. Tomorrow she would find a suitable weapon. One thing was certain, he'd already taken so much more from her than she'd ever been willing to give.

Chapter Seventeen

Only a numbing silence surrounded her, as if perhaps her ears had been filled with water. Her feet felt wet and cold, and as she looked down at them, she realized that the ground she stood on was covered in blood. Bending forward, she glanced at the reflection that stared back at her, only to discover that it was that of a child—a younger version of herself.

She gasped then and drew back, her eyes roaming across the vast expanse of emptiness that stretched to infinity around her. There was nothing but her; not a tree or a bird could be seen. She had no idea how she'd gotten there, but she knew that she had to find a way back home. Mama and Papa would be worried about her. But there was so much blood . . . it was deeper now, almost reaching the hem of her nightgown. With a deep breath, she stepped forward and began to walk, and as she did, buildings began to rise on either side of her until she found herself once again in that awful alley, a scream splitting the silence as a masked stranger appeared before her. "Where are you going?" he asked, his voice dark and menacing.

Swallowing hard, she tried to stop herself from glancing

up at the window that she knew she'd find, but her eyes failed to listen, and as she turned to look she saw her mother's body turn around and fall away.

"You can't stop me, Lucy. I'm cleverer than you," the assassin warned as he took a step closer.

She wanted to kill him, but with what? She had no weapon, and besides, she'd promised her mother she'd run. So she did—or tried to at least, but as she spun away and started to move the blood held her back. It was up to her hips now, making it impossible for her to do anything but wade forward. She looked back and saw that he was gaining on her with an efficiency that she couldn't possibly match, and as she readied herself to start swimming, she felt the chilling grip of his hands upon her shoulders pushing her down. She wanted to scream but found that she couldn't. Something was covering her mouth . . . his hand perhaps? In desperation, she started to struggle, but his weight was holding her firmly in place, and she suddenly realized with startling clarity that the dream was gone and that this was real—her very own living nightmare.

"Open your eyes, Lucy," he told her in a dangerously low whisper. "You and I need to have a little talk."

Terror sprang to life once more, but she still couldn't scream—not against the cold, leather-clad hand that was firmly pressed against her mouth. She dared not look, and yet she feared what he might do if she disobeyed him, so she slowly opened her eyes into two small slits, only to come face to face with that awful, black mask—one side shrouded in darkness, the other reflecting the flickering flame of the oil lamp that stood next to her bed. She did scream then, her eyes widening against her own volition as she tried to free her arms from his grasp, but his hand muffled whatever sound she made, and his weight, as he straddled her, made all her attempts at escape futile.

"I must admit that I'm a bit disappointed, Lucy." His voice was leering and cold. She couldn't recognize it, but then again she suspected that he'd probably intended it that way. "I was hoping for a bit of a warmer welcome after such a long time. At least *I* was gallant enough to send you a present."

Lucy blinked. Was this it then? Was she about to be brutally murdered while her husband, his family, and guests enjoyed their Champagne downstairs? It hardly seemed fair, and though she'd no desire for this brute of a man to see her cry, she simply couldn't hold back the hot tears that threatened behind her eyes.

"Oh, Lucy," he said, "don't be so sad. It's not over yet, you know. However, I did come here to give you your final warning." He stroked his thumb slowly across her cheek—a caress that would have seemed loving had it come from anyone else. Gooseflesh rose along her arms in response to it. "You aroused too much attention today with your little episode out there on the moor; we can't risk that happening again. As it is, you're lucky that you were able to explain the matter away, but the minute I begin to feel threatened . . . Well, you read my note, but just in case William and Lady Ridgewood aren't enough of an incentive for you to keep quiet, I thought I should warn you that I may decide to take my anger out on someone else entirely . . . on little Vanessa perhaps."

Lucy stilled. He couldn't possibly mean to harm an innocent child. Nobody could be that cruel. But then, *she'd* been an innocent child once.

"Doubt me all you want," he said, as if reading her mind, "but you'll be the one risking the lives of those around you, and just so we're clear, I have indeed just added Mr. Summersby's daughter to the list."

Lucy wondered if a place worse than hell existed. She hoped so, for this man deserved a far harsher fate than to merely burn for all eternity.

"Now, I have to leave you, unfortunately, but we'll meet again soon enough. You mustn't worry about that, Lucy." He leaned a little closer, and when he spoke again his voice sounded hollow. "I have no choice but to let you go, but hopefully our little conversation has made you realize that I'll succeed in my task by all means necessary. Do you promise not to scream?"

With tears blinding her eyes and her breath coming in rapid bursts, Lucy quietly nodded. "Why are you doing this?" she asked, as soon as she was free to do so. He still pinned her down, but at least he'd removed his hand from her mouth, allowing her to breathe normally again.

A moment later, he was across the floor with his hand resting on the door handle. He turned back to face her and merely shrugged. "The same thing that gives most people an incentive to work—money."

"This was a . . . a job?" She couldn't believe that she was having this conversation, but she needed answers, and he was the only one who could give them to her. But this time he didn't reply. Instead he quietly cracked opened the door, looked out to ensure that no one was coming, and then exited her room without another word or backward glance.

Lucy wasn't sure how long she'd been lying there under

the covers before the shock of it all had dissipated enough for her to move—half an hour most likely, although it felt like much more. With shaky hands, she pulled back the covers and sat up. She couldn't let him win. The thoughts of revenge that had crowded her mind for so long came flooding back. This was it, she decided. He might have sought her out instead, but that didn't mean that she had to cower helplessly in a corner while he threatened everything around her. Yes, he terrified her because she had no doubt of what he was capable of, but she also knew that her only way forward would be to stop fleeing and to turn around and face him.

Drawing a deep, resolute breath, she stepped down onto the floor. She could no longer wait until tomorrow in order to obtain one of the daggers that she'd imagined she'd borrow from William's collection in the study. Now that the assassin had visited her in her bedroom, she realized the imminent danger and the importance of being able to protect herself.

Shivering from the cool night air that surrounded her, she padded across to her wardrobe to retrieve her dressing gown. The fact that she'd been completely naked beneath the covers while that beast of a man had held her down and threatened her was not a thought she cared to entertain at the moment. Instead, she forced it back as she began slipping her arms through the sleeves, pulling the garment tight around her waist as if she hoped it might somehow shield her from harm.

She couldn't go back downstairs now—not like this and certainly not with guests still milling about. She hadn't checked the clock, but if William wasn't back yet like he'd promised he would be, then that could only mean that he was still busy entertaining their friends. Her eyes settled upon the door that connected her room with William's; it was standing slightly ajar. Surely a man like him, trained to be a soldier and a spy, would keep a weapon close to where he slept.

Without another moment's hesitation, she crossed the floor, picked the oil lamp from her bedside table, and pulled the door wide open. She then paused for a moment on the threshold, knowing that with one more step she would violate William's privacy, betraying his trust yet again. A deep breath strengthened her resolve. She could turn to no one for help in this matter and was therefore forced to protect herself and her loved ones by whatever means necessary.

Her movements were quick and determined this time as she walked through to her husband's sanctuary—a room she'd visited on only one previous occasion. Her eyes went directly to the couple of chairs where they'd sat and shared a glass of brandy together two days earlier. She doubted that he'd be inclined to share anything with her again if he discovered her rummaging through his things like a thief in the middle of the night.

Turning about, she wondered where to start. It was one thing to be in his room without permission but far more difficult to actually open a drawer and peek inside. It would also be a lot harder to explain such an action if she got caught.

With a forceful mental shove, she pushed her misgivings aside and carefully opened the top drawer in William's dresser. Peering inside, she found some handkerchiefs, all neatly folded and stacked on one side. Next to them were his cravats, and next to them, a few different accessories—pocket watches, a monogrammed cigar case, three pairs of gloves, and a couple of leather wallets. Closing the drawer back up again, she moved on to the next one, finding only crisp, white shirts this time. By the time she was done looking, she was forced to concede that if William did have a dagger or a pistol hidden away in his room, then it had to be somewhere else.

She paused to think as her eyes swept over the four-poster bed, the metallic threads on its burgundy colored quilt shimmering in the glow from the oil lamp that Lucy had placed on top of the dresser. A bedside table with a couple of drawers stood on either side. Stepping toward the one on the right, Lucy reached out and pulled open the drawer. A book was the first thing to catch her attention—Bensley's *The Officer's Manual in the Field*. A slow smile pulled at Lucy's lips as she stared down at the leather-bound edition. Of course her husband would have such a book by his bed rather than a novel or a collection of poetry, for which she knew he cared very little.

Reminding herself of her task at hand, she pushed it gently aside and reached inside the drawer until her hand found something cold, hard, and metallic. Her breath was one of relief as she pulled the object out, revealing a single shot Manton pistol. Careful to point it away from herself, she turned it over in her hands, studying it as she wondered whether it might be loaded. She supposed it must be in case William happened to need it in a hurry, but she couldn't be sure. For that matter, she wasn't even completely certain that she'd be able to figure out how to use it if she had to. With a frown, she reached back inside the drawer and pulled out a small box of shot and powder. She'd have to examine everything more closely, but she'd do so in her own room and with the door locked.

Closing the drawer, she went back to retrieve the lantern

from the dresser and was just about to exit the room when the door opened and William stepped inside, his eyes widening with momentary surprise as he spotted her. Concern abandoned his features, and he gave her a warm smile of appreciation as he started toward her, but then his gaze dropped to her hand, and he slowed until he stood completely still. "What are you doing?" A frown transformed his features into a mask of worry, though his voice remained completely calm.

"No . . . nothing," Lucy stammered as a flash of heat rose to the surface of her skin and her hands began to tremble.

He was in front of her in a second, his much larger body looming over her as he braced his hands on either side of her slight figure, keeping her trapped. "You've taken something of mine without my permission—a rather dangerous weapon— and all you can tell me is that you're not doing anything?" His voice was a low rumble. "Do you think me a complete imbecile, Lucy, or perhaps blind?"

Unable to speak for the painful knot that now clogged her throat, she quickly shook her head.

He drew back a little and took a deep breath. "I thought we'd moved past this, Lucy, yet here you are, sneaking about and purposefully lying. Will you please tell me what's going on?"

"I . . ." Words failed her, and when she tried to breathe, her voice quivered and broke instead, practically choking her. With a loud sob, she sank to the floor and cried until she could no longer see. What could she possibly tell him without putting everyone around her in danger? William was too observant; he'd know that she was being dishonest with him no matter what excuse she tried to fabricate.

"Lucy?" His voice was hesitant, but a moment later he was beside her on the floor, his hands reaching around her body and pulling her toward him until her head was nestled against his chest. It was a long time until he spoke again, but when he did it was with concern marking his voice. "I can tell that something's troubling you, Lucy. Why won't you tell me? Why won't you trust me?"

Easing back a little, she raised her gaze to meet his, brushing the tears from her eyes. "I cannot," she whispered, her eyes darting toward the dark corners of the room as if she half expected the assassin to leap out and attack them for this small truth. His eyes narrowed, and the words that she needed to say suddenly gushed from her mouth. "Please, William . . . don't be angry with me. As hard as it is, you must believe me when I say that I *cannot* tell you." Locking her eyes with his, she implored him to understand.

His gaze turned contemplative. "Nobody acts like this unless they're truly terrified," he muttered. "Your jumpiness . . . your uneasy behavior during dinner last night . . . the incident during our ride earlier in the day . . . This isn't just about your nightmares or the fears caused by your parents' deaths, is it Lucy?"

Closing her eyes against the sympathetic glimmer in his eyes, she sank back against the dresser and shook her head.

"Who has threatened you?"

Again she shook her head, determined not to disclose anything further. As it was, his assumption based on her behavior alone was likely to place him in danger.

"Very well," he said, relenting, "it seems you're in enough of a state right now without me pressing you any further, but as I've told you before, I'll stand beside you against whatever trouble you have to face. It would just be a lot easier for me to do so if you tell me who has put you so ill at ease. For now, however, I shall show you how to use the pistol in case you need to, and then you shall remain here with me for the rest of the night. Until I know exactly what it is that's putting you in such a state of panic, I've no intention of leaving you unattended." Leaning forward, he placed a tender kiss upon her brow. "I apologize for my reaction before, but I don't respond well to backhanded behavior or to being lied to—especially not when I was under the impression that there would be no more secrets between us."

Lucy blinked. Was he really forgiving her for sneaking into his room, stealing his pistol, and then serving him an obvious lie? Surely this man was too good for a woman like her to deserve. "I'm sorry," she said. "It was badly done of me. I know that. But I didn't know what else to do."

He nodded, hesitated a moment, and then said, "I have to tell you something as well." He drew a deep breath. "Before you told me about your past, I asked my father to write a letter to the first secretary of the Foreign Office, asking him to investigate you."

"Oh God." Lucy felt her heart slam against her chest. This could ruin everything. If the assassin found out that the Foreign Office had become involved there was no telling what he might do.

"I'm sorry, Lucy, but I had to know who I was married to."

Of course he did. She was a fool for not considering it before. "You have to stop them," she said, her eyes locking on to his.

"I'm afraid it's too late for that. The letter was sent out two days ago. I'm sure the agent has already discovered everything he could about you."

Heaven help her. Heaven help them all. She felt herself grow suddenly hot and short of breath. The light in the room began to swim before her eyes, and it almost seemed as if the walls were closing in on her. Swallowing hard, she managed to say, "Nobody can know about this, William. Nobody can know you did this."

He stared back at her for a moment and then nodded. "All right," he muttered. "I'll take care of it. You have my word."

She knew he meant it, and yet she couldn't help but worry. "Come," he said as he pulled her to her feet and into his arms. "Let's not think about it anymore tonight." Bending his head, his lips found hers, gently at first and then with growing urgency.

All worries of the masked assassin fled Lucy's mind as William's tongue entered her mouth and his hands pushed away the fabric of her silk dressing gown, leaving her bare in the glow of the flickering flame. And when she felt his fingers stroke against her soft and aching flesh, it became impossible for her to think of anything but William and the passionate moment they now shared.

CHAPTER EIGHTEEN

Thanking the maid for the coffee she'd brought him, William added some milk and sugar as she took her leave before settling back against his chocolate-colored armchair. He hadn't slept a wink last night, his mind constantly working to try to solve the puzzle surrounding his wife. Hoping to contemplate the matter even further, he'd skipped breakfast, escaping quickly and efficiently to the peace and quiet that his study offered.

If someone was threatening Lucy as he now suspected, then there could be only two possible explanations. She'd either received a letter from the blackguard—perhaps with the intent to blackmail—or if not, then it had to be one their guests. A letter seemed most plausible of course, since it was hard to believe that any of the people he knew would be capable of alarming her so. Still, he couldn't dismiss her serious reaction to Reinhardt yesterday or the fact that she felt it necessary to arm herself against a possible assailant. With a heavy sigh, he took a sip of his coffee just as a knock sounded at the door.

"Enter!" His voice sounded too loud to his own ears, but there was little he could do about that now except hold silent and wait.

The door opened, and his father stepped inside, nodding a quick greeting to his son before closing the door behind him. "Thank you for joining me," William said, waving him forward. "Come have a seat. There's coffee if you'd like some."

"Don't mind if I do," Bryce said as he reached for the pot and began to pour. "Splendid ball last night, by the way. You must remember to praise your wife, William. She did a marvelous job, especially on the canapés."

"Yes, it was rather smashing, wasn't it?" William studied his father for a moment. "And I couldn't help but notice that you managed a dance too, in spite of the trouble that your legs keep giving you."

Bryce shrugged, but however indifferent the old man desired to appear, William couldn't help but notice the hint of a smile. "Lady Ridgewood was a wonderful partner, and therein lies the difference, my boy. You see, she was quite willing to move at a slower pace, not caring one way or the other if we annoyed anyone else with our dalliance."

"You're rather enjoying her company, aren't you, Papa?"

Bryce frowned. "I've told you so before, William. You know that I both appreciate and admire the woman. She is a lovely lady after all."

William feigned a cough to keep from grinning. "And after this house party is over, do you suppose you might desire to develop your acquaintance with her further?"

"So many questions, William. Tell me, what exactly is this about?"

William knew that his father's patience would soon wear thin and that the time for honesty had come. "I need to speak to Lady Ridgewood, Papa, and when I do, it might get ugly. I've no desire to damage your growing relationship with her, though she's highly likely to connect the dots once I'm through. She may be furious with you for seeking her company under false pretenses."

"Perhaps I ought to—"

"No." He grimaced at the wariness that rose in his father's eyes, but in light of everything that had happened and with Lucy unwilling to cooperate, he could only hope that Lady Ridgewood might be able to tell him something—anything at all—that would help shed some light on who was threatening Lucy. "Things have progressed since you and I last spoke, and I need answers—answers I'm unable to get from Lucy."

"I see," Bryce muttered. "Shall I ask her to come and join us then? She's just finished breakfasting and is currently waiting for me to take her for a ride in the barouche."

"Yes," William replied, regretting that his father's outing would have to be delayed. "Unfortunately, this can no longer wait. I hope you understand."

Five minutes later, Lady Ridgewood was seated across from William with Bryce at her side. Although William didn't know her too well, having spoken to her on only a few occasions, he'd developed an instant liking for the countess. This had not changed. If anything, the way in which Lucy spoke of her had served to increase his admiration for the woman who'd taken his wife in when she had nobody else to go to.

A tray with tea and biscuits was brought in by the same

maid who'd brought the coffee earlier. Again, William waited for her to take her leave before commencing. "Forgive me if what I am about to say offends you in any way, my lady," he said, "but there has been a development, so to speak, and because of this I must insist on knowing if there is anything my wife may have kept from me. Are you aware that she has told me about her past?" William couldn't help but notice the frown that crossed his father's face. Carefully setting down her teacup with the elegance and poise of a true aristocrat, Lady Ridgewood offered him a calm smile. "She did mention that she has told you everything. Whether or not she truly has, I cannot say."

"Then perhaps you would be kind enough to tell me yourself, in your own words?"

Lady Ridgewood's eyes narrowed, though her smile did not fade, and when she spoke again her voice was clear and even. "My first duty lies with Lucy, my lord, so unless you give me a compelling enough reason to betray her trust, I fear that I must remain silent, even to you."

She would not be bullied, he realized, and noting the hard stare that his father was giving him, he silently cursed himself for assuming that she would. "Very well then, I have reason to believe that Lucy may be in grave danger." From her stiffening posture and taut expression, it seemed that he now had Lady Ridgewood's full attention. *Good.* "She's been acting quite strange for the past couple of days, and last night I happened upon her as she was trying to make away with my pistol. She was terrified of something."

Lady Ridgewood closed her eyes briefly, nodded, and then took a deep breath, which she exhaled before saying, "That changes everything. I must protect her, even if she doesn't want me to. Tell me, Lord Summersby, what exactly do you wish to know?"

William blinked, then shook his head and tried to focus. "From what she's told me, her father was the Earl of Hampstead, British Ambassador to the Ottoman Empire. When he and his wife were brutally murdered, Lucy managed to escape back to England where she's spent the last six years in your care. She married me so that I could accompany her back to Constantinople, find the man who did it, and bring him to justice."

Lady Ridgewood offered a thoughtful nod in response. Her gaze was distant for a moment, but then her eyes met William's and she said, "All of this is true, though there's one significant thing missing from your account. Did she tell you that the man who killed her parents wore a mask? She has no idea what he looks like."

William paused as he reflected upon the conversation he'd had with Lucy. No, she hadn't told him about a mask, though he didn't believe the omission had been deliberate. Talking about the incident had visibly shaken her. Still, he couldn't help but ask, "How did she expect me to help her find him when she has no idea what he looks like?"

"You are an excellent spy," Lady Ridgewood told him seriously. "It's the reason why Lucy picked you, you know. I advised her to be honest with you and to seek your help, but she feared the consequence of what might happen if her existence was made public. I'm glad she eventually did confide in you though. You're a good man, Lord Summersby. I know you'll do what you can to help her." Picking up a biscuit, she took a bite while both men's attention remained riveted upon her. She glanced at Bryce. "I suspected that you sought my company with the intention of discovering as much as you could about Lucy, but I couldn't betray her trust. I hope you'll understand, just as *I* understand *your* motivation."

"It was only my reason for instigating our friendship. It's not my reason for wishing to maintain it, for in all truth, I hold you in the highest regard," Bryce told her as he reached for her hand and placed a kiss upon her knuckles.

"And I you, Lord Moorland," she responded with a smile.

They certainly seemed to handle the situation in a mature fashion, William noted, deciding that a person's ability to forgive and forget probably grew in accordance with their age.

"How long have you known that Lucy was the Earl of Hampstead's daughter, William?" Bryce asked, his eyes narrowing just enough to suggest that he didn't like being lied to either.

"A couple of days," William told him.

Bryce nodded. "You might have mentioned it. I could have called off Percy's agent."

"I was sworn to secrecy, Papa. Besides, as far as Percy's agent is concerned, it was too late to stop him by then. You sent the letter three days ago." He hesitated only a moment before adding, "No one can know when a reply arrives, however. The mere thought of it sent Lucy into a panic when I told her about the possibility. I'll ask the butler to keep all correspondences on his person and to deliver them to me only and in private.

Again Bryce nodded. He took a sip of his coffee, frowned a little, and said, "I thought she was dead."

"As do most people, I'm sure," Lady Ridgewood remarked with a wry twist of her lips, "but her body was never found, as you well know, and she's done her best to keep it that way. It was quite an ordeal for her as you can well imagine—twelve years of age and forced to flee a foreign country after witnessing her mother's murder."

William sank back against his chair and, elbows resting on the armrests, arched his fingers in front of him. "Considering her father's position as ambassador, coupled with his rank as a peer in general, there may have been many who disliked him."

"It could have been the bloody locals for all we know," Bryce muttered. William knew that Hampstead had been a good acquaintance of his and that his father had mourned both his and his wife's deaths. At least there was some measure of comfort to be had in discovering that their daughter had not been a victim as well.

"It's possible, I suppose," William remarked. "However, the mask does suggest that not only was it a planned attack but also that the assassin knew he might be recognized and took preventive measures in order to avoid it."

"But it does sound rather unlikely that an incident that occurred so long ago and so far away would be the reason behind Lucy's recent displays of nervousness. Surely there must be another explanation," Lady Ridgewood said as she looked to each of the gentlemen for an answer.

"I have to agree," Bryce said. He paused for a moment before saying, "She seemed all right until . . . well, the day before yesterday I suppose. Except when Reinhardt mentioned the pendant . . ."

"I asked her about that when I went to check up on her yesterday. It was her mother's, you see, and I dare say I haven't seen that gold heart since I last saw Eugenia eight or nine years ago—before they left for Constantinople. Lucy claimed she'd kept it hidden away in her jewelry box all this time." Lady Ridgewood suddenly frowned. "And then she changed the subject all together. Do you think it's possible that . . . No, it can't be."

"We can't dismiss anything," William said, feeling uneasier by the second. "Consider what we've deduced so far, Lady Ridgewood: Lord and Lady Hampstead's murders were not incidental. Six years later, Lucy marries me, venturing back out into society and perhaps even drawing the attention of the man she escaped from so long ago. Then the pendant suddenly shows up after last being seen on Lucy's mother, and when we factor in Lucy punching Reinhardt when merely he sought to cut her loose with his knife, her sudden need to keep a pistol by her bedside, and her odd behavior in general, I cannot help but think that not only is something very wrong but that Lucy might be in terrible danger as we speak."

"Dear Lord," Lady Ridgewood murmured, her teacup rattling against the saucer as she returned it to the table and prepared to rise.

William held up a staying hand. "I've asked Alexandra to keep her company until I return to her side. They're upstairs in Lucy's bedroom right now, so I do believe they're quite safe for the moment. In the meantime, I've also asked Ryan to entertain the guests with a game of croquet outside in order to keep them occupied and consequently prevent drawing attention to Lucy's absence. The fewer questions asked the better."

Bryce concurred with a nod. "What's your next move, William? Anything that we can do to help?"

William nodded and then took another sip of his coffee. It was tepid by now, making him wince slightly in response to it. "Lucy and I will be joining you for a ride in the landau. Your trip in the barouche will have to wait, I'm afraid. There'll be less cause for suspicion if we venture out on a group picnic than if Lucy and I head out alone." Picking up a biscuit, he bit into it to remove the taste of the coffee. "You'll drop us off at a fair distance from the house and then enjoy a pleasant country ride while Lucy and I go for a walk."

"You think you can make her talk?" Lady Ridgewood asked, her voice sounding hopeful while her eyes remained wide with concern.

"I hope so," William said as he rose to his feet and straightened his jacket "because the more I consider the matter, the more inclined I am to believe that her life may very well depend upon it."

CHAPTER NINETEEN

Lucy stared stiffly out of the window as the carriage rolled down the driveway and away from Moorland Manor, swaying slightly as it rounded a bend in the road, the loose gravel crunching beneath the wheels. She was sitting next to William, with Constance on the opposite bench with Lord Moorland. Nobody spoke, and although Lucy's eyes were fixed upon the passing landscape, she didn't register any of it. All she could think about was her encounter with the masked assassin the night before, not to mention her conversation with William after he had caught her in the act of stealing his pistol. He'd kept her under close guard ever since, insisting that she breakfast upstairs in her room along with his sister.

Lucy hadn't minded the confinement too much. Indeed, she'd felt too rattled to entertain anyone and too nervous at the prospect of having to face Reinhardt, Galensbury, Stanton, or Fairfield with a smile upon her face. One of them had killed her parents six years earlier, and the thought that she'd entertained and laughed with the man had made her sick to her stomach.

Now, William's insistence upon taking this drive filled her with trepidation, for she sensed that he had an ulterior motive behind it—that he wished to speak with her privately.

"This was a splendid idea," Constance suddenly remarked, startling Lucy out of her reverie. "The weather's wonderful— perfect for a picnic."

"I couldn't agree more," Lord Moorland said cheerfully.

Lucy wasn't so sure she agreed. She eyed her husband, who looked completely calm and collected as he sat there beside her. He was no fool; his job was to solve riddles, for heaven's sake. There was no way that he would be satisfied by what she'd told him last night. As it was, she doubted that he'd slept much, for he looked more tired than usual. And if he hadn't slept, then he must have been thinking . . . contemplating and deducing.

As if to confirm this nagging suspicion, he suddenly leaned out of the window on his side of the carriage and called for the coachman to halt. "This is far enough," he said as he reached down and opened the large picnic basket that stood on the floor between their feet.

Turning to look, Lucy saw him pull out a smaller basket from inside the larger one, realizing that he'd asked Cook to pack two separate meals. Apparently he meant to get her completely alone.

For some reason, she'd imagined that he'd merely pull her aside at some point or take her for a walk, away from the others. But no—he didn't seem to desire anyone else's company at all. She forced herself to remain calm. If he only knew the danger that he was placing them all in with this stubborn determination of his. Rising, he grabbed one of the carriage blankets and then moved toward the door. "Come back for us in a couple of hours, will you?"

"Certainly," Lord Moorland agreed, tipping his hat toward Lucy. "Enjoy your outing."

Feeling ambushed, Lucy's eyes shot toward Constance in alarm, but her friend simply smiled. "Go on, Lucy—we'll see you later." And before she had time to fully analyze the situation or issue any form of complaint, she felt herself being pulled out of the carriage by William who was already on the ground waiting to assist her.

"I needed to get you alone for a while without drawing too much attention," he said as she helplessly watched the carriage roll away into the distance. "We have a lot to discuss, without prying eyes or anyone close enough by to listen. Come—let's go this way."

As if in a daze, she started walking, her hand resting firmly upon his arm as he led her forward along a path that quickly took them away from the road and through a thicket of trees. As the path narrowed, he went ahead of her, turning occasionally to offer his hand as they stepped over some rocks and fallen trees that were blocking their way. Eventually, the path widened into a clearing, and as William moved aside, Lucy stilled, her breath catching in her throat, as the beauty of the scenery around her filled her with awe.

"I used to come here as a child," he told her as he took her hand in his and led her forward toward the small lake, the surface of which was dotted by pale, pink water lilies in full bloom.

Towering trees, lush with bright green leaves, flanked the edges of the lake like soldiers, while dense vegetation filled the embankment on all sides except for where they stood. Here the ground was flat and firm, covered by grass and moss instead. A gentle breeze moved the air, rustling the leaves, and Lucy instinctively tilted her head backward to stare up at the pale, blue sky overhead, her eyes squinting against the sun as it weaved its way in and out between the branches. "Thank you for sharing it with me," she whispered, squeezing William's hand as she turned back to face him. "It's a very special place."

"And completely private," he quietly added, meeting her gaze.

Lucy felt her stomach flutter, once again wary of what he might say. But he said nothing yet. Instead, he set down the small basket he'd been holding and spread the blanket out upon a sunny patch of ground.

Crouching down and opening the basket, William then pulled out some ham and cheese, two rolls of bread, a small bowl filled with slices of apples and pears, a couple of scones, and finally a bottle of red wine. "Hungry?" he asked, handing her a plate and a napkin once she'd settled herself on the opposite corner of the blanket.

"As a matter of fact, I am feeling rather peckish. My appetite wasn't too big during breakfast. After last night's . . ." She realized too late that she'd just offered him the perfect opening for the conversation that she felt certain they were about to have and returned her attention to piling ham, cheese, and apple slices onto her plate—anything to keep her hands from fidgeting.

"I spoke to Lady Ridgewood this morning, Lucy," William told her quietly after a moment's pause. She didn't have to look to know that he was sitting quite still and watching her. "I needed to know if there was anything you'd neglected to tell me—not just because of our relationship, because I know that you've had your reasons for secrecy, but because I'm worried that if you don't tell me exactly what it is that's going on, you'll be facing danger alone, with no one to help you."

Looking away, Lucy stared out over the flat water. She knew he was right, of course, but at the same time it felt like such a big risk to take. "Lady Ridgewood mentioned the mask," William told her softly. Reaching across the blanket, he placed his hand over hers. "And from what I've managed to piece together based on what she's told me and my own observations, it does appear as though the man who did it is still after you."

Closing her eyes, Lucy drew a quivering breath. She should have known that William's astuteness would give him reason to question everything he saw. "He sent me this pendant." Her fingers rose to clasp the gold heart that hung from the chain around her neck. "And warned me against giving rise to suspicion if I valued the lives of my friends and family . . . I couldn't tell anyone that he'd found me, and when he . . ."

"When he what, Lucy?" William urged, reaching for her chin and turning her face back toward him.

Lucy blinked back the first few tears, her whole body beginning to tremble from the flood of memories that came pouring back into her head. "Last night, he visited me in my room while you were downstairs attending to our guests." Her voice was cracking with emotion, and she drew another deep breath to calm herself, but when she spoke again, it was in a heartbreaking whimper. "He was wearing the same ugly mask that he wore the night he stabbed my mother."

"Did he hurt you in any way?" William's eyes were dark now, his mouth drawn in a grim line.

Lucy shook her head as she wiped at the tears, but as much as she tried, she couldn't seem to stop them from flowing down her cheeks. "No, but he terrified me. That's why I took the pistol, William. He's toying with me as he waits for the right moment to strike. I can just imagine the kind of twisted pleasure he takes in watching me unravel. I'm so sorry that I couldn't tell you, but he threatened the life of even Vanessa." Burying her face in her hands, she allowed the pain she'd forced back for so long to rise to the surface, and her whole body shook with the anguish of it all.

A heartbeat later, she felt William's strong arms wrapping themselves around her, hugging her against him the way he'd done last night. "It's all right," he whispered as he gently stroked the top of her head. "You did the right thing."

His words of kindness forced another sob from deep inside her chest. "I don't know what to do, William. I'm so scared."

"We'll figure it out together," he promised. "I'll do whatever it takes to protect you and keep you safe from this murderous dog, but we need to lure him out somehow, and it must be done carefully so as not to alert him. A man like that is likely to act rashly if he feels threatened, and we cannot allow that, not when he has no qualms about killing."

A shiver raced down her spine at his ominous words. Straightening her back, she eased away a little and stared in wonder as the expert agent who'd been lying dormant in her husband's body rose to the surface. Though her heart still pounded in her chest, she felt herself calmed by his sudden air of command. "What do you propose?"

He fell quiet for a moment, as if contemplating the issue, but then his eyes brightened with devilish glee, and his lips curled upward into a devious smile. "A scavenger hunt."

"What?" Lucy couldn't begin to imagine what he hoped to achieve with such a thing.

"Consider the mask, Lucy." His eyes were wide with excitement now. "If we find it, we'll find the killer. The mask is the evidence we need, and he brought it with him into our home. It must be in his room somewhere. It's so simple, Lucy. All we have to do is find it, and we can do so easily enough and without detection while we keep him occupied with the hunt."

"And since *we'll* have written the clues," Lucy added, warming to the idea, "we'll have the perfect excuse not to participate in the hunt ourselves."

"We'll send everyone off to the conservatory or to the stables even . . . somewhere that will keep our assassin at a safe enough distance while we conduct our search. And then, once he's been unveiled, we'll have him bound and gagged while we send for the local constable. Just another day in which to keep you safe," he muttered as he pushed a loose strand of hair back behind her ear and met her gaze. "Tomorrow you'll be free, Lucy. I promise." Leaning forward, he then placed a soft kiss upon her lips before moving back to his spot on the other side of the blanket.

Lucy's heart fluttered in response to his attention, and she found herself wishing that he had stayed close to her for a little while longer. But when her stomach growled a moment later, she was reminded that she was in fact quite hungry. Picking up a piece of cheese from her plate, she sank her teeth into it and began to eat, noting that William had already finished off his ham and cheese and was presently in the process of opening the bottle of wine. He offered her a glass, which she accepted without pause. "To your parents," he told her solemnly as he clinked his glass against hers.

She hesitated a moment while she reminisced, hoping that William was right in his assessment and that she'd finally be able to put the whole ordeal behind her. Of course he was; this was his area of expertise after all.

Shaking off her misgivings, she took a sip of the wine instead, enjoying the powerfully rich flavor that it offered as it flowed down her throat, warming her from the inside out. Gazing across at her wonderful husband, she contemplated telling him how she felt about him, but she hesitated a moment too long, and suddenly her chance to confess how much she'd grown to love him had passed. He was on his feet tearing off breadcrumbs from his roll and tossing them to some eager ducks out on the lake.

Lying back on her elbows, Lucy stretched her legs out in front of her and nibbled on her apple slices while she quietly watched him—his tall frame so handsomely clad in a snug pair of caramel-colored breeches and a dark green, tight-fitting jacket. He wasn't wearing a hat, and his hair, which had probably been neatly arranged by his valet that morning, had become tousled in the meantime—a look Lucy remembered from when she had kissed him a couple of days earlier in the garden. It was a look that made her insides melt and her heart beat faster, for it gave him an air of masculinity like no other—something elementary that drew her to him like nothing else ever would. "As sorry as I am for the way in which it happened, I'm truly glad that I married you, William." Her voice was soft as she spoke.

He turned back to face her, a little startled perhaps, judging from his expression, but then he smiled and his whole face lit up. "And though I didn't care for your approach to the matter, I find myself forced to admit that you make a far better match for me than Lady Annabelle ever would have done."

Well, it wasn't exactly a declaration of his affection for her, but it was close enough. He no longer resented her for trapping him, and for that she could only be thankful.

Tossing the last bit of bread in the water, he turned back toward her once more and began tugging off his jacket and pulling at his cravat. "We still have a lot of time to spare before my father returns with Lady Ridgewood. How about if we make the most of it and go for a swim?"

"A swim? William, you cannot be serious." And yet she knew that he'd never been more so, for there was a look in his eyes that spoke of trouble and mischief and . . . something far more wicked.

He pulled his shirt from beneath his waistline and went to work on the buttons. "Absolutely," he told her seriously.

"But . . . someone could happen upon us at any moment." Her mouth was beginning to grow dry from looking at him. His shirt was now gone; he'd pulled off his boots and had begun unfastening his breeches. Heaven help her if she didn't feel terribly hot all of a sudden. Where on earth was her fan when she needed it?

"Nobody's ever come this way when I've been here, so the only person who'll be looking at your lovely body will be me, and I plan to do a lot of looking, for this will be the first time when I see you in the light of day." With a quick tug, his breeches and unmentionables were suddenly both removed, leaving him completely naked before her. "But as you can see, it's highly unlikely that all I will do is look."

Indeed.

Lucy forced herself to swallow. Heat flooded her veins, and her breasts tightened against her bodice as she reminded herself to breathe. Their lovemaking last night had felt wonderful, she remembered, and as every thought of their wanton behavior together filled her mind, a sense of longing sprang to life inside her, and she grew unexpectedly brazen. "You'll have to help me undress," she murmured on a sultry breath of air.

William's grin turned sinful, and when he spoke, his voice was low and guttural. "Nothing would give me greater pleasure, my dear."

CHAPTER TWENTY

Instinct told him to rush forward and rip the gown from her body, yet somewhere amidst the rush of heat pumping through his veins and the heady desire that numbed his mind, he found the restraint he needed and stepped forward slowly instead. Her back was turned to him now, but before she'd turned away, he'd glimpsed the deep blush in her cheeks as she'd studied his naked form. A slow smile tickled the corners of his mouth as he came close enough to touch her—the neat row of buttons lining the curve of her back, beckoning to be unfastened.

Reaching out, he let his fingers trail along the length of her spine. She shivered in response, her breath just ragged enough to ensure that he was having the desired effect. With one more step, he pressed his chest against her back, circled her waist with his arms and pulled her against him. Lowering his lips to the sweep of her neck, he then kissed her until she swayed against him with a moan of pleasure.

His breath had grown short, and he had no choice but to close his eyes momentarily while he sought for control. It was almost too much to bear—the billowing folds of her gown caressing him, bringing him to the height of arousal. He'd have to take care not to embarrass himself. In fact, the sooner they made it into the lake, the better. His fingers began to toy with the first button, urging it through its hole before moving on to the next. He'd never been intimate in a lake before, and the prospect of being so now with Lucy was becoming more enticing by the second.

Unfastening the last of the buttons, he pulled her gown wide apart, drawing a tremulous breath as he eased the sleeves from her shoulders, allowing the garment to fall away—discarded and forgotten. He hadn't realized until now that the only thing that remained to be removed was her chemise. "No corset?" His voice was raspy to his own ears while his hands traveled up and down the length of her sides, crumpling the delicate fabric that remained until it was up around her waist.

"Not today," she murmured. She offered no further explanation, but her voice was soft and sensuous when she spoke, and when he paused again, reminding himself to breathe, she stepped nimbly out of his grasp and pulled the chemise over her head.

With his mouth gone dry and his heart knocking against his chest, William stared in wonder as the flimsy fabric fluttered in the breeze before sailing to the ground beside her. Returning his gaze to Lucy's alluring figure, he felt his groin tighten with need as she turned around to face him. And as if his self-control wasn't hanging by a thin enough thread already, she served him the most wanton of gazes as she stepped toward him, her hands not limp by her sides but traveling over her hips and buttocks instead in a most tantalizing fashion.

Bloody hell!

To think that she'd been but an innocent maid a mere day ago ... Well, he'd apparently brought out the minx in her, and while nothing pleased him more, he was also alarmingly aware that his desire to have her was now undeniably urgent. Without a word, he closed the distance between them and swept her up in his arms in one swift move. She gasped—her eyes wide with surprise—but he ignored it. There was only one thing on his mind right now, and nothing was going to delay him any further. With brisk steps, he found himself waist deep in the cool water of the lake, and then, without warning, he plummeted under, taking Lucy with him in a violent splash.

Resurfacing a moment later, he shook his head free from water before glancing about in search of her. He'd lost his hold when she'd wriggled against him, but a squeal close by brought his attention just in time for him to catch a spray of water aimed directly at his face. "Why you little ..." He reached for her, but his hand grabbed the water instead while his lovely little quarry darted backward on a bubble of laughter.

Diving under, he chased her with long, even strokes until he felt the movement of her feet pushing against the water. This time, he caught her by the ankle, and as he rose back out of the water, he pulled her back, his hands moving up to her waist until he had her firmly secured in a tight embrace. Her breath was coming in rapid bursts, and there was mischief in her eyes—something meant to tease and tempt him. But what affected him the most was the feel of her plump breasts pressed firmly against his chest and the softness of her stomach as it met with his hardness.

Drawn like a sailor to a siren, he bowed his head and lowered his mouth over hers. Her response was immediate and intense—her arms snaking their way around his neck, drawing him closer while her lips parted to allow him entrance. He was quick to react, and as his hands slipped over her shoulders and down her back, pushing at her buttocks to force her hips forward, his tongue drove into her mouth to stroke against hers. He could feel her fingers raking through his hair, speaking of the same growing restlessness that had started to consume him too, and it excited him to no end.

Nipping her lower lip gently between his teeth, he removed his mouth, kissing his way along her jawline instead, and as he licked the lobe of her ear he rocked toward her, eliciting a soft murmur from the back of her throat. With one hand rising to her breast, he toyed with her nipple, tugging and squeezing it, while his other hand drifted down between her buttocks to stroke her from behind. She arched her back in response, straining against the touch of his fingers, and in doing so, she brought her breasts higher, offering them for him to devour. And devour he did—his tongue lapping at the moist surface of her skin, circling its hardened center as she begged him for so much more. "Soon," he muttered, the words muffled against her chest, "very soon."

He was a man of experience, and as much as he wished it, he knew that entering her out here in the middle of the lake would be a difficult feat to accomplish, not to mention uncomfortable, awkward, and perhaps even unsafe. No, for them to make love properly, they would have to return to dry land, but he feared that doing so would dampen the mood somehow, for there was no denying that both he and his wife had reached the point of arousal where all inhibition and sense of propriety had been mercilessly stripped away. He'd no desire to lose that now. Instead, he reached for her hand and brought it down between them, licking his way up toward her neck and back along her jawline as he placed it over his straining flesh.

"'Touch me, Lucy." His words were a low, suggestive whisper in her ear. It took a moment for her to respond, but then her delicate fingers wrapped themselves around him, and the crackling embers that poured into his groin sent sparks of energy coursing through his veins. It was all he could do to remain upright, and when she started moving her fingers back and forth, touching him like he'd shown her to do the night before, a loud groan escaped from the depths of his chest.

"Dear God," he gasped, his fingers harder and faster against the juncture of her thighs. "Tell me you're close, Lucy . . . please tell me."

"Yes," she said as she spread her legs wider and arched her back further to offer more access. Increasing the movement of her own hand, she forced William to grit his teeth as he held back with all his might; he would not beat her to it . . . he would stay with her until . . . "Now," she rasped, erasing all thought from his mind, "I feel it coming."

He felt her tremble against him within the next second and finally let himself go—an explosion of static energy so violent that he felt all his muscles strain in response, the loud groan of pleasure he emitted swallowing whatever sounds Lucy might have made.

"You're much naughtier than you let on," he told her a short while later as he pressed a kiss against the top of her brow.

"And you, sir, are far more wicked than I would have imagined." Her voice had a playful edge to it as she spoke, and William knew that if they kept this banter up, they'd easily have another frolic or two before they had to dress and get ready again.

"You've no idea," he told her, beginning to wonder how well she'd fare if she rode him. Remarkably well, he decided, feeling himself begin to stir once more.

"Is that so?" She'd begun striding toward the embankment, but as she spoke, she tossed a tempting smile in his direction.

Lord help him, if she only knew about half of his wild imaginings. They were countless to be sure and would certainly require the lack of any inhibitions on her part—more so than any gentleman could ever expect from a lady. But as he started after her, he couldn't help but acknowledge that she'd already shown herself to be quite willing, and, as it was, they'd only just begun.

"You'd better remove that ridiculous grin from your face, Lucy, before we return to the house," Lady Ridgewood warned a while later when they were all once again seated in the carriage. "It's quite clear for all to see that the two of you have done far more than eat and chat, which will only make anyone with a pair of eyes in their head deduce that we did not all picnic together, as we tried to make it appear, but rather that we went to great lengths in order to fake a joint outing."

"A valid point," William concurred as he turned to regard Lucy. "If the assassin is watching, you will make him wary. Try to frown."

She did, but her features became contorted instead and did not look the least bit convincing. William could hardly blame her. As it was, he was finding it bloody hard not to look like a lovesick pup after making love to her once more upon the blanket just as he'd envisioned, but, unlike her, he'd trained himself to force whatever expression was needed in a given situation to the surface.

"You're just making it worse," Lady Ridgewood said. His father nodded silently at her side.

"I'm sorry," Lucy said, biting on her lip as if she thought that might help; it didn't. "I just . . ." She covered her mouth with her hand, concealing what William knew to be another smile, for her eyes betrayed her.

"Oh for heaven's sake," Lady Ridgewood moaned.

"I dare say you'd best do something fast, William. We're approaching the driveway," Bryce said.

"Right." William turned his attention back to Lucy. "Think of the man we're about to trap, and what he's done to you— of what he did to your parents. We mustn't give our hand away—not now when we're so close. He can't know that I've won your trust. We must give the impression that you've revealed nothing to me. Do you understand?"

He'd seen her smile drop away and her eyes begin to glisten at the mention of her parents, and while he regretted causing her pain, it had to be done. She nodded as the first teardrop spilled from the corner of her eye and trickled down her cheek. "Good. Now, whatever happens, whatever I say, you must remember that I care about you a great deal, Lucy. You're my wife, and I'll do anything to protect you—anything at all."

He saw the question in her eyes, but there was no time left to explain. They were home again and with numerous eyes upon them as footmen came forward to set down the steps and assist in whatever way possible. Stepping down, he donned his gravest expression before turning to offer Lucy his arm.

"You had an easy time of it," Andrew said as William stepped into the library after asking Lady Ridgewood to escort Lucy back upstairs. "The rest of us had to play croquet!"

Carefully eyeing the rest of the gentlemen present, William crossed the floor to the side table and poured himself a large brandy. "Sorry I missed it. Who won?"

"Lady Amanda, if you can imagine that," Charles told him. "She's not so shy when it comes to taking a good whack at a wooden ball."

"Hm," William muttered, frowning. "People aren't often what they seem to be. Even *you* know that."

"What the devil's the matter with you?" Ryan asked. "You were in a pleasant enough mood when you left, but now you seem . . . irritable somehow."

Tossing back his brandy, William paused for a moment as he looked back at his friends. "Maybe that's because things aren't as wonderful as they seem," he said bitterly as he turned back to refill his glass.

"What are you talking about?" Stanton asked. "You've married a wonderful woman and—"

"You'd think so, wouldn't you?" He laughed then, but there was no joy behind it. "I've never encountered a bigger liar or schemer in all my life, and believe me, I've encountered a lot."

Silence settled like a cloud upon them. Everyone stared back at him with shocked expressions.

Galensbury was the first to speak. "I don't understand," he said. "You seemed quite . . . enamored with each other last night when you danced."

With a heavy sigh, William dropped into the last remaining armchair and passed his hand over his face in agitation. "I see no point in keeping up the pretense. You're not idiots, any of you. Surely you know as well as I do that she trapped me into marriage! What could possibly be more conniving than that?" Taking a deep breath, he forced his voice back under some measure of control. "She begged me to give her a chance—to forgive her so we might be happy together. Instead she fed me one lie after another."

"What exactly are you saying?" Trenton asked, looking quite ready to wring the neck of any person who threatened his or his wife's family.

"I'm saying she's evasive . . . She refuses to tell me anything about herself or about her parents. For all I know, she could be a fortune hunter . . . some poor soul's by-blow intent on climbing the ranks. I know what she's not, however; she's not Lucy Blackwell." Everyone looked completely taken aback by this new piece of information. He could tell that they held their breaths while they waited for him to continue. He waved the letter the butler had handed him upon his return and forced back a smile. Lucy had been so worried about the assassin discovering that the Foreign Office had become involved, yet it was about to work in their favor—an important piece in their plan of deception. "Word just arrived from Sir Percy, but his guess regarding her identity is as good as mine." This, of course, was a lie. If Lucy hadn't revealed her true identity, he would have discovered it from Percy; the man had been quite thorough in his investigation.

"So then her behavior..." Stanton said, "her episode during the ride yesterday?"

William looked across at Charles. "She must have feared that you were on to her. After all, it did happen only the day after you commented on her mother's pendant."

"Hardly the sort of jewelry a woman of lowly birth would have in her possession," Andrew remarked.

"I suppose not," William concurred, "but maybe she stole it from somebody. You did say that your mother had one just like it, did you not?"

Charles merely frowned as he took a sip of his own brandy.

"Come now, Summersby," Galensbury said, aiming for a lighthearted tone, which quickly died when he met William's stare. "Lady Ridgewood was her guardian until the two of you married, after all, and she's a highly respectable lady. You cannot think that she would have taken in such a child, much less have allowed her to marry an unsuspecting earl."

"Perhaps not," William muttered. "I don't know what to think anymore, but I do know that she cannot be trusted."

"And I thought my relationship with your sister got off to a rocky start," Trenton muttered.

"I take it your picnic did not go so well then?" Ryan offered.

William gave him a scowl. "What do you think?"

"And she's given you no explanation for her elusiveness?" Charles asked.

"None."

"Well, perhaps she'll come around, William," Andrew said, his voice a little gruff. "We all know that the goings on in a woman's head can be difficult for any man to comprehend. But Lucy's not stupid by any means, so whatever it is you think she's keeping from you, I'm sure she has good reason."

"I hope you're not defending her," William growled.

"I certainly am. I tend to judge people based on my own experiences with them, William, and your wife has been nothing but pleasant and hospitable toward me. If anything, she's suffered your reproachful stares with the grace of a true lady, but just when it seemed that the two of you had put your differences behind you, you—"

"She forced my hand, Andrew." William's voice had dropped to a dangerous tone.

"Be grateful that she did," his friend remarked with startling fierceness for a man who was generally all smiles. "For if she hadn't, you'd now be married to that wet towel Lady Annabelle."

"He's right, you know," Ryan said. "Lucy does seem like a better match."

"And as far as I can tell from observation alone," Andrew added, "she seems frightened more than anything else."

William glanced around at the rest of his friends, all nodding their agreement with Andrew. It was impossible for him to say which of them was guilty of murder, for whoever it was, he was concealing his true nature exceedingly well. William had hoped that this little pretense of his would offer him a small glimpse of the man he sought, but it had not. That aside, it was still necessary for him to convince his friends that he and Lucy were drifting apart and that she'd revealed nothing. For now, until they put their plan in motion, it was the only thing that he could think of to keep her safe.

"Of course she's bloody frightened. She's undoubtedly terrified that I'm going to discover whatever it is she's so bent on concealing from me." With a heavy sigh, he rose to his feet and made for the door. "Think what you will," he told them, "but I've had enough of her games, and as soon as this house party is over, I'm heading back to London without her. My devious wife can go to the devil for all I care."

Dinner that evening was by no means a pleasant affair. William was all doom and gloom, and whenever anyone asked him a question or attempted to engage him in conversation, his responses were terse.

"Is Lady Summersby still unwell?" Miss Scott suddenly asked, nodding toward Lucy's vacant seat.

"She seemed all right last night at the ball," Lady Amanda pointed out in her usual quiet voice.

William frowned and the young woman instantly returned her attention to her plate. "She's had a relapse." Silence followed while knives and forks scraped loudly against the plates. Picking up his glass of wine, William glanced around at his guests and expelled a deep sigh. "Forgive me. I'm being a terrible host."

"We completely understand," Miss Cleaver remarked.

"Considering your wife's ailment, it's only natural for you to be worried about her. But at least you have your brother and Lady Steepleton to turn to for help. I assume they've seen to her?"

"I did indeed visit with Lady Summersby right before dinner," Mary said from the other end of the table. "She's much better now and resting."

"What a relief," Andrew said, glaring across at William. "Perhaps we may have the pleasure of her company again tomorrow then."

"I believe so," Mary said.

"And from what I gather," William remarked with as much indifference as he could muster while he took a sip of his wine, "she insists on going ahead with the scavenger hunt she had planned, which I dare say will entertain you all to no end."

The four young debutantes immediately squealed with delight and clapped their hands together, which was of course to be expected. Regarding his friends, he couldn't help an inward smile at the sight of their morose expressions.

"I hope we're not all expected to participate," Charles said with a frown.

"I can't say," William replied, adding just a touch of sarcasm to his words, "but considering how *persuasive* my wife can be when she sets her mind to something, I do believe you'll have a hard time refusing her if she insists."

CHAPTER TWENTY-ONE

Lucy woke the following morning to gray clouds hanging heavily in the darkened sky overhead. With her face still snug against her fluffy pillow, she turned onto her back and reached across for William, only to find an empty space; he'd apparently already risen. Stretching her arms before sitting up and swinging her legs over the side of the bed, she reflected on the day that lay ahead—of its importance.

She'd remained in her room the previous evening with the door lock firmly in place, but William had joined her as soon as he'd finished his dinner and had told her about the conversation he'd had with his friends. Hopefully his display of anger and mistrust for her would put the assassin at ease enough for them to carry out their plan undeterred.

Pulling the curtains aside, she stared out at the dreary scenery of the garden below. The bright colors of the previous days had faded to tones of gray. With a heavy sigh, she reached for the pendant about her neck and enfolded it in her fingers. She then closed her eyes and drew a deep breath. Today she would find him, face him, and move on with her life. She would be free from his torment, and she would finally find peace—or so she hoped.

A knock sounded, and Lucy blinked. Stepping toward the door, she quietly asked whom it was before admitting her maid.

Together they picked out one of her long-sleeved day dresses—a cream-colored creation, dotted by a pattern of tiny rose buds, and with a square neckline trimmed with a thin piece of lace. It was simple but pretty, and according to Lucy's own opinion, suited her quite well.

By the time she made her way downstairs for breakfast, the clouds had ruptured, giving way to a steady downpour that, while being good for the garden, meant that the scavenger hunt she had planned would have to be limited to the house alone.

Reaching the door to the dining room, she stopped momentarily and drew a deep breath. Her stomach had begun to twist and turn into a tight knot, while her heart, which had been perfectly calm only a second ago, was now fluttering quite erratically. Somehow, she had to overcome this bout of nervousness. She had to face her guests without looking like a scared little girl whose only desire was to run away and hide. No, she was strong, she reminded herself, and she'd been through a lot already. Today she would have William by her side, and together they would get through this.

With renewed determination, she stepped inside the dining room and attempted a smile. "Good morning," she said, addressing those present—a cheerful assembly that comprised all the women (with the exception of Constance) and Lord Fairfield, who added a touch of male presence from behind his crackling newspaper.

Lady Lindhurst shot her a smile. "Good morning, Lucy. You look well rested and so much better. Indeed, there's a touch of color to your cheeks today. It suits you."

Lucy thanked the viscountess as she took the empty seat beside her and waited for the attending maid to bring her a cup of tea. "As your hostess, it just won't do for me to remain in bed, especially not when I have such a splendid activity planned for you all today."

"William mentioned something last night about a scavenger hunt," Alexandra said from across the table as she buttered a piece of bread. Looking up, she offered Lucy a thoughtful stare. "Seems like a good choice with the weather being as dismal as it is."

"I love those!" Lady Amanda remarked with more enthusiasm than Lucy would have expected from a woman so shy. She was sitting quite secluded at the far end of the table with a couple of seats placed between herself and the next person and seemed instantly flustered as everyone turned to face her, for she stirred her tea with increasing rapidity, as if the motion would create a whirlpool large enough to swallow her up.

When she unexpectedly continued to speak, she did so with a timid voice and without raising her gaze from the movement of her spoon. "I enjoyed a very lovely scavenger hunt during the Christmas holidays when my family and I were invited to attend a house party at the Earl of Birdbrook's estate. It was such fun."

"It's always been my understanding," Lord Fairfield remarked from behind his newspaper, "that these sorts of things are especially designed as an excuse for couples to sneak off and steal kisses with one another in hidden corners."

A gasp arose from all the debutantes, while Miss Scott underlined their shared astonishment with an "Oh my!"

Lucy, on the other hand, felt her cheeks grow hot as she recalled having done that very thing with her husband in the garden, not to mention so much more by the lake only yesterday. She took a bite of her bread to mask her discomposure before saying, "Then it is fortunate that our scavenger hunt shall take place during the day when there are few dark corners to be found."

Alexandra chuckled, and Lucy looked across at her to find her eyes bubbling with mirth. "A private room would serve just as nicely, you know."

"Alexandra, that is quite enough," Lady Lindhurst remarked, her eyebrows arching in a rather intimidating fashion. "You will not put any unsavory ideas into these young ladies' heads."

"My apologies," Alexandra said as she trained her features into something of a more serious nature. She then turned her attention to the debutantes, who seemed to be following the whole exchange with very keen interest. "No sneaking off to steal kisses in private rooms or corners—understood?"

They all nodded.

Lady Lindhurst gave an exasperated sigh. "You couldn't possibly have bated them any better than you just did, Alexandra."

"And I assure you that if there's to be any kissing in dark corners, I'll be most happy to oblige," Lord Fairfield said, lowering his paper just enough to serve them all a cheeky smile as he waggled his eyebrows.

A chorus of giggles erupted from the debutantes, to which Lady Lindhurst responded with a very disapproving shake of her head. "There will be no kissing by you or any of the other gentlemen present, Lord Fairfield. I am supposed to be chaperoning these young ladies, along with Lady Ridgewood. We all know that a kiss can lead to so much more." She served Alexandra a pointed stare. "And I for one have no desire to explain anything to these young ladies' mamas. I won't have them ruined. Do I make myself clear?"

Everyone nodded, aware of the authoritative tone behind the viscountess' words.

There was silence for some time after, and Lucy found herself searching for something to say, but her thoughts on the matter ended at the sound of another voice. "Have you written the clues yet?" The question came from Miss Scott, who'd leaned forward in her seat in order for her to look directly at Lucy, since Lady Hyacinth was sitting between them.

"Not yet," Lucy said with a slight shake of her head as she bit into a piece of toast with a slice of cheese on it.

"I'd be happy to offer my assistance," Lord Fairfield said, lowering his newspaper once more and meeting her gaze. He smiled, and his whole face emanated a kindness that most men tended to keep well hidden beneath a mask of gravity.

"That is very kind of you," she told him, "but I've already asked William to help, and he has . . . agreed." She hesitated before saying the final word, hoping it would reinforce the story of their strained relationship.

It must have worked, for a frown settled upon Lord Fairfield's brow, and he opened his mouth as if to speak but must have changed his mind, for he simply smiled instead and said,

"Very well then," before returning his attention to whatever riveting piece of information it was that he was reading about.

Lucy breathed a sigh of relief. She didn't think that Lord Fairfield was the man with the mask, but she mustn't take any chances. As it was, she and William were balancing a dangerously delicate line between a strained marriage and the united front that the situation called for. They had to appear to be at odds with each other while still seeming willing enough to stand together for the sake of their guests—not an easy feat to accomplish when one look from William was enough to make Lucy's heart race with desire.

She took another bite of her toast, conscious that a conversation was taking place around her but too preoccupied with her own thoughts to pay much attention to it. Instead, she finished her tea, excused herself from the table, and headed toward the parlor. If they were going to have a successful scavenger hunt later in the day, it was about time that she started planning for it.

Half an hour later, she was still sitting at her escritoire, trying desperately hard to come up with some clues for the scavenger hunt, only to realize that doing so was definitely not her forte. She wanted the riddles to rhyme, but when she tried *painting*, all she could think of was *feinting*. It was no use. She desperately needed William's help and had sent the butler to find him, but that was already fifteen minutes ago according to the clock on the mantle.

She was just about to put pen to paper in yet another attempt when a low voice coming from directly behind her caused her hand to still in midair. Her stomach flipped while a rush of heat flittered down her spine. It was William, and in the next instant she felt his firm hands upon her shoulders and his breath tickling the side of her neck.

"You mustn't," she muttered, scarcely able to breathe for the rush of sensations coursing through her body as he leaned closer still.

"The men are busy in the study with a game of cards, and I've taken the precaution of closing the door," he whispered, his lips grazing her skin in a soft caress. But just as she thought she might melt beneath his touch, he moved away and came to stand beside her instead. "You're right though. This is a bit too risky, and besides, I'm here to help you with the clues—not to have my way with you upon the floor. There'll be lots of time for that later." He gave her a wink and a cheeky smile before turning serious once more. "Mind if I take a look at what you've come up with?"

How he was able to sound so casual when the effect his words were having on her was enough to make her mouth go dry, her stomach to flutter, and her legs to turn weak . . . thank God she was sitting down. With a hard swallow, she made a stoic attempt to regain her composure so she could focus on the task at hand. She pushed the paper she'd been working on toward him while he pulled up a chair and sat.

Leaning forward, he read her meager attempts at riddles and frowned. "We need to ensure that we keep everyone downstairs for this, so that leaves us with a limited number of rooms." He returned the paper to Lucy. "How about something like this: *Higher than the keys . . . Go and search among the trees.* And then we'll place the next clue on the frame of one of the landscape paintings in the music room."

Lucy had to concede that it was far better than what she'd come up with so far and was more than happy to let William compose the rest of the clues while she wrote them down. Besides, it was a task that would keep her mind away from William, his close proximity, and his oh so intoxicating scent of sandalwood. She drew a deep breath, deciding to concentrate on his voice instead.

A little less than an hour later, they both agreed that the clues they'd managed to prepare for the hunt would serve quite nicely in terms of keeping the guests occupied for a decent amount of time. Lucy turned to face William, only to find him studying her intensely.

"Are you ready for this?" he asked her. His voice was soft and quiet, but his eyes remained serious.

The nervousness she'd felt earlier surfaced, but she forced it back and managed a smile. "I believe so."

He looked skeptical but finally nodded.

"Are *you* ready?" she then asked in return. "After all, it is one of your friends that—"

"Whoever this turns out to be, the man we seek is no friend of mine, and when we discover his identity, Lucy, he'll be fortunate if he leaves this house alive." His voice was fierce, but it filled her with courage, for there was strength and determination behind it—a promise that they would succeed. And then he reached out and pulled her toward him for a hard and passionate kiss that wiped all fear and misgivings from her mind. His forehead was pressed against hers when he spoke again, his breath warm against her cheek while his hand supported the back of her head. "You're stronger than you think, Lucy, and we're in this together. He cannot win."

Reaching up, she fisted her hand through his dark blonde hair and pulled him back, touching her lips against his for another, much softer, kiss—a kiss that reflected the contents of her heart. His eyes were wide with wonder when she pulled back to meet his gaze, and her voice quivered and shook when she finally spoke. "Do you have any idea how much I love you?" Creases appeared upon his forehead, as if he was actually giving the matter some serious thought, and she smiled, realizing that her declaration had struck him completely by surprise.

He shook his head a little and appeared on the verge of saying something when the door opened and Alexandra popped her head inside. "Are you almost finished? Luncheon will be ready soon." She stepped inside and nudged the door shut, then leaned back against it as she studied each of them in turn. "You don't appear your usual self, William. Indeed, it looks like you were about to swoon. Are you all right?"

William cleared his throat and rose, offering Lucy his hand as soon as he'd straightened his jacket. "Yes. Quite. Thank you." Whatever it was he'd planned to say, Lucy realized that it would have to wait until later. She *had* expected him to look a little more pleased, however, and the fact that he didn't—the fact that his face showed no sign of pleasure whatsoever as he guided her from the room filled her heart with a slow and aching pain.

Lucy ate her food in silence, allowing her guests to fill the room with cheerful chatter while she in turn did her best to ignore the whirlwind of emotions that was churning inside her. The man who'd haunted her nightmares for so long would soon be unveiled and brought to justice, but the man she now dreamed of every night did not appear to reciprocate her feelings. She told herself that it was only natural, considering she'd had two weeks to get to know him, while he'd only just discovered who *she* was the day before. But she couldn't deny that it hurt all the same. A hand tugged at her sleeve, and she realized in a haze that it was Constance, that the meal was over, and that most of the guests had already departed from the table.

As if in a trance, she rose from her chair, linked her arm with Constance's, and allowed her friend to lead her to the parlor, where William was already in the process of issuing instructions for the hunt. "Lady Amanda will be paired with Miss Geraldine, Miss Cleaver with Lady Hyacinth. Stanton, you'll be partnering with Lord Fairfield, and Charles with Lord Galensbury. Those of you who are married will work with your spouses, making a total of . . . six teams to be exact. Lady Ridgewood and Lady Lindhurst will supervise the hunt with me and my wife, while Papa and Uncle Henry will remain here, guarding the prize."

"There's a prize?" Miss Scott squealed as she clapped her hands together with much enthusiasm.

"Well, it wouldn't be as much fun if there wasn't," Stanton remarked dryly, earning a frown from all four debutantes. William seized the proffered moment of silence to issue a clue to each of the teams.

"*I can be open or closed as I stand in my bed,*" Miss Scott began reading after unfolding the piece of paper that she'd just been given. *"Some like me pink and some like me red . . .* Any idea of what it might be, Amanda?"

Lady Amanda pondered the riddle for a moment before saying, "I do believe we ought to have a look in the conservatory."

"What does our clue say, Mary?" Ryan asked urgently, his competitive spirit appearing to rise as he watched his sister hurry off with Lord Trenton.

"Two armies face each other for battle. When players engage, there's no time for prattle," she said and then raised her gaze to her husband while Bryce chuckled from his seat in the corner. "Surely that must be the chess set in the library."

"We'll know soon enough," Ryan remarked as he grabbed her hand and pulled her along behind him, his long strides forcing her into a near run.

As soon as the last of the contestants had left, with Ladies Ridgewood and Lindhurst on their heels, William reached for Lucy's hand and gave it a tight squeeze. "Come on," he said, his expression one of severity mixed with excitement, as he led her out into the hallway and toward the stairs. "Let's get this over with."

Chapter Twenty-Two

With a tight hold on Lucy's arm, William guided her briskly up the stairs. He'd been careful to check that the hallway was empty before leaving the parlor and was now eager to escape out of sight before someone happened to see them. They had no time for delay or, even worse, questions.

Reaching the landing, he relaxed a little and loosened his grip on Lucy's arm. He felt her tug against him and released his hold completely, allowing her to pull away. She'd looked preoccupied during luncheon, and he now lowered his gaze intending to judge her expression, but she'd already started toward the first guestroom, her face hidden from view.

Do you have any idea how much I love you? The words resonated in his head. He didn't know—hadn't even considered that she might care for him so strongly, although somewhere deep inside him, he'd secretly hoped. The thought that she did took his breath away. They'd already been through a lot together, and while she'd kept her guard up, it was impossible for him not to admire or respect her. There had been no ill intent on her part. On the contrary, the reasons behind her actions were most honorable, though perhaps a bit naïve.

But, she had needed his help, and she had consequently done what she'd thought necessary in order to get it, and it probably had been necessary, for there was no doubt in his mind that he would have married Lady Annabelle instead, leaving Lucy to chase after the assassin on her own. That the situation had changed in the meantime and that the assassin had found *her* was not something anyone could have predicted, but he was still thankful to be by her side now so he could protect her.

However, when she'd spoken of love in the parlor, he'd been stomped. He hadn't taken the time to analyze his own feelings for her yet, so he'd paused momentarily in order to consider what they might be, and then his sister had interrupted, and he'd lost his chance to respond. Now was not the time either. A better moment would present itself as soon as all of this was over. He'd make damn sure of it.

He followed her without hesitation, stood behind her as she paused, watched her knock just in case the room wasn't empty. No one responded from within, and she gently pushed down the door handle and eased the door open to peek inside. "This is Galensbury's room, I believe," she whispered, stepping gingerly over the threshold and moving sideways so he could follow.

Galensbury . . . He wasn't a close friend of his, and William would never have thought to invite him had it not been for the letter he'd received. He'd wondered for some time now if the man had a more sinister reason for asking to attend the house party. His character was a bit difficult to judge, as if he always kept his guard up. Was it possible that he was the assassin?

Opening the top drawer of the dresser, William began to search while Lucy walked across to the wardrobe. He couldn't see her, but he could hear that she was rummaging about, looking for clues. "I don't see anything unusual," she said a few minutes later.

William sighed. "No, me neither." He'd looked through all the drawers and come up empty handed. "Have a look under the bed perhaps—under the pillows even." He walked across to the window as she did so and pulled the curtains aside to look behind them. Nothing.

Looking to Lucy, he watched her shake her head. If Galensbury was their man, then he'd hidden the mask somewhere else. "No point in wasting any more time here," he said as he gestured for Lucy to follow and headed for the door.

The next room was Andrew's, and as they stepped inside, William felt his whole body tense. Andrew was his friend, and, like Charles, they'd known each other since Eton. There was a bond between them, forged from sharing the sting of a beating each time they'd gotten themselves into trouble, and they'd gotten into trouble a lot.

Opening drawers and searching through Andrew's belongings, William pushed aside the memories of sneaking out of their dorm at night. They'd done it for the thrill in the beginning, but as they'd grown older, they'd done it to rendezvous with the local girls.

Spotting a large-sized box in the bottom drawer, William's hands stilled as he touched the lid. It was just the right size to contain the sort of mask that Lucy had described.

He hesitated, drew a deep breath, and quickly moved the lid aside. A gush of air escaped from his lungs at the site of a brand-new pair of shoes. He'd never felt more relieved. "Did you find anything?" he asked, closing the drawer back up and rising to look across at Lucy. Her expression was serious as she moved about the room in much the same way that she'd done in Galensbury's.

"Not a thing," she said, offering him a crooked little smile. "I didn't think he was the one, but I'm glad to have it confirmed."

William nodded. "I couldn't agree more," he said, taking her hand and pulling her back out into the hallway. His eyes met with hers briefly before he turned to stare across at the two doors on the opposite side of the hallway. Well, they might as well get on with it, and with his suspicions beginning to lean toward Stanton, another man whom he did not know well enough to properly assess, he led Lucy across to his room and opened the door.

It looked the same as the rest, but while the other's had been decorated in blue and green tones, this room was dominated by red. William scanned the space before stepping tentatively forward. Each of his senses seemed on alert, as if he half expected an attacker to leap from the wardrobe or from under the bed and cut them to ribbons. It had to be Stanton. He was sure of it now and moved to the dresser with more determination, confident of what he would find. But with each drawer he opened, he found nothing more than another stack of shirts or some other piece of clothing.

"Tell me you've found it," he muttered, slamming the last drawer shut and spinning around to face Lucy. She was searching the wardrobe, the doors wide open on either side of her, but she straightened to the sound of his voice, turned her head to meet his gaze, and quietly shook her head. He marched forward and pushed her aside, determined to find her mistaken. "It has to be here!"

"It's not," she whispered, and he knew that she was right, even as he stood there hopelessly pushing Stanton's jackets aside, as if the mask might somehow be hidden among them. It was not, and he had no choice but to acknowledge that the culprit was, indeed, one of his friends: Charles.

"It's still possible that whoever wore the mask hid it somewhere else entirely like you suggested earlier. It would be the smartest thing to do," Lucy said.

He stared at her, and he knew that, in spite of what she said, Charles was the man she suspected the most, and while he appreciated her attempt at trying to mollify him, there was little point in doing so. "We have to check, Lucy—no matter what we might risk finding."

She nodded and took him by the hand, squeezing it gently as if she knew exactly how difficult this must be for him and hoped to offer some measure of comfort. Startling really— they were very likely about to uncover the man who'd killed her parents in cold blood, and here she was trying to assuage him because it might turn out to be one of his friends. She truly was a remarkable woman.

Once inside Charles's room, they went through the same motions as before, and with each drawer William pulled open, he expected to find a mask staring back at him, but he didn't. The wardrobe came up empty too, save for clothes and shoes of course. "I don't get it," he muttered, turning about as if hoping to spot something he'd missed, but the room seemed neat and sparse—nothing stuck out.

A scuffling sound caught his ear, and he realized that Lucy was nowhere to be seen. "Where are you?" he asked.

Her voice came from the other side of the bed, and stepping around it, he saw that she was lying with her stomach pressed against the floor and with most of her head and right arm under the heavy frame of the bed. "There's a box," she explained, her voice straining as she reached for it.

A moment later, she managed to bring it out and quickly stood, brushing a bit of dust from the lid. William could see that her hands were trembling and thought to help her, but before he managed to do so, she took a deep breath of air and lifted the lid just enough for her to glance inside.

William could scarcely comprehend what happened next, for it happened so fast: Lucy shrieked, then tossed the box from her hands as if she'd just been burned, her eyes closing firmly as if to block out what she'd seen, and as it landed with a thud on the floor, the lid flew off and a ghastly black mask fell out.

William couldn't move. It was as if his feet had been nailed to the floor, his body frozen in time. Charles . . . it couldn't be, and yet it was. He shook his head and closed his eyes against the evidence just as Lucy had done, but when he opened his eyes, it was still there, grinning back at him, and it was then that anger assailed him. Hot rage poured into his chest, slashing at his heart, and he felt himself begin to shake, felt the pressure build in his head until he thought it might explode. When he turned to look at Lucy, the black loathing that he felt for Charles in that instant must have shone in his eyes, for she immediately took a retreating step backward.

"I'm going to kill him," he muttered, his voice a low growl that sounded foreign to his own ears, and Lucy's eyes widened in response. He knew she was shaken, but he didn't have it in him to offer comfort right now. Hell, he could barely even speak, he was so furious. And he'd meant what he'd said. Charles was about to find himself skewered.

With a swift swoop, he gathered up the mask and headed for the door, pausing only for a brief glance in Lucy's direction, just to be sure that she was following. She was right behind him, for which he was grateful. The less he had to say the better, especially since he felt his control wavering. It wouldn't be fair at all to unleash his wrath on her, but he feared he might not be able to help it if she forced him to speak. It was better—safer—to remain silent.

Returning to the parlor, the door almost flew off the hinges as he yanked it open, garnering a look of surprise from both his father and Uncle Henry. His father was the first to speak, his eyes narrowing as they settled upon the mask that he was gripping in his hand. "I trust you found what you were looking for?"

William felt his jaw clench and it was with sheer willpower that he managed to nod, his eyes scanning the room before he stepped forward and crossed the floor, tossing the mask onto his father's lap.

"Christ!" Bryce flinched, and that just about said it all because William's father was not the sort of man who was easily disturbed by anything. He raised his head and looked at Lucy. "I would have nightmares too if I were you."

William didn't have to look at his wife to know that she was trembling. He wished he could draw her against him, hug her, and kiss her to soothe away her pain, but all he could focus on was his anger. "Get them all back here," he heard himself say, his voice growing to a near roar. "Get them all back here right now!"

His guests must have known that something was amiss, for they spoke in soft whispers as they returned to the parlor one by one, and with one look at William, they quickly averted their gazes and kept quiet. But William was interested in only one man, and when he stepped through the door with a cheerful demeanor, William was directly before him in two long strides. "You bloody bastard," he flared, watching as the smile fell from Charles's face. "You murdering scoundrel!"

Charles frowned and attempted to sidestep, but William was there to block his path. He could hear the murmurs coming from everyone present, but he didn't care; he was out for blood now, and he was damn well going to get it. As it was, his muscles strained and flexed, itching to be put to good use by pummeling the man who stood before him—the man who'd killed Lucy's parents and terrorized her for six long years. He held up the mask instead. "We found this in your room, Charles."

Seeing what is was, Charles took a step backward, a look of horror upon his face. "Bloody hell," he muttered, shaking his head from side to side as if searching for someone to come to his rescue. Nobody would, not when William told them what he'd done. He hadn't thought it possible to become more enraged, but to his surprise, he did when Charles said, "That's not mine."

William could have sworn he saw red, and before he could stop himself, he'd tossed the mask aside, leaned back, and directed a punch at Charles's face. It landed squarely in the jaw with perfect precision and such force that Charles was knocked backward and onto the floor. William was on him in a second, hitting him wherever an opening allowed, ignoring the gasps of horror that came from the ladies while the men yelled for him to stop. He wouldn't stop—couldn't stop—and kept on hitting while Charles writhed from side to side beneath him in a desperate but impossible attempt to get away, his blood already flowing from a gash in his lip, his one eye swollen shut.

It wasn't until he felt himself yanked backward and upward by strong hands that William's nerves began to settle. He stumbled a bit, coughed, and looked around at all the shocked faces that were staring back at him while he searched for the one that he needed to see the most . . . Lucy. "Where is she?" His breath was coming in fast bursts. "Where's Lucy?"

A murmur rose as everyone looked about, but nobody answered. She must have left—too horrified and stricken by what she'd witnessed, no doubt. He couldn't blame her, and his eyes shifted toward Charles who was being hauled off the floor by Ryan and Trenton. His temper began to rise once more, and he took a step forward, intent on finishing the man off, but his father stepped between them and took him firmly by his shoulders. "Stop this right now," he hissed. "You're all riled up, and it's clouding your judgment, William. You're a good agent, but you've tossed your reserve and your ability to think because this is personal."

William had no desire for a lecture at present and tried to shove him aside, but Bryce held fast. "If you kill him, there'll be hell to pay for you too—better let the constable deal with him when he arrives."

The constable . . . ?

William nodded his head numbly, acknowledging the truth behind his father's words. If he killed Charles, he'd probably face a trial himself or perhaps even prison. He doubted he'd hang for killing a murderer, but what if he did? He couldn't do that to his family. No, the authorities would have to handle the matter instead, and he and Lucy would move on with their lives together. He needed to see her, be with her, talk to her . . . Where the devil was she?

"I believe Stanton went to tell one of the footmen to fetch him," Galensbury said, stepping forward to join in the conversation.

"Who?" His father was right. He couldn't think straight anymore.

"The constable—he said something to that effect before stepping out into the hallway."

William looked at Charles. His childhood friend was staring back at him in disbelief, as if he failed to comprehend what was going on. Perhaps he didn't. William blinked as the room began to swim before his eyes. He reached out and grabbed onto Galensbury's arm, steadying himself while Stanton's charming smile invaded his mind. A cold sweat descended in a sheen upon his flesh, and a shiver raced down his back. "You're innocent," he muttered as his mind cleared, sharpened, and drew on the analytical skills he'd garnered for so long.

Charles nodded, accepting the brandy that was thrust into his hand by Trenton. "And I wouldn't mind an explanation . . . or an apology."

Both would have to wait. With the fear of a man about to

lose everything, William raced out the door and ran down the corridor as fast as his legs could carry him, the heels of his boots clicking loudly against the floor. He should have trusted his instinct instead of what he'd seen. He should have . . . Dear God . . . Lucy. Skidding to a halt in the foyer, he thrust open the front door and hurried down the steps toward the driveway, only to see a horse galloping away with a cloud of dust churning about its legs as it went.

"Saddle my horse!" he yelled to nobody in particular. Precious time had been lost already due to his own stupidity. He had to get moving if he hoped to rescue his wife from the clutches of that devil. He started toward the stable at a run, only to find Ryan keeping pace at his side. "Stanton has Lucy," he explained, not knowing how much everyone else had managed to piece together. "Tell Papa that I'm going after him."

"Not bloody likely," Ryan muttered, his face creased in a grim frown. "I'm going with you."

"The devil you are," William almost shouted, reaching the stable door and issuing instructions to the two grooms. "You have a wife and a small child. You're staying right here and out of harm's way."

"I'm a physician, remember? You might need me."

William was about to object when Trenton appeared in the doorway. He was holding up three saddlebags. "I brought some hastily packed provisions as well as some money. We'll need it."

"We?" William looked from one to the other.

Stepping forward, Trenton shoved one of the saddlebags toward him, and he instinctively grabbed it. "You'll have a hard time stopping us, Summersby, so you may as well accept that we're tagging along. Your father's agreed to keep Moorland running in your absence. Alex and Mary will take care of your guests."

The horses were brought out, and William swung himself up into the saddle, kicking his stallion into a rapid gallop. He'd no intention to wait for anyone, so if Ryan and Trenton meant what they'd said, they'd best hurry, because right now his life had only one purpose, and that was to save Lucy.

CHAPTER TWENTY-THREE

Lucy wanted to scream, but she couldn't. She wanted to lash out and flail Lord Stanton until her fingers started to bleed, but she couldn't do that either. Her hands were tied behind her back, her mouth gagged so tightly that it almost choked her, and to add to this discomfort, she'd been tossed over the horse's back so that she lay across it, the front part of the saddle digging painfully against her abdomen—the increasing soreness punctuated with every move the horse made. There was no longer any question as to whether she'd turn black and blue from this but rather how long it would take for her to recover.

The horse veered sideways, and Lucy felt Stanton's hand on her back, holding her firmly in place so that she wouldn't fall off, but the movement forced the hard edge of the saddle into her ribs, and she winced. Whatever tears she might have cried were whipped from her eyes by the wind as it gushed past her face. He hadn't killed her—not yet, anyway—and she began to wonder why. Maybe he had simply elected to do it somewhere with no one around to watch or interfere.

She thought of William and wondered if he had noticed her absence by now. Surely he must have—if he'd stopped pummeling Reinhardt that was. She hadn't seen more than the first punch, but judging from William's fearsome expression, Reinhardt would be lucky to walk away with his head still attached to his neck. It was then that Stanton had suggested they fetch the constable. Taking her gently by the arm, he had guided her to the door and quietly asked if she would mind issuing the order to have a horse brought around.

Of course she hadn't minded—the last thing she wanted was for things to escalate to the point where William would have to face charges as well. But as soon as they'd walked out of the house and the door had closed behind them, Lucy had spotted a horse already saddled and waiting. She'd pondered the matter for only a second before a thick, wadded piece of fabric had been lowered over her mouth, and while she'd fought like a hellion to the best of her abilities, she'd been no match for a man of Stanton's strength.

At least the rain that had pelted down earlier in the day had now ceased, though the sky remained dark and the air quite chilly. There were deep puddles on the ground, and each time they galloped through one, the water sprayed upward, staining Lucy's face with its muddied wetness. Closing her eyes against the ground as it rushed by below, she tried to ignore the pain in her torso, the gag that pulled on her jaw threatening to make her cast up her accounts, and the cord that dug against her wrists. It was an impossible feat of course, but at least the thought of William brought some measure of hope. He would come after her; she was certain of it.

It was dark by the time the horse's movements slowed to

a steadier pace, clopping along while Lucy's head lulled back and forth. And then they finally came to a complete halt, the horse's breath coming in hard bursts while Lucy breathed a sigh of relief. She felt Stanton move his legs as he shifted position, and then his hands were on her, pulling her up and down onto the sturdy ground below. Her legs buckled, but he kept her upright with a firm grip on her upper arm. "You're mine now," he muttered, low in her ear, "and if you try anything stupid, I'll serve you the same fate as I did your beloved parents. Do you understand?"

The sob that left Lucy's mouth in response to his threat was muffled by the gag, but she could feel her whole body tremble while her skin prickled with gooseflesh and tears strained against her eyes. Weak from the journey, she submitted and nodded her response. The gag was swiftly removed, and she found herself led forward on hard cobbles, only now realizing that they'd arrived in a town. Her eyes began darting about, searching each building for some sign of where they might be. It was almost impossible to tell without the light of day, but as they kept on walking and rounded a few more corners, a pungent smell of salt water and seaweed filled the air, assaulting her senses.

Her mind whirled as Stanton guided her through the crowd of people and toward a mid-sized vessel. How would William find her? If he'd been close behind in pursuit, he should have reached them by now, which could only mean that he'd lost their trail. She had to find a means by which to signal him if he happened to pass this way, but how? She tried to think, only to find herself distracted by a large, broad-shouldered man with a wiry beard, a bulbous, wide nose, and two beady eyes. His shirtsleeves were rolled up past his elbows, revealing a pair of thick, muscular arms, while his legs reminded her of tree trunks. "Is this the cargo you mentioned?" he asked as he stared her up and down, his lips smacking together as he openly studied her chest.

"Will that be a problem?" Stanton asked, pulling her possessively against himself and hardening his grip.

The other man's gaze swept over her once more, and then the left corner of his mouth drew upward to form a crooked smile. "Not at all. But you'd best keep a steady eye on her, for the crew might get an idea or two with such a beauty on board." He grinned now, revealing an uneven row of tainted teeth. "Wouldn't mind toppling her myself, though I do imagine you'd have a thing or two to say about that."

"I'll slit you from ear to ear if you lay one grubby hand on her," Stanton growled, leaning slightly forward to punctuate his threat with his height.

The man didn't budge, and Lucy drew a tight breath, wondering if the two of them were about to come to blows. The tension in the air seemed ripe for it. Perhaps she'd manage to escape? But then the man simply nodded and shrugged his broad shoulders somewhat resignedly. "Yes, I've no doubt you would." He then fell quiet for a moment as if contemplating the situation but eventually shook his head in defeat and pointed toward the gangplank. "Take her on board. Lord knows I can do with the blunt. One of my men will show you where to stow her, but one sign of trouble from either of you and I'm tossing you overboard."

"Just keep your men under control," Stanton warned as he pulled Lucy past the man whom she had now guessed to be the captain of the ship and, pushing her ahead of him, marched her up the gangplank until she was faced with no other choice but to jump down onto the deck. "Why are you doing this?" she asked as soon as she was on board. She tried to twist her head around so she could look at him, but he gave her a rough yank that forced her to face forward instead.

"Quiet," he hissed, giving her a hard shove that made her trip, but his grip kept her upright, and as she found her footing once more, she reluctantly began to walk. What could she do? She had no weapon of any kind, and she was now outnumbered by a burly group of ruffians because, from what she'd seen so far, the crew seemed no less threatening than their captain.

"This way," a stout fellow called to them. His face was gruesome beneath the black cap that he wore, and Lucy turned her head to look away from the eyes that bulged from their sockets, the wide scar that marked his right cheek, and the gaping cleft in his lower lip. This was a man who'd seen his fair share of fights—no doubt about that. Thudding across the deck, he lifted a hatch and pointed to a ladder that disappeared into the darkness below. Lucy's heart pounded against her chest as she watched him reach out his arm, grab a lantern from on top of a barrel, and hand it to Stanton. "So you don't fall and break your necks," he explained in a gruff tone of voice.

Leaning slightly forward, Lucy stared into the murky hole with growing horror and trepidation as reality began to sink in. She tried to twist around again in the hope of catching another glimpse of the shore. Perhaps she'd find William galloping to her rescue. But it was impossible for her to see much of anything in the split second that she was offered before Stanton pushed her forward once more. Her hands were still tied behind her back, and she probably would have plummeted straight inside the hatch, head first, if Stanton hadn't pulled her back at the very last second. She heard him chuckle—that same aristocratic chuckle that he'd otherwise used to charm and cajole. "In you go," he said, his hand still steady upon her arm as she placed her foot on the first rung of the ladder. She hesitated before taking the next step, attempting to buy some more time, hoping and praying that William would still manage to come. But by the time her feet touched the planking of the hull and the hatch closed above her head with a loud clunk, she was forced to realize that he would not, and the thought of it—that he had failed—filled her with despair.

At her side, Stanton raised the lantern, spreading an orange glow across their surroundings. There wasn't much to see down here—boxes and crates mostly, some fishing nets, and some reels of rope. "I suggest you make yourself comfortable," he told her as he nodded toward one of the crates and indicated that she should take a seat. His tone was pleasant, in stark contrast to his actions. The man could not have seemed more devoid of a conscience. "It's going to be a while before we reach dry land again."

It was colder down here—a wet chill that went straight to the bones—and Lucy shivered as she followed his instructions, her eyes trained on her muddied slippers and the filthy hem of her gown. She heard Stanton move around and was surprised to feel a blanket being settled over her shoulders a moment later. The pain in her belly from the ride still irked her, but at least she might be safe from catching her death. "Why?" she asked simply, her gaze still downcast.

"I thought I explained that already," he muttered, and though she wasn't watching him, she sensed that he'd sat down on one of the other crates.

"The money—yes, I know. But that doesn't explain why I'm still alive. I thought you intended to kill me as well."

He chuckled, and she hated the sound of it—hated that he could sound so jovial, so charming, so normal when in truth he was anything but. "I have something far more interesting in store for you, my dear Lucy."

She lifted her gaze to meet his, and as she did, she poured all the anger and hatred that she felt for him into her eyes. "I'll kill you the first chance I get."

He was before her in an instant, his face close, callous, and full of malice as he stared back into her eyes. She didn't see the blade he held, but she felt its sharp edge against the pulse of her neck and immediately caught her breath. "Then I'd better make sure that doesn't happen, hadn't I?" He eased back slowly and went back to sit on his crate. "As long as you behave, I'll let you live."

Lucy tensed. If his plan wasn't to kill her, then what on earth did he have in mind? The uncertainty of what awaited her filled her with dread. She couldn't comprehend his reasoning, couldn't seem to figure out what his motive was or what he hoped to accomplish. But if money was what he was after, then he must have been paid dearly for killing her parents and now for . . . she looked at him again and found him studying her with much interest. "Who hired you?"

His brows rose up, and he smiled. "Ah, I see you're beginning to put the pieces together—took you long enough." He paused, looking as though he was considering her question, but eventually shook his head. "I don't want to spoil the fun, but if you think long and hard on it, I'm sure you'll come up with a name."

Fighting for control of her emotions, Lucy pushed back the tears, forced her body under some measure of control, and tried to think. Unraveling in a fit of hysterics would get her nowhere. Who would have had the motivation to kill her parents? Who stood to gain from it? It was impossible for her to contemplate, so she decided to ask a different question instead. "I take it that you were well compensated for the job?" He was a lord, so she assumed he would only have taken the assignment in exchange for an exorbitant amount, especially if his aim was to rid himself of debt or keep up with a lifestyle that had become beyond his means, for whatever reason.

"Not yet," he said dryly, "but I will be . . . soon."

What on earth did he mean by that? Her eyes suddenly widened, and she jerked her head up to look at him. "You're taking me to someone, and once you do, you'll receive your payment?" She was thinking out loud now, trying to piece the puzzle together as best she could.

A slow smile slid across Stanton's lips, and he began a monotonous and patronizing clap. "Well done, Lucy. Well done, indeed. You've practically cracked the whole case wide open. A shame you weren't this astute earlier or you might actually have managed to save yourself."

No wonder he'd kept on looking for her all of these years. Her mother had been correct in her warning, and Lucy had been a fool to think that the man had remained in Constantinople, waiting for *her* to find *him*. His face might appear calm on the outside, but Lucy knew better. He hated her just as much as she hated him. "How much?" She couldn't believe she was sitting there conversing with him like this, but she wanted as many answers as she could possibly get, and since she had no means of killing him, at present anyway, she might as well try to understand the situation as best she could.

He didn't answer her at first but crossed his arms and then his legs before settling back against a large, over-stuffed sack. He then tilted his head, appearing to somehow assess her worth, and when she shivered this time, it was not from the cold. "You ought to fetch me roughly three hundred thousand pounds—perhaps even more with your hair and eye color taken into account."

Lucy's jaw dropped. She was speechless. This was far more money than she would have expected, which could only mean that the man he planned to deliver her to must be extraordinarily wealthy. She swallowed hard and tried to think once more of whom it might be, but they were leaving England now. She sensed that the ship had already begun to move, and she could think of no one abroad who might have had ill intent toward her father or otherwise hoped to gain from his death. It didn't make any sense, and the more she thought about it, the more muddled her mind became.

She was tired, truth was, so with the wood of the ship creaking around her while the crew thudded about overhead, Lucy pulled a heavily loaded sack closer and settled herself against it. There wasn't much she could do now anyway, so she might as well rest and gather her strength because, for some reason, she sensed that the journey ahead would be a long one.

Closing her eyes, her thoughts returned to William. She could see his handsome face before her, so vivid she could practically reach out and touch it. Her throat tightened, and again the tears burned, but this time it was for a different reason. He'd assured her that everything would be all right—that he'd protect her. Yet here she was, alone in the hold of a ship with this cold-blooded killer and with no hope of rescue. She hadn't dared imagine that William felt as strongly for her as she did for him, but she had thought that he had at least cared enough to try to help. What if she was wrong? Of course any number of things might have happened to prevent him from showing up before it was too late, but she knew his career history and knew, therefore, somewhere deep down inside that if he'd really wanted to find her, he would have done so. The acknowledgment of it broke her heart.

CHAPTER TWENTY-FOUR

Constantinople, six weeks later

He'd told her that everything would be all right, that she mustn't worry, because he would protect her. William paced restlessly back and forth in the confines of the salon, a handsomely decorated room in the guest house where they were staying. Low benches backed with plush cushions lined the walls while larger cushions meant for sitting upon lay strewn about the floor, the glass and metal beads that adorned them shimmering in the sunlight as it drifted through the windows.

With a sigh of frustration, William dropped onto one of the silk-clad divans the room had to offer and buried his head in his hands. "I promised her that she would be safe," he muttered, feeling once again that deep-rooted sense of fear that had plagued him ever since they'd left England. It was stronger than it had ever been before, now that the trail had gone cold.

Following Stanton had been no easy task. He hadn't traveled to Portsmouth like the road he'd ridden along had suggested, and it had taken some backtracking and questioning of the locals to discover that he'd taken Lucy to a neighboring town instead.

Arriving in France, they'd once again wasted valuable time on questioning anyone who claimed to have seen a tall, dark-haired man riding off with a red-headed woman. Most had been willing to fabricate a story in return for a bribe, and weeding out the facts from the lies had led them astray more than once.

But when they'd gotten as far as Novi Sad, William had been fairly certain of where Stanton and Lucy were heading. However, he still suspected that they had arrived in Constantinople three days after them—three extra days for Stanton to do with Lucy as he pleased. William shuddered.

"We can still find her," Ryan quietly told him. "We know she's here somewhere."

William laughed, but it was a laugh of hopeless defeat. Lifting his head, he spread his arms wide. "Where do you suggest we look? She could be anywhere. It's impossible for us to search every house."

Trenton stepped forward and held a glass out to William. "Here, drink this." He waited for William to take it, which he eventually did with a lengthy sigh of resignation. "Let's try to analyze the situation from a logical point of view. We know Stanton hasn't killed Lucy, which can only mean that he wants her alive for some reason. Why bring her all the way back here? What's his goal?"

"He must have something to gain from it," Ryan ventured.

William, frustrated, turned it all over in his mind again. They'd been down this road before, pondering all the possible reasons behind Stanton's behavior in the hope that understanding him would somehow lead them to Lucy. *Unless . . . Bloody hell.* He was on his feet in a heartbeat, his drink forgotten as he reached for his jacket and headed for the door. Why hadn't he thought of this before? His hand already on the door handle, he said, "Women fetch a handsome sum on the slave market here." His voice was tinged with the excitement of his insight.

"Christ," Ryan exclaimed, hurrying after him with Trenton following close behind, their heels clicking sharply against the tiled floor.

Stepping out into the busy street filled with horses, carts, and people jostling to and thro, William took a sharp turn to the right and started walking. He hadn't the faintest idea of where he was going, but his eyes roamed over the many faces in the crowd as he went, until he spotted a middle-aged man of heavy girth, dressed in a richly embroidered caftan. Squeezing his way past a vegetable cart in order to reach him, William signaled for the man to stop and then addressed him in French. "*Excusez-moi.* My friends and I are new in town. I was hoping that you might be able to direct us toward the market. We desire to purchase a woman."

The man stared back at William with obvious incomprehension before finally pointing a finger toward something in the distance and muttering words in Turkish that William couldn't understand. He then hurried on his way. Turning around just in time to step out of the way of a horse and rider, William tried to locate Ryan and Trenton. He spotted both of them a little further down the street and started toward them.

"Do either of you happen to speak the local language?"

he asked hopefully, knowing full well that the answer would be no.

Confirming this, Ryan and Trenton both shook their heads. "I can get by in Latin," Ryan offered, "though I doubt it will do us any good unless we happen to stumble upon another physician. Wouldn't mind having Mary along right now. I believe she speaks enough Turkish to make herself understood. She's also familiar with the town, having spent a little over a year here with her father."

Trenton turned to Ryan. "I take it her father was busy harvesting knowledge. Perhaps he worked with some of the physicians, and they would be able to help us. Do you recall any names? Did she happen to mention a location . . . the name of a hospital, perhaps?"

"No, her descriptions were not so detailed, and besides, she was here a long time ago—five years or more, I believe." He stopped to think, and William knew that he was wracking his brain for any small piece of information that might be of use to them.

Impatient to find Lucy, he began walking again. He knew it was probably a wasted effort since he'd no idea where he was heading, but at least he felt as though he was doing *something*. They needed a translator of some sort—someone who knew the town in and out and could both interpret the language and help them deal with the culture because even if they did happen to find Lucy standing on an auction block, they'd have no idea of how to partake in the bidding. In all likelihood, they would just end up getting their heads lopped off as soon as they tried to steal her away.

"I've thought of something, and though it may be a long

shot; there is a man who would be capable of helping us." It was Ryan who spoke as he came up alongside William.

William halted in his tracks, almost colliding with Trenton who was right behind him. "Who is it?" He asked, his eyes locking with his brother's in a hard stare.

Ryan leaned close to William's ear. "The sultan," he whispered.

"Are you mad?" William gasped, drawing both Ryan and Trenton to the side and out of the path of those trying to get past them. "We can't just walk up to the sultan and ask for an audience."

"Why not?" Trenton asked, his expression quite serious.

"Because the way I see it, it wouldn't surprise me in the least if *he's* the very man behind all of this. Think of it: if we're correct in our assumption that Stanton has returned here with the intention of selling Lucy, then he must be expecting to receive a huge amount of money. The fact that he was still searching for her after six years indicates that he had a lot to gain from finding her, and if that's the case, then a man like the sultan would certainly have the funds to compensate him for his troubles, not to mention that the murder of Lord and Lady Hampstead might have been political."

Trenton shrugged. "I suppose so. But if that is the case, then we've even more reason to seek him out." He turned to Ryan. "Were Mary and her father well acquainted with the sultan?"

Ryan nodded. "Mary speaks highly of him. From what I understand, she and her father resided in the palace for a lengthy period of time as his guests. Naturally, Mary would have been little more than a child back then, but she says that her father and the sultan spent much time in each other's company and that he considered him a friend."

William sighed in response to the look that came over Trenton's face as Ryan spoke. It wouldn't be so bad having the sultan on their side, but it could be detrimental if he turned out to be their enemy. He was their fastest chance for success though, and as it was, William dared not consider what Lucy might be facing with each passing moment that he spent looking for her. He had to find her fast. "Very well," he said, as he began to rise to the familiar thrill of adventure. "Let's pay a visit to the palace."

As it turned out, their plan was by no means as expeditious as William would have hoped. For some absurd reason, he hadn't imagined having to wait for more than an hour to meet with His Majesty, but it had already been three hours since their arrival and William had long since lost his patience. "We should leave," he said as he got up for the hundredth time and paced across the mosaic tiled floor. "This is getting us nowhere."

"We'll be no better off roaming aimlessly about the city in search of one woman when we don't even speak the local language," Ryan said with an edge of exasperation. "We need help, and as far as I can tell, this is our best chance."

"We can stop more people on the street," William insisted. "Surely we must be able to find somebody who speaks French, Latin, or English. We could try the harbor for instance; sailors often speak a variety of different languages."

"That may not be such a bad idea," Trenton muttered. He pulled out his pocket watch and studied it. "Let's give it another fifteen minutes. If nobody shows up, we'll make our excuses and leave."

William drew a deep breath to calm himself. The thought of Lucy in the company of Stanton alone was enough to make his stomach roil. What on earth would happen to her if he sold her off to some wealthy pasha? She'd become a concubine in his harem, would have to . . . He swallowed hard and squeezed his eyes shut to force away the disturbing images that swept through his mind. No, he would find her first. He simply *had* to, not only to ensure her safety but, blast it all, to tell her that he loved her too. If he'd learned anything at all over the course of the past six weeks, it was that his life would be empty and meaningless without her in it.

A door opened and a short, slim man with a hooked nose entered. He was dressed in a pair of dark blue şalvar and a matching cropped vest, edged with gold thread. Upon his head, he wore a turban of sorts—its style not entirely dissimilar to some of the ones being paraded about by London women, though William had never approved of the fashion himself.

"Bu şekilde." The servant gestured toward the door, indicating that they should follow.

With a glance in both Ryan's and Trenton's directions, William strode after the little fellow, knowing that they would be right behind him. They'd been searched for weapons upon their arrival and had been told that their daggers and pistols would be returned to them as soon as they left again, but William did not enjoy the feeling of venturing into unfamiliar territory without any means of protection. As a result, his eyes took in every little detail as they passed, observing all possible escape routes and the location of all the guards. It was an exercise that couldn't be helped even if he'd tried, for it had become second nature to him now—a result of many years of service to his king and country.

Bird song reached his ears, and a moment later, he stepped out into the sunlight and followed the servant across an open courtyard shaded by orange trees, their crowns densely filled with ripe and heavy fruit. Entering a colonnaded walkway paved with marble, they continued onward until they arrived at a tall, open doorway, arched at the top and surrounded by an elaborate mosaic.

Drawing a tight breath, William glanced back for good measure, ensuring that Ryan and Trenton were still with him. He then entered behind the servant and found himself in a vast hall with gilded ceilings that seemed to arch at precarious angles. The walls were covered with elaborately painted tiles that shimmered and gleamed with intricate floral designs. The floors were flooded with plush silk carpets overlapping one another in a rich frenzy of pattern. The furniture was sparse, save for four divans facing one another to form a square with a table in the middle, each one beckoning with a bounty of cushions that scarcely allowed for a place to sit.

William's gaze shifted to the man already spread out upon one of the divans. He seemed to be of average height, though it was difficult to tell since he did not stand up. His dark brown eyes were set on either side of a long, slim nose, his mouth almost entirely concealed by a thick, black beard. His clothes were similar in style to what they'd seen other men wear but appeared to have been made from expensive silks, the edges trimmed with gold thread embroidery. A young girl with a multitude of bracelets about her slim wrists was seated at his feet, her back perfectly straight and her chin held high as she delicately balanced his glass of wine in her hand.

Stepping forward, the servant they'd been following began calling out a long string of words that William took to be an elaborate salutation of some sort. He then fell to his knees before the sultan's feet and spoke in a low tone. The sultan said something that William once again did not understand.

As the servant rose and bowed back down again, William, Ryan, and Trenton all took their cue and swiftly performed a series of sweeping bows before the regent. They straightened and waited for the sultan to wave them forward, which he did without too much preamble, much to William's relief.

"Please be seated," he spoke in French, surprising William with a perfect accent as he gestured toward the other divans. He then reached for his glass and ordered the slave girl to fetch some more wine for his guests. Directing his attention toward the servant who was still present, he issued what William presumed to be a series of orders, to which the servant performed a low bow before backing out of the room on shuffling feet and vanishing altogether.

William took the glass of wine offered to him and leaned back against the cushions in a hopeless attempt to find a comfortable position. British fashion was clearly far too restrictive to allow for such a thing, so he eventually sat back up, discreetly eyeing his brother and Trenton before turning his full attention on the sultan.

"As you will no doubt understand," the sultan began, lacing his fingers together and resting his chin upon them as he stared at each of his guests in turn, "I've been rather busy today with some political issues. It is unfortunate that such matters must come in the way of life's greater pleasures, but such is the case. Thus, the reason for the delay—you will accept my apologies, of course."

William hesitated only a moment before inclining his head and saying, "Naturally, Your Majesty."

The sultan nodded his approval and lowered his hands to his lap. "Then let us proceed with business. I understand that there is a matter you wish to discuss with me. I assume it is of great importance and that you are not wasting my time?"

"We have come to seek your assistance," Trenton told him as he took a sip of his wine. "There is a woman . . ."

The sultan chuckled and then plucked a grape from the fruit bowl on the table and popped it into his mouth. "There is always a woman. Is that not so?"

A jingling of tiny bells filled the air, and William instinctively turned to watch as a group of women enter, all dressed in flowing veils and translucent fabrics that left little to be imagined. His breath caught at the unexpected display, and his eyes widened as they all started singing and dancing, their bodies writhing like elegant serpents as they moved their hips and bellies most seductively. They really were a long way from England, William realized. Intent on ignoring the visual distraction, he turned his back on the lot of them. "This one is special," he told the sultan pointedly, "for she is my wife, and she has been kidnapped. I wish to get her back." He opened his mouth to add more, but the sultan cut him off.

"She is here in Constantinople?" he asked. William nodded. "You are certain of this?"

"Yes, Your Majesty," William replied, his stomach a tight knot of nerves.

He watched as the eased back against his divan. "And you wish for me to help you find her. What makes you think I won't just toss you back out into the street? If you've traveled all of this way to find your wife, then she must be quite exquisite, indeed. Perhaps *I* should find her and install her in my harem."

A growl of rage left William's lips, and he instantly rose, intent on strangling the arrogant bastard with his own bare hands.

It was enough that he had Stanton to contend with; he didn't need this as well. But he hadn't made it more than half way out of his seat before a gleaming blade touched his abdomen, and he froze. He lifted his gaze, only to be met with a fearsome expression coming from a bald guard with a broad chest. Glancing sideways, he saw two other guards with their hands ready on the hilts of their yatagans. He didn't stand a chance if he decided to take them on and chose instead to settle back down again.

Once more, the sultan chuckled. "As you can see, I am thoroughly protected." He sipped his wine with an annoying slowness.

Ryan cleared his throat as if readying himself to speak. He took a cautious look at William and then turned away to face the sultan. "Your Majesty, coming here today was my suggestion. In fact, I believe you are acquainted with my wife and her late father." William tried to gauge the sultan's reaction, but he merely appeared bored if anything. The situation did not look promising at all. "Indeed, my wife speaks quite highly of you. Her name is Mary, and her father was John Croyden, a rather exceptional—"

"By all that is holy, why didn't you just say so from the start," the sultan exclaimed, tossing back his wine and waving for one of the servant girls to refill his glass. "John was a good friend, and as I believe you were about to say, an exceptional surgeon. His daughter was remarkable too, both smart and determined and at such a young age. I trust they are well?"

"Mary is quite well, but my father-in-law unfortunately died before I had the opportunity to make his acquaintance."

A shadow flickered across the sultan's face. "I am so sorry to hear it."

"We were hoping that, in light of our relationship with Mary, that you would be kind enough to consider helping us find Lady Summersby, my brother's wife." Ryan gestured toward William with a bit of a sympathetic expression.

"Yes, yes of course," the sultan waved his hand, dismissing Ryan's words as if they were completely inconsequential. "But first things first, you must call me Mahmud, for we are friends now, yes?"

Trenton was the first to reply. "We are, indeed," he said with a smile as he then began to indicate each of them in turn, "and we are Michael, Ryan, and William." He gave William a look of warning.

"Now then . . ." Mahmud clapped his hands together, and the dancers stopped singing and dancing before quickly filing back out of the room, leaving only a couple of servant girls and guards behind. He leaned forward, and there was an intense gleam in his dark, almond-shaped eyes. "Tell me everything you can about your wife, William. The more I know, the easier it will be for my men to locate her. Tell me what she looks like."

William quickly did, and as he spoke, he painted a verbal picture of Lucy that was so vivid he could practically see her standing there before him. He suddenly frowned, realizing that he'd inadvertently left out the most relevant detail. "She is the daughter of Lord and Lady Hampstead, our former ambassador to your country, and the man who has her is the very one who killed her parents."

Mahmud finally looked well and truly shocked, for his mouth had dropped open and his hand had paused in midair on its way to the fruit bowl. He blinked, abandoned whatever piece of fruit he'd planned on sampling this time, and sank back against his plump cushions with a dark expression upon his face. "You tossed me a bone before when you mentioned John Croyden and his daughter, but I have just now realized how much meat there's on it.

"Lord Hampstead was a guest in this country. I knew him well and considered him a friend. We met on many occasions, both publicly and privately. Following his death, my men searched for over a year for the culprits who did it, but they came up empty handed and ... well, we eventually allowed the case to rest." His eyes met William's in a shockingly sincere expression. "Helping you find your wife and the man who killed her parents will be most satisfying."

Chapter Twenty-Five

Confined to a small, sparsely furnished room, Lucy stared out of one of the three small windows that lined the wall. They offered her no means of escape, for she would never be able to fit through any of them, and even if she did, she'd likely break a limb or quite possibly her neck in an attempt to jump, for she was quite high up. Even if the windows did not give her hope, they did serve to distract her from what had become of her life—a thin thread connecting her to the outside world.

There were people down there, each of them going about their business, completely oblivious to her existence as she stood there watching them go by. She'd noticed a few days ago that a family of six lived across the street, and she now followed their daily routines with keen interest—the father as he left the house in the mornings in order to go to work and the children when they came out to play in the afternoons.

A slow ache tugged at her heart as she wondered if she would ever have children of her own. She'd long since lost whatever hope she'd had of William coming to her rescue, though she hadn't decided on the reason for him not showing up. Had he simply been unable to find her? Or was it because he didn't care enough? She took a deep breath and expelled it again as she strained her neck to watch a group of women walk by, their heads covered by scarves and their faces concealed by veils.

It no longer mattered *why* he hadn't come, just that he hadn't. Thinking about him only made the pain so much worse, so she tried not to remember how safe and warm she'd felt in his arms—the way her heart had leapt and her stomach fluttered whenever he was near. She thought of his tender kisses, the touch of his hand, and she shook away the memory, knowing that she was only adding to her own torture if she did. And to what avail? She would never see him again.

Determined to think only of the present, she forced her mind back to her current situation and to Stanton. He had told her very little about what was in store for her, but he'd kept her alive. A deep, blinding rage trickled through her veins at the very thought of him. She'd had one chance at revenge during the last six weeks—one moment when he'd left her unguarded in the room of whatever inn it was that they'd been staying at for the night. Having finished his meal in her company, he'd stepped outside for only a few moments, but when he'd returned, she'd been ready for him. She'd smashed the carafe that had been forgotten on the table, grabbed the longest shard, and waited for him to come back.

Tears burned before spilling down her cheeks as she recalled her failure. She'd been so close, but he'd been swift to dodge her attack, sustaining only a minor cut to his arm while her fingers had taken the worst damage. She lowered her gaze to the palm of her hand and to the two bright lines that now crossed it. Blood had gushed from the wound, the pain of it overshadowed only for a moment by the beating that Stanton had delivered to her in a fit of fury. Lucy drew the now trembling hand to her face, intent on wiping away the tears, when she heard a key scrape against the lock in the door.

"Wallowing in self-pity again, I see," Stanton remarked as he stepped inside the room, locked the door again, and popped the key inside his jacket pocket.

Lucy drew a deep breath as she turned to face him. She hated that he had seen her cry, and she hated herself for being too weak not to.

He stood before her now, studying her with that same charming smile of his that merely suggested that they might be old friends. She wanted nothing more than to rip it from his face and trample on it until it turned to dust.

"Your confinement has done you good," he said as his eyes roamed over her. She shifted a little but refused to turn away. She would be brave, she told herself, and not a coward. "The bruises have completely vanished from your face. Show me your hand."

Hesitantly, she lifted the scarred palm and fingers and turned it toward him so he could have a closer look. His jaw clenched as he stared down at it, and when he raised his eyes to meet hers, they were black with anger. "That was a foolish move, Lucy. You should have known better."

He stepped away from her again, and she noticed now that he was holding a dark green bundle under his arm. Her gaze went to it, and she immediately heard him chuckle. "As you can see, I've brought you a gift." He tossed the bundle carelessly on the bed, the movement unraveling it enough for her to see that it was some sort clothing. "Now then, why don't you try it on?"

She waited for him to leave, but instead he came toward her until he was so close that she could feel his breath upon her face. She shuddered and instinctively drew away, but his hands came up to grasp her arms, preventing any hope of retreat. "Turn around," he told her in a low voice as he pushed against her, urging her to do as he asked.

Squeezing her eyes shut to block out this nightmarish reality, she complied with his wishes, trembling as his hands ran down her back, his fingers working the buttons of her gown until she felt the weight of her dress lifted from her shoulders and fall to the floor. She was standing in nothing but her chemise now, and an unbidden flash of standing in much the same way six weeks earlier while William undressed her by the lake flickered through her mind.

Determined not to unravel in front of this monster, she buried the memory and focused her attention on one of the windows instead. She would get through this somehow, just as she'd gotten through everything else before.

"I believe you can manage the rest of it on your own," Stanton said, and when Lucy turned back around, she saw that he was now sitting on the bed with his arms and legs crossed while he stared at her with great intensity. He'd refrained from forcing himself upon her during their time together, and for that she was grateful, though she couldn't quite understand why he hadn't, for the look that he gave her now suggested that it was *not* from lack of desire. And when he spoke again, his voice was low and deliberate. "I suggest you begin by removing your chemise. You won't be needing that anymore."

"I . . . I cannot," she muttered, knowing how silly it was, for the sheer fabric hid nothing from his view. Still, she knew that she felt more protected with it on than she would with it off.

But without as much as offering her a response, Stanton had leapt to his feet and ripped the garment away from her, his eyes widening ravenously as he gazed upon her naked form. "You might as well get used to it, my dear. I shan't be the only man perusing your lovely attributes today."

She felt sick and suddenly dreaded that he might have changed his mind and decided to have her after all. To her complete and utter relief he backed away slowly, while she in turn did her best to hide herself from him with her hands, but her desperate attempts at some measure of modesty only made him laugh. "And as skittish as you are, you certainly do have a body to be admired. Now then, put these on, will you? We're beginning to run late."

Only too eager to find herself clothed again, Lucy grabbed the garments from Stanton's outstretched hand while he mocked her with a scornful grin, his eyes still feasting on her each and every curve until she felt sullied beyond compare. She turned each of the items he'd handed her this way and that as she tried to figure out how to put them on, horrified to find herself blushing profusely as she fastened the last of the buttons on the cropped . . . She'd no idea what to call it, for it was unlike anything else she'd ever seen—something like a bodice without the skirts attached, ending just below her bust line and leaving her belly completely bare.

The trousers she'd been given were full and billowy and similar to what she'd seen many of her parents' servants wearing. But in contrast to the ones she'd seen in the past, these were of such thin fabric that each and every outline of her legs, hips, and bottom remained visible beneath. They sat low on her pelvis, the waistband adorned with strings of metal beads that jingled with every move she made. Lucy drew a sharp breath. "I cannot go anywhere like this," she murmured as she tugged and pulled on the skimpy bodice in the hope that it would somehow cover more of her. It did not. Instead, her breasts squeezed together beneath it, bulging against the tautness of the fabric.

Stanton's lips curled into a smile. "I think you look perfect. In fact, I'm quite confident that the bidding will escalate to an astronomical amount, but you're right of course, you cannot be seen in the street looking so . . . inviting." He tossed her another garment, which she caught against her chest—a long tunic made from a denser fabric. "Put that on and tie the red sash around your waist. There's a scarf too, for covering your head. I suggest you wear it so you don't draw too much attention to your hair. I'd like to leave that as a surprise."

He turned to go but paused before reaching the door. "I see no point in keeping the truth from you any longer, Lucy. Tonight, I'll be auctioning you off to a wealthy pasha, and then I'll be on my merry way while you remain here . . . the prize of his harem, I'm sure."

Lucy stilled. She'd known this would happen—feared it each and every day—but she was still shocked to hear him say it. She closed her eyes for a moment and tried not to panic, and when she spoke her voice was detached and calm, as if it was coming from someone else entirely. "Will you tell me who's behind this? Will you tell me who it was that ordered you to kill my parents?"

He took his time, and the silence that filled the room in that instant was almost suffocating. But then he finally tilted his head, gave her a most pleasant smile, and said, "It seems as though your dear Uncle George didn't enjoy being the spare as much as he let on."

Lucy's skin began to prickle. A shiver raced down her spine.

"He didn't appreciate putting so much hard work into an estate that wasn't his. He wanted the title, the fortune, the land . . . So he came to me, and we struck a deal." He shrugged as though the whole matter was of little importance. "I was falling into debt at the time and desperately needed the money. But, your uncle apparently had a soft spot for you. However, it can't have gone very far, can it?" Stanton said as he grinned. "Selling you into slavery hardly seems a better fate. I, however, cannot complain, for I am free to collect whatever profit I can make off you, and to ensure that I get the job done, your uncle promised me another hundred thousand pounds once I return and present him with a proof of sale."

Lucy couldn't breathe. It was as if someone had just ripped her lungs from her chest. She felt faint, light-headed, confused . . . The world she knew had spun completely out of control. Her uncle? The man she'd loved so dearly? The very one who had made her laugh as a child as he'd raced around the garden with her on his back? He'd helped her father build the tree house for her in the garden. "I don't believe you," she whispered.

The left corner of Stanton's mouth drew upward to form a sneer. "How very trusting of you." He pulled a piece of paper from inside his jacket pocket, unfolded it, and held it up for Lucy to see. "My orders, as you can see, were to ensure that you did not return to England. I believe you'll recognize the signature on the bottom there—my guarantee, if you will, that your uncle intended to keep his word in regard to my payment."

It was unfathomable . . . unthinkable. But as the thought of George callously deceiving them—of so cruelly betraying them—began to sink in and settle in her head, she found herself consumed by a worse sort of anger and hatred than she'd ever felt for Stanton. Her whole body shook with it; her jaw clenched, and her heart pounded in her ears.

"So you see," she heard Stanton say, and it was as if his voice was coming from some distant place, far, far away, "I've been more than patient. Six years is really a very long time to wait in order to get paid."

Without another thought for herself or anything else, she flew at him, her fists pummeling against his chest while desperate sobs of grief and anguish escaped her throat, but he soon had her overpowered with his strength, holding her in a tight embrace and grinning with unabashed amusement while she struggled and writhed against him. She wanted him dead—to watch the spark of life that flickered in his eyes dwindle and die as he drew his final breath. And then she would return to England, somehow, and face George. She'd burn down the whole bloody estate if that was what it would take to see justice served. "I suggest you learn to guard your emotions well, you little hellion," Stanton whispered in her ear as he tightened his hold on her. "The man who buys you will have no qualms about giving you a daily lashing or two until you learn to submit and behave."

With one last, quaking sob, Lucy went limp. She knew she couldn't win. She simply didn't have the means or the strength necessary. So when he eased her back on her feet and took her by the arm in order to lead her out of the room, she allowed him to do so without further complaint, and it was then that she sensed that her soul must have left her body, for she'd never felt more empty, more numb, or more hollow inside than she did at that very moment.

The carriage ride did not take long, and as it pulled through a large archway and into an open courtyard with colonnaded walkways on each side, Lucy stared out of the window, realizing that the man who lived here must be one of great wealth and affluence.

"Come now," Stanton said, already standing on the ground below. He was reaching up to take her hand and help her down, his gentlemanly façade firmly back in place.

With a sigh of resignation, she placed her hand in his, a sense of finality creeping over her as she did so. This was it. There were guards and servants everywhere. If she'd hoped to make a run for it at any point in time, she should have done so long ago. She shook her head against the thought of it. What was the point in punishing herself when the opportunity for escape had never arisen?

Stanton's grip upon her arm was hard and firm as he guided her forward in order to follow a short, potbellied man who disappeared through a doorway and up a flight of stairs. The air was cooler inside, a result of the many open windows stoking a gentle breeze that made white, veil curtains drift back and forth.

Reaching the top of the landing, they were greeted by a tall, slim woman dressed in a richly adorned caftan that had been cinched at the waist in the same manner as Lucy's. She was wearing a similar pair of şalvar trousers that peeked out beneath the hem of it, and on her feet she wore a pair of pointed gold slippers. Her eyes were two uninviting black slits that disdainfully swept over Lucy from head to toe. Her nose was slim, her lips even slimmer.

The servant they'd been following exchanged a few words with her, and Lucy's knowledge of the language was good enough to understand that Stanton would be taken further upstairs to the pasha's salon, while she would remain down here to wait.

The sour-faced woman gestured for Lucy to follow her as she departed through another doorway and strode down a long corridor into a large, open room. Lucy had imagined that she would have been relieved to find herself separated from Stanton, but as she gazed around the room at all the plump cushions that lay strewn about with more than a dozen women lazily reclining upon them—all turning to stare at her with unabashed curiosity—she was surprised to realize that she was not.

She knew that she was being silently weighed and measured as she continued after the woman who'd brought her here. She'd no idea who the woman might be, but judging from the way in which the other women shrank away from her as she passed, Lucy guessed that she must be someone of importance. "Oturmak," she said to Lucy while she pointed to a low divan, and Lucy obediently sat. She wanted to know what to expect next but feared that her Turkish wouldn't be good enough and chose instead to remain quiet.

The woman left, and a servant appeared with a tray carrying a carafe of wine and an empty glass. She set it down on a small, round table in front of the divan and quietly began to pour. "Içmek." Lucy knew that the word the servant had spoken meant drink, but if she'd had any doubt, she would have understood from the gesture the servant made toward the glass and then toward Lucy's mouth. With a frown, she offered a small bow before shuffling away to another corner of the room, and Lucy became once more aware of all the eyes that were trained upon her, as if they thought she might do something unexpected.

Lucy imagined that more than an hour must have passed when a series of shouts suddenly rose through the air and all the women who had otherwise been lying about without a care in the world suddenly sprang into action. Whatever it was that had been said, Lucy hadn't managed to make out the exact words, but judging from the sudden frenzy the women were now in, she imagined that a fire must have broken out somewhere in the building, for they were hurrying to and fro as if in a panic.

She was just preparing herself to make a run for the door when one of the women caught her by the arm and said, "Sultan burada—the sultan is here." And before she could manage to work out the significance of that or how it might affect her, she found herself whisked away from the rising chatter now filling the room by the same man who'd taken Stanton to see the pasha a short while ago. He led her brusquely down the corridor through which she'd arrived earlier and toward the stairs. "Where are we going?" she tried to say in broken Turkish.

He gave her a look of surprise but quickly hid it beneath a frown. "You have come here dressed like that. I think you know where we are going."

Of course she did. They were going to see the pasha, and she supposed the sultan too if what the woman had told her was true. Reaching a wide door with elaborate carvings of animals on it, the servant paused and turned to look at her. "Remove the caftan and your scarf," he said. His voice was sharp but not unkind, and Lucy found herself doing as he asked. His gaze swept over her, but if her hair color had surprised him, he hid it well. With a nod of approval, he knocked on the door and waited to be granted entrance before pushing it open and stepping inside.

Lucy followed hesitantly behind him, her eyes scanning the room, which was far more lavish than any other she'd seen so far. As the servant moved aside and she saw the five men sitting before her in a wide semicircle, her feet grew heavy, and she desired only to turn and run. Beside her, the servant fell to his knees, and she swiftly followed suit because she not only knew that it would be expected but also suspected that she'd fall over at any moment anyway.

"Rise!" a strong voice demanded.

Lucy lifted her head and looked up at the group of men who were sitting before her. All were dressed in long, richly embroidered tunics, their legs crossed beneath them as they reclined against some large cushions. All had beards while their heads were covered by turbans. The only one who stood apart was Stanton, who appeared to be having some difficulty getting comfortable in his tight jacket and trousers.

Ignoring the rapid beat of her heart and the overwhelming sense of anxiety that she feared might swamp her at any second, she forced herself to take a deep breath and comply. Pulling her feet beneath her, she pushed herself upward until she stood, perfectly poised like the graceful aristocrat she'd been raised to be. Her red hair flowed over her shoulders, and as her gaze swept across each of the faces before her, she knew that Stanton had been correct in his assessment. He would walk away from this a very wealthy man, indeed, for their eyes gleamed with greed, as if they'd just discovered a vast pirate's treasure, and the only thing Lucy could think of was which of them would confine her to his golden cage.

CHAPTER TWENTY-SIX

Two days had passed since they'd arrived at the Topkapi Palace and Mahmud had promised to help find Lucy. He'd assured William that his spies had been sent out all over the city in an attempt to gather information, but they had not yet returned with anything useful, and William had long since grown tired of waiting. He wanted to act, not sit around eating grapes and drinking wine while women danced about. It was beyond frustrating. Lucy was in trouble, and his instinct was to rush forward and slay everyone in his path until he found her.

"You're wearing down the rug," Ryan muttered from the divan he was sitting on.

William stopped and turned to him with a frown but couldn't help but take a glimpse at the rug in the process. It was true; the ply seemed thinner and more trampled in the middle where he'd been striding back and forth. With a sigh of annoyance, he sank down next to Trenton, who was sitting on the adjacent divan, sharpening his dagger. "What are you reading?" he asked Ryan, not because he particularly cared,

but because he felt he needed to say something—anything—
to take his mind off the tedious wait.

"Words and phrases," Ryan replied, offering William
a sideways glance while his nose remained immersed in the
book he was holding.

William rolled his eyes and slumped back against a cush-
ion, crossing his arms in the process. "Really?" His voice was
thick with sarcasm.

With a small sigh, Ryan lowered the book to his lap and
turned to look at his brother. "Yes, I asked Mahmud if he
happened to have a dictionary that I might be able to borrow.
He lent me this one, which I believe belongs to one of the
princesses."

"Will you ever stop studying?" The question was not
spoken unkindly. If anything, William was very impressed
by his brother's ability to absorb knowledge.

"Probably not, and besides, I am now quite capable of
asking for something to drink in case either of you gets thirsty."

Trenton looked up from his dagger. "I'd rather you learn
to ask for directions so we can find our way back home again."

There was a knock at the door, and a servant entered,
bowing as he did so before saying something that William
once again could not understand. He looked to Ryan to see
if he'd managed to grasp any of it, only to find that he was
already on his feet. "He wants us to follow him," he said.
"Something about food, I believe."

"Well, we'd better not disappoint then. I'm sure Mahmud
must be expecting us," William said, also rising and signal-
ing for Trenton to put his dagger away. Mahmud might have
offered them his friendship, but William wasn't about to test

the limit of such a friendship. They were still under his roof, having remained at the palace as his guests in case word arrived about Lucy. William had no desire to give the sultan a reason to doubt their loyalty toward him. After all, he was quite fond of his own head.

"Please, be seated," Mahmud said as soon as they stepped into his presence. He was already sitting on a pile of cushions on the floor and with a low table containing what appeared to be a bountiful feast in front of him.

"*Merci*," William said as he sank down onto another pile of cushions. How anyone might find this more comfortable than a proper chair and table was beyond him. His own discomfort was soon forgotten though as he watched Ryan and Trenton fold their legs beneath them like a couple of awkward contortionists. His lips twitched with amusement while Ryan shot him a warning glance; apparently, his brother did not share his humor.

As soon as they were seated, Mahmud clapped his hands together, bringing two servant girls forward. Instructions were swiftly issued, upon which they both began attending to the men, pouring wine and filling their plates with the delicacies that the table offered. From the corner behind them, music began to rise, and, taking a glance, William noticed a man with a long, slim string instrument.

"*J'ai des nouvelles*—I have news," Mahmud told them, bringing William's attention back to him. He watched as the sultan cut slices from a fig and put them in his mouth one by one . . . William wanted to take him by his tunic and shake him until he told him what news he happened to have come across. His patience was at an end.

"About my sister-in-law?" Ryan asked, his voice sounding as strained as William felt.

"*Oui*. One of my spies has informed me of an auction that is to take place in the home of one of my pashas. A red-headed woman of unsurpassed beauty has just arrived there—"

"We must go at once," William said, already starting to rise, but Mahmud placed a staying hand upon his arm.

"All in good time, *mon ami*. Mahmud goes nowhere in a hurry. *Non*—we shall enjoy our meal so our bellies are full, and then we will go." He met William's gaze. "The house is not far."

William reached for his glass and took a long sip of his wine, wishing he had something stronger with which to calm his nerves. He longed for his brandy. "What if they proceed without us? What if another man buys Lucy before we manage to save her?" Dear Lord, it didn't bear thinking about. She was close—scared, most likely—and they were sitting here having a feast.

Mahmud chuckled. "Ismet Pasha has been specifically instructed to wait for us to join him before proceeding any further. He will not dare defy my wishes, and besides, he already knows he's in trouble for not inviting me to partake in the auction in the first place. I dare say he hoped to keep your wife for himself." He tilted his head a little while he studied William. "You must not fret, *mon ami*, or you will act rashly. Be calm. Your wife will be returned to you before nightfall. You have my word on it."

Another half hour crawled by before Mahmud finally decided that he'd had his fill and was ready to go. "My servant Amir will fit you with an appropriate disguise," he told William. "Your brother and Lord Trenton will remain here to await our return."

This was news to him and not something that William felt at all comfortable with. *A disguise?* "May I ask why?"

"We desire discretion, *oui?* I don't usually bring more than one companion with me on such outings. Bringing three would look suspicious and may give rise to alarm. As for the disguise, you are not from here, and though you have my protection, the others might be hostile toward you. Besides, this man you speak of—the one who took your wife—if he recognizes you, he may do something drastic. This I cannot allow, just as I cannot allow for you to rush in and slay him in front of my pashas, as I know you desire to do. I may be sultan, but such an act performed by an outsider and sanctioned by me would reflect most poorly. I must act according to the law, William."

It wasn't what he wanted to here, but William knew that he was right. This was a personal issue for him, and because of it, he was letting his emotions run away with him. He wanted Stanton's blood, no doubt about it, but he would have to accomplish it some other way. If nothing else, he knew that Stanton would be arrested for committing murder in this country and that his sentencing would be swift. Still, it would be easier if the matter could be settled out of court. He'd have to think on it.

"You look very convincing," Mahmud told him a short while later as they sat across from each other in the Sultan's carriage. William was no longer dressed like a British gentleman but was wearing a pair of gray şalvar trousers instead, beneath a deep blue caftan. His dark blonde hair had been perfectly concealed by an equally blue turban, and on his face he wore a fake beard. Even Ryan had failed to recognize him.

"Just as long as nobody tries to engage me in conversation," he said, knowing full well that it might be considered odd if he didn't respond to a potential question.

Mahmud waved his hand, dismissing his concern. "All you have to do is look threatening. Nobody will dare speak to you then, for they will realize soon enough that you are present merely to protect me."

"I also won't have any idea of what is being said." This bothered him the most. He hated not being in full control of a situation.

Mahmud frowned as the carriage jostled through an open archway and into a large courtyard. "Parts of the discussion will naturally be conducted in Turkish; that is unavoidable. However, I shall try to say as much as I can in French. I'm sure that Lord Stanton will offer the necessary excuse for this."

The carriage rolled to a halt, and the steps were set down, affording no more time for William to ponder the situation. Stepping down to the ground, he waited for Mahmud to follow, and the moment the sultan's head appeared through the doorway, a holler went up, heralding his arrival. Other shouts and cries filled the air from the open windows above them, and William knew that the Ismet Pasha's home had just been turned on end by their arrival.

A tall and stocky man of William's height came out to greet them, bowing his head with respect as he muttered words that William presumed to be some sort of greeting. Mahmud said something in return, upon which the man rose to his full height and beckoned for them to follow. They were shown up a wide staircase until they reached the third floor. Here, two more men waited, both rising the minute they walked through the door—one was Stanton.

William's hands clenched and unclenched at his side, his palm brushing lightly against the hilt of the yatagan that was strapped to the sash around his waist. He could feel his heart rate begin to rise and drew a deep breath, forcing himself to remain calm. A lot was at stake and he couldn't afford to risk failure just because he found himself incensed by Stanton's arrogant demeanor. So he nodded a greeting instead and then followed Mahmud over to a pile of awaiting cushions.

Wine was poured for each of them by a young, blonde-haired girl who floated around the room with unusual grace, while Mahmud exchanged a few words in Turkish with Ismet and the other guest whom William presumed to be another pasha, judging from his clothing. He then turned his attention toward Stanton. "It has come to my attention that you have brought a young lady with you—one whom you consider too valuable to sell in the common market."

"*Oui*, Sultan," Stanton replied, bowing his head in a show of reverence. "You will see that she is quite exquisite."

"Hm . . ." Mahmud snapped his fingers, and the blonde girl appeared by his side. He issued an order, and she immediately left the room. "Who is she, if I may ask? Where did you find her?"

"The story is a little sad," Stanton said with a pitiful smile. "She is from my homeland, but her family is terribly poor. They needed money, so . . ." He shrugged his shoulders to indicate that there wasn't much else to tell.

"In other words, she is not a woman that will be missed . . .

not a woman that somebody might come looking for?" Mahmud asked.

"On the contrary, she will no doubt have a much better and easier life here than she would have had if she would have remained in England, and so will her family."

William felt hot rage thrumming through his veins at the audacity of the man before him. He wanted to reach out and strangle him and felt his whole body stiffen as he tried to hold himself in check. He had to think of Lucy.

"Well then," Mahmud said, "let us not waste any more time, for it is precious, and I have grown weary of waiting. Ismet, tell your servant to show her in."

The pasha did as he was asked, and a small, thin-looking man scurried off to do his bidding, passing the blonde-haired servant girl in the door; she had returned with a large bowl of fruit, which she immediately set before Mahmud. He nodded and muttered something beneath his breath—a thank you perhaps.

The sound of voices drifted toward them, coupled with the shuffle of scurrying feet—then silence. And then, the door opened again, admitting the same slim man who'd run off just a moment earlier.

From his position on the floor, William could see another pair of legs and feet behind him, but he couldn't make out a face. His breath caught, and he was certain that his heart must have stopped as the man stepped aside, giving way to the woman who stood with the poise of a soldier about to defeat an entire army.

Lucy.

He barely managed to get a proper look at her before she

was on the floor, performing a series of bows similar to what the servant was doing.

"Rise!" Mahmud said from beside him, and she slowly did, her body stretching itself upward while her fiery red hair cascaded over her back and shoulders.

She was wearing ... William stifled a low growl at the sight of how she was dressed in front of these men. Indeed, she might as well have been standing there stark naked for all the good the sheer, green fabric was doing to cover her body. She was still as lovely as he recalled, perhaps more so if such a thing were possible. But there was a deep-rooted pain and fear in her eyes that could not be dismissed, and it only made him want to kill Stanton so much more for having done this to her.

Ismet said something, to which the other pasha nodded. Mahmud regarded Stanton with a scrutinizing slyness. "How much is the opening bid?"

Stanton smiled and William could practically see the greed burning in his eyes. "Three hundred thousand pounds."

Silence filled the room. William felt certain that he must have misheard. It was an astronomical amount. Surely more than either of these men ...

"Three hundred and fifty," Ismet said, speaking in French.

Stanton gave him a slow nod of approval, but Mahmud raised his hand and said, "She looks familiar." He then rose to his feet and stepped toward Lucy.

William wanted nothing more than to join him, for he knew she must be well and truly terrified by everything that was going on—her fate exacted in such businesslike fashion by men she did not know and with, as far as she could tell, no sign of him to save her. But he steeled himself for a moment, like a general holding back his army until the right moment to strike presented itself.

"I don't see how that might be," Stanton replied with the skill of a natural liar. "I doubt that Your Majesty has ever visited the slums of England."

Mahmud circled Lucy, and it seemed to William as if everyone in the room held their breath as he did so. "*Non*—my memory is quite superb when it comes to faces. Tell me, *Cheri*—who are you really?"

William saw the look of uncertainty that flooded her eyes, replaced a moment later by hope, and then snuffed as her gaze found Stanton's. Her lip quivered, and she shook her head. "*Je suis désolé*. Lord Stanton is right. I am nobody of consequence."

"And yet you speak French perfectly," Mahmud pointed out, and Lucy appeared to shrink away, like a small child about to be punished for her disobedience.

William's jaw clenched, and he wondered how much more of this he could take—how much more he could possibly allow her to suffer. But they had Stanton within their grasp, and William saw Mahmud's plan now. At present, he had no reason to act against him—not without causing scandal and a potential political uprising. He would need proof first or perhaps something that might cause Stanton to make a mistake. As difficult as it was for him to do, William chose to watch the situation unfold.

"Unusual perhaps," Stanton replied with a casual shrug of his shoulders, "but not unheard of."

Mahmud appeared to accept his excuse, but then his fingers went to the gold heart pendant that Lucy wore about her neck, seemingly admiring the trinket with great approval as he turned it back and forth. "A gift from you, I presume?"

William watched as Stanton's face turned slightly grimmer, but then he smiled and nodded. "I thought it fitting, given the circumstances. It is also my belief that a lovely woman should always be adorned with pretty things."

William's eyes returned to Lucy. She looked as stiff as a starched cravat and about ready to topple sideways onto the floor. But Mahmud seemed not at all affected by her or by Stanton or anyone else for that matter. He was completely calm and collected as he returned to the table, bent down, and picked up a bunch of grapes, which he then began popping into his mouth one by one. He chewed about seven of them while everyone watched in silence until a look of confusion finally settled upon his face in the form of a deep frown. "Hm . . . And yet I recall seeing one exactly like it a few years ago, although it hung about a different woman's neck then."

Ismet and the other pasha must have sensed that something was afoot, for they both shifted with exceptional uneasiness, scooting away from the center of conflict until they found themselves backed up against a wall. Stanton's eyes grew dark and angry. "What exactly are you suggesting, Your Majesty?"

But however frightening Stanton might have looked, it was nothing compared with the quiet hatred that seeped from Mahmud's eyes as he turned on the earl in disgust. "I believe you know well enough." He gestured toward Lucy, his eyes still trained on Stanton. "I am suggesting that she bears a startling resemblance to her mother, the Countess of

Hampstead, that she speaks French because she was raised as an aristocrat, and that the pendant she wears was a gift from Lord Hampstead to his wife—a special order that was acquired with *my* assistance. So do not feign ignorance with me, Lord Stanton, for I know exactly who this woman is."

Mahmud turned away, and it was then that William noticed that Stanton had begun to seethe with rage. In one swift move he was on his feet, holding a tiny dagger that he'd pulled from the back of his boot. He charged toward Mahmud in a fit of fury and with a growl so full of loathing that it would have frightened away the vilest of creatures. Mahmud turned, eyes widening as he realized Stanton's intent. With the instinct of a man who'd honed his skills in battle, William sprang forward, drew the yatagan, and didn't even pause to think as it sliced through the air and made contact with Stanton's torso.

A cry of anguish escaped from Stanton's lips, his eyes widening as he fell forward against the blade—a spray of blood dotting everything around him. With a hard shove, William pushed Mahmud out of the way, preventing the dagger that Stanton still clasped from burying itself in the sultan's neck.

Shouts rose from those around them, undoubtedly in Turkish, though William's mind was too numb to tell. He sensed that feet were shuffling back and forth, but he couldn't focus on any of it as he looked down at the man who'd threatened his wife for so long. His eyes were still open, but the life behind them was gone. An ugly gash gaped open at his navel, deep and wide enough to reveal something that William guessed to be the stomach. A strong hand grabbed his arm, lifting him to his feet until his eyes met Mahmud's.

"*Merci, mon ami,*" the sultan told him in a low whisper

and with a meaningful expression upon his face. "Thank you, my friend." He then added, to nobody in particular, "This auction is over. I'm taking the girl and returning her to her family. Ismet!"

The pasha came forward, his face completely red while he spoke a whole series of words that William could never hope to understand but which he surmised to be a long apology, for he looked about ready to leap out of the window if that was what Mahmud desired for him to do.

But Mahmud just waved his hand, said a couple of words, and then dismissed him. William reached for Lucy's arm and paused for a moment before grabbing hold of her. She looked frazzled, shocked, and frightened. And then his fingers closed around her, and she gasped as if he'd startled her out of a private reverie. "Shh . . ." he told her as he guided her forward. He wanted to reveal himself but thought better of it. This was not the place for them to have their reunion, and since he knew that she must have realized by now that she was safe, he decided that the situation would not worsen if he waited until they returned to the privacy of the palace.

CHAPTER TWENTY-SEVEN

Lucy moved as if in a daze. Everything had happened so fast that she'd barely been able to grasp what was going on before Stanton had been felled by the sultan's bodyguard. She didn't want to look at him, but her head turned of its own accord until she caught a glimpse of Stanton's glassy eyes. Her body trembled, and she felt her lips begin to quiver, but she did not cry. This was what she'd hoped for, what she'd dreamt about for so long, but now that he lay on the ground before her, split open and with no life left in him, she did not feel the sense of relief she'd imagined would flood her body to replace all the pain and anguish. She felt empty, numb. Her parents were dead, and she realized that nothing in the world would ever bring them back. Nothing would ever be able to compensate for their loss. Not even this.

A hand grabbed her arm, startling her, and she looked up to find that it was the sultan's guard, and that he was trying to lead her away. The sultan had said that he would return her to her family. From what she'd gathered, he'd not only known her parents but had also considered her father a friend. Perhaps there was still hope then? She felt it flicker to life inside her, like a fragile little flame.

Her thoughts went to William, and as she placed one foot in front of the other and began to walk, she wondered what he might say when she returned to England, wondered once more if the reason why he hadn't come for her was because he'd been unable to find her or because he simply didn't care about her enough. The uncertainty gnawed at her heart, for she loved him with such desperation that she knew it would destroy her if she discovered that he did not feel the same about her. And yet, she reminded herself that she was probably hoping for too much. William had never been anything but honest with her, while she, on the other hand, had repeatedly lied. She sighed heavily as she stepped inside the awaiting carriage and turned to look out of the window. She had no desire for conversation right now, not even with the men who had saved her.

The ride back to the palace was short. When they arrived, the steps were set down and the sultan and his guard stepped out, the guard reaching up his hand to help her down. She allowed his kindness, but she did not smile as she placed her hand in his and began to alight, realizing then that she was incapable of any sensation right now. It was almost as if she was floating somewhere above her body, but as strange as it felt, she did not try to force it away, for she knew that it was protecting her from the onslaught of emotions that threatened to attack at any given moment.

"*Mon ami*," the sultan said, addressing his guard as soon as they'd stepped inside the palace walls. "Lucinda Hakim ought to be taken to the harem until she is ready to depart for

England, but under the circumstances . . . and in light of the fact that you saved my life today . . . we will make an exception to this rule."

The guard said nothing but merely bowed his head as if to say thank you. Lucy was puzzled. She'd thought the man to be nothing more than a servant, but the way in which the sultan spoke to him—the way he addressed him as a friend— was really quite odd. And why would the sultan make an exception about the harem because he'd saved his life? It all seemed so confusing.

"Follow Amir. He will direct you to a suite of rooms that have been made available." He paused as he looked at Lucy, and his lips drew upward into a kind and gentle smile. "Guard her well, *mon ami,* for she truly is a ravishing beauty."

"I shall protect her with my life," the guard muttered, bowing once again before giving her a light tug on the arm to indicate that she should follow.

Lucy didn't know what to make of it all. Should she feel frightened or comforted by what was going on? The sultan had said nothing about when or how he would facilitate her passage back to England. Based on his interaction with the man who was now accompanying her, she assumed that he would be traveling with her as some sort of protector.

The servant whom the sultan had referred to as Amir arrived at a beautifully carved door that arched into a sharp point at the top. He opened it and stepped aside, gesturing for Lucy to enter. With a small breath of apprehension, she moved forward, her eyes widening at the opulence of what she saw. What a change from the small and simple room that Stanton had kept her locked away in. This was so incredibly lavish by comparison, with piles of fluffy cushions in rich silks and velvets, beckoning for someone to sit or lie upon them. Rugs in vivid displays of pattern and color brightened the floors. The windows stood open, their soft, veil curtains drifting back and forth with whispery airiness. There were low tables with brass trays carrying fruit bowls and wine glasses upon them, each with its own intricate design carved into it.

"Is it to your liking?" A deep voice rumbled from behind her.

"It's incredible," she muttered, stepping further into the sanctuary and looking around at all the details. A moment passed, and then she realized something. The question and her answer had not been spoken in French. She paused, hesitated, and then turned around to face the guard who was quietly standing a few paces away and regarding her. "You speak English?"

He nodded, and she breathed a sigh of relief—not because she didn't speak French fluently, but because there was something very comforting about being able to converse in her native tongue. She studied him for a moment and was just about to ask how long it would be before they traveled when he stepped toward her instead and pulled her into a tight, and very unexpected, embrace. "What . . ."

"I've missed you so terribly much, Lucy."

His voice was a low murmur, but it was also familiar. So was the body that she was being pressed against, she realized. She loved that voice and that body—had missed them both so terribly much these past six weeks. "William?" It seemed impossible, ridiculous even, given the way the man who was holding her looked. And yet she knew it to be true, and as her mind registered the facts, her arms circled around his chest to hug him against her with all her might. He'd come for her after all and had saved her. Tears welled in her eyes, and she allowed them to fall.

"I've been so worried about you, Lucy," he whispered against her hair. "I'm sorry it took so long, but we lost track of you and . . . Bloody hell." She heard his voice falter and choke and knew that he was crying too. He cared about her . . . more than she had ever dared believe.

"We?" she suddenly asked, frowning a little as she eased away from him so she could look into his eyes. He looked strange and unfamiliar with the beard he was wearing, and she reached up and gave it a gentle tug. "Does this come off?"

He grinned a little, lifted his own hand, and began pulling it away, revealing the handsome face that she loved so dearly. "Ryan and Trenton are here too—couldn't have kept them away if I tried." The beard came away with one last tug, and he began unraveling his turban until the fabric was in a heap on the floor.

Lucy's heart drummed in her chest as he pulled her toward him once more, that same familiar heat diving beneath her skin. Her breath caught and her stomach fluttered with expectation as her hands swept over the well-defined muscles of his back, and then he finally lowered his mouth to hers, sweeping her off her feet. It was a kiss unlike any other that they'd ever shared before—full of longing, hope, and love. It was rough, and it was desperate, but it spoke volumes about their feelings for each other.

"Lucy," he murmured as he kissed his way toward her neck. "I love you so very, very much." He pulled back a little, and as she met his gaze, she saw the truth behind his words, and her heart swelled with happiness. He wiped his thumb across her cheek, and she realized that she was once again crying. "I was a fool not to tell you sooner, but I thought we had time . . . I thought I could keep you safe, protect you. I'm so sorry that this happened to you."

"Things didn't exactly turn out the way we'd expected, did they?" She gave him a sad little laugh. "But the important thing is that I love you more than words can say, William, although I must admit that I'd begun to doubt that you would come. I'm sorry."

"I would probably have been skeptical too if I was you. It took much longer than I had anticipated." He pulled her back against him and kissed the top of her head.

"None of that matters anymore." She nuzzled her face against his chest, inhaling the rich, musky scent of him. "Right now, all I want to do is forget. Will you please help me?"

It was clear that he knew her meaning, for his mouth closed over hers once more, and his tongue swept inside to tangle with hers. So lost was she in the heat of the moment that she didn't even realize that she'd been picked up off the floor until she found herself being settled upon the bed. And while he undressed her, William never stopped kissing. He kissed her cheeks and her jawline, the curve of her neck and her collarbone. His kisses scorched her chest while her fingers raked through his hair.

Before she knew it, her clothes were completely gone, and a moment later, so were his. She wanted to stop for a moment to look at him, but he kept on worshiping her with his mouth, and as his tongue swept across one of her nipples, she knew that looking at him would have to wait. She was lost now and could think of nothing but the feel of his body against hers, the touch of his fingers as they drifted over her hips. And as he gently nudged her legs apart and kissed his way along her inner thighs, she could not stop herself from rising to meet him. This was heaven—complete and utter bliss.

That devilish tongue of his swept over her in slow, easy strokes, stoking a fire within her so furious that she thought she'd surely burst. He stopped, denying her release, and rose over her until he was staring down at her with adoration in his eyes. He said nothing, but the look upon his face spoke volumes about his love for her as he carefully eased himself inside her. And then it was gone, replaced by lust and the same burning need that she could feel swimming through her own veins. She wrapped her legs around him, forcing him closer and urging him to move—slowly at first and then with faster and harder thrusts.

"Lucy," he muttered, his voice was low and guttural, "I can't . . . I mean, I don't . . . Christ, Lucy, I'm about to . . ."

"Me too," she said, panting for breath as the first tingles began to rise up her legs. They trickled through her and settled in her groin, intensifying and expanding until they finally shattered on a burst of energy. A groan of pleasure escaped her lips at the same time as it did from his, the tremors of passion rippling through both of their bodies.

As their breathing slowed and their bodies returned to a calmer, more sedate state of being, William rolled to the side and pulled her up against his chest, hugging her against himself with an arm and a leg. "You're just as eager as I remember," he said, chuckling against her hair, sweeping it aside a little so he could kiss her neck.

"Mmm . . . I missed this, William. I missed us. It will be good to get home again, so we can do this more often."

"How often are you thinking?" His voice was teasing in her ear.

She smiled but knew he couldn't see it, so she added a coquettish ring to her voice instead. "At least once a day, my lord, perhaps even more."

"More?" He spoke in a near growl, and she knew that she'd just stoked his desire again. His hand trailed over her stomach and down toward the soft curls between her legs.

She turned onto her back and reached for him. "I believe my appetite for this . . . ahem, activity . . . has become quite insatiable."

With a bark of laughter, he rolled on top of her. "It seems I have my work cut out for me, my dear, but to tell the truth," he said as he lowered his head and kissed her gently on the tip of her nose, "nothing in the world gives me greater pleasure than pleasuring you."

Chapter Twenty-Eight

"Do you really think that the sultan helped my father procure this pendant for my mother?" Lucy asked as she lay wrapped in William's arms after yet another bout of lovemaking.

He ran his fingers slowly up and down her arm, watching as her fingers brushed against the gold heart that lay nestled at the base of her throat. "I've no idea," he told her honestly. "We can ask him if you like. In any case, we probably should rise. I'm certain that both Ryan and Trenton are quit eager to see you again."

Lucy nodded, then bit down on her lower lip as if she was contemplating saying something more. William didn't press her, and after a couple of minutes, she turned her head enough to meet his gaze. "I found out who's behind all of this," she said. There was a sadness to her voice that was mirrored in her eyes, and it immediately had William on alert. He frowned but again said nothing, though his hand had paused its playful movement, forgotten as suspense took over. "Stanton told me that it was my uncle. I can't prove it of course, so he'll probably get away with it. I just . . ."

"Shh . . ." he whispered, spotting the tears in her eyes and pulling her closer in a tight embrace. He hated seeing her so miserable. "I'm sorry to hear it, Lucy. We'll think of a way in which to make him pay for what he did."

"How?" Her voice was desperate. "We can't just march into his home and accuse him of murder. He'll only deny it and have us escorted out. There's no evidence."

It was a difficult situation, to be sure, but William was not about to give up so easily. He wanted Lucy to be happy—or at least as happy as she would ever be. There was no doubt that she would always be haunted by the memory of what had happened and by the knowledge that her closest living relative betrayed all of them for material gain. It would definitely be a difficult burden to bear, but perhaps it would be easier for her to move on with her life if she knew that justice had been served. It was a hope worth fighting for. "Come," he told her as he sat up and swung his long legs over the side of the bed. "Let's dress. We have a great deal to discuss with Mahmud if we are to return to England before Christmas."

Lucy frowned. "Christmas? I've had no sense of time here. After everything that's happened, it would be lovely to celebrate the holidays in our own home."

"Then you'd better get a move on," he said with a grin as he walked across to some clothes that had been neatly laid out on one of the divans. His shirt, jacket, and breeches were there, along with a pretty, white cotton gown intended for Lucy. He held it up for her to see, noticing the way her lips curved into a warm and appreciative smile. There was no question that she would be happy to abandon the cropped top and şalvar trousers forever.

As soon as they were both dressed and William had helped Lucy fashion her hair into something that didn't reveal their recent activities too much, he opened the door to their room and found Amir waiting for them. He immediately wondered how long Mahmud's servant had been standing there but decided not to dwell on it. "His majesty awaits," Amir said as he gave William a small bow. "*Suivez-moi.*" He then started down the corridor while William reached for Lucy's hand, settling it in the crook of his arm so he could escort her like a proper English gentleman.

They followed Amir for what seemed like an eternity through vast rooms and across two courtyards until they were led out onto a large balcony that had been shaded by a canopy. It was mid-October, but the Mediterranean sun still shone brightly in the sky, warming the air to a pleasant enough temperature. Looking around, William spotted his brother, Trenton, and Mahmud, already seated on cushions upon the ground, and with a low, square table between them. They immediately got up to greet Lucy, Ryan ignoring all etiquette as he gathered her up in a tight embrace. "We were so worried about you," he said. Trenton, standing a little to the side, blinked, and William hid a smile. There was something heartwarming about the otherwise serious earl forcing back a tear or two, though William was not about to say as much; he'd likely earn himself a beating if he did.

"Please," Mahmud spoke, gesturing toward the table that stood ready with a vast meal upon it, "let us celebrate with a feast."

They each took their seats and allowed a couple of servant girls to fill their glasses with wine. "Thank you for your help, Your Majesty," Lucy said after taking a sip in response to a toast made by Mahmud. Her voice was soft and meek. "You have been most kind toward all of us."

"It was the least I could do," Mahmud replied with a note of sympathy to his voice. "I considered your father a friend. And to think of what that beast did . . . I am glad that there has been put an end to him."

"I was wondering . . ." Lucy's voice was hesitant. "You said that you recognized my pendant because it was a special order item that you helped my father obtain. Is that true? For some reason I thought my mother had it long before we even came here."

Mahmud chuckled as he placed a pancake upon his plate and began pouring honey on top of it. He shook his head and reached for some chopped almonds. "Your memory is correct. Your mother already had the pendant when I first met her, but Lord Stanton had no way of knowing this, so I set out to deceive him in the hopes that he would make a mistake." He folded the pancake neatly around the honey and almonds. "You must agree that my plan worked out quite well."

William stared at Mahmud as it all began to make sense. "You wanted him dead."

"Like I said, it would have been difficult to convict him without proof. I certainly couldn't have allowed you to kill him without punishing you as well, unless of course you had good reason to act. I merely nudged things along a little, and once he threatened my life . . . Well, nobody will begrudge you your actions, *mon ami.*"

"But you could have been killed yourself," Lucy said in a voice of pure and utter amazement while Ryan and Trenton both appeared dumbfounded.

"A chance I was willing to take," Mahmud assured her, "though I had every confidence in your husband's ability to act swiftly. Say what you want, William, but you were desperate for Stanton's head. The only thing you needed was an excuse, which you were given. Shall we leave it at that?"

William blinked. He hadn't realized how shrewd Mahmud could be until now and found himself admiring his strategy. "Perhaps it is our turn to bluff," he muttered as he picked up a slice of melon and bit into it, savoring the sweet, juicy flavor. His eyes found Lucy's. "I think I've just figured out how to get your uncle convicted. We don't need proof, Lucy. We just need to convince him that what we're saying is true."

Chapter Twenty-Nine

England, December 22, 1817
Two miles from Hampstead House

"Try to relax," William said as the carriage rocked back and forth on the uneven road. "It will all be over soon."

Lucy drew a quivering breath. "My stomach is in uproar, William. I'm so nervous that I fear I may be ill at any moment."

"Shall I ask the driver to stop for a while so you can get some fresh air? It might help."

"No." Lucy shook her head. She pulled the heavy blanket further up around herself. "The sooner we get out of this cold, the better."

William nodded and pulled her closer against himself, hoping to offer her a little warmth. A thin layer of snow had settled upon the landscape all around them—a scenery quite different to what they'd left behind in Constantinople only a few weeks earlier. He was now plagued by frost biting at his toes and could only wonder how Lucy must be feeling with her much thinner slippers. They really should have stopped by Moorland on the way, but Lucy had insisted on having the matter pertaining to her uncle settled immediately so it wouldn't be hanging over their heads for Christmas.

Instead, William had sent Ryan to Moorland in order to inform their father and the servants of their imminent arrival. Trenton had parted ways a little later, eager to return to Whickham Hall, where they all knew that Alexandra would be anxiously waiting, forever worrying about her husband's safety.

Another carriage carrying the local constable followed behind them. William had stopped in town to have a word with him while Lucy had remained in the landau. He'd explained the situation as quickly as possible, adding that they lacked the proof that would be required in order to make an arrest, but that they hoped to obtain a confession, and that it might be prudent for the man to accompany them. The hundred pound note he'd offered (not as a bribe, of course, but as means of payment) had probably helped as well, he thought with a wry smile as Hampstead House came into view in the distance. It was similar in size to Moorland Manor, but the architecture appeared more austere and foreboding—not at all the sort of place that he would have envisioned Lucy growing up in.

He squeezed her hand to offer some measure of comfort, for he could feel her trembling against him, and while it might as easily have been from the cold, he sensed that it was more likely because she would soon come face to face with her treacherous uncle. "Don't let him unnerve you, my love," he whispered against the crown of her head. "You're stronger than he is, and you're not alone."

Rolling up to the front steps of the house, the carriage

came to a complete stop, and William gave Lucy a quick kiss of reassurance before the door was opened by the driver and the steps set down. William quickly alighted, his boots squeaking in the snow as he turned to assist Lucy. A moment later, they were both heading toward the front door, accompanied by the constable who trailed a few paces behind.

The imposing front door was already open, with a butler waiting immediately inside by the time they arrived at the top step. "We have come to pay a social visit to his lordship," William said in a curt, matter-of-fact tone that he hoped would dismiss any argument the butler might consider making.

"Unfortunately—" the butler began to reply. His posture was stiff and unflinching.

"I am confident," William continued, cutting him off completely, "that his lordship will be most thrilled to have his niece returned to him after so many years of absence."

The butler's otherwise blank expression instantly transformed into one of shock. His eyes moved past William to Lucy, who was standing a little behind him and with the hood of her cloak still covering her head. "Lady Lucinda," he said, gasping a bit for air, "is it really you?"

William stepped aside to let his wife past. She drew her hood back to reveal her fiery red hair, and with tears glistening in her eyes and a quivering voice she said, "Yes, Peterson, it is."

Peterson appeared to struggle with his own emotions for a moment and then stepped aside to let them enter. "It's so good to see you again," he said, nearly choking from astonishment. "If you'll please follow me through to the parlor, and I'll inform his lordship that you are here. He'll be ever so pleased."

William wasn't so sure about that but decided to keep quiet. Steeling himself, he stepped forward and urged Lucy along with him, but as soon as they entered the parlor, he felt her hesitate. "It's exactly the way I remember it," she whispered. She left William's side and moved further into the room, her eyes wide with wonder as she reached out to trail her fingers along the back of one of the chairs.

"Would you care for some tea?" Peterson asked, sounding a little awkward.

Lucy turned to him with a sad little smile. "Yes, thank you. That would be lovely."

He quickly left the room, and William surmised that he was probably relieved to be afforded with a moment or two in which to compose himself and return to his usual butler-ish demeanor. Remembering the constable who hadn't said a single word thus far, William turned to him and gestured for him to join them. "Let's have a seat while we wait for our host to make his appearance."

The constable frowned at the pale blue silk armchair that stood before him but eventually nodded and stepped toward it. Sitting down across from him, William regarded Lucy who was still in the process of reacquainting herself with each of the objects in the room. "Won't you join us?" he asked, feeling certain that she would fare much better if she was sitting down when her uncle stepped through the door.

She turned toward him as if in a daze and slowly nodded. The door opened again, and Peterson returned carrying a tray containing a teapot, cups, and a plate of biscuits. "His lordship is on his way," he told them, appearing to be once more in perfect control of his features.

Seating herself on the corner of the sofa, as close to William as possible, Lucy took a careful sip of the tea that had just been poured. "Thank you, Peterson," she told the butler, to which he nodded as he departed the room. He appeared just as dispassionate as when they'd first arrived, although it did seem as if his eyes now sparkled with happiness.

Reaching for his own cup, William settled back against his chair. He'd barely managed to do so, however, before the door swung open and an older gentleman stepped inside. He was of average height, with dark brown hair that now showed traces of gray. His eyes were blue, narrowing at the sides so that it looked as if he was squinting. As soon as he found Lucy, his lips drew together in a thin but wide smile. "Lucy! I cannot believe that it is you. I dared not hope that I would ever see you again." His arms went wide as if he meant to embrace her. William stifled a groan. But when Lucy remained frozen on the sofa with her teacup suspended in midair, her uncle's eyes narrowed even further, and he frowned. "Will you not come and greet me?"

William hazarded a glance in her direction. She looked pale and as though she might either leap from her seat and flail her uncle alive or simply collapse in a dead faint. Either way, William decided that it was a very good idea to take the teacup she was still holding out of her hand and set it on the table before she dropped it on the floor. He then looked at the constable who didn't seem as though he had any intention of saying a word, so William decided to take matters into his own hands and rose to his feet. "Allow me to introduce myself. My name is William Summersby. I am the Earl of Moorland's son and Lucy's husband."

"Indeed?" the earl said, his features melting into a soft expression. "Then I must congratulate you it seems, though I must admit that I'm a little disappointed that you didn't invite me to the wedding."

"Lucy had her reasons for desiring discretion and privacy. She's suffered greatly since her parents' murder."

"Such a tragedy," the earl muttered. "I cannot begin to imagine what you must have had to endure. How did you even make it back to England?"

"With difficulty," Lucy whispered, her eyes focused on the floor.

"She's a very determined woman," William added. "I admire her greatly. For six long years the only thing that kept her going was the desire for revenge, and when she finally found the man responsible and—"

"I beg your pardon?" the earl said, nearly choking on his words. "You . . . you have found the man who killed my brother and his wife? I've been searching for years but to no avail. You must tell me everything at once. Who is he? *Where* is he?"

"He was apprehended a couple of weeks ago at my estate when he attempted to kidnap Lucy. He apparently intended to take her with him to Turkey and to sell her there as a slave—a partial payment for services rendered."

"Dear Lord," the earl muttered as he sank down onto the seat behind him, "he's told you this?"

"He's told us a great deal more, my lord." William could hear his own voice grow angry and cold. He'd had enough of this game. It was time to spring the trap. "In fact, he didn't seem to be able to stop talking . . . about *you.*"

The earl's eyes shot up to meet with William's. "What are you saying? If you're implying . . ."

"I'm not implying anything. I am simply stating the facts, and the facts are that Lord Stanton killed Lord and Lady Hampstead in cold blood as per your orders."

"It's not true!"

But William had seen that look of desperation on many men's faces before—the kind of look that was tinged with guilt and fear. Lucy's uncle wanted the title and the fortune, but he was a coward who'd sent another man to do the dirty work for him and now dreaded the punishment that was to come.

"Lord Stanton is presently being held in a cell at Newgate. He was supposed to hang for murder but has been offered a life sentence instead, in exchange for any information he might have, implicating someone else. He immediately mentioned you, so you see, there's really no use in denying it."

The earl's face drew together in an angry scowl. "You can't prove any of it. Whatever Stanton might have said holds no water. Don't you see, he'll say anything to save his own neck."

"Perhaps," William acquiesced, reaching inside his jacket pocket and pulling out a worn piece of paper. He unfolded it and studied it for a moment while the whole room fell into silence. "But he did give me this letter, signed by yourself and promising an exorbitant amount of money in exchange for, and I quote: 'ensuring that Lady Lucinda remains behind in Constantinople once the matter pertaining to her parents has been settled.'"

"But I . . . That's not what I wrote." His eyes widened in alarm as he realized his misstep. "I mean, whatever that piece of paper there says, it must be a forgery. It will never stand in a court of law."

William's eyebrows rose, and he handed the piece of paper over to the constable who also appeared to study it with much interest. Ignoring the earl's claim that the letter was a fake, William zeroed in on the first thing he'd said instead. "Then what exactly did you write, my lord?"

"This really is rather compelling evidence," the constable muttered, with a most serious expression upon his face. "Most compelling, indeed."

The earl frantically raked his fingers through his hair. "I didn't mean to . . ." His eyes were panic stricken now as they looked from one person to the other. "It was Stanton's idea. I'll tell you everything if you will assure me that I will not hang. After all, I have killed no one. It was all his doing."

William clenched his jaw, the rage building, and prayed that he would have enough self-control not to pummel this pathetic excuse of a man. "Unfortunately, Lord Stanton is already dead and offers you no opportunity to bargain for your life."

"What? But I . . . You just said that—"

"I lied," William told him in a rather casual tone. He moved a little closer to the earl and held the letter out toward him. "Take it—as a reminder of who it was that convicted you."

It was a shaky hand that snatched the letter away from William. Taking it, the earl stared down at the page, a frown appearing upon his forehead as he turned it over. "It's . . . it's blank," he muttered.

"Hm, quite so," William concurred. "So you see, in the end, you really have only yourself to blame."

"No," the earl exclaimed. He seemed ready to grasp for words—anything that might help him. "No, you cannot do this. The evidence you claimed to have in your possession is non-existent. It is precisely as I told you. You have no proof."

"Ah, but you have already said more than enough to merit a trial, isn't that right, Constable?"

The constable nodded. "It most certainly is." He got up and pulled a pistol from his jacket pocket. "And we can do this the easy or the hard way. It's entirely up to you."

The earl nodded submissively and began to rise from his chair, but just as he reached his full height, he made a grab for the pistol, attempting, as far as William could tell, to wrench it out of the constable's hand. "Get down, Lucy!" His words of warning could not have come any sooner, for in the next second, the pistol went off with a loud boom. Lucy screamed and William jumped forward, wrestling the earl to the ground and pinning down his arm so the constable could retrieve his pistol. "Lucy—are you all right?"

A quiet squeak from behind the sofa table followed by a raspy "Yes" confirmed that she was indeed unharmed. William breathed a sigh of relief, but he did not relax his hold on the earl. "Get up, you bloody bastard," he growled, easing off of him and hauling him to his feet. Spotting the hole above the sofa where the lead shot had struck, he clenched his jaw, realizing just how close they'd come to absolute disaster. "You almost killed her."

"Is everything all right? I thought I heard a . . . Good heavens!"

Turning his head, William found Peterson standing in the doorway staring in bewilderment from one person to the other. "I shall be escorting his lordship out to the constable's carriage, Peterson. Would you please remain here with Lucy while I do so. I believe she's had quite a shock."

"Erm . . . yes, yes of course," Peterson muttered as he stepped forward.

William turned to go, but Lucy stopped him. "A moment, if you please." She walked up to her uncle, who was looking more terrified and helpless by the second. "How could you do such a thing? Have you no conscience at all? My father loved you . . . I loved you . . . Yet you betrayed us all in such a cruel and despicable way. It's beyond comprehension, and, unfortunately for you, it's beyond forgiveness as well." She then turned her back on him and walked back to the sofa, sat down, and averted her gaze from the man who'd taken so much from her.

When William returned ten minutes later after escorting the constable and her uncle out, she still hadn't moved, but the redness around her eyes and the wet streaks upon her cheeks showed visible signs of crying. Given the circumstances, William would not have been the least bit surprised if she would have collapsed in a fit of hysterics. Her parents had been brutally murdered, the man who'd done it had kidnapped her, dragged her across Europe, almost sold her into slavery. As if that wasn't enough, she'd discovered that the man behind it all was none other than her dear uncle. It was more than anyone should have to endure.

"Is he gone?" she asked, her gaze still focused on something far away in the distance.

"Yes, Lucy, he's gone."

She nodded her head and then turned to look at him. "Thank you for everything, William."

Relief was visible in her bright green eyes—so much so that William found himself catching his breath. He was suddenly afraid to speak, fearing that he would choke on the words, for the emotions that suddenly whirled through him were so powerful that he found himself struggling for control. Rising to her feet, she came to him and wrapped her arms around his neck. "Let's go home," she whispered as she pressed a tender kiss against his lips.

He nodded, drew her closer, and hugged her in a tight embrace. "What an excellent idea," he murmured, ignoring Peterson's discreet cough, which he knew was meant as a reminder of his presence. William didn't care; the only two things that mattered to him at that moment were that Lucy was safe and that she was his.

CHAPTER THIRTY

They had left Hampstead House after promising Peterson that they would return for a visit after the holidays. There would be a lot to see to including a search for another heir to the estate, but for now, Lucy was simply happy to have the matter of her parents' murder resolved, even though she would have wished for another outcome.

Snow was falling heavier than it had done earlier in the day, and while she still felt the cold, chilling her to the bone, she had to admit that there was no place she'd rather be at that very moment than wrapped in William's arms as they rolled steadily toward Moorland Manor. William had assured her that they would be home before dark, but the clouds overhead had already blocked out most of the sun, and they had stopped only a couple of miles back to light the lanterns that hung from the sides of the carriage.

"Do you suppose that your brother and sister might be there with their families when we arrive?" Lucy asked, turning her head slightly so she could gaze up into William's blue eyes. The plan had been for Lord Trenton to fetch Alexandra and their two children, while Ryan, after informing their father about their arrival, was supposed to fetch Mary and baby Vanessa.

"Considering the weather, not to mention the time it will take for them to prepare for a two-week absence from their homes, I don't believe that we will see any of them before to-morrow at the earliest."

But as they pulled up to Moorland Manor, they spotted another newly arrived carriage. "Quick, open the door, William." Lucy hadn't felt this excited about anything in a long time. She was part of a family again, and she was suddenly very eager to see her sister-in-law who was presently waiting for her to alight with a big grin upon her face.

"Lucy! It's so good to see you again," Alexandra exclaimed, handing baby Claire over to her husband so she could wrap her arms around her in a very sisterly hug. "Michael told me about your ordeal. Thank heavens you're all right. Come, let's go inside and warm ourselves by the fire."

"Don't worry about us," Lucy heard William call out as she and Alexandra started up the front stairs. "Trenton and I will be right behind you." She could hear the laughter in his voice and couldn't help but smile in response to it.

They were barely through the front door when the sound of voices shouting and footsteps scurrying along reached their ears. A moment later, Constance came into view, almost top-pling Lucy to the ground in her excitement. "Thank God you're safe," she whispered, hugging her so fiercely against her that Lucy felt her lungs constrict. "I've been so terribly worried—you cannot possibly imagine. But now you're home, and that's all that matters. Come, let's get both of you inside so you can get some color back in your cheeks."

"I wouldn't mind a cup of tea," Alexandra said as she took the lead and headed toward the parlor.

"Oh, I can do so much better than that," Constance remarked. "I asked Cook to prepare a large pot of mulled wine for when you arrived. I'll have it brought in straight away."

"I hadn't expected to see you so soon," Lucy said as she and Constance followed Alexandra. "I'm so glad you're here."

Constance served her a secretive smile. "Me too, Lucy. There's something that I must tell you . . ."

"Lucy!" A loud voice boomed the instant they set foot inside the parlor. Lucy immediately recognized the voice as belonging to Lord Moorland. He came toward her with a wide smile upon his face, reached for her hand, and placed a gentle kiss upon her knuckles. "It's good to have you home with us again."

"Thank you, my lord. It's a great relief to be back."

He nodded, and as he smiled, Lucy sensed that it was almost as if he knew precisely how she felt. She wondered how many times he must have gone off to war, fearing that he might not return, and being as relieved as she was now whenever he did. He turned to Alexandra who was standing by Lucy's side. "It's good to see you too, Alex. But where are my grandchildren? You didn't forget to bring them did you?"

"They're right here," Trenton said with a chuckle as he and William came into the room. He strode across to his father-in-law and handed baby Claire over to him while Richard ran to hide behind Alexandra's skirts.

"Please," Constance swept her arm toward the sofas and armchairs, "won't you have a seat? We still have so many questions about everything that happened to you, Lucy. You must tell us everything."

Lucy drew a deep sigh and then turned a pleading gaze on William who stepped forward to claim her arm and escort her toward one of the sofas. "So much has happened, Lady Ridgewood, and it's been a terrible strain on all of us. Would you mind overly much if we simply enjoy each other's company for the remainder of the day? I'll be more than happy to fill you in later."

"No, of course not," Constance said, looking quite sorry that she'd broached the topic at all.

Lucy quickly offered her a smile that she hoped would calm away her worries. "Perhaps we could talk about how to celebrate the holidays instead. I imagine that you must have some traditions, and I'd really love to hear about them."

"What a splendid idea," Lord Moorland remarked as he gently tickled baby Claire under her chin. The infant responded with a delightful squeal that brought an instant cheer to the room.

"I was thinking that we could fell an evergreen tomorrow. We'll use the trunk for our Yule Log and the branches to fashion some boughs and wreaths," William said as a maid entered carrying a tray with cups and a large pot of mulled wine, the cloves and cinnamon filling the air with their rich aromas.

Setting down the tray, the maid proceeded to pour, handing each of them a cup before departing again with a curtsy.

"We usually decorate and light the log on Christmas Eve," Alexandra said, blowing on her wine before taking a hesitant sip, "and then on Christmas Day, we'll go to church in the morning and return home for a lovely dinner complete with roast pig and plum pudding."

"It sounds wonderful," Lucy said, already eager to set off in search of the evergreen.

"I hope we didn't miss too much," came a voice from the doorway. Turning her head, Lucy spotted Ryan and then Mary, who was carrying baby Vanessa in her arms. They both welcomed Lucy back with as much enthusiasm as everyone else had done before taking their seats on one of the sofas next to Constance and Lord Moorland.

"I must admit that I'm mighty relieved that you've finally arrived, Ryan," Lord Moorland said, handing Claire back to her mother. "I wasn't sure how much longer I would be able to keep this bit of news bottled up inside me."

"What news?" William asked, setting his cup down on the table and placing his elbows upon his knees as he leaned forward.

Lucy couldn't help but notice a slight blush rise to her father-in-law's cheeks and immediately wondered if this had something to do with what Constance had been meaning to tell her earlier.

He hesitated a moment, looked to Constance, returned his gaze to each of his children, and finally said, "You know that I will always love your mother with all my heart. Nobody will ever be able to take her place. But I have also grieved for such a very long time, and, as you know, there were many dark moments when I thought I'd never be capable of going on without her." Lucy found herself holding her breath as he spoke, his eyes appearing to mist over, though he'd probably deny such a thing. "However, the years have dulled the pain, and after meeting Constance ... ahem ... Lady Ridgewood, I have discovered that it is possible for me to find not only happiness again but also love. I love her, and I have asked her to be my wife."

There was only a moment's silence before Alexandra was out of her seat with Claire once again delivered into Trenton's arms as she leapt to embrace her father. "I wish you so much happiness, Papa," she said as she wiped at her own tears.

"I was afraid that you might be upset with me for marrying again," he muttered somewhat bashfully.

"No, Papa," she whispered as she gave Constance a big smile. "You deserve every happiness in the world. Mama has been gone from us for so long. It will be easier knowing that you've found a new kind of joy with Lady Ridgewood at your side."

"She looks too young to be my stepmama," Ryan said as he heartily shook his father's hand before reaching for Constance's and lifting it to his lips for a kiss.

Constance immediately laughed. "I'll take that as a compliment, Ryan."

William stepped forward next to offer his congratulations while Lucy walked over to Constance and put her arm around her waist in a little sideways hug. "I'm so pleased for you," she said. "I have every confidence that Lord Moorland will be the perfect husband for you."

"Thank you, Lucy." Judging from her smile, there was no doubt that Constance thought so too.

"What a lot of weddings this year has had to offer," Alexandra exclaimed as she took baby Claire back into her arms.

"We're not married yet," Lord Moorland muttered,

though the gleam in his eyes told everyone that he intended to marry Constance at the first available opportunity.

"No," Alexandra agreed, "but I was also thinking of my brothers and Michael's sisters."

"Lady Caroline and Lady Cassandra?" William asked.

"Quite so," Lord Trenton remarked, looking rather pleased with himself, "though I still have to meet the men who captured their hearts. I'm not familiar with either one, and from what Alex tells me, Cassandra's wedding was particularly rushed."

"Well, Ryan and I attended both weddings with Alexandra," Mary piped up, "and I must say that both men looked rather ... ahem ... handsome. Is that not so, Alex?"

"Most assuredly," Alexandra quickly agreed, "although Cassandra's wedding did have a bit of an unfortunate incident, so to speak."

"What?" Lord Trenton asked, his head snapping around to stare at his wife. "You mentioned no such thing before."

"Forgive me, my love, but everything has been so rushed since your arrival, and besides, it's nothing for you to worry about now. Rest assured, I'll tell you all about it later."

Lord Trenton frowned. He did not look convinced but was afforded with no opportunity to press the matter any further when Ryan suddenly said, "Oh, I almost forgot!" Reaching inside his jacket pocket, he pulled out something green, holding the object high in the air for all to see.

Lord Moorland frowned. "That looks suspiciously like a sprig of mistletoe."

Ryan's smile widened to a grin. "So it is, and I say that you and Lady Ridgewood will be the first couple to kiss beneath it." And without further ado, he held it over their heads, leaving them with very little choice but to comply while everyone else cheered and clapped in support of the newly engaged couple.

"Give me that," William muttered, snatching the sprig from his brother's hand. He then reached for Lucy, whose heart had begun that old familiar fluttering beat that it always made right before William kissed her. And then he did, and it was the most marvelous kiss of them all, for she was home now, spending Christmas with her family and with the man not only whom she loved but also whom she knew loved her in return.

ACKNOWLEDGMENTS

Of all the books I've written so far, this was the most difficult one for me to finish due to plot-related issues, yet when I called my editor virtually in a state of panic, I remember hanging up the phone and thinking, "OK, I can do this." Thank you so much, Esi, for your help and support—you're awesome!

Having a husband who's ready to help me with all aspects of my work, from tips on advertising to ironing out plot issues and willingly forgoing our TV time together whenever I had a deadline looming has added tremendously to the whole experience. Thank you so much for all your encouragement, your support, and for making me feel like a superstar whenever I doubted myself. I love you!

And as always, a BIG thank you to you, dear reader, for allowing me to follow my dreams.

Keep reading for the can't miss first
Summersby Tale,

LADY ALEXANDRA'S
EXCELLENT ADVENTURE,

and be sure to read
Ryan Summersby's story in

THERE'S SOMETHING ABOUT
LADY MARY,

available now from
Avon Impulse

An Excerpt from

LADY ALEXANDRA'S EXCELLENT ADVENTURE

London
May 15, 1815

Sir Percy Foxstone took a slow sip of his single malt whiskey, savoring the rich flavor as it warmed his chest before he sank down into one of the deep leather armchairs in his office at Whitehall.

Lazily swirling the caramel-colored liquid, allowing it to lap against the edges of his glass, he regarded his friend with caution. "I'm deeply sorry it had to come to this, old chap," he told him quietly.

Bryce Summersby, Earl of Moorland, nodded, his forehead furrowed in a thoughtful frown. "Do you see now why I never wanted Alex to get involved?" He shook his head in disbelief.

Bryce's son William had joined the Foreign Office four years earlier when he was twenty-three years old. He'd had a number of successful missions during that time and had been personally thanked by the Prince Regent for uncovering a French spy who'd managed to infiltrate parliament.

Which is why it was so difficult to now believe that William was handing over valuable information to the French.

He'd gone to Paris in March, as soon as news of Napoleon's escape from Elba had reached the British shores. Accompanying him on his mission was his longtime friend, Andrew Finch, who'd joined the Foreign Office a couple of years earlier, on William's recommendation.

Percy picked up the most recent letter that Andrew had managed to send out of the country. "Judging from the tone of this, it seems Mr. Finch was completely caught off guard by William's behavior."

Bryce grunted before taking a swig of his whiskey. "I'm just not buying it," he muttered, piercing his friend with a hard stare, his mouth set in a grim line.

"Is that an objective opinion or one based on the fact that William's your son?"

"Bloody hell, Percy!" Bryce shouted, glaring at his friend. "Do you seriously believe William has betrayed us—that he's a traitor?"

Percy let out a deep sigh as he leaned forward, his elbows resting in his lap as he studied the glass between his hands. "I have to accept all possibilities." His eyes settled on Bryce's in a hard stare. "My position demands it."

"Who are you sending, Percy?"

Percy paused for a moment. The only reason he'd sent for Bryce in the first place was because he considered him a close friend. He'd already shared the details regarding William's mission with him and was beginning to wonder how much more he ought to divulge. "I've settled on Michael Ashford, Earl of Trenton."

"Thomas's boy?"

Percy nodded, knowing Bryce was familiar with the Duke of Willowbrook.

"Thomas is a man of great integrity," Bryce said rather stiffly. "I hope the apple didn't fall too far from the tree."

"Would you like to meet him?"

"What's your *plan*, Percy?" Bryce asked, ignoring his question. "Are you sending this Ashford fellow to kill my son?"

Percy sighed. "I'm not sending Ashford to assassinate your son, Bryce. I'm sending him to bring William back home so that he may face the charges against him. My hands are tied, old chap. You know treason's an unpardonable offense."

"And if he resists?"

"Let's hope he's wise enough not to," Percy said softly, giving Bryce a meaningful look.

"Michael will assume he's guilty of all charges and will do what must be done by all means necessary. Is that it?"

Percy nodded reluctantly. "Something like that," he said, in little more than a whisper.

"Then by all means, show Lord Trenton in so I may meet the man."

It was a delicate situation—one that Percy wished to have no part in. But now since he'd started down this road, what could he do other than hope it would soon be over?

He was inclined to agree with Bryce when it came to William's character. William had always been an honorable man. It seemed unthinkable that he might have turned traitor. Then again, Percy had seen it happen before. As he went to the door and called for Michael to enter, he sent up a silent prayer that he would somehow manage to bring William home in one piece.

A moment later, Michael strode into the room with a confidence that made it clear this was no fledgling.

Before them stood a tall figure of a man, well over six feet, with broad shoulders, a powerful chest, and strong arms. In short, he looked like he could slay a dragon with one hand while protecting a damsel in distress with the other. His hair was dark and ruffled, his eyes sparkling with boyish anticipation.

"Gentlemen . . ." Michael followed his greeting with a slight nod.

"Lord Moorland," Percy said, "may I present Michael Ashford, Earl of Trenton?"

Bryce rose to his feet, all the while assessing the man who'd soon be determining the fate of his son. After a moment's pause, he grasped Michael's outstretched hand in a firm shake.

"I've heard a great deal about you, Lord Moorland, from my father in particular," Michael said. "He's a great admirer of your military endeavors—says you're quite the strategist." He released Bryce's hand with a wry twist of his lips. "He also says he's never managed to beat you at chess."

Bryce feigned a polite smile. It had been a while since he'd last seen Thomas, but he had fond memories of the poor man's numerous attempts at beating him at his favorite game. "How is your father?"

Michael shrugged as he reached for one of the decanters on the side table. "Do you mind?" he asked Percy.

"Not at all. Help yourself."

Pouring a glass of port, Michael glanced over at Bryce. "Still going strong," he told him. "He will be sixty-two in a couple of months, but he's still running around like a young lad. Trouble is, his limbs are stiffer than they used to be. I can't help but worry he might hurt himself. In his mind, he's no more than twenty years of age."

"Just wait until you are as old as we are," Bryce told him. "You won't believe your eyes when you happen to catch yourself in a mirror. Indeed, you will most likely draw your sword wondering who the devil that stranger is staring back at you." He raised his glass to Michael. "Enjoy your youth while you have it, Trenton. Lord knows it will be gone before you know it."

"I briefed Trenton on his mission this morning," Percy said, apparently deciding that it was time to get on with the business at hand. Bryce could only hazard a guess at how uncomfortable this whole dratted business must be for him. Nothing could be nastier than having to decide the fate of somebody's child—especially not when that child was like family. But he also understood that responsibility weighed heavily on his friend's shoulders. Percy would not be able to leave the matter alone—he *had* to investigate. As Bryce watched him sit back down in his dark brown leather chair, he desperately hoped that he truly did know his son well enough, and that Andrew was somehow mistaken about William's actions. "He'll be ready to leave in the morning."

Bryce moved to the side table to refill his glass. "How long have you and my son known each other?" he asked Michael.

"Well, er . . . actually, I . . ."

"Trenton has never actually met your son, Bryce. You know we don't allow our agents to meet unless they are working on the same assignment. It helps protect their identities when they are in the field."

"Well, I don't mean to point out the obvious," Bryce remarked, his voice laced with annoyance. "But how the devil is he supposed to find him when he doesn't even know what he looks like?"

"There are ways."

Bryce scoffed. "We both know that William is quite skilled at deception. He works well undercover—hence the reason you gave him such an important assignment in the first place." Bryce took a large gulp of his whiskey to calm his nerves. "I want Ryan and Alex to accompany him."

Percy's mouth dropped open. "But you always said—"

"That was then and this is now. They will be able to identify their brother."

"And you are certain that you want Alex to go as well?"

Bryce had no desire to let his daughter get muddled up in this mess, but she was a better horseman, a better swordsman, and a better shot than Ryan had ever been. In fact, the only reason he was sending Ryan at all was to act as her chaperone. "Quite certain."

Both men turned to Michael. His expression was impossible to read as he absorbed the news that Bryce's children would be tagging along. "It will be a perilous journey," he stated. "They will have to hold their own. I have no desire to babysit anyone."

"You won't have to," Bryce grumbled. "Alexa—"

"Is the best swordsman you're ever likely to come across," Percy said as he cut off his friend.

Bryce followed his lead and held silent, realizing that it would probably be a cold day in hell before Michael would ever agree to bring a woman along, no matter how much he and Percy might vouch for her. In truth, he'd likely quit first, and if Bryce knew Percy as well as he thought, then that was not a risk that he was willing to take.

"Henry Angelo is a good friend of mine," Bryce added. "He's spent a number of years at Moorland Manor polishing Alex's skills."

Mentioning the famous dueling master had its desired effect. Michael nodded his approval. "But what if Summersby *is* guilty of treason? . . . What if he fights back? I can't afford to have his siblings standing in my way if I'm forced to take action." He paused. "Do you think they'll be willing to stand idly by while I kill their brother, or will they turn on me in a foolhardy attempt to save him?"

Bryce's blood ran cold at Michael's detached tone. He didn't doubt for a second that the man before him was prepared to carry out his orders. Would Alex and Ryan let him kill their brother, even if he were a traitor? Absolutely not, but they gave him hope that he might see William again, and for that reason alone, he was prepared to say anything to ensure that they would be in a position to help their brother. "If they were to discover that he has been consorting with the French, then I cannot imagine that they would try to stop you."

"Very well then," Michael acquiesced. "We leave at dawn. Will they be ready by then?"

Bryce nodded. "I have already told them to prepare themselves in the event that they would be joining you."

"There's a tavern on the outskirts of town—The Royal Oak. Are you familiar with the place?"

"I am."

"Good. Tell your sons to meet me there at five. I have no intention of waiting for them, so if they're late—"

"They will be there," Bryce told him sharply. "You have my word," he added, reaching out to shake Michael's hand.

"And you have my word as a gentleman that I shall act fairly," Michael responded. "Sir Percy tells me that both of you find it unlikely that William's a turncoat. I will discover the truth of the matter, and I hope you will trust me when I say that I would never dream of harming an innocent man. Furthermore, my prerogative is to bring him back alive, so if all goes well, you will see your son soon enough, Lord Moorland."

"Thank you," Bryce told him sincerely. "I shall await your return." He raised his glass in a final salute before gathering up his coat and heading for the door. "You will keep me informed?" he asked as he looked back over his shoulder at Percy, his hand already on the door handle.

"You will hear from me as soon as I have any news. I promise."

With a heavy sigh and a thoughtful nod, Bryce left Percy's office with growing trepidation. He wasn't a gambling man, yet here he was, willing to risk everything dear to him in order to save his firstborn child.

Though he had faith in both Alexandra and Ryan, he hated having to sit idly by in anticipation. If only he could go in their stead, but that was impossible. He'd grown too old to be of use on rescue missions, particularly with his left leg paining him as much as it did these days.

No . . . he had no choice but to send his children, and in spite of himself, he suddenly smiled. This was exactly the sort of thing that Alexandra had been dreaming about for years, and now he was finally ready to indulge her. If only the stakes weren't so high.

Born in Denmark, Sophie spent her youth traveling with her parents to wonderful places all around the world. She's lived in five different countries, on three different continents, and speaks Danish, English, French, Spanish, and Romanian. She has studied design in Paris and New York and has a bachelor's degree from Parsons The New School For Design, but most impressive of all, she's been married to the same man three times, in three different countries, and in three different dresses.

While living in Africa, Sophie turned to her lifelong passion: writing. When she's not busy, dreaming up her next romance novel, Sophie enjoys spending time with her family, swimming, cooking, gardening, watching romantic comedies, and, of course, reading. She currently lives on the East Coast.

You can find Sophie Barnes on Facebook and follow her on Twitter at @BarnesSophie. Visit her website at www.sophiebarnes.com.

Visit www.AuthorTracker.com for exclusive information on your favorite HarperCollins authors.

About the Author

Born in Denmark, [illegible] has spent much of her life operating wonderful places all around the world, living in in five different countries, and in two different languages, and speaks Danish, English, Dutch, Italian, and Romanian. She has made her home in Italy and New York and has studied for a degree in Patisserie at Le Cordon Bleu, London, and in pastry work, she has catered to all sorts needs in cuisine in three different restaurants and to three different kitchens.

While living in Africa, She volunteered to help the poor tion centre. When she is not busy sitting up by her own romance novel, She also enjoys mending one's own true friends, swimming as a regular pastime, watching romance comedies and, of course, reading. She currently lives in the city that never sleeps and her life and [illegible].

Visit www.AuthorTracker.com for exclusive information on your favorite HarperCollins authors.

Give in to your impulses . . .
Read on for a sneak peek at seven brand-new
e-book original tales of romance
from Avon Books.
Available now wherever e-books are sold.

THREE SCHEMES AND A SCANDAL
By Maya Rodale

SKIES OF STEEL
THE ETHER CHRONICLES
By Zoë Archer

FURTHER CONFESSIONS OF A
SLIGHTLY NEUROTIC HITWOMAN
By JB Lynn

THE SECOND SEDUCTION
OF A LADY
By Miranda Neville

TO HELL AND BACK
A League of Guardians Novella
By Juliana Stone

MIDNIGHT IN YOUR ARMS
By Morgan Kelly

SEDUCED BY A PIRATE
By Eloisa James

An Excerpt from

THREE SCHEMES AND A SCANDAL
by *Maya Rodale*

**Enter the Regency world of the Writing Girls
series in Maya Rodale's charming tale of a
scheming lady, a handsome second son, and
the trouble they get into when the perfect
scandal becomes an even more perfect match.**

Most young ladies spent their pin money on hats and hair ribbons; Charlotte spent hers on bribery.

At precisely three o'clock, Charlotte sipped her lemonade and watched as a footman dressed in royal blue livery approached James with the unfortunate news that something at the folly needed his immediate attention.

James raked his fingers through his hair—she thought it best described as the color of wheat at sunset on harvest day.

He scowled. It did nothing to diminish his good looks. Combined with that scar, it made him appear only more brooding, more dangerous, more rakish.

She hadn't seen him in an age . . . Not since George Coney's funeral.

Even though the memory brought on a wave of sadness and rage, Charlotte couldn't help it: she smiled broadly when James set off for the folly at a brisk walk. Her heart began to pound. The plan was in effect.

Just a few minutes later, the rest of the garden party gathered 'round Lord Hastings as he began an ambling tour of his gardens, including the vegetables, his collection of flowering shrubs, and a series of pea gravel paths that meandered through groves of trees and other landscaped "moments."

Charlotte and Harriet were to be found skulking toward the back of the group, studiously avoiding relatives—such as Charlotte's brother, Brandon, and his wife, Sophie, who had been watching Charlotte a little too closely for comfort ever since The Scheme That Had Gone Horribly Awry. Harriet's mother was deep in conversation with her bosom friend, Lady Newport.

A few steps ahead was Miss Swan Lucy Feathers herself. Today she was decked in a pale muslin gown and an enormous bonnet that had been decorated with what seemed to be a shrubbery. Upon closer inspection, it was a variety of fresh flowers and garden clippings. Even a little bird (fake, one hoped) had been nestled into the arrangement. Two wide, fawn-colored ribbons tied the millinery event to her head.

Charlotte felt another pang, and then—Lord above—she suffered *second thoughts*. First the swan bonnet, and now this!

James had once broken her heart horribly, but could he really marry someone with such atrocious taste in bonnets? And, if not, should the scheme progress?

"Lovely day for a garden party, is it not?" Harriet said brightly to Miss Swan Lucy.

"Oh, indeed it is a lovely day," Lucy replied. "Though it would be so much better if I weren't so vexed by these bonnet strings. This taffeta ribbon is just adorable, but immensely itchy against my skin."

"What a ghastly problem. Try loosening the strings?" Charlotte suggested. Her other thought she kept to herself: *Or remove the monstrous thing entirely.*

"It's a bit windy. I shan't wish it to blow away," Lucy said nervously. Indeed, the wind had picked up, bending the hat brim. On such a warm summer day as this, no one complained.

"A gentle summer breeze. The sun is glorious, though," Harriet replied.

"This breeze is threatening to send off my bonnet, and I shall freckle terribly without it in this sun. Alas!" Lucy cried, her fingers tugging at her bonnet strings.

"What is wrong with freckles?" Harriet asked. The correct answer was *nothing* since Harriet possessed a smattering of freckles across her nose and rosy cheeks.

"We should find you some shade," Charlotte declared. "Shouldn't we, Harriet?"

"Yes. Shade. Just the thing," Harriet echoed. She was frowning, probably in vexation over the comment about freckles. Charlotte thought there were worse things, such as being a feather-brain like Lucy.

Charlotte suffered another pang. She loathed second thoughts and generally avoided them. She reminded herself that while James had once been her favorite person in England, he had since become the sort of man who brooded endlessly and flirted heartlessly.

Never mind what he had done to George Coney . . .

An Excerpt from

SKIES OF STEEL
THE ETHER CHRONICLES
by Zoë Archer

In the world of The Ether Chronicles,
the Mechanical War rages on, and
appearances are almost always deceiving
… Read on for a glimpse of Zoë Archer's
latest addition to this riveting series.

He *had* to be here. His airship, *Bielyi Voron*, had been spotted nearby. Through the judicious use of bribery, she had learned that he frequented this tavern. If he wasn't here, she would have to come up with a whole new plan, but that would take costly time. Every hour, every day that passed meant the danger only increased.

She walked past another room, then halted abruptly when she heard a deep voice inside the chamber speaking in

Russian. Cautiously, she peered around the doorway. A man sat in a booth against the far wall. The man she sought. Of that she had no doubt.

Captain Mikhail Mikhailovich Denisov. Rogue Man O' War.

Like most people, Daphne had heard of the Man O' Wars, but she'd never seen one in person. Not until this moment. Newspaper reports and even cinemagraphs could not fully do justice to this amalgam of man and machine. The telumium implants that all Man O' Wars possessed gave them incredible might and speed, and heightened senses. Those same implants also created a symbiotic relationship between Man O' Wars and their airships. They both captained and powered these airborne vessels. The implants fed off of and engendered the Man O' Wars' natural strength of will and courage.

Even standing at the far end of the room, Daphne felt Denisov's energy—invisible, silent waves of power that resonated in her very bones. As a scholar, she found the phenomenon fascinating. As a woman, she was . . . troubled.

Hard angles comprised his face: a boldly square jaw, high cheekbones, a decidedly Slavic nose. The slightly almond shape of his eyes revealed distant Tartar blood, while his curved, full mouth was all voluptuary, framed by a trimmed, dark goatee. An arresting face that spoke of a life fully lived. She would have looked twice at him under any circumstances, but it was his hair that truly made her gape.

He'd shaved most of his head to dark stubble, but down the center he'd let his hair grow longer, and it stood up in a dramatic crest, the tip colored crimson. Dimly, she remembered reading about the American Indians called Mohawks, who wore their hair in just such a fashion. Never before had she seen it on a non-Indian.

By rights, the style ought to look outlandish, or even ludicrous. Yet on Denisov, it was precisely right—dangerous, unexpected, and surprisingly alluring. Rings of graduated sizes ran along the edge of one ear, and a dagger-shaped pendant hung from the lobe of his other ear.

Though Denisov sat in a corner booth, his size was evident. His arms stretched out along the back of the booth, and he sprawled in a seemingly casual pose, his long legs sticking out from beneath the table. A small child could have fit inside each of his tall, buckled boots. He wore what must have been his Russian Imperial Aerial Navy long coat, but he'd torn off the sleeves, and the once-somber gray wool now sported a motley assortment of chains, medals, ribbons, and bits of clockwork. A deliberate show of defiance. His coat proclaimed: *I'm no longer under any government's control.*

If he wore a shirt beneath his coat, she couldn't tell. His arms were bare, save for a thick leather gauntlet adorned with more buckles on one wrist.

Despite her years of fieldwork in the world's faraway places, Daphne could confidently say Denisov was by far the most extraordinary-looking individual she'd ever seen. She barely noticed the two men sitting with him, all three of them laughing boisterously over something Denisov said.

His laugh stopped abruptly. He trained his quartz blue gaze right on her.

As if filled with ether, her heart immediately soared into her throat. She felt as though she'd been targeted by a predator. Nowhere to turn, nowhere to run.

I'm not here to run.

When he crooked his finger, motioning for her to come toward him, she fought her impulse to flee. Instead, she put one foot in front of the other, approaching his booth until she stood before him. Even with the table separating them, she didn't feel protected. One sweep of his thickly muscled arm could have tossed the heavy oak aside as if it were paper.

"Your search has ended, *zaika*." His voice was heavily accented, deep as a cavern. "Here I am."

An Excerpt from

FURTHER CONFESSIONS OF A SLIGHTLY NEUROTIC HITWOMAN

by JB Lynn

Knocking off a drug kingpin was the last thing on Maggie Lee's to-do list . . . Take three wacky aunts, two talking animals, one nervous bride, and an upcoming hit, and you've got the follow-up to JB Lynn's wickedly funny *Confessions of a Slightly Neurotic Hitwoman*.

"I see a disco ball in your future." Armani Vasquez, the closest thing I had to a friend at Insuring the Future, delivered this pronouncement right after she sprinkled a handful of candy corn into her Caesar salad.

Disgusted by her food combination, I pushed my own peanut butter and jelly sandwich away. "Really? A disco ball?"

If you'd told me a month ago that I'd be leaning over a table in the lunchroom, paying close attention to the bizarre premonitions of my half-crippled, wannabe-psychic coworker, I would have said you were crazy.

But I'd had one hell of a month.

First there had been the car accident. My sister Theresa and her husband, Dirk, were killed; my three-year-old niece, Katie, wound up in a coma; and I ended up with the ability to talk to animals. Trust me, I know exactly how crazy that sounds, but it's true . . . I think.

On top of everything else, I inadvertently found myself hurtling down a career path I never could have imagined.

I'm now a hitwoman for hire. Yes, I kill people for money . . . but just so you know, I don't go around killing just anyone. I've got standards. The two men I killed were bad men, very bad men.

Before I could press Armani for more details about the mysterious disco ball, another man I wanted to kill sauntered into my line of vision. I hate my job at Insuring the Future. I hate taking automobile claims from idiot drivers who have no business getting behind the wheel. But most of all I hate my boss, Harry. It's not the fact that he's a stickler for enforcing company policy or even that he always smells like week-old pepperoni. No, I hate him because Harry "likes" me. A lot. He's always looking over my shoulder (and peering down my shirt) and calling me into his office for one-on-one "motivational chats" to improve my performance.

I know what you're thinking. I should report his sexual harassment to human resources, or, if I deplore the idea of workplace conflict (and what self-respecting hitwoman wouldn't?), I should quit and find another job.

I was getting ready to do just that, report his lecherous ass and then quit (because I really do despise "helping" the general public), but then the accident happened. And then the paid assassin gig.

So now I need this crappy, unfulfilling, frustrating-as-hell clerical employment because it provides a cover for my second job. It's not like I can put HITWOMAN on my next tax return. Besides, if I didn't keep this job, my meddling aunts would wonder what the hell I'm doing with my life.

An Excerpt from

THE SECOND SEDUCTION OF A LADY

by *Miranda Neville*

Enter the thrilling, sexy world of Georgian
England in this splendid Miranda Neville
novella—and catch a glimpse of Caro, the
heroine of the upcoming *The Importance of
Being Wicked*, on sale December 2012.

"Eleanor!" She looked up. He stepped forward to meet her
on the bridge. "Eleanor!" He should ask her how she was, why
she was there. But he didn't care why she was there. All he
wanted to do was take her into his arms and tease her stern
mouth into returning his kisses.

His outstretched arms were welcomed with a hearty
shove, and he landed on his back in cold water.

"What—"

She looked down at him, grim satisfaction on her elegant features. "I beg your pardon, Mr. Quinton, but you were in my way. I have things to attend to."

As he struggled upright in the thigh-deep water, she completed her crossing. Cold soaked through every garment, chilling his skin, his ardor, and his heart. "Wait! You are trespassing," he called, a surge of rage making him petty. He'd been wrong, yes, but his intentions had ultimately been honorable. She had sent him about his business with a cold rebuke. And returned all his letters unread.

"Oh? Is this your land?" she said with a haughty brow, knowing well that his home was over a hundred miles away, near Newmarket.

"Effectively, yes," he said, clambering up the bank. "I have control of the Townsend estate for another three weeks, until my ward reaches his majority."

"In that case," she replied, "I'll collect *my* charge and be off."

Ignoring the squelching in his boots, he reached for her again. In the bare second his wet hand rested on her lower arm, warm under his chilled fingers, longing flooded his veins. "Eleanor," he whispered.

"Get your wet hands off my gown." She shook him off.

"Won't you forgive me?"

Her grey eyes held his. He'd seen them bright with affection and wild with ecstasy. Now they contained polished steel.

"I think, Mr. Quinton, it would be better if we both forget that there is anything to forgive."

Max deliberately mistook her meaning. "Good," he said. She watched him unbutton his clammy, clinging waistcoat with the outrage of a dowager. Yet she'd seen him wearing even less. Or felt him, rather. It had been dark at the time.

The garment slid down his arms. "I'm ready to apologize again, but I'd like it even better if we could begin a new chapter. Can we start again? Please, Eleanor."

Eleanor watched Max Quinton drape his wet waistcoat over a branch, in fascinated disbelief that, meeting her after five years, he should be stripping off his clothes. She trusted he wouldn't be removing all of them. The entreaty in his voice affected her, but only for an instant. Giving him a dunking had blunted the edge of anger that his appearance provoked, that was all. Nothing else had changed.

"I made it clear in the past," she said coldly, "that our acquaintance was over. Forever. Should we meet again, which I trust won't be necessary, you may call me Miss Hardwick."

"Don't you think that's absurd, given what we once were to each other?"

She stepped farther away from this unpleasantly damp man. Never mind that his figure was displayed to advantage beneath clinging linen, fine enough to limn the contours of his chest and reveal an intriguing dark shadow descending to the waist. It was true that his thick, wavy hair looked quite good wet, but she no longer responded to the lilt of laughter in his deep voice. "Our past relationship was founded on falsehood and meant nothing. I never think of you, and I'd like to keep it that way. We meet as indifferent strangers."

A smile tugged on his lips. It was one of the first things she'd noticed about him, that hint of humor in an otherwise grave face. "Do you often push strangers into rivers?"

"You deserved it."

An Excerpt from

TO HELL AND BACK
A LEAGUE OF GUARDIANS NOVELLA
by *Juliana Stone*

All Logan Winters wants is to be left alone with the woman he loves. But fate isn't on his side . . . Logan and Kira are back in the latest League of Guardians novella from Juliana Stone.

Priest knew he was in trouble about two seconds after they exited the bed-and-breakfast. Up ahead, just past the giant pumpkin display, stood a pack of blood demons. They'd donned their human guise, of course, but it did nothing to hide the menace they projected. A family of five gave them a wide berth as they traversed the sidewalk, and he watched as the mother hustled her children past.

Smart humans.

The damn things looked like a bunch of thugs—all of

them well over six feet in height, with thick necks, tree trunks for legs, and shoulders as wide as a Mack truck.

They were mean and strong, but dumb. Bottom feeders who kissed the asses of most of the underworld. He wondered who they called boss.

Normally, Priest wouldn't have blinked. As an immortal knight of the Templar, he was used to dealing with all sorts of otherworld scum. In fact, it had been a few months since he'd flexed his muscles and connected his fists with demon hide. Normally he looked forward to this kind of shit because life, such as it was, gave him only a few moments to feel truly alive. Making love to a hot-blooded woman did that. Waking up to the smell of fresh rain did that. Killing a bunch of punk-ass demons did that. He glanced to his side.

But normally he worked alone.

Casually he leaned his tall frame against the brick façade of the coffee shop to his right and kept Kira out of view. The woman didn't say anything—she didn't have to. Her pale features and large, exotic eyes couldn't hide her fear. But there was something else there, and it was that something else that was going to make all the difference in the world. Anger.

He reached his hand forward, as if to caress her cheek. All the while, his eyes scanned the immediate area looking for demons. To anyone glancing their way, they appeared to be a couple deeply involved in each other. Lovers.

Priest ignored both her flinch and her quick recovery as his gaze swept along the street behind him. His liege—the Seraphim Bill—hadn't told him much of this assignment, but he knew enough. He knew where Kira Dove had been.

The gray realm.

It was a place he was all too familiar with, and he had to give it to her, the little lady had spunk. Anyone who escaped purgatory in one piece was strong. He'd never met the hell-hound, Logan Winters, but his woman had guts.

His eyes hardened when he spied a second pack of blood demons hunkered down near the bed-and-breakfast they'd just left. When he felt the unmistakable shift in the air that spelled real trouble, his insides twisted.

Lilith's crew.

Just fucking great. His Harley was nowhere near where he needed the damn thing to be. He was surrounded by demons, in the middle of a large crowd of innocents and this little bit of woman had the very bowels of hell on her trail.

A new scent drifted up his nostrils. Lilith's pack hounds were here somewhere, and their human disguises would be hard to penetrate. Those guys were pros.

Priest straightened and dropped his hand from her cheek until he drew her delicate fist into his large palm. Damned if he was gonna let the queen bitch of hell get to Kira Dove. Strong white teeth flashed as he smiled and looked down at her.

"You ready to rock and roll?"

Huge eyes stared up at him, their dark depths hiding a hell of a lot more than pain and fear. There was strength there . . . determination, and—he smiled—a fuck-you attitude.

She nodded and then whispered, "Let's do this."

An Excerpt from

MIDNIGHT IN YOUR ARMS
by Morgan Kelly

**For fans of *Downton Abbey* and readers
of Jude Deveraux and Teresa Medeiros
comes the brand-new tale of a love
that crosses the boundaries of time . . .
from debut author Morgan Kelly.**

Laura collapsed on top of him with a weak moan that he sucked from her lips as he withdrew and coiled himself around her, face to face, his arm cradled along her spine. They were both slick with sweat, drenched in the only substance that quenched what it had ignited.

"One doesn't learn *that* in finishing school," he murmured appreciatively into her ear, when he could speak. She giggled, hiding her face in his shoulder.

"I suppose you think me utterly wanton?" she said. "Isn't that a word you use these days, to describe women like me?"

"There are no women like you," he said, tucking a damp curl behind her ear.

"Not here," she agreed, snuggling against him.

"Not anywhere," he said.

Laura smiled and pressed her lips to his chest. He ran his fingernails slowly up and down her back, and she nearly purred. He loved the way their skin stuck together, as though they were truly fusing into one person. His eyes grew heavy, and he blinked, afraid that if he fell asleep, she would simply disappear. He didn't know the rules. He didn't know if there were any. They seemed to be making them up as they went along.

"In this time," he said, "are you truly not yet born?"

"Not for years and years."

"Then how is it you can exist, here and now, with me?"

She looked up at him, her head arched against the pillow. "I really don't know, Alaric. I only know that I do, and that I have never felt more alive than when I'm with you."

"If you . . . stayed, here, with me, what would happen when you *are* born?"

Laura rolled onto her back, her leg still hooked around him and her body pressed alongside his. She cradled her head on her arm, the sinuous curve of her underarm upraised. Tiny beads of sweat pearled her collarbone, a necklace of her own making. "I don't know. But my time isn't a good one, Alaric. It's a dangerous time, when the whole world has been at war with itself. I've seen things I can't erase from my mind. People have done things that take away their humanity—and now they are expected to carry on like decent citizens."

"I know what war is," Alaric said.

"Not war like this," Laura said quietly. "We can never be the same, any of us. Being here with you makes me feel like none of that could ever happen."

"Maybe it won't," he said gently, running his palm over her sweet flesh.

"Oh, it will," she said. "And then it will happen again. Time isn't the only endless cycle."

An Excerpt from

SEDUCED BY A PIRATE

by *Eloisa James*

**In Eloisa James's companion story to
The Ugly Duchess, Sir Griffin Barry, captain
of the infamous pirate ship *The Poppy*, is back
in England to claim the wife he hasn't seen
since their wedding day . . . but this is one
treasure that will not be so easy to capture.**

"You're married to a *pirate?*"

Phoebe Eleanor Barry—wife to Sir Griffin Barry, pirate—nearly smiled at the shocked expression on her friend Amelia Howell-Barth's face. But not quite. Not given the sharp pinch she felt in the general area of her chest. "His lordship has been engaged in that occupation for years, as I understand it."

"A pirate. A real, live pirate?" Amelia's teacup froze, halfway to her mouth. "That's so romantic!"

Phoebe had rejected that notion long ago. "Pirates walk people down the plank." She put her own teacup down so sharply that it clattered against the saucer.

Her friend's eyes grew round, and tea sloshed on the tablecloth as she set her cup down. "The *plank*? Your husband really—"

"By all accounts, pirates regularly send people to the briny deep, not to mention plundering jewels and the like."

Amelia swallowed, and Phoebe could tell that she was rapidly rethinking the romantic aspects of having a pirate within the immediate family. Amelia was a dear little matron, with a rosebud mouth and brown fly-away curls. Mr. Howell-Barth was an eminent goldsmith in Bath, and likely wouldn't permit Amelia to pay any more visits once he learned how Sir Griffin was amusing himself abroad.

"Mind you," Phoebe added, "we haven't spoken in years, but that is my understanding. His man of business offers me patent untruths."

"Such as?"

"The last time I saw him, he told me that Sir Griffin was exporting timber from the Americas."

Amelia brightened. "Perhaps he is! Mr. Howell-Barth told me just this morning that men shipping lumber from Canada are making a fortune. Why on earth do you think your husband is a pirate, if he hasn't told you so himself?"

"Several years ago, he wrote his father, who took it upon himself to inform me. I gather he is considered quite fearsome on the high seas."

"Goodness me, Phoebe. I thought your husband simply chose to live abroad."

"Well, he does choose it. Can you imagine the scandal if I had informed people that Sir Griffin was a pirate? I think the viscount rather expected that his son would die at sea."

"I suppose it could be worse," Amelia offered.

"How could it *possibly* be worse?"

"You could be married to a highwayman."

"Is there a significant difference?" Phoebe shrugged inelegantly. "Either way, I am married to a criminal who stands to be hanged. Hanged, Amelia. Or thrown into prison."

"His father will never allow that. You know how powerful the viscount is, Phoebe. There's talk that Lord Moncrieff might be awarded an earldom."

"Not after it is revealed that his son is a pirate."

"But Sir Griffin is a baronet in his own right! They don't hang people with titles."

"Yes, they do."

"Actually, I think they behead them."

Phoebe shuddered. "That's a terrible fate."

"Come to think of it, why is your husband a baronet, if his father is a viscount and still living?" Amelia asked, knitting her brow. Being a goldsmith's wife, she had never been schooled in the intricacies of this sort of thing.

"It's a courtesy title," Phoebe explained. "Viscount Moncrieff inherited the title of baronet as well as that of viscount, so his heir claims the title of baronet during the current viscount's life."

Amelia digested that. Then, "Mrs. Crimp would be mad with glee if she found out."

"She *will* be mad with glee," Phoebe said, nausea returning.

"What do you mean?"

"He's back," Phoebe said helplessly. "Oh, Amelia, he's back in England."